Spencer Hill Press

Contact:
Spencer Hill Press, PO Box 247, Contoocook, NH 03229, USA

Please visit our website at www.spencerhillpress.com

First Edition: July 2013.

Lisa Amowitz
Breaking Glass : a novel / by Lisa Amowitz – 1st ed.
p. cm.

Summary:
When the girl he loves disappears, a seventeen-year-old tries to call her back from beyond the grave to solve her own murder.

The author acknowledges the copyrighted or trademarked status and trademark owners of the following wordmarks mentioned in this fiction:
Absolut, Advanced Placement, Advil, Arizona Iced Tea, Bluetooth, BMW, C-3PO, C-Leg, Discovery Channel, Dorothy, Dracula, Facebook, Frankenstein, Hair Club for Men, History Channel, Hulk, iPhone, Ivy League, Jeep, Jockey, Ken, Lego, Little League, Lone Ranger, Magic 8 Ball, Manolo Blahnik, Matchbox, Mob Wives, Monday Night Football, Netflix, Old Farmer's Almanac, Oldsmobile, Otto Bock, Paralympics, Parker Brothers, Phantom of the Opera, Photoshop, Post-it, PowerBar, Ralph Lauren, Rhode Island School of Design, SATs, Sears, ShopRite, Six Flags, Sleeping Beauty, Sports Authority, Star Wars, Superman, Tin Man, Tonto, Vicodin, Volkswagen Jetta, West Side Story, Wii, Wite-Out, Wizard, Yankees, YouTube

Cover design by Lisa Amowitz
Interior layout by K. Kaynak

ISBN 978-1-937053-38-3 (paperback)
ISBN 978-1-937053-39-0 (e-book)

Printed in the United States of America

BREAKING GLASS

LISA AMOWITZ

SPENCER
HILL
PRESS

For my parents, Gene and Sherry, who nurtured the spark.
For my children, Benjamin and Rebecca,
to whom I pass it along, with love.

Now (November 17th)

Outside the dinner theater lobby, the glow of street lamps barely penetrates the thick mist that shrouds the parking lot. It's the kind of night that Jack the Ripper might have prowled the cobblestoned streets of London searching for victims.

In the lobby, fresh from the standing ovation he's received as Tony in our production of *West Side Story*, my best friend Ryan Morgan is surrounded by a crush of people. For two weeks running, his performance has been drawing crowds from all over Westchester County.

I glance around furtively, but no one notices the lighting guy. Truth is, my heart's not in theater. I'm only working weekends to pad my college applications, and my wallet. So, I take a minute to study the latest text from Susannah Durban, Ryan's girlfriend of three years. Heat creeps into my cheeks.

For the past year, Susannah's been inexplicably texting me with YouTube links to her haunting stop-action animations. I watch her body drift across the screen draped with filmy gauze, her dark bronze hair and golden skin amid floating leaves, graveyards, ballet dancers, Indian goddesses, and scattered words in Hebrew and English, most of which make no sense.

But other than telling me the link is private and to keep it our little secret, Susannah never mentions them when I see her. Neither do I.

Yet if I could dive into my iPhone and swim beside her, an exotic fish in her private world, I would do it and never look back.

And Ryan would kill me. Best friends don't want to *do* their best friend's girlfriend. I think that's written somewhere. So is not cheating on your girlfriend. And so is not ratting him out.

I glance behind me. Ryan is intertwined with Claudia Herman, the community college girl who plays Maria. Claudia's hot. And she's slept with our whole track team. I think of Susannah, mercifully out of town on a college visit.

My phone vibrates. Susannah again. This time it's an actual text.

I clench my jaw and look away from Ryan and his latest fling, sworn to silence by the Guy Code of Honor.

Jeremy! guess what. i'm here! got n earlier flight

I peer out into night, then glance at Ryan again.

Shit.

Claudia has one leg coiled around Ryan's tall frame, like a boa constrictor. I fumble with my phone. Texting under pressure has never been my strong suit.

Heart pounding, I gulp in air and think of my water bottle, nestled in the glove compartment of my car. I can feel my lips pressed to its cool rim, imagining the warmth of its contents sliding down the back of my throat.

But no. I have to stay sharp. I'm sensible, I tell myself. *Sensible Jeremy Glass.*

Besides, there's no time. Susannah emerges from the parking lot mist carrying a single red rose. A circuit flips on inside me; a familiar volt of current sizzles through my core like heat lightning. I stuff the phone in my pocket and try to position myself to block Ryan from view. My palms are slick. At first, I identify the heaviness behind my eyeballs as guilt. Only as Susannah pushes through the glass doors, droplets beaded on her hair like diamond chips, do I recognize the cold hollow thing that claws up into my throat for what it really is.

Shame.

Panic cramps my insides. The water bottle beckons.

"Jeremy!" Susannah hugs me, smelling of rain and vanilla. She flashes a smile, her clear eyes bright, but at the temples her deep golden skin is almost transparent, stretched just a bit too tight. And her raincoat hangs loose. "I thought I should be here for the big night, so I booked an earlier flight," she says. "Surprised?"

"A little. I know Ryan certainly will be." I'm buzzing like I've just downed a fifth of Absolut, the damp ache inside me incinerated to ash. The idiotic smile still frozen on my face, I notice a scarlet string around her wrist. Buying time, I ask, "What's that?"

Susannah shrugs her bronze curls behind her shoulders. She takes a step closer and tilts her head toward me in a way that causes a shudder to run up my legs.

"It's a souvenir from the Kabbalah fair I stumbled onto this weekend. Can you believe it?" She gazes at me as if this bit of information should hold some significance. We are both part Jewish, at least in lineage, though Susannah has always been more into the occult. I keep the Magic 8 Ball she gave me for my fifteenth birthday in a place of honor with the first track medal I won. For me, her fascination with the spiritual realm has always added to her mystique and made me want her all the more. "Oh, the trendy spiritual stuff," I say, stalling for time. "Isn't Madonna into that?"

Susannah narrows her eyes. My heart stutters. The way she looks at me sometimes, I wonder if she sees through the placid mask I've worn all these years. With my hands-on experience, I figure I'm probably a more accomplished actor than Ryan is by now, so I should be able to hide how I really feel.

But Susannah smiles, roots around in her giant handbag, and hands me a pen with a clear top and a little floating carousel horse inside. "Since you made such a stink about Rhode Island having the oldest carousel still in use in America."

"The Flying Horse Carousel. Wow. Thanks, Suze." I pocket the pen and wipe the dampness from my palms. "I love it." I don't mention that I will probably rearrange my shelves to find a special place for it among the historic relics, personal and otherwise, I collect the way birds gather twigs. My shelves are crammed with artifacts people bring me from their travels: old baseballs, gravestone rubbings, arrowheads, even chunks of brick from buildings where significant events took place.

You don't have to worry about what's going to happen with history.

Because it already happened.

Then it dawns on me. I'd been so wrapped up in the details I'd missed the main point. "What happened with your portfolio review at Rhode Island School of Design, Suze? Isn't that why you went in the first place?"

Susannah looks away. "I can't afford that place."

"Can you say *scholarship*? Your art is amazing," I offer, avoiding mention of her strange but genius animations.

"With my grades?" She smiles and meets my gaze, emotions I can't read flickering in her green eyes. Her smile falls away. "Besides. I'd never fit in there."

I reach for her hand. "I thought you said your filthy rich half-brother was going to pay. Suze, you can't just—" I start to say. Until I remember what's happening right now, about twenty feet behind us. I'm afraid to look.

"I never went to the interview," she mutters, sniffing the rose.

"Are you kidding?"

Susannah scans the crowd for Ryan. For the past two years, RISD was all Susannah talked about. She'd trudge every weekend to that portfolio class in the city, just to get ready for it.

"So was he awesome?" she asks brightly.

I swallow hard and try to answer, but my mouth is dry as pavement. Even though it's ripping my insides apart, I'm still covering for Ryan.

"Bet you were great on the lights, Jeremy," Susannah adds quickly. She cranes her neck, trying to spot Ryan in the crowd. "So where is he?"

Heart pounding, my mind hiccups through its storehouse of facts. I reposition myself to block her view. There's no time to try texting Ryan a warning.

I could tell Susannah. Tell her how Ryan has been sneaking around behind her back for over a year, even hooking up with two college juniors in a motel room during one of our out-of-town meets. But defying the Morgan machine by pointing this out would take too much energy. Instead I blurt, "Did you know the Flying Horse Carousel in Watch Hill was once part of a traveling carnival?"

She laughs and shakes her head. "What? Jeremy, sometimes you can be such a—"

But her voice trails off as her gaze wanders past mine, her smile crumpling like a paper bag. I follow her line of sight and I know this is it. The crowd has thinned around Ryan, enough for her to see him with his mouth smashed against Claudia's.

"Oh, man," I gasp. I turn to comfort Susannah, but she is already gone.

I stand, dithering, wanting to run after her and apologize for letting her walk into this ambush.

But, no. This is something Ryan needs to take care of. I might have signed on to sweep his mess under the rug, but I'll be damned if I'm going to clean up after him. I push through the crowd to get to him.

"What? She *what*? Did you know she was coming back early?"

I feel my face heat. "No."

Ryan pushes a pouting Claudia off him, his stage makeup still glistening and thick, traces of Claudia's lipstick smeared on his lips. "Good job, Jeremy. You could have at least texted me."

My hand curls into a fist. I stuff it in my jacket pocket. "She ran out," I say. "Maybe you can catch her."

Ryan shrugs, and without a coat, stalks out of the theater into the night. I wait a few minutes, then follow. Susannah's car is gone, and so is Ryan's. I try to call Susannah, but she doesn't pick up.

I get in my car and focus on resisting the water bottle's siren call, panicked glimpses of my waking nightmare crashing through the floodgates, the terrifying memories swept through with it. The rain and the torrents of water sweeping past, draining into the Gorge, forcing me to remember. To relive it. No. Not *now*. I need to stay clear.

Since eighth grade, when I discovered that liquor dulls my terrors, I have been a master thief and spy.

Not even Ryan knows.

Just a sip to calm my shaky nerves. One tiny sip to beat back the rising waters that threaten to drown me. I can do it. I pride myself on my steely self-control and my ability to remain stone-cold sober, even when the track team holds a victory keg party. They call me Jeremy the Teetotaler, Jeremy the History Nerd, who never partakes.

I snap open the glove compartment. The innocuous silver bottle is shoved behind the owner's manual, gas receipts, and a collection of PowerBar wrappers. I raise it to my lips and gulp once, twice, three times, the cold liquid igniting as it hits my throat. It takes two, three more gulps to slow my heart to normal speed. The bottle is nearly empty. I cap it and return it to the compartment, warmth flowing to my cold fingers. I'd need to drink three times as much as that to lose focus.

Swerving through the deserted black roads, slick with rain over the ice, I follow my usual running circuit. This is familiar turf. Practically my backyard.

Yes. I can do this. Susannah knows my route, so I hope she's come this way and parked, knowing I'd find her. She wants me to find her. To comfort her. I'll tell her everything. How I'm sorry for lying to her. For letting Ryan hurt her. And maybe, at last, she'll accept that it's not Ryan she wants, but me.

But there's no sign of her.

After driving and searching fruitlessly, my mind churning with outcomes, the now-driving rain blurring my windshield, I can't stand it anymore. My heart is racing. Just one last sip to fortify myself is all I need.

When I round the next hairpin curve, my headlights flash on Ryan's car parked behind Susannah's, both engines running. I squint through the rain and mist and spot them behind the guardrail, illuminated in the headlamps' cone of light. There's no shoulder on this side of the road, so I pull over when I can, about twenty yards past them.

When I finally get out of the car, I can hear her shouts over the racket the rain makes. My head is buzzing, but my thoughts are clear.

In fact, they've never been clearer, as the roots that entangle me fall away.

The damp air smells like freedom.

Susannah screams, and pounds at Ryan's chest with her fists. He shoves her hard and she falls backward. I don't see her get up again. Raucous arguments are nothing new between Susannah and Ryan, but I've never seen him hit her before.

There's a steep decline into the woods where they've chosen to have their argument, and I worry Susannah could have gotten hurt. Ryan disappears now, too. *What the hell are they doing?*

I begin to run at full tilt. I still have some distance to cover, but that's no problem for me, even with the Absolut pumping heat through my veins. But my boot heel catches on a wet leaf and slides out from under me.

I'm flying, but I land softly.

I should have worn my running shoes, I think crazily, then scramble to my feet.

There are blinding lights. The squeal of brakes. Breaking glass.

I don't make it to the other side.

Then

Art class was mandatory freshman year, and I'd spent most of my summer griping about it. I preferred to be out running, not cooped in a smelly room with Mr. Wallace, the creepily silent art teacher who looked like an iguana, but with even less personality.

None of my track buddies were in the class with me, so I fidgeted on my stool, trying to figure out a way to get an extra period of gym.

Five minutes after the late bell rang, a bronze-skinned girl with a cloud of hair a shade lighter flounced in. She wore a tight-fitting black T-shirt and baggy black cargo pants tucked into lace-up combat boots. Mr. Wallace's iguana-eyes followed her to the empty stool next to me. When she got closer, I could see the tiny white hand-written letters on her shirt that said "laugh."

I'd never seen anything so beautiful in my life.

"Is that an order, or a noun?" I whispered once Mr. Wallace looked away, busying himself with the attendance roster.

A slim eyebrow arched over one bright green eye. "You don't remember me, do you?"

"If I'd met you before, I wouldn't have forgotten you."

I rubbed my sweating palms against my jeans. Scrawny as I was, I knew I had no chance with this girl. But at least I could charm her with my biting wit.

"I looked a little different back then," she said, leaning in so close I could almost taste the scent of vanilla on her skin. She pulled away just as Wallace began to read off the attendance.

After my name was called, she leaned in close again and said, "Jeremy Glass, say hello to your Pirate Queen."

I had no idea what she was talking about, but I did learn her name was Susannah Durban. The syllables sat on my tongue like melting sugar.

Now

There's some kind of fog in the room. Through the fog I see my father's eyes.

"Jeremy," he says. "Can you hear me?"

The fog is heavy. It bears down on me, forcing my eyes to close.

"Jeremy. Stay with me." Air hisses in my ears. I'm losing the sound, too.

It seems like a long time later when my eyes flutter open again. My gaze lands on my father. I struggle to understand why I am lying on my back trying to focus my vision on my dad's bloodshot blue eyes.

"Jeremy," he says. "There was an accident last night."

My mind scrambles to piece together the last thing I remember. Susannah and Ryan fighting. Oncoming lights. I struggle to sit, but everything, every inch of me screams with pain.

"Did something happen to Susannah?" I think I am shouting, but instead it comes out as a muffled croak. I sink back on the pillow and let my eyes slip closed.

"Nothing happened to Susannah, as far as I know," Dad says.

I sigh, my eyes still closed, the harsh light stabbing through my eyelids. My heart is starting to race and I remember the flask.

And how buzzed I was as I stepped onto the road. My memory stops there. Had I ever made it across? "Was her car still there?"

The chair scrapes the linoleum as he slides it closer to me. "I have no idea. Susannah Durban isn't really my main concern right now, Jeremy."

My eyes blink open and scan the fluorescent tableau. Machines purr, hum, and bleep. Wires and tubes sprout from me like I'm some kind of space-age hookah pipe.

It's me. I'm the one in a hospital bed. Not Susannah. I'm numb, floating, but I can feel my weight sinking into the hard bed. One foot pushes up from under the blanket and I wiggle my toes to make sure it works. The other leg, mottled and swollen as a raw sausage, is suspended above the bed, enclosed in a configuration of rings and pins. It tingles vaguely, but doesn't actually hurt.

"She was there. With Ryan," I say.

Dad stares at me, his eyes weary and filled with something vague. It dawns on me that it is resignation. It's the same expression he dons before a particularly tough trial, along with one of his expensive but slightly worn suits. His calm demeanor makes me want to vault from the bed, run into the hall, and keep going.

No way that's happening.

Dad sighs. "Actually, Susannah's mother, Trudy, called this morning to tell me Susannah never did come home last night, as if I could do anything about it."

Was she on the run again? Susannah had run away seven times since Freshman year Dad had had to intervene on Mrs. Durban's behalf to stop child services from placing her in foster care.

"I told her that, at the moment, I had more pressing things to attend to," he adds.

"Shit." I glance at my engineering feat of a leg and realize that I won't be running anywhere for a while.

Dad pushes away the salt and pepper flop of hair from his forehead. His face is creased and the skin under his eyes puffy beneath his lawyer's composure. "Don't worry about Susannah. Worry about yourself."

He looks away. I can tell by the way he swallows he has more to say, but I'm too tired to ask. I want to know if they found the water bottle full of vodka, then I realize a simple blood test will tell them the whole story. But mostly I want to know where, exactly, Susannah is. I reach for my phone. No texts from her.

I don't even think about Ryan, until he walks into the room.

—⁓—

Dad has ducked out for coffee. It's me, Ryan, and the beeping of the machines.

Ryan pulls up the chair Dad has just vacated. "I came as soon as I heard."

I furrow my brow and search my memories. "Dude. Weren't you there?"

Ryan twitches the sandy curls out of his eyes. He studies me, confusion and sorrow mingling on his face. "I was so busy having it out with Susannah we didn't even hear you. Then she started to run, so I chased her."

I stare back at his uber-sincere expression. This from a guy who was pissed I hadn't lied well enough for him. I grind my teeth. "She *ran*? I thought I saw her fall. It's all rocks, and then there's that steep slope to the reservoir."

Ryan shrugs. "She tripped, got up and started running like a mad cow."

"She tripped, or you pushed her?" I try to sit forward, but pain lances through my leg as if a team of chainsaw-brandishing dwarves have crash-landed on it. I fall back shakily onto the pillows.

"Take it easy, Jer."

I search my mind for details, but the night is hazy, a mix tape of rain, vodka, and bright lights. And then Susannah's face is in front of me—glistening lips, autumn leaf eyes, tears sparkling on their rims. The urge overtakes me, like it always does when there are things I can't face—the urge to run. But I'm pinned to the bed like a butterfly specimen. "Where is she now, Ryan? My dad says she never got home last night."

"Jeez, Jeremy, how should I know? I *did* follow her. It's pretty rough going on those rocks. It hasn't changed since we used to fish there. And the weather last night was hideous. The ground was slippery. I lost my footing and wrenched my ankle. I couldn't keep up. I just lost her."

"So, she vanished into thin air. And a high school track star like you couldn't keep up with her. You expect me to believe that?"

"C'mon, Jeremy, what's up with you? It wasn't like I didn't try to follow her. She was hysterical and I was worried because she cut her head when she fell. But I could barely walk with my ankle, you know, and I lost track of her. I figured she probably doubled back to where her car was and took off. I got back to the road just as they were loading you into the ambulance. You can check the police report. They asked me if I'd seen what happened, but I didn't find out it was you in there until later."

"You left a bleeding girl stumbling around in the woods and you didn't wonder why her car was still there," I say in a monotone. "And your ankle looks okay today," I add.

The nurse comes in, adjusts my drip bag, then leaves. Ryan leans forward, his voice soft. Reasonable. "She wasn't that hurt. Just a scratch. Shit, Jeremy. You know Susannah. She pulls these stunts all the time. She used to run away all the time."

"Right. I saw you hit her, Ryan."

Ryan turns a bit green. "C'mon, Jer. It was just a little shove. If you saw us, then you know she was slamming me with her fists first. I wasn't going to *do* anything with Claudia Herman. Suze is just—*oversensitive.* You know how she gets."

I'm getting fuzzy. It must be the drugs they keep pumping into me. The words kick out like a knee to the groin. I'm shouting now, my voice hoarse, my mouth flooded with a sour taste.

"You mean how she gets when you *fuck around* behind her back?"

I want to suck the words back in. In all our years as The Lone Ranger and Tonto, I've never violated the sidekick rules. Even when I had to bite my tongue so hard it bled.

Outside my room, I hear voices speak rapidly in urgent tones, too low to understand but loud enough to recognize. It's Patrick Morgan, *Esquire*, talking to Dad. I'd know his booming voice anywhere. Ryan's uber-influential father is probably here to make sure the Morgan interests are safeguarded—as in, Ryan's name is kept clean. He had to have heard my outburst and now Dad is most likely supplicating himself and pleading to the Almighty for forgiveness on my behalf.

Clouds of cotton breeze over me, my eyes closing. The drugs are claiming me again. I almost forget Ryan is still here, beside me.

"That's not what we fought about, Jer," he says softly.

Behind my closed lids, I still see only Susannah's face. "Then where the hell is she, Ryan?"

Then

"Pirate Queen?" I repeated, at a loss for words. My brain, which was used to snapping facts into place like Lego bricks, groped helplessly for something to latch onto.

"In the playground. With the bossy kid. I gave you a Buffalo nickel. I bet you still have it."

I scratched my head and blurted, "Wait. How long ago was this?", just before Mr. Wallace turned around to glare menacingly at us.

Then it all comes back to me. We were eight, Ryan and I. Ryan's babysitter and my mother were sitting on the playground bench, yakking with the other babysitters and parents. Ryan and I were deep into an epic Pirate Quest. Ryan was Captain Hook. I was the first mate. *Of course.* We had a six-boy team of trusty crewmen at our command. We'd just landed on the deserted island, and according to the map (the one I'd scribbled in crayon on a napkin in the lunchroom earlier that day), we were getting close.

The last thing we needed was a girl intrusion. Girls were gross. Yucky. Annoying. A pathetically skinny girl with dark skin, a mop of lighter curls, and eyes like lime-green lollipops swung silently from the monkey bars, watching our every move. We ignored her. Until she jumped down and stalked over to us, all knees and elbows, topped with a ridiculous orange bow that was almost as big as her head.

"I'm the Pirate Queen, and I bet I know where the treasure is."

Ryan leaned on his long pirate's staff, a big stick we'd found in the woods that lined the playground. My gaze shifted between the girl and Ryan as he sized her up. He squinted. I squinted, too.

"No, you don't," he said. "Girls don't know anything."

"Oh, yeah? If you let me on your treasure hunt, I'll tell you where it is. Take it or leave it."

Ryan swung the sweaty curls from his eyes and squinted harder, his lip curled into an exaggerated sneer. "First, you have to pay us a pirate bounty," he said. Even then, he was great at playing a role.

But the girl was, too.

She shrugged and pulled a four-leaf clover and a Buffalo nickel from her pocket.

Ryan pocketed the clover and tossed the nickel to me.

She seemed to be on her own at the playground. After an hour of intense play, a car pulled up and honked. The Pirate Queen bounced off with a quick goodbye.

"I would marry that girl," I said to Ryan, watching her go, the Buffalo nickel in my pocket.

"You're a dork," Ryan said. "Girls are stupid."

We never saw her at the playground again.

And there she was. The Pirate Queen. And her name was Susannah.

Susannah Durban.

After class, in the hall, Susannah pulled me aside. "So, do you?"

"Do I what?"

"Still have the nickel."

In my mind, I scanned my cluttered shelves full of mementos. I never threw anything out, especially something potentially valuable. I knew just where it was, but I hesitated. I didn't want her to peg me for the geek I was. "Um, probably."

"I'd like it back."

Proximity to this girl was pumping icy fire through my veins. I was helpless under her command. If she'd told me to walk down the hall like a chicken, I'd have probably done that, too. But I summoned my cool and kept my head together. It was a skill I'd be perfecting over the years. "Sure. Okay. I'll look."

"Will you walk me to my next class, Jeremy? I have no idea where West Hall 3 is."

I cleared my throat, honored, yet disturbed that in my feverish state I hadn't offered to be her knight in shining armor first. "Sure," I bumbled. "That's the Bio Lab. I have that fourth period."

She glanced at me and smiled a darkly shy cat smile, as if she knew she'd just taken permanent possession of my soul.

On the walk to West Hall 3, I tried to make casual conversation and wondered if she could detect the tremor in my voice. I'd had crushes before, fleeting little fancies that blew in and out with the breeze, all, of course, unreciprocated. But this was different. This was not a breeze. This was a hurricane gale. "So, uh, what brought you back to Riverton after all these years? The thriving cultural scene?"

Riverton has exactly three restaurants, a nature preserve, an ice cream shop called Awesome Cow, a library, a supermarket, and the Riverton Historical Society. The Society was founded through the largesse of the Morgan dynasty, primarily to document and showcase their near century-long stranglehold on the town and to preside over the properties they'd donated to the state. In it you can see old photos of the whole Morgan brood, from their original dry goods store to the three mansions overlooking the river, one now a historic site. There's a young and handsome Patrick Morgan on his wedding day when he married Ryan's mother, Celia. If you squint, you can even see my parents holding hands in the background. You can see pictures of Patrick, with numerous athletic trophies. There's a graduation photo on a framed yearbook page, Patrick and his friends in caps and gowns, beaming megawatt smiles in black and white.

"Ha! My mom's a realtor. She was showing a house in Riverton that day when I told you I was the Pirate Queen. Last month, she found out that the house she grew up in was on the market. So she grabbed it, and back to Riverton we are."

I struggled to focus and connect this exotic creature to the little waif from the playground. The pointy ankles and skinny ribs were all smoothed over in streamlined curves. I was actually short of breath, as if I'd just sprinted a mile. "Your mother grew up here? So did my parents. Maybe they all knew each other."

"Maybe," she said, her gaze suddenly distant, then added, "Hey. Where is that bossy kid with the big stick? Does he still live in Riverton?"

"His name is Ryan. Ryan Morgan. If your mother is from here, then she has to know the Morgans. They basically own this town."

Now

Time in the hospital is formless. Shapeless. People come and go, but coherent thoughts are hard to come by. I drift slowly up from my dreams to find Dad by my bedside, his eyes even more shot through with red veins than before. I have a fleeting thought of how quiet the house must be with him rattling around alone without me to hassle.

"Jeremy," he says. "They've operated."

The words shock me off my cloud of cotton fuzz. "On *me?*"

Dad gives me his sorrowful one-cornered smile, as if there's a tax on using both sides of his mouth. Or maybe they don't work in tandem. I realize I can't even remember what his two-cornered smile looks like, or if he'd ever had one.

"On your leg, Jeremy. The break was very serious. Your tibia was fractured in three places. The doctors say you have compartment syndrome, which is when—"

It's a known fact that Dad reverts to jargon during times of stress. Usually it's legal jargon, but medical terminology is more suited to the occasion. I cut him off with my own trademarked brand of issue avoidance. "Did you know that there are historic records of bones being set all the way back to 3000 BC?"

"Jeremy." He sighs. "This is serious. You're going to be off your feet for a while. And—and they won't know if the surgery took for about a month."

The last words sting like the peeled skin of a blister. "*Took?* What does that mean? My leg wasn't cut off and reattached, was it?"

Dad's face is blotchy and purplish. The breath whistles out through his nose. "No. It's all there." He stands abruptly. "I'm going to send the surgeon in to speak to you. Maybe she can explain things better than I can."

"Dad, just a second. Was Ryan there when they loaded me into the ambulance? He says he was. And his car should have been there. He says it's on the police report. Did you see the report?"

He stares at me for a beat as if I'm speaking a different language. "Does that really matter right now, Jeremy? Look at you."

"It matters to me."

Dad heaves a sigh. "I saw the police report, Jeremy. The truck driver that hit you called the accident in and waited with you until the ambulance came. There won't be any charges filed. There was no one else there. Ryan went for dinner with his parents after the show."

"But, Ryan was there with Susannah! I saw his car. I saw him. He says the police talked to him after the accident. Asked him if he'd seen it. Why would he lie?"

My father's face grows red. "Jeremy. Please. You were in a terrible accident. What you think you remember may not have been what actually happened. I'm an attorney, so I know—people have been convicted on the false memories of witnesses. Be careful about what you claim you saw, because your recollections may be faulty."

"I know what I saw. Ryan was there. We just talked about it. Ask him."

"Patrick Morgan made sure I got a copy of the report, and there's absolutely no mention of Ryan being a witness at the accident scene." Dad wipes his brow and continues in a low and soothing tone. "This will all blow over when Susannah turns up. So settle down. You have other, more important things to think about right now. Like your health. The doctor will be along in a minute."

Dad scoots out of the room, leaving my confused mind to make sense of the conflicting accounts. *Why would Ryan say he was there if he wasn't?*

Instead of the doctor, a very small person, her tiny face lost in a fury of dark hair, shuffles in hesitantly, like Dorothy approaching the Wizard. She's wearing a white uniform and holding a package.

"They said it was okay to come in. Is this a bad time?"

I glance at my leg. It's swathed in white gauze and suspended by an elaborate system of wires and pulleys the Brooklyn Bridge would envy. "Are you a nurse?"

She shakes her head. "I'm Marisa. I work for Mrs. Durban."

Mrs. Durban. Susannah's mother. I'd met her maybe three times, but we'd barely spoken. Something about her fierce eyes and harsh features put me off. I can't imagine working for her, and feel pity for this slight girl.

I detect a faint accent. Her eyes are large and luminous. She looks about eleven. She looks like she's about to pee her pants.

I check out her boobs. Definitely not eleven.

I know this girl. She goes to my school. But she's nearly invisible there, someone who slips from shadow to shadow, barely stirring the air as she moves.

She hands me the package, messily wrapped in brown paper and covered in marker scribblings. I turn it over in my hands and spot my name in the jumble.

Marisa is skittish, like a cat at the edge of a riverbank. "Mrs. Durban found this in Susannah's room. She asked me to bring it to you."

"So no one's heard anything from Susannah yet?" I ask, still turning the package over and over. My fingers tremble. I've lost track of time in the hospital. How many days have I been in here? Two? Four? A week?

"No. Not that I know of." Marisa says, and turns to leave.

"Do you want me to open it now?" I ask, though I regret it instantly. The package is meant for me. Susannah wrote *my* name on it. Me.

I glance at my phone on the bed table. My calls to Susannah have gone to voicemail, text messages unanswered. Where is she? Is anyone looking for her? Suddenly, I'm afraid to open the package.

"I have to go now," Marisa says. And she does.

I'm alone with my trussed-up leg and a package from Susannah.

The phone shuddering beside me nearly jolts me off the bed. It's a text. A YouTube link from Susannah.

I click the link and it directs me to another one of her animations. Leaves float through black space in the herky-jerky, stop-action way that is Susannah's style.

She wanted to study animation, I think. She'd just come back from visiting her way older half-brother, Dennis, in Rhode Island. One of her mother's cast-offs, Susannah called him. She'd often wondered how many more there were. Going to RISD meant everything to her. Why on earth would she run away now, when she was almost free? Where would she go?

I think of her face as she told me she skipped out on the college tour, and watch the small screen cluttered with Susannah's personal iconography. Old gravestones. Torn lace. Faded cigar boxes.

Before she'd left, I'd barraged her with interesting tidbits about Rhode Island and she'd scribbled them in the ratty little notebook she took wherever she went. The first circus pitched its tent in Newport in 1774. The world's oldest operating carousel is in Watch Hill. Hence, the pen from Watch Hill.

And, sure enough, a carousel horse flies past an eerie circus tent.

I shudder.

This is recent.

And I wonder—has Susannah been keeping secrets of her own from me? From everyone?

The scene closes in on a mound of dirt. A pair of disembodied hands unearth a peeling cigar box. The box opens. Inside is a word in old wood-type lettering. And I have my answer.

SECRETS

Shaking, I rest my phone upside-down on the bedside table.

My eyes close, and all I can see is her face, watching me, asking me silently what I'm going to do, forcing me to relive the many ways I've failed her.

I lie there, the package sitting on my lap. An hour. Two hours. Time here is, again, shapeless, measured by the beeps of the equipment I'm connected to. I step onto the cloud that has lowered itself like a magic carpet.

Then

As if she'd conjured him just by the mention of his name, Ryan ambled down the hall, headed straight for us, his eyes locked on Susannah. I guess I might have wished somewhere deep inside my animal brain that Susannah would have been as mesmerized with me as I was with her, but that tiny hope was quickly snuffed out when I saw the look in her eyes.

I knew that look. It was the glazed expression most girls got when they laid eyes on Ryan Morgan.

Susannah's lips had fallen open, as if she'd been struck dumb by a holy vision, and I wondered where that tough little Pirate Queen had gone. Gritting my teeth, I imagined Ryan as he looked at her, the saintly corona glowing around his head full of wavy gold hair.

I wanted to pull her aside and warn her that, though I loved him like a brother, angelic Ryan was already, even in ninth grade, hell on girls. In eighth grade he'd torn through about five relationships, leaving a trail of flaming wreckage behind him, broken-hearted nymphettes who followed me around, hungry for any little crumbs of information about him I could provide.

But I did no such thing. Despite his flaws, my loyalty was to Ryan. Steadfast and true, I squeezed my sweaty hands into my pockets, clenched them into fists, and clamped my mouth firmly shut.

Now

The weight of the package on my lap pulls me back. So does the persistent throb in my leg. Where are the nurses when you need them?

I tear open the package.

Inside is another package wrapped like a gift. On it is a label. The word SECRETS is stamped across it.

I tear it open, terrified, yet desperate to know what's inside. Terrified to learn what burden she wants to place on me. Terrified that I owe her and that I'm partly to blame for her pain.

It's a wine-colored velvet pouch with a flap. Inside are five candles, a pendant on a red cord, a piece of chalk, and a parchment envelope. The pendant is the Kabbalah one Susannah always wears. The one Ryan gave her. I strain to recall if she was wearing it the night she disappeared, but there is no way to know for sure; she'd been wearing a jacket. My hands sweaty, leg grinding with pain, I pull the paper from its envelope.

There's a Post-it note stuck to it, written in Susannah's neat hand.

I'm entrusting my secrets to you, Jeremy.

The pain chews its way up my leg. I read the title of the paper under the Post-it.

To Summon The Dead

Where the hell are those nurses?

The pain shoots pointy roots up my spine and into my cranium. I reach for the call button and stuff the package under my pillow, squeezing my eyes against the tears.

In the time it takes to blink, the pain brings a flash of crystal clarity. And I know.

I may never run again.

History is only a crutch that won't support me any longer.

But history, because of my love of it *and of her*, is why Susannah is entrusting her secrets to me.

CHAPTER

four

Then

The look of rapture on Susannah's face was reflected in Ryan's. It was a look of curiosity and wonder, a look of such intensity that I knew anything I did to come between them was pointless. Right there in the hall near West Hall 3, I witnessed two people falling in love.

It felt like horses were trampling over my chest, like my ribs were cracking, the bone shards jammed into the soft tissue of my lungs.

But I kept the smile pasted on my face and managed to speak between painful breaths. It was a skill I'd come to master over the next three years. "Susannah. This is Ryan Morgan. The bossy kid from the playground. Ryan, meet the Pirate Queen."

Ryan's blue eyes dilated, his mouth falling open like he was about to take a bite of the most luscious ice cream cone ever. "Huh?" he said, eloquent as usual.

"From the park. It was like five, six years ago? Remember when we used to play pirates, and this girl came along and you said that girls were—"

"Yeah! I remember. I said girls were stupid."

I didn't mention that I was the one who'd vowed I was going to marry her.

Susannah smiled and flipped some stray curls out of her face. "You really said that?"

Ryan chuckled. "What did I know when I was eight? Where's your class? I'll take you there."

And just like that, he slipped a muscled arm over her slim shoulder and they drifted away as if I wasn't there. As if they'd been standing alone. I watched them go, the ridiculous smile clamped on my face like a too-tight mask.

Now (November 26th)

Six days later, I'm carted out of the hospital, a pincushion on wheels.

I've had no further contact from Susannah and there's been no sign of her. Search teams have combed the reservoir banks and turned up nothing. Trudy Durban has been on the news nightly, pleading for information about her whereabouts, leaving me to ponder why she's never called to ask me what was in the package.

Dad rolls my chair out to the car, my casted leg pointing the way like a battle standard.

My leg, the doctor tells me, is on probation. Okay, that's not how she put it. Compartment syndrome. Nerve endings starved for oxygen. Potential tissue death. I heard every other word, but I got the point.

Wrapped in gauze and held together by pins and rods, my leg has a month to plead its case.

I'm sent home with a set of crutches, metal ones, with cushions to support my armpits and protruding rubber grips that comfortably fit my grasp. There's a sturdy permanence about them, unlike the one-size-fits-all wood crutches you can buy in the local drugstore.

I don't trust them.

Dad's had a narrow makeshift wood ramp built over half the steps so I can roll in through the back door. His study-slash-den on the first floor is to be my home while I recuperate. I maneuver the wheelchair to the window and watch the sparrows land at the feeder Dad and I set up on the ancient gnarled oak at the end of our driveway last winter. I want to fly away too, but instead I'll be collecting dust like the artifacts on my shelves.

Days pass. I don't want to think about what's going on with the crushed bone beneath the raw skin of my injured leg. I can't feel my toes, but even after three painkillers my shin still announces its throbbing presence. A forbidden sip from the Civil War canteen from last year's re-enactment, cleverly hidden behind the towers of DVDs in the wall unit, can't stop it, either.

I rise on the crutches and stumble around the room, back and forth, back and forth, dragging my Eiffel Tower of a leg. It's good resistance training, I tell myself. By the time I get the cast off, my other leg should be made of iron.

Then I bench press. Ten times. Twenty times. Fifty. Until my arms burn and my neck sinew is about to snap.

I fall into the chair, soaked with sweat, and watch the birds some more.

It doesn't work. The pain is still there.

I flick on the TV and turn to the local news. The media feeding frenzy over Susannah's disappearance has reached a fever pitch. Trudy Durban's pleas have hit a chord. She is convincing, a grief-stricken mother, begging for word of her daughter. Even the town which had rejected her thaws to her pleas. But there's no sign of her. Thirteen days and counting since Susannah disappeared. Since my leg began its battle for survival.

Kabbalah. Susannah's latest in a continuum of shifting passions. Before her trip, I'd found an old book on it. I'd made a passing effort to bone up on it so I could appear interested, but it's not enough to help me now.

Are the clues to her disappearance somehow linked to her interest in ancient Hebrew mysticism? Lately, Susannah's art had taken on a distinctly spiritual quality. She'd started an amazing drawing, a brightly colored diagram of numbers, circles, and Hebrew letters superimposed over a gnarled tree drawn with gray ink on black paper. She'd smiled cryptically and told me it was the Tree of Life. She'd never shown me the finished art.

I think about what little I learned of Kabbalah, or know about the Jewish religion in general. Dad never pushed for much except for a menorah at Chanukah and Passover dinners at my aunt's in New Jersey. Mom wasn't much of a Christian, either, except at Christmas, when her exquisitely traditional ornaments emerged from attic boxes. Every December they'd hung from a live spruce Dad and I chopped down from the woods behind our house. It has been a long time since we've had one of those.

I close that door fast. Memories of my mother are not safe terrain.

Religion was never a big factor in my upbringing. As far as I knew, it was even less so in Susannah's; according to her, her mother was raised Jewish, but converted to Catholicism. Susannah claimed she was everything and nothing.

But while I immersed myself in history, running, and other less acceptable pursuits, Susannah was searching for something more.

What was she looking for? Had she found it?

I review what I've learned and find nothing to help me. The writings of the Kabbalah are highly spiritual teachings intended to explain the workings of the universe, the connection of the earthly plane to the divine, and the human soul's relationship to all of it. Very positive stuff. Nothing diabolical or demonic in there that I could find.

Yet I remember Susannah was particularly interested in the explanation of what happened to the soul after it passed to the next plane.

I shiver and think of the velvet pouch, buried at the bottom of my gym bag. What other, darker roads had Susannah's quest led her down?

During my hospital stay, someone from Durban Realtors kept calling my cell and hanging up. Probably Mrs. Durban or Marisa, wanting to know what was in the package Susannah left me. I wonder if Marisa ever told Trudy Durban about the package in the first place. I imagine she would have torn it open, even if it was addressed to me.

I shudder. I can't face Mrs. Durban. Then I'd have to admit I was there that night. That I failed to help Susannah because I'm a drunk.

Time is rapidly taking on a new shape. Instead of the smooth lake of history, a place I can wade into and do the backstroke, it's a whirling funnel that tapers to a single point, impaling me on the memory of the night Susannah disappeared.

Suddenly, I can't get away from the surge of memories that press against my skull, threatening to crack it wide open. I fight the useless urge to run. Birds with clipped wings can't fly.

Then

Ryan didn't call, text, or show up on Facebook that night. But I did see he'd added a new Facebook friend to his impressive stable. I stalked Susannah's privacy protected profile, learning nothing and not daring to add her. At midnight, the friend request from her came in, and without hesitation, I accepted and jumped to her page. Photos of her. Photos of her art. Crazy art. Wild art. Towering constructions of junk teetering in unknown backyards, a much skinnier, younger Susannah smiling beside them. And then a chat window opened.

Hey, thanks for adding me. Sorry about what happened today. I get easily distracted.

I was seething, aching, worse than the aftermath of any marathon run. But I knew from the start that girls like Susannah didn't go for dorks like me. It wasn't the natural order of things. And there she was, offering an olive branch. Maybe even offering a chance at friendship.

And so, for fear of getting blocked from her circle, I became a satellite, a planet caught in her orbit. Agreeable Jeremy Glass, who didn't care if his heart was passed through a meat grinder, as long as he got to breathe the same air.

No problem. I typed, each idiotic keystroke like a nail hammered into a coffin of my own making. **See you in class tomorrow.**

Now

My phone trembles on the unmade bed. A text. Probably Ryan again. He's been checking in every day, sometimes twice, along with a few other kids from the track team. After pressure from Dad, I'd long since apologized for my outburst, claiming it was the drugs that loosened my tongue. Under the circumstances, Ryan forgave me. Now he and the guys want to visit, but I'm just not in the mood to see anyone.

I propel my wheelchair to the bed, rolling over and around the clothes and other crap scattered across the floor. Though Dad has tried to straighten up, the mess has grown to epic proportions and leaning down from the wheelchair to pick up my clothes makes my leg explode with pain.

I freeze, staring at my phone until my eyes burn.

The text is from Susannah.

Maybe, I tell myself, she's finally getting in touch. Maybe this entire episode really is an elaborate prank of hers, some ill-conceived attempt at the performance art she'd admired after a class trip to visit trendy galleries in Chelsea. Eventually, everything Susannah saw, learned, or thought about filtered into her art.

She wouldn't go back to her brother in Rhode Island. Maybe she's got other half siblings, or estranged uncles. Maybe she's located her mysterious father. By now, she's realized the whopper of a mistake she made by running off. Maybe this whole thing is about punishing Trudy Durban, payback for being a lousy mother. It's a well-known fact that Trudy is a bitch with a dangerous temper and a violent streak. In one notorious incident, Trudy shot a neighbor's dog that had wandered into her yard, claiming the dog was possessed. Susannah claimed that one time Trudy had even threatened her.

Improbably, I picture Susannah by the ocean in a white dress, her bronze curls lifted in the salty breeze.

The vision crumbles. Instead, I see her closed eyelids, paper-thin and bluish, dried leaves and bits of dirt caught in the snarled strands spread around her like seaweed.

My temples throb. I open my eyes and read the text. I'm breathing hard. No actual response to my repeated texts. No confirmation that she's read them. Nothing but another private link to a stop-action animation.

Ryan does a herky-jerky hula across a colorized photo of a backyard. It's my backyard. He stops at my tire swing and strikes an Egyptian-like pose by the gnarled oak tree at the end of our driveway, and pulls off his smiling face like a mask to reveal a frowning face beneath. A flowering bush sprouts. A sign is pitched into the ground.

SECRETS—DIG HERE

Shaking, I sit in the chair and watch the sun sink between the naked trees. I doze and wake up, my neck cramped, back stiff. It's late now. Dad has left me dinner on a tray and probably gone to bed. We've spoken so little since I got home. What is there to say that won't dredge up the stuff we can't talk about?

I lie back on the reclining leather lounger in front of the flat screen and flick on an old movie from Netflix. Some study. I'm pretty sure this is where Dad kicks back and watches porn, though sadly I can't find any evidence of that. Instead, I watch some stupid eighties movie about girls and nerds, which hits a bit too close to home.

I don't realize I've fallen asleep again until I wake gasping, heart thudding against my ribs. My lungs are filling with water. I claw at my throat, unable to breathe. Unable to scream, until I finally choke out a cry for help.

It's starting again.

With my usual defenses stripped away, I'm powerless to stop it. Now there's nothing to hold back the return of the terrors.

Then

I was nine when Mom picked me up from camp that afternoon, the summer after encountering the Pirate Queen. It was just an ordinary day and Mom was there, like always, but that day something sharp scraped inside my stomach, ordering me not to get in the car. On occasion, Dad left the office for a bit and drove me home for Mom. For some reason I couldn't explain, I distinctly remember wishing this were one of those days.

Even though the loop of that day has replayed so many times in my head, I can't remember anything particularly unusual about Mom as she strolled over to my cluster of unruly campers. She was neatly groomed as always, prettier than most of the other moms, that army of frowzy, chubby, and harried women who emerged from their refrigerated SUVs, clutching their containers of iced coffee, to claim their young.

Mom's blond hair was pulled into a crisp ponytail, her refined features free and clear of makeup. She patted my head and kissed me on the cheek. I caught a whiff of her French perfume and a splash of cinnamon mouthwash, but as she pulled away I saw that feral wildness in her eyes, the empty hopelessness I'd sometimes glimpse when she thought I wasn't looking; the glazed look of a wounded deer as it lies dying on the forest floor.

Her hands gripped the steering wheel so tightly the knuckles were white. She glanced at me in the rear-view mirror and smiled, but her eyes were puffy and red.

If I'd refused to get in the car with her, maybe it never would have happened.

Mom might still be alive.

Now

I hear myself screaming.

Hair unkempt, Dad comes skidding into the study in his bathrobe. I fight to draw breath into my constricted airways. He settles beside me on the chair's armrest and pulls my sweaty head against his chest. "It's okay, Jeremy. It's okay," he murmurs.

I force my breathing to calm and pull away.

"Was it one of those nightmares again? I thought you stopped having those."

My heart speeds up again. I want to run. I want to run.

I want to drink.

"I'm okay, Dad," I finally manage to say. "It happens sometimes, but not as much as—you know—when it happened. I'm kind of used to it, I guess."

He stands, pats my head, and then steps back and stares at me for a beat before he speaks. "The doctor tells me that these things are normal after a trauma. And you've just been through another..." He stops, the words that almost slipped out trapped safely behind his teeth. "Get some sleep. You sure you don't want me to help you onto the daybed?"

I meet his gaze, questions sizzling on my tongue. The ones I'll never ask.

Why? Why did she do it?

Dad looks so earnest. So concerned.

Yet no words have ever been spoken between us about what caused my mother to drink every afternoon—and drive her car off the road into the Riverton Gorge with her nine-year-old son strapped into the backseat.

I feign sleep and listen to his slippered feet retreat to the hall, back to the world beyond this room.

And now I can't stand it anymore. Dad's study has become the inside of Mom's car as we sailed over the embankment and plunged into the Gorge, dark waters rising to my eyes, filling my mouth and throat. The pressurized silence as Mom's hair floated free from its binding in slow motion, like the sea anemones I'd seen at the aquarium.

—⁂—

I wait a half hour until the house noises go silent. Until I'm certain Dad has gone back to sleep. Grabbing the crutches, I throw them over my lap and wheel myself into the kitchen.

Dad's stash is in the pantry. He thinks I don't know that he's never tossed out the contents of Mom's well-stocked bar, the rows of Absolut lined up like my collection of tin soldiers. He's hidden the treasure trove behind a few massive bags of barbecue charcoal. Over the years I've been refilling them with water.

I can't imagine why he keeps them.

A shrine to Mom? A test for me?

I raise myself gingerly onto the crutches, appalled how tough it is to balance, even with my workout regimen. I hobble into the dark pantry, careful not to scrape the crutches or fall. I'm shaky; the need for the liquor's cold warmth calls out from deep inside my bones, drowning out the shame I feel as I reach for what killed my mother and almost killed me eight years ago.

I find the bottle I've marked as having the purest undiluted vodka. I've only turned to the pantry as a last resort, so there's plenty to last me.

Uncapping the bottle, I take a swallow, knowing how the liquid will dull my mind, slow my reflexes and make balancing on these crutches an Olympic challenge. But I've run marathons after downing half a bottle. And won.

Then

The next day at school, Susannah was wearing an identical black T-shirt, this time with white cargo pants and flip-flops. Her toenails were painted black; though I tried not to stare at her feet, I couldn't help but notice there were tiny words painted on each nail. Her hair was piled high on her head and it took all my strength not to reach over and pull out the contraption that held it all there, so it would tumble around her shoulders in a shimmering waterfall of curls.

Her T-shirt had the same tiny word "*laugh*", which was now joined by two other words, "*and the...*"

"Is that a time released T-shirt?" I asked, and was treated to a Mona Lisa smirk.

She pointed her foot and wiggled her toes. "Look."

I leaned in closer and read the message on her toenails. "... *world laughs with you. Weep, and you weep alone.*"

"Is that your motto?"

"Yep," she said, already bent over a box of found material, from which we were all expected, under the reptile gaze of Mr. Wallace, to create a self-portrait that was both breathtakingly original and meaningful.

"It's mine, too."

I stared miserably out the window, pondering the exact number of crows that perched on the telephone pole, trying not to think that my self-portrait should be a rusting old car at the bottom of the Gorge.

By the time I'd snapped out of my reverie, Susannah had constructed a figure with a protruding rib cage and outstretched arms entirely from tiny bits of windshield glass and a coat hanger.

"Is that a portrait of me?" I asked, smiling. "You know, Jeremy Glass?"

Susannah slanted her head, dead serious. "You're a real kidder, aren't you? Where's yours?"

"I'm still thinking." I said, actually wondering why this sunshiny girl was making a portrait of herself with broken glass. "I guess I'll do a running shoe. That's what I am. A runner."

She smiled, then said, "Aren't we all?" Returning to her efforts, so deeply engrossed in her work that she didn't even notice when the bell rang.

When I think of Susannah, this is how I like to see her—deep in concentration, her brow furrowed. I wonder if art for her is like running is for me, an escape from the dark things that always threaten to black out the sun.

Now

The sharp edge of my panic dulls. I'm ready to face Susannah's treasure hunt now.

I hobble unsteadily to the back door and peer out. A black void looms beyond the three steps from the stoop to the driveway and the oak tree beyond. Navigating the steps with crutches is a skill I've yet to master. Doing so with a half-bottle of vodka sloshing through my veins is a whole other level of challenge.

But I have to know if there really is a message in the animation, or if Susannah is just playing with me. Why would she send me animations and not get in touch? Anger flares unexpectedly.

She's abandoned me in my time of need.

Where the hell is she? I have to know.

One precarious step, two steps, three. My sneaker touches asphalt a few seconds before the rubber crutch tips catch up with it. I'm still standing.

I pause, mustering the courage to cross the dark driveway to the old oak tree that was so clearly the one in the animation. I imagine the air rushing by my face as I run, muscles pumping as the pavement purrs beneath my rubber soles. The ground slants. It's the longest few yards I've ever faced. Longer than the final leg of the marathon I'd run last summer, gripped by fever and violent stomach cramps.

Across the dark gulf of pavement, I reach the tree. My tree. I wonder if the animation is a map to guide me here. *But why?*

I'm at the base of the tree, moonlight falling on its tangled roots. The night wind nips at my T-shirt and flaps my pajama pants. Ragged clouds frame the moon's taunting smile. A few raindrops fall. My shattered leg registers nothing, only the steady ache from within the crushed bone, pounding its ominous drumbeat.

The vodka is wearing off and I'm hit by a wave of exhaustion. If I could run, I'd sprint back into the house and crawl under the covers. But coming out here is a commitment. Now I have to follow through.

I glance up to the second-floor windows. Dad's room is still dark. The wind kicks up. Cold rain slaps the driveway, plastering my hair to my scalp. Gingerly, I lower myself until I am sitting on my butt, the scaffolded leg jutting out like a bridge to nowhere. Rain muddies the place where the growth of moss has been disturbed not so long ago.

Using the tip of my crutch as a spade, I loosen the dirt. The rubber tip bonks something hard. Swiveling, I dig with both hands and feel the corner of what appears to be a box or something.

Rain slams me with repeated thuds. Muddy water fills the hole I've made as I pull a cigar box out of the ground. Though the colorful paper label has nearly disintegrated, I recognize the box as the one from Susannah's animation. I open it. There's nothing inside except a plastic baggie with a photo of Ryan sealed within. Someone has defaced it with markers and Wite-Out to give him long eyelashes and a mouthful of Dracula teeth. There's a strip of paper in Susannah's neat printing that reads:

Ryan has secrets, too.

I close the box, let the rain wash away the grime, and tuck it under my arm. My mind revs, but then stalls. It's as oversaturated as my T-shirt, unable to process the fact that the box in Susannah's video link actually exists.

Water eddies down the slope, pooling around my butt. Cold liquid streams off the metal contraption holding my leg together. I feel nothing but a vague burning itch as I laboriously make my way back inside the house.

CHAPTER

five

Now

I wake to quiet. Slivers of light creep across the clothes and papers strewn around my floor. I'm sprawled on the daybed, naked save for the strip of sheet draped over my privates like in a Renaissance nude. I don't remember peeling off my soaked clothes or where I'd put them. My head vibrates like a rhapsody played on steel drums. My leg thrums, the swelling skin between the pins hot to my touch.

Dad has left my daily fix of Vicodin on the mini-fridge with a glass of water, a banana, and a bowl of dry cereal. There is a carton of milk inside.

I dress and chase down the two pills with gulps of water before the grumble of pain becomes a scream. I settle on the bed and wait for the Vikes to kick in and keep the gnawing pain at bay.

Watching my chest rise and fall, I imagine Susannah wiping my brow with a cold compress. What I really need right now is a nurse. A very pretty nurse.

My thoughts skim through lazy fields of memory and imagination. Susannah cavorts through the tall grass flinging flowers at me. My stomach rumbles. I'm starved.

But I'd rather drink before the golden memories turn ugly, grow fangs and bite me.

I consider reaching for the few remaining dregs of vodka in the canteen above my head, but nix that idea. Too much effort. The Vicodin will have to do.

Hours drift by. If I don't move too much, the numbing haze of my meds masks the grinding gears in my leg well enough that I'm almost comfortable. I reach for the Civil War history book on the night table. Mandatory reading for some, guilty pleasure for me. My thoughts flow back to a different age as I pore over battle trivia and primary documents. At first, I think the rapping at my door is artillery fire. The book flies from my hands.

"Dude! It's me!" says a muffled voice through the closed door. "The back door was open. Can I come in?"

Ryan. "This isn't a good time," I call out weakly. My leg slowly heats like a sausage on a spit. I realize it's been hours since I last took a painkiller. There's an aching heaviness between my ribs. My hands are like weights at the ends of my arms.

"You in there, Jer?" Ryan calls through the door.

I try to answer, but before I have the chance, the door bursts open. Ryan peers at me, arms folded. "Dude. You look like crap."

"Thanks for clearing that up. I was just sitting around wondering if I really do look as shitty as I feel. "

"Sorry." Ryan smiles and sets a box on the night table. "The guys and I thought you'd like the complete set of Ken Burns' Civil War documentary. To kill the time while you recuperate, you know?"

My gaze flits to the boxed set of DVDs on the table. I'm kind of touched they picked something I'd really like. Normally my heart would leap at such a treasure. But it can't even muster a flutter. "Cool. Tell them thanks."

Ryan slants his head. "You must really feel like turd if even Ken Burns can't get a rise out of you."

I prop my back against the wall. The words fly out before I even realize I thought them. "How hard did you look for her? Did you go back there?"

Ryan's shoulders slump. He plops heavily into Dad's recliner and sighs. "Me and some of the guys went back to Reservoir Road a couple of days later and walked up and down along the shore. Then the searchers and their dogs came. There's no sign of her. What else do you want me to do?"

There's a cold lump in my throat. I consider the photo of Ryan, defaced to make him look like a bloodsucker. I can't fathom what Susannah is trying to say, but one thing is clear. She was furious. I can't say I blame her.

"You're the one that's supposed to care." I close my eyes briefly, then open them and meet Ryan's wounded gaze. "If anything happened to her, it's our fault. You know that, right?"

Ryan scowls, his brow furrowed. "That's completely and totally nuts. You're all doped up and you're not making any sense."

"I'm making perfect sense. You fucked with her head and I helped you do it."

Ryan rolls his eyes. "C'mon. This is the painkillers talking, dude, not you."

Something stirs beneath the damp sludge of my stupor and shoots to the surface. "Just leave, okay?" I say coldly.

"What is this shit, Jeremy? What's gotten into you?"

"Too much Vicodin and not enough vodka."

Ryan stands, his hands balling into fists. "I didn't ask you to follow us that night. If you hadn't stuck your nose into my business you wouldn't be in this—"

"Is *that* what you think I'm pissed about? *Myself?*" I grab the closest thing to me, the Civil War tome I'd dropped, and in a sudden burst of strength fling it at him. Yeah. I'm fucked for life. But it's my own fault and I can't throw a goddamned book at myself. Ryan makes an easier target. "Get the fuck out of here."

Ryan ducks. The book sails past him and falls at the feet of the girl who stands in my doorway, her mouth falling open.

It's Marisa, the girl who works for Susannah's mother.

"Enjoy the Ken Burns marathon." Ryan brushes past Marisa and stomps out.

"This is a bad time," she says in her softly accented voice.

"Yeah." I say, overwhelmed by the slicing agony that knifes up my leg.

"I should go."

But Marisa doesn't leave. She stands in the doorway, the Civil War book at her feet. Her arms are full of more books.

"That would be a good idea," I say.

I'm feeling lame for lashing out at Ryan. He's probably still in shock. Reasonable Jeremy never yells. Reasonable Jeremy is always in control. Reasonable Jeremy is happy in his role as human doormat and Enabler-in-Chief.

"Your father asked me to speak to your teachers. You, uh, have a good chunk of AP Calculus to catch up on."

"So, you're working for him now?"

"I go where the money is," Marisa says curtly.

"Great," I say. "I should have known. AP-fucking-Calculus. The Holy Grail. It wasn't my idea to take it, but Dad figured it would better my scholarship chances. I'll never catch up at this point."

Marisa looks down, her tiny face lost in the dark curls. "I can help, if you like."

Not wanting to insult her, I try to smile, but sour thoughts tug my mouth into a sneer. "It's not worth your time."

She raises her chin and there's the barest glimmer of a challenge in her coal-black eyes. "I'm very good at math. I took AP Calc last year. Let me know if you change your mind."

Marisa whirls around and leaves. The upended Civil War book rests exactly where it landed.

I stare at the empty door, then grope for the Vicodin. I pop four of them in my mouth, gulp down the last of the water, settle back, and wait for the lava flow in my leg to cool.

—⁂—

It's Dad's turn to host poker night. Once a month, he and his buddies gather at one of their homes for their raucous, drunken, testosterone-laden card game. I remember Mom used to have an aversion to poker night and always hid in her bedroom. Because of that, I thought it was some kind of terrible man ritual until I started to realize it was kind of fun. I got to sneak some rum into my bottle of cola and slink off with my booty, unnoticed.

But tonight, I dread it. And the thing I dread the most is facing Patrick Morgan and his pretend pity.

The men set up in the dining room and I listen to their laughter, the pain in my leg intensifying with each passing minute. I swallow two Vicodins and have managed to immerse myself in a book about Revolutionary war hero Nathan Hale when I look up to see Patrick Morgan standing in the doorway to Dad's study.

"Jeremy, my boy!" he booms with a broad, cheery grin, liquor fumes radiating from him in waves. I lick my lips, thinking how much I could use a swig of whatever's sloshing around in his stomach.

He's holding a basket brimming with snack foods and candy. "Celia knows you have a sweet tooth, so we thought these goodies might help you convalesce."

He strides into the room, places the basket on Dad's messy desk, and pulls up a chair next to my wheelchair. "So," he asks softly, his grin vanishing, "How are you feeling, Jeremy? How's the leg?"

"Kind of busted up, but okay, I guess, Mr. Morgan."

"Jeremy, you've known me your whole life. You are permitted to call me Patrick. In fact, I insist."

"Okay, Patrick." I stare at him, without any idea of what I should say. Patrick Morgan always manages to render me speechless, his burning blue eyes and shock of movie star grey hair making him seem larger than life.

"Good book?" he asks.

"Um, yeah, if you like reading about tragic heroes who died senselessly."

"Hmmm," says, Patrick, suddenly lost in thought. "You, on the other hand, are a pretty lucky guy. You could have been flattened by that truck, Jeremy."

"Yeah, I guess." I neglect to mention that Susannah wasn't as lucky, since she hasn't been seen or heard from since that night, which was now over two weeks ago.

Patrick Morgan stares at me, and it's as if his eyes can cut through the layers of my silence like scalpels. "Ryan misses you, but I understand if you're not up for company these days."

I glance at my leg, which still throbs despite the Vicodin-induced veil of numbness settling over it. "I'm sorry if I've been kind of rude to Ryan. But I've been in a bit of pain. It's hard to be sociable."

"Ryan is your best friend. You don't have to do anything." The eyes don't leave me, like a knife pressed against my throat. I gasp for air, the room suddenly stuffy and close.

"I know, but..."

Patrick Morgan stands. "It's okay, Jeremy. Not a problem. Ryan's just concerned about you. As we all are."

"Thanks, Mr. Morgan—uh—Patrick. I'm sure the leg will be fine."

"I wasn't referring to your leg."

"Huh?"

Patrick Morgan heads for the door, but turns back around. "You don't suppose the doctors didn't register your extremely elevated blood alcohol level, do you?"

His words are like a slap. How stupid *am* I? I should have known there'd been a Morgan intervention.

"What?"

"Jeremy. You were driving a car while heavily under the influence. You could have killed someone. Instead, you got yourself hurt. Under the circumstances it was easy to have the medical report vanish."

"What are you saying? Does my father know?"

"As always, your father has chosen to avoid reality. And you have enough other problems to deal with right now, don't you?" Patrick Morgan pauses, jettisoning the frozen smile. He leans in close, his voice velvety soft. "What I'm saying, Jeremy Glass, is to look carefully where you step. It's easy to take a fall when you're hopping around on one leg."

—m—

I weigh Patrick Morgan's words and wonder if I heard him right. If the drugs are making me paranoid. Was he trying to extort me into keeping quiet? Or is he just playing his part as the influential family friend stepping in to save my precarious reputation?

It's hard to say.

Once the house clears, I lie awake, unable to sleep. Dark thoughts flood my mind like a broken water main. Images float by—my mother's blond hair slipping free of its ponytail in slow motion, the thin bluish skin of Susannah's temples. My heart pumps a soundtrack to the looping slide show. Sweat coats my forehead. The need to run burns through my stagnant muscles.

If I had any sense, I really should be worrying about what was going on with my leg under its cast. It can't be anything good.

Finally, the pain subsides. I'm up on one crutch, precariously reaching with my free arm for the canteen. Every shred of sense I possess screams that mixing four Vicodin and vodka is a recipe for an overdose.

It's really just a few swallows, I tell myself. There's my famous self-control.

I down the stuff.

A short time later, swaddled in a warm fuzz, my mind settles, then is drawn like dead leaves to a sewer drain toward Susannah and the mysterious Kabbalah package. She went to the trouble of burying the cigar box, so apparently she had some kind of a plan. I can't help but wonder if it included dying.

I fish out the package from under my bed and stare at it.

A dead-summoning kit.

What kind of game is Susannah playing? Is this some weird test of my loyalty, a personal hazing? Or a penance for my betrayals?

Either way, I've got to play out my part in her little psychodrama.

I sit a long while, the velvet pouch resting on my lap, debating whether I should call Mrs. Durban and tell her about the package. I'm pretty sure Marisa smuggled it out of their house without her knowing. I wonder, irrationally, what would happen if I used it to bring back my mother instead. My mother who killed herself and almost took me with her.

I must be insane to believe this cheap kit will do anything. It's no Kabbalah spell. It's probably something Susannah bought at one of those occult shops she frequented in the East Village, on the hunt for props for her animations. I look for a trademark, just to make sure it doesn't say Parker Brothers or something.

But I'm feeling crazy enough to try using it.

The contents of the baggie within the velvet pouch are pretty flimsy for such a solemnly monumental ritual. Which makes it kind of difficult to take the thing seriously. But since Susannah apparently has, I resolve to continue.

There's a note on parchment printed in an overly pretentious script, five tapered white candles, a diagram of a pentagram, and a snip of hair in a small baggie. Susannah's hair. Tucked inside the folds of the velvet pouch is the Kabbalah necklace she always wore. The one that Ryan gave her.

I swallow hard, growing convinced that this has to be some elaborate prank of hers. She'll probably tape me as I do the stupid ritual. The video will go viral on YouTube and I'll be the laughingstock of Riverton.

I soldier on. To not do so would be the ultimate disloyalty. She entrusted her secrets to me. I can't fail her again, even if it means making a fool of myself. Besides, hopped up on Vicodin and vodka, it all seems to make sense.

The instructions direct me to position the five candles in a pentagram formation that's big enough for a human to stand in. I dutifully carry out the task. One toppled candle, I realize, can burn down the house with me in it. But there are candlesticks in the pantry, a holdover from the era of Mom's gracious dinner parties, the ones she quit hosting years before her death without explanation.

It takes me awhile to get the ritual set up—five candles at the corners of the pentagram diagrammed in masking tape. In the center of the symbol, I arrange the snip of hair. My forehead is clammy with a thin film of sweat. My breathing feels thin and labored. I'm just nervous, I tell myself.

I glance at my watch. Dad's probably dead asleep by now, so there's little chance he'll pop in and catch me in the act.

I slump over in my wheelchair, the last of my energy drained, and stare at the dancing flames. I wonder if I've totally lost my mind—if the pain, vodka, and Vicodin have finally evaporated the last drops of my sanity.

Clutching Susannah's pendant, I begin, hoarsely and deliberately, to recite the incantation. There's a strange power in the words as they rise from my chest. The floor beneath me tilts and lists, like I am on the deck of a storm-tossed ship.

I summon thee
the one to be,
the one who lost her life,
her happiness,
family and friends
I call now in the night.

I repeat the spell three times. When I am done, I am a hollow vessel filled with light. There is no sign of Susannah in spirit form, or anything else for that matter, just flickering candles and the darkness that tugs at my extremities, pulling me toward an abyss. I struggle to focus but the room is blurred. Time slows to a grainy Susannah-style stop action. I'm fading and my leg burns as if acid has seeped under the cast. Shivering, I slip down into cold waters.

Now

Objects and debris float by. I half expect to see the Wicked Witch pedaling past. Up ahead, incongruously, is a dining room table set with five candles. A woman sits, her back turned to me. I hesitate, because once I draw another foot closer, I recognize my mother.

She turns, her hair coiffed in its neat blond bun, not a strand out of place. Dressed in a prim white tailored shirt, just the way I remembered her most mornings. She is sipping coffee from a teacup. She smiles at the sight of me as I paddle toward her, and I'm struck by the realization that I must be dreaming. Candles are burning underwater and I'm about to have a nice chat with my dead mother.

Her delicate features are expectant, hopeful. "You called for me, Jeremy?"

She gestures toward one of the brocade-upholstered dining room chairs. It's as if our whole dining room has been transported to the bottom of the Riverton Gorge.

"I, uh—not exactly, but I was thinking about you." Not wanting to offend, I hedge, my heart racing. "I'm always thinking about you, Mom," I stammer.

"I know you are, honey. I did leave rather abruptly." She smiles, studying me. In this dream, my cast is gone. My damaged leg radiates an eerie bluish glow. Refracted by the underwater tableau, it casts our faces in bluish light.

"You've grown so much, Jeremy."

I nod. Of course I have, I think. Eight years will do that to a boy.

I hear a ticking noise, as if a timer will soon go off and then something horrible will occur. Like, maybe I've cast the wrong spell. "I'm not dead, am I?"

Mom shakes her head, still beaming as if she is at my high school graduation. "No, honey. Not at all."

"Do you know where Susannah is? Is she here with you?"

Mom shakes her head sadly. "I'm sorry. I can't say I know what you're talking about. But you really should take care of that leg, Jeremy. It's giving off the strangest light."

Mom disappears—dining room table and all. I sink lower into the frigid depths of the Gorge, my leg glowing like an electric eel.

—m—

Now I'm floating upward in an ocean of seamless white, propelled by a jet stream of warm milk. Instead of the pale blue glow, my leg is blurred, as though my dream is a video and the camera lens couldn't focus in on it. Confused, I paddle through the thick white expanse, headed somewhere, wondering idly if I really am dead and Mom was too polite to say so. But I'm kind of too relaxed to care.

I come to rest on a soft surface enclosed in a white membrane, a chrysalis inside its fuzzy white cocoon. It's warm and cozy in here. I think I'd like to stay indefinitely. But something tells me the world outside of my casing is not heaven. Not by a long shot.

A voice pierces the gauze of my white world. Shapes move as if behind a plastic shower curtain. I struggle to understand the words, to understand where I am.

There is that familiar smell. Those familiar beeping sounds. The hushed voices. The scrape of a chair on linoleum.

Had I ever left?

"He's coming to," says a woman's voice.

My eyes blink open and the light hurts like razors are slicing into my corneas. I close them fast, but not before recognizing Dad, his tired eyes peering over a surgical mask.

"Hey, kiddo," he says softly.

I peel open one eye and peer at my leg. Instead of seeing it and the pins sticking out of it, there is a flat section of blanket clear up to the hip. A wave of sudden nausea hits. I squeeze my eyes closed and sink deeper into the pillow, hoping I'll open them again to find myself on the debris-strewn floor of my father's study, the acrid stench of burnt candles riding up my nostrils.

"I'm going to let the doctor speak to you, Jeremy, if that's okay. She can explain." Explain? Like what they did with my leg? Did it have a proper burial? I never even had the chance to say goodbye.

"Why, Dad?" I moan.

"It had to be done," Dad mutters. "The leg was already in danger. The infection came on so fast. I'm—I'm so sorry."

I hear the scrape of his chair and the soft pad of his shoes as he exits my room. I smell the doctor's perfume as she pulls up a chair beside me and gives me the lowdown. Her voice is tender and soothing, but the words she utters are far from it. Fast-moving infection in an already severely compromised limb. Tissue death. How they tried to save the knee, but couldn't. How with the right rehabilitation and prosthetic I can walk again. Maybe run.

Yeah, sure, I think. In the Special Olympics. But I say nothing. Only nod with my eyes still closed and catalog how I've lost the only things I'd ever loved. My mother. Susannah. Running.

But I have plenty of history. No shortage of that.

She leaves me staring at the inside of my eyelids, listening to the beep-beep of the machines and thinking about how I would very much like a drink.

But for now, massive doses of painkillers will have to do.

An orderly comes in with a pitcher of water and a cup. Once he leaves, I prop myself up and pour the water. For some reason, I am fascinated by the condensation that collects on the cup's circumference.

The curtain around my bed rustles gently, followed by a faint waft of vanilla. My heart speeds up.

"Is someone there?"

Then I see it. And blink because I can't be sure I'm not dreaming.

Words are forming on the cup as if written with a finger.

I'm sorry.

I study the words and they vanish, filling in with more condensation.

I lean back onto the pillow, convinced the painkillers are causing me to hallucinate.

Now (December 4th)

If I thought recovering from a leg amputation meant that the hospital staff would just leave me alone to vegetate, discarded like a banana peel, I was wrong. I don't even have time to brood over the bandaged appendage that measures half the length of my one remaining foot. It's barely worth calling a stump. It's more like a stub. Or to be more specific, a nub. It's not even as long as my—I can't even finish that thought.

I'm told repeatedly the bone infection had come dangerously close to killing me, as if the entire hospital staff feels the need to explain that they didn't just get excited with a handsaw. It was necessary to remove all of the diseased bone. Saving the hip joint was considered a big win. I'd come perilously close to losing that as well.

My days post-surgery are chocked with dizzying changes of dressing, merciless massages, pokes, prods, and painful scrubdowns by a woman with hair growing out of a mole on her chin. I am no longer handled like an egg. Instead, muscular people of indistinguishable gender move me around and make me stand on my one leg to the point where I feel like their Ken doll, or at least an over-sized stork. And peeing on one leg may very well be the low point of some very low days.

The room fills with flowers from well-wishers, but I refuse to see anyone but my father. I want the whole damn town to leave one-legged Jeremy Glass alone. I imagine the clucking tongues of the Riverton wags sitting at Awesome Cow, whispering about that poor unlucky boy and his tragedy-plagued life.

My father glances at me with a wounded gaze that rarely fixes on mine. He says little beyond slight words of encouragement when I manage to hop around the room on my crutches. My balance is good for a beginner, the physical therapist tells me, but it's harder than I would have thought. I am lopsided. Asymmetrical.

The desk nurse informs us that we have a visitor who won't take no for an answer. It's Patrick Morgan. I tell Dad I don't want to see him, or Ryan, or anyone else for that matter, but Dad insists. Patrick Morgan is not a person you deny. He *owns* Riverton, as well as the building in which Dad's small law office is housed, my father reminds me. As if he needs to.

I'd always thought my dad and Patrick Morgan were friends from way back, the pre-cursor to Ryan and me. These days, I'm not sure. Dad seems skittish. Under his mild words, I catch the implied message. My destroyed physical condition is not a free pass. I'd better patch things up with Ryan for the good of our family's future economic health.

In the moments before Mr. Morgan arrives at my room, Dad turns to me, face grave and splotchy.

"Do you take me for a fool, Jeremy?"

"What do you mean?"

"You think I don't know how, after the accident, the medical reports on your blood alcohol level miraculously vanished? You can thank Pat Morgan for that."

Heavy footsteps approach, growing closer. "So he told me."

"I just didn't think that issue was a priority, given your condition. But by no means are you off the hook, Jeremy," Dad hisses in my ear in the seconds before Patrick makes his entrance, his arms laden with a giant tower of cookies wrapped in purple cellophane and tied with a perfect white bow. His feet are festooned with the most pretentious cowboy boots I've ever seen. Red alligator with black snakeskin. I know it's crazy, but I can't help but think he's subtly rubbing it in that he has two legs and so does Ryan.

Over the years, Patrick Morgan has been my Little League coach, soccer coach, and unofficial running coach. In fact, he was the first person to tip off my spectacularly un-athletic father about the speed of my running stride. He just never expected me to be a better runner than his perfect son.

Today, the thought of pity from him makes me cringe. More likely, he'll be secretly happy to have me off the team so I can't make Ryan look bad with my faster miles. Those days are gone for good.

Win for Team Morgan.

Dad takes the cookies from his hands, cookies that I know Ryan's mother Celia baked just for me. Mr. Morgan's pointy boots clop to my bedside. He leans over, brow furrowed, his eyes, vividly blue as a lit gas burner, filled with deep concern. He says, in a solemn whisper, "Ryan understands now why you were so abrupt with him the other day. You must have been in terrible pain. We're all so very sorry this happened, Jeremy."

"Thanks," I say. His pity is like sandpaper on my eyeballs. I think I want to scream or rap him over the head with a crutch, but I keep my face composed in a pleasantly flattered expression.

"Celia would have come, but you know how she gets. She's very choked up over your—over your situation—and didn't want to upset you. So she sent these cookies instead." Patrick Morgan pauses a minute to look up at Dad, who starts to fidget as if he's standing barefoot on hot sand. Mr. Morgan adds, "We all love Celia's cookies, don't we?"

Dad coughs into his hankie, like he's suddenly got a chicken bone lodged in his throat, and ducks out into the hall. I fight back the ridiculous tears that well in my eyes. For a long time, Celia Morgan's tried her best to fill the Mom-shaped hole I was left with. I wish fervently that it is her standing there instead of Ryan's father, but she is an emotional person, known to cry at funny movies, and would most likely be bawling her eyes out over me. Not what I need at the moment.

"It will be tough for Ryan without you on the team to keep pace for him."

No. I do not need to be reminded of all the things I won't ever do again. I look away.

"But don't worry, son. You'll be back. We heard that your dad's insurance only covers a cosmetic prosthesis. The team is taking up a collection for one of those high-tech titanium types the soldiers get. It was Ryan's idea. He's already collected two thousand dollars."

I turn to look back at him. "Seriously? He didn't have to do that."

Patrick Morgan shrugs. "He thinks he does. I know you boys have had your differences lately. But—well. Ryan would really like to see you."

Differences. *What's one missing girl between friends?*

I look down at my ex-leg on the blanket. I can still feel its weight pressing into the mattress and wonder how long my nerve endings will take to understand it's gone for good.

"Soon," I manage to choke out. "Real soon. Tell him thanks, okay?"

—w—

Shortly after Patrick Morgan leaves, my dad hovers at the door, half in and half out. He looks perplexed, like a man who's been sucker-punched looks right before he keels over.

"Jeremy. Obviously the possibility of a track scholarship is off the table."

I nearly laugh. "Obviously."

So that's what's on his mind. Not that I'm going to have to hop through life as a half-man. That I will probably never have sex unless I pay for it, because who wants to date a circus freak? No. It's the tragic realization that he will have to shell out extra cash for my education. Provided he still wants me to get one.

"After you're healed a bit more, we'll discuss our options."

"Right, Dad. Let's call a meeting. Maybe we can negotiate a better contract for my former leg. If the scale is generous enough, maybe it'll agree to be reattached."

Dad's eye twitches. "Good night, Jeremy. Sleep well."

—⁂—

It's ten minutes before visiting hours end. I am nearly asleep when a flummoxed nurse enters and explains in a soft voice that I have a female visitor who is adamant about seeing me and refuses to leave. Would I mind? Just for a minute?

It's Trudy Durban, Susannah's mother.

"Okay," I mutter, barely coherent.

Trudy Durban has let her youthful beauty weather into a thing of the elements, her angular face like a wind-sculpted rock structure, hazel eyes wary as a hawk's. Wiry blond hair laced with gray falls around her face like barbed wire.

Then

The first time I'd ever laid eyes on the mysterious Mrs. Durban was at the Morgans' annual Christmas extravaganza, three years ago. I'm not sure what I expected, but the pale-as-milk white woman who stalked into the Morgans' stadium-sized house sure wasn't it. I'd always imagined Susannah's mother as a dusky bronze beauty, an older version of her. I knew Susannah was mixed race, but I'd always imagined her father as the white half, a wayward Jewish guy who'd left her single mom to raise her alone, not the other way around.

Miraculously, Susannah and Ryan had not actually hooked up at that point. There had just been the daily ritual of heavy flirting, batting eyelashes, and posturing I'd endured from behind my carefully constructed mask of I-don't-give-a-crap. I could still keep my lame fantasy alive—that it was me Susannah really wanted.

At least in art class, she was still mine—a completely different person from the airheaded, hair-flinging girl she became around Ryan. In class we talked politics, history, ethics, aesthetics, and spirituality while she made twisted masterpieces from string, wire, papier-mâché, and whatever else was lying around. Then she turned to paper and ink, creating her own universe of bizarre whimsy, totally at odds with the smiling face she presented to the world.

But she didn't seem to get it. And I died a little each day as I watched her eyes light up at the sight of Ryan. I was just there, a comfortable chair for her to flop into—reliable Jeremy Glass, everyone's friend, steadfast and true.

I hated myself for hating Ryan. It wasn't his fault that he was the sun, and dark souls like us were drawn to his orbit.

Yet we'd made it all the way to December without Ryan and Susannah becoming an official couple. By this time, though no one knew it, I was well on my way to becoming an official alcoholic, raiding Dad's liquor cabinet in the sleepless hours when the nightmares stormed out from the shadows to swallow me.

And Susannah, I told myself, was the only one who could make the nightmares go away.

—⁂—

The Morgans' annual Christmas party was the chance for the town's elite to kiss the ring and show their loyalty to the dynasty that owned them. It was a formal dress affair, the men in black tie, the women in silk skirt-suits or sleek sequined gowns. At fourteen, I was a sapling whose branches had grown longer than its trunk. Dad had tried to stuff me into my bar mitzvah suit, but ended up having to spring for a new one since I'd grown about five inches and could now look him straight in the eye.

That year, the Morgans were honoring some noble cause in a wildly tasteless way no one had the nerve to criticize. The party was a benefit for a local AIDS foundation and the massive Christmas tree was strung with syringes and condoms. Liquor flowed like water from a tap. It goes without saying that I made the most of these parties.

The Morgans' cavernous living room echoed with laughter and clinking glasses, but everything quieted the second Susannah, looking like a golden goddess in a ruby taffeta gown, entered with her mother, Trudy. I could barely scrape my eyes off Susannah, but I caught Dad's sneer.

"Why the hell is everyone gawking at them?" I asked.

Dad continued to pile caviar on a cracker, but his hand was shaking. "The mother used to live in Riverton."

I was totally piss drunk, but was already a master at hiding it. "Duh. I already know that. Why is everyone hating on them?"

"Trudy Durban left some loose ends, Jeremy."

"What is that supposed to mean?" My gaze tracked Susannah as she glided across the room while her mother stood frozen in the foyer.

"She left a lot of bad blood behind. To be honest, I have no idea why she would move back here. It's not like she has any friends."

"What did she do?"

"Made trouble."

If Dad elaborated further, I didn't hear it over the ringing in my ears. Susannah had made her way to where Ryan waited under the mistletoe. While the other partygoers slowly recovered from the shock of Trudy Durban's unwelcome appearance, Susannah and Ryan made out like their lives depended on it.

And I ran to the bathroom to puke up my guts.

Now

Susannah had once pointed out that her mother's wardrobe palette was beige, cream, mauve, and gray, always in monochrome. Today it's tasteful beige, suitable for visiting the infirm, but the illusion of professionalism is warped slightly by the tangled bramble of folk art crosses, chains, and charms she wears around her neck. It's like she'd been given ten minutes to grab all she could carry in a flea market shopping spree. The bouquet of flowers she carries contrasts riotously with her neutral backdrop.

"Hello, Jeremy," she says in her deep rasp.

I squirm. Pat Morgan is supposed to be greeted like family, at his own insistence. I opt for formal with Susannah's mother. "Hi, Mrs. Durban."

"I'm not going to ask how you're feeling. It's obvious you're in your own private hell," she says. From the haggard lines around her eyes, it's apparent the last few weeks haven't been a picnic for her, either.

"Pretty much, I guess."

"Patrick Morgan denies it, but I heard you got hurt trying to save Susannah from that bastard Ryan. Was he there or wasn't he?"

"I—well. Not really. I—they were fighting and I just wanted to—" I stop talking because Mrs. Durban's gaze has drifted. She's still talking, but not to anyone in the room.

"I warned her not to take up with the son of that devil. I begged her. But Susannah is an obstinate girl. She always does the exact opposite of what I tell her. She did it to defy me."

She pulls a crumpled tissue from her pocket and noisily blows her nose.

I watch her, uncomfortable, wanting to sleep. I want her to leave and take her mean eyes and jangly necklaces with her. But curiosity keeps me awake. I doubt her reason for visiting me is to check up on the healing progress of my stump.

Her gaze snaps back into focus. "The police aren't helping any more. No evidence of wrongdoing, they say. The press has moved on to more interesting stories. But I shouldn't be surprised. No one will touch the Morgans."

I prop myself up on my pillow, completely awake now. "What do you mean, Mrs. Durban?"

She stares straight into my eyes, her mouth set in a firm line. "Someone in this town killed her."

My palms are sweaty. "Why would anyone want to kill Susannah?"

"Lots of reasons."

"Such as, Mrs. Durban?" I lean forward. "Susannah is my friend, and I want to know where she is, too."

"Of course you do." She stares absently down at me, then snaps out of it again, her gaze burning with renewed intensity. "Maybe you can tell me what was in the package Marisa gave you. Little bitch admitted she brought it to you before I could unwrap it."

I knead the blankets, cornered, wanting to run, wanting to fly. Anything to escape this woman's incinerating stare. "It was just some art."

She squints. "She seemed to be on a big art giveaway kick."

Mrs. Durban withdraws a large envelope from the shopping bag on her arm and slips out a sheet of thick paper. My heart almost stops, then resumes its rickety thumping. She places it in front of me on my one half of a lap.

I recognize one of Susannah's lavishly detailed ink and watercolor masterpieces, white ink on black paper. A huge pile of finely crosshatched skeletons, bones, half-eaten apples, dead babies, bottles, and sneakers crowds almost the entire page. At the top of the pile is a small gnarled tree with roots that sink into the debris. The tree sprouts a single green leaf, but the leaf is not an actual image, but a tiny word printed in green ink. "TRUTH", it says. At the bottom of the page, scrawled in white across the delicate inkwork, a message is written in script:

This is for you, Jeremy Glass.

Trudy Durban removes one of the beaded crosses from around her neck and rests it on top of the drawing.

"Your mother was Episcopalian," she says, "but I thought you might need this." She fingers her jumble of necklaces and stares down at me, her mouth a hard line.

"Were you and my mother friends?"

"For a time." Her eyes glaze over and she stares past me. Then her gaze snaps back into focus. "But there are dark forces at work in this town."

C H A P T E R

e i g h t

Now (December 10th)

I'm sent home after five days with detailed directions for proper care of the stump and lots of good wishes. From the way the miserable nub is fussed over and swaddled, you'd think I was bringing home a newborn baby.

It's Monday, December 10th. Over three weeks since Susannah went missing.

A light film of snow coats the winding roads of Riverton. Holiday lights twinkle from the houses we pass. I imagine happy intact families composed of happy intact people, enjoying the season and each other inside their cozy homes.

We pass the Morgans' massive house, ablaze with lights, a cross between a circus and a stadium. The circular drive is populated with more reindeer than they have in Alaska. Shrouded in snow, it's Riverton's very own winter wonderland.

I try to envision the Morgans inside, Ryan and a bunch of our track buddies watching Monday Night Football in the den. They're all talking about what a shame it is about their star runner. Or, maybe they're laughing about it. There's something ironic about a one-legged track star. Even I have to admit that.

The Morgans' house is always full of people, as if cramming the cavernous thing with bodies makes up for the fact that three people have an obscene amount of living space all to themselves. Susannah always insisted that Celia and Patrick Morgan were like the ideal parents she'd never had. I could see it with Celia Morgan. Her motherliness had a way of softening Patrick Morgan's imperious presence. There are always cookies baking in their vast, stainless steel kitchen.

But Patrick Morgan? I guess with a mother like Trudy, just about anyone would seem like an improvement.

We pull up the steep driveway and I see Dad has made the feeble attempt to string some colored lights on the house. It's almost laughable compared to the Morgans'. But it's clear he tried, so I keep a lid on the sarcasm for once.

"Nice, Dad. Is this for me?"

He turns to me. "I thought you'd like it. You always complain I'm lousy at Christmas."

"You're a Jew. You're not supposed to be good at it."

Dad chuckles and flashes me a rare full-cornered smile. "Well—you're only half a Jew. I thought the other half would enjoy the lights."

His smile drops away as it slowly dawns on Dad that he's fed me my next line.

"So which is the half that's left?" I say with a sideways smile. "The Jewish half or the Christian one?"

Dad reaches over and places a hand on my shoulder. "Feeling sorry for yourself is understandable, but it's not going to solve anything, Jeremy. You still have to think of your future."

"That pesky thing again."

Dad turns off the ignition. "Let's go inside. I've ordered an Indian takeout feast in your honor. After all that lousy hospital food, I thought you'd be famished."

It's not just my loss. It's his, too, I realize. Which makes me feel even worse.

"Thanks, Dad," I say. "Indian food sounds great."

—m—

The trip from the car to the house is a heroic 3-D action-adventure movie. The snow is coming down hard. Dad decides that it's too risky for me to navigate on crutches, and the wheelchair can't roll on snow, so he slings my arm tightly over his shoulder. Clutching his waist, I hop in small, mincing leaps, a human pogo stick, until, wet and exhausted, we finally make it inside.

We eat our Indian feast in the dining room. Dad's got a pathetic little tree and an electric menorah set up. I slap on a smile as he tries to distract me with a story about a flaky client, but the heaviness bears down on me so hard I can barely taste the lamb korma, my favorite. I feel Mom watching from the shadows.

"Are you even listening to me, Jeremy?" Dad asks.

"Actually I was thinking about this Civil War general, Dan Sickles. His leg got shot off in battle. He had the bones of the ruined leg wired together so it could be put on display at the Army Medical Museum. Maybe I could have mine put on display in the school trophy case next to last year's State Championship Cup."

Dad stares at me a beat, then lays down his fork. "Look, Jeremy. We can either tiptoe around each other and act like everything's fine, or we can be realistic about things."

"Tiptoeing may be difficult."

Dad slams down his glass of water. "Jeremy!"

"Okay. Sorry. I didn't mean that. It's just a reflex."

Dad shakes his head. "No more jokes."

"Okay."

"Jeremy, your grades matter more than ever if you still want to get into Cornell. Do you? You can, if you want."

"I haven't thought that far ahead. Right now, I'm kind of wondering who we should donate all my left running shoes to."

Dad stands up and slams his fist on the table. The water glasses jiggle. "Damn it, Jeremy! It's not funny. None of this is funny. I've tried to help you, tried to steer you down the right path, and yet, you—you *did this*." Dad's voice rises to the point where veins are popping in his neck and he is yelling. "How could you drink, with your mother's history? *How could you?* You've done this to yourself," he finishes quietly, tossing his napkin onto the table and striding out.

I close my eyes and hang my head. "Because I'm an asshole," I say to the empty room.

A few minutes later, as I pull myself up on my crutches, Dad returns. His eyes are puffy and red, his hair damp, like he's splashed his head with water.

"I've arranged for Marisa Santiago to help you with your schoolwork. She's a senior and has finished most of her requirements, so she has some free time to work with you. She aced her SATs, by the way."

"Her?"

Dad slants his head. "Are you implying because she's an immigrant that she couldn't have anything to offer?"

"No," I say softly. "I was just surprised, that's all."

"She's extremely bright. And she needs the money. Without her help, you're up the creek. You've got to ace that AP Calculus if you want a shot at Cornell, and there's very little time to finish your college applications. You've already missed more than three weeks of school."

I'm so tired, and I don't want to tell Dad that I'd much rather drink myself into a stupor as I zone out on history books. That I don't care about calculus, or Cornell. That I want to drink until I'm numb. But I just nod my head so I don't set him off again. "I know."

He looks at me warily. "Get some rest. And don't forget that stump massage regimen. It's important if you want to get fitted for a prosthetic leg. You have the physical therapist coming to work with you in a few days."

"Sounds like fun," I mutter, too low for him to hear.

—⁓—

Dad stays home with me for the next two days. We don't talk much. Mostly, I sleep, trying to forget, trying not to think of what they've done with my leg. A nurse comes by to review the changing of dressings and the proper wrapping of the stump.

By the time he goes back to work on the third day, my eyeballs are nearly popping out of my head from thirst.

I stagger clumsily on my crutches to visit the stash in the pantry. I don't want to hurt Dad, but the panic is swirling in like the black waters of the Gorge. I imagine my lost leg sinking and vanishing into the murky depths. I open the pantry door, heave the giant bag of charcoal out of the way, and cry out.

Gone. The bottles are all gone.

I stand, leaning on my crutches so that with my one leg they form a tripod, and wait for things to quiet. My heart is racing. Since the painkiller dosage has been gradually decreased, panic has started to announce itself at the edges of my drug-induced equilibrium like an ominous organ chord in a cheesy old movie. Soon, the chords will be loud enough to drown out all other sound.

These are the times I used to run.

But what am I going to do now?

I feel myself shattering inside, like a clay figurine that has been broken, holding my shape before I crumble to dust. I ease myself to the floor and rest my head in my hands.

"What the fuck am I going to do with my life?" I ask the cereal boxes.

The door creaks ever so slightly and a soft breeze whisks past my cheek.

I raise my head. "Suze?"

Nothing.

Then I hear it, the softest of whispers, little more than a breath.

At least you still have a life, Jeremy Glass.

Did I really hear that, or was it just my guilty conscience misfiring?

I scrape myself off the floor and clump back to the study.

I've been so busy starring in my own drama since the amputation, I haven't really thought much about Susannah. She's been missing for four weeks, and at one point it was all I cared about. And now her mother thinks someone might have killed her.

So what have I done about it? Nothing, except distract myself with nonsense rituals and hallucinate evidence that I've brought her back from the dead. To start with, there's no evidence that she is even dead.

But what if Ryan actually killed her and, just like always, I'm letting him get away with murder? Meanwhile, the poor bereaved boyfriend has been busily raising money for my new super-advanced high-tech leg, texting me once a day to update me on his progress. As always, I text him back a quick thank you and refuse to see him, though he asks each time. Today, instead of texting me he's sent a link to a video of a guy walking with the state-of-the art leg he's hoping to get me.

I consider calling him and asking some pointed questions. Like, where did she run? How far did he follow? My dad insists the police report says Ryan wasn't there at the accident scene. That his car wasn't there. Leaving nothing to trace him to Susannah's disappearance except my very shaky and unreliable word.

I search my memories for clues and wonder how accurate they are. Could anything I remember be trusted? What if I had it all wrong? With the amount of drugs I'm on, I'm starting to doubt everything. Even what I've seen with my own eyes.

But if Patrick Morgan can doctor my medical report, why not a police report?

I'd have to do some serious poking around to uncover the real truth. Which is no easy task in Riverton. But one I'm not above trying.

With me occupying his study, Dad's turned the dining room table into a precarious mountain of papers, his ad hoc home office. Before I took over his space, he must have still worked at his desk. In his haste and upset over my accident, he probably stuffed the police report in the bottom desk drawer, his catchall for bills and whatnot, and then forgot about it. Dad's not exactly Mr. Neat.

I hobble over to his desk. It's my lucky day. The bottom drawer is unlocked and I don't have to look far. In a crumpled manila envelope is a copy of the report, filed by Sergeant Evan Barnes, one of Dad's occasional poker buddies.

There is no mention of the four vehicles that should have been at the scene if Ryan's account is accurate. There are just three recorded as present—mine, Susannah's, and the truck that was involved in the collision.

There is no eyewitness account of the accident, save for that of the truck driver. The officer notes he was quite distraught, insisting that he didn't realize I was in the road until he hit me.

I stare at the paper. Either the report is a fake, or Ryan flat-out lied to me. He'd left Susannah alone in the woods. Or he'd killed her and scrammed.

Or my memory is playing tricks on me. Either way, none of this adds up. Susannah is missing. Her mother thinks someone killed her.

And maybe so do I.

Then

Susannah and Ryan became the "it couple" that Christmas, and I took my place as the ever-present third side of our triangle. We were Susannah and Ryan, and Jeremy. My mask fit so well, I started to believe it was my actual face.

The stark reality that Susannah had chosen Ryan over me stuck in my gut like a blade.

I had to admit, as Susannah's boyfriend, Ryan thrived and unexpectedly developed the nerve to step away from his persona as Ryan the jock. He started auditioning for school plays, getting bigger and bigger parts. Ryan could sing like crazy and commanded the stage as though it belonged to him.

I finally understood that there was much more to my old friend than met the eye. And that Susannah saw clearly what I'd completely missed. Ryan really had star potential.

Still, it didn't make my agony any easier. But instead of drifting away, idiot that I was, I kept coming back for more.

Susannah started designing the scenery for the school plays. Not wanting to leave poor, faithful Jeremy out of the equation, Susannah drafted me to do lights, since I sucked at everything else besides running and knowing shit no one cared about. And the most surprising thing of all was that, although Trudy was still the town pariah, Susannah was accepted into the Morgan household like a long-lost relative.

Ryan got his first lead role in the school's production of *Pippin* and it took up most of his time. Susannah complained that Ryan's dad didn't seem to get how brilliant an actor he was and that it bugged her.

"Figures," I said. "Patrick Morgan's a competitive guy. That's how he built the family empire. Acting is a joke to someone like him."

"That's a rotten thing to say, Jeremy. Mr. Morgan is an amazing human being."

"I'm sure your mother would totally agree."

Susannah went quiet.

"What? Did I say something wrong?"

"Just leave my mother out of this," she snapped.

"Okay." I should have known better than to bring up Trudy Durban, but it bugged me the way Patrick Morgan seemed to have Susannah eating out of his hand. She'd made it clear how her mother bitterly disapproved of her dating Ryan. That they fought about it all the time. One night, Trudy had chased Susannah down the street with a cooking pan. The cops had been called; if Dad and Patrick Morgan hadn't stepped in, Susannah might have been removed from her home and placed in foster care.

Susannah cleared her throat, her eyes bright. "My mother is an asshole. The Morgans treat me better. They're my real family."

One week later, that March, a month before her fifteenth birthday, Susannah ran away for the first time.

She didn't get far. Just to her half-brother's house in Rhode Island. She had only been gone four days before she'd called her mother to come pick her up and bring her home.

When Susannah got back, she seemed changed in some subtle way I couldn't put my finger on. There was a ferocious gleam in her eyes I hadn't seen before. She smiled and joked around as always, but in class she attacked her art with a silent fury that set my teeth on edge.

"Jeremy," she asked, looking up from her work one afternoon. "Do you ever think about what happens to the soul after we're dead?"

"No," I lied, staring out the window. I'd never talked to her about how my mother died, how I relived the horror each night. I figured someone had to have told Susannah by now. Everyone in Riverton knew all about brave Jeremy Glass and his life of tragedy. "I can't say I have."

Susannah continued pushing bits of colored mosaic tile into the weird many-armed figurine she'd been working on for weeks. "I've been doing some reading."

"Cool." I'd been bending her ear about the five or so books I had going and hoped my nerdish habits were rubbing off. "What about?"

"Oh, world religions and stuff. This is me as Kali, Goddess of Destruction."

"But you're not a destroyer, Suze," I said, laughing. "You're a creator."

She stopped working and turned to look at me, a delicious smile curling her lips. "Nature is destructive and creative, all at the same time."

It was such a Susannah thing to say. Holding back on the urge to kiss her, right there in art class, felt like swallowing knives.

Later that period, Mr. Wallace announced to the class that Susannah had received a full scholarship to participate in a summer Digital Arts seminar in the city, where she would study animation and graphic design.

I was truly happy for her. Happy for Ryan and his theatrical success. Basking in my own status as a track star. We secretly started calling ourselves the Awesome Threesome.

But I was drinking more than ever.

Now

An insidious thought creeps into my head. Maybe Ryan killed Susannah and wants to buy my silence with the promise of a new leg. My head spins.

It's too much. All of this is just too much.

I. Need. A. Drink.

Finally, under the last shelf, nestled behind a carton of Arizona Iced Tea, I see the glint of a bottle. When Dad destroyed the reserve of Absolut, he must have kept one for himself and hidden it where he figured I wouldn't find it. He didn't count on how tenacious I can be when I'm thirsty.

I pry out the bottle, twist open the cap and, like a parched man in the desert, start gulping. I can't stop until I slug down half the bottle.

I watch Ryan's video again and again, repulsed by the bionic limb, yet fascinated by the simple act of running. I'm far too sloshed to stand steadily. Finally, my bursting bladder forces me to haul myself up on my crutches and stumble to the bathroom. Somehow, head spinning, floor tilting, I get there, possibly dragging myself part of the way on my butt. I'm not sure how I manage to aim my pee in the right place. At least, I think I do.

Reflected in the full-length mirror, the sight of me catches my attention. I'm in a T-shirt and flannel pajama pants, the empty pant leg rolled up and tucked into the waistband. I strip to my underwear, and for the first time since the surgery, take a good look at myself. All these years pushing myself to the limit, and I never appreciated how my once-scrawny frame had become sinewy and powerful. Until now—all my efforts rendered useless, a gleaming chassis with no wheels.

Maybe I could have made my move when I was whole, if I wasn't such a wimp. I could have had Susannah for myself. Changed the course of our histories. She'd still be here. Alive. I'd be standing on two legs.

The shuddering tears come on like a summer squall. My lungs fill with liquid as the room floods with the dark waters of the Gorge.

I should join Mom. Dive to the bottom of the Gorge and settle in the crevices between the jagged stones, the place that was meant to be my grave eight years ago.

I sink to the freezing tile floor, instead.

I'm not sure how long I lie curled in a fetal position on the bathroom floor, too spent to haul myself upright. The effects of the Absolut are receding and all I can think about is how I want some more.

There's a tingling pressure next to my ear. A soft murmur beside me, inches away.

I'm here, Jeremy.

I sit up, heart racing, and glance crazily around.

There's no one.

Great. I've finally snapped and gone over the edge. There was talk that my mother was crazy. Had always been crazy. Now I'm losing my mind, too.

I haul myself upright and lean over the sink. Run water and wet my head to shake it off. The vodka does this to me. Fogs my mind, blurs the sharp edges. That's what I want it for, isn't it?

But the voice was so real.

I'm still smashed, I realize. Flat-out wasted. I've never let myself get this bad.

I shake my head, spraying droplets everywhere, and face myself in the mirror. Sunken brown eyes circled by bruised rings, my face so gaunt and pale it's nearly blue. Scraggly stubble peppers my chin. I look like my own ghost.

"Here lies Jeremy Glass," I say to my reflection. "May you rest in pieces."

I know I hear it this time, despite the haze that clings to my senses like cloud cover. The voice is garbled, as faint as leaves rustled by a light breeze.

But you're not a ghost, Jeremy.

I pivot wildly, slipping, and nearly lose my balance.

"Susannah?"

It was her voice. *It was.* Maybe she's been here all along, hiding out. Playing games. One rainy afternoon when we were fourteen, she had evaded Ryan and me in her cavernous old house for two hours.

But there's no answer.

Just the faintest wisp of vanilla perfume.

CHAPTER

ten

Now

I clump back to Dad's study, fling myself onto the bed, and drop into sleep...

...and wake, the windowpanes framing solid squares of ink-black night. The bedside light is on, and all too quickly I realize what woke me.

Pain spirals up my phantom shin, coils around my absent thigh, and explodes at the stump. I reach for the Vicodin, pop three in my mouth, and settle back on the pillow. Gradually, my body cools. The pain ebbs. I drift, barely registering the feather-light touch that brushes my cheek.

Jeremy.

"Dad?" I murmur, peering through slitted lids.

My eyes snap open and I sit up. There's a static charge pulsing in the room like the air right before lightning touches ground. My scalp tingles, but there's nothing to see.

I search the room's shadows for some kind of a sign, unsure of what I'm looking for—or if I want to find out.

"Suze?"

The room prickles with silence. I want to run. My heart skips as the dark waters close in. I struggle to breathe.

If Susannah really is here then my worst fear is true.

71

She's dead.

And I've called her back.

—⁓—

"Jeremy? You okay?" It's my dad. "I thought I heard you call out."

I swallow hard, my eyes squeezed shut. "Yeah," I grunt.

I hear his light step. I feel his gaze on me. "You sure? The doctors said the healing process would be tough."

"I took some meds. I'll be okay." I manage to pry my eyes open.

He's looking at me doubtfully. "Try to get some rest. And I hope you're being careful with the Vicodin. You seem to be going through them a little too quickly. I have Marisa coming to see you in the morning, after your physical therapy session."

He turns to leave. I almost call out and ask him to stay, but with the pain pleasantly snuffed I settle under the blankets, finally comfortable.

Then

The second time Susannah ran away was in the third week of sophomore year, after a very public fight between her and Ryan.

It was right outside the school building. Ryan held Susannah while she flailed wildly. Sobbing, she broke free and smacked him hard in the face, then ran away like a madwoman. Ryan gave chase and, overcoming her easily, tackled her to the grass. With everyone watching, they lay that way for about fifteen minutes until Susannah stopped struggling. Finally, Ryan got up and walked away, leaving Susannah lying face-down on the schoolyard lawn.

I considered approaching her, but decided against it. The temptation to drape myself on top of her and cover her with gentle kisses was too strong.

That time, Susannah was gone for an entire week. After two days of sulking around, Ryan showed up on my doorstep at one in the morning, totally out of his mind drunk.

I was drunk, too, like I was pretty much was every night, but that was easy enough to hide from someone who was more dead drunk than me. Ryan never held his liquor as well. Especially at fifteen.

I ushered him into the living room and plopped him on my couch.

"She's too good for me," he blubbered, his face in his hands. "It's my fault she's gone. Last week I ended up backstage with Tania Davis."

My hands curled into fists, but I kept my tone even. *How could he steal her out from under me, and then just throw her away?* "Whoa, dude. Why and how?"

"I don't know. I swear. Things got carried away after rehearsal. Tania came on strong. I guess she caught me at a vulnerable moment. It just happened. We were talking, and then we were all over each other. I felt so bad I told Suze. She didn't take it so well."

"So I noticed."

Ryan looked up, eyes glistening on his tear-streaked face, the soul of misery. Even if his wound was self-inflicted, I couldn't help but feel his pain. There was no way she was going to run into my arms.

"Will you talk to her?" Ryan asked.

"Why? You think I can hypnotize her into forgiving you?"

Ryan cradled his face in his hands. "You'll think of something clever, Jer. You always do. Susannah thinks you're brilliant."

"She does?" I tried not to sound too enthusiastic, but the compliment floated like a bubble of happiness at the bottom of my stomach.

"You are, you fucking a-hole. Please. Just come up with something to calm her down. Something to let her know it won't happen again."

I settle onto the couch beside him. "You could get her a nice symbol of how sorry you are. Like, I don't know, a piece of jewelry?"

Ryan stands suddenly. "That's it! Dude, you are a fucking genius. Last weekend we went to the city and there was this crazy store in the Village with all kinds of weird new-age stuff. You know how she likes all that mystic crap. I couldn't drag her out. We spent an hour in there. There was this necklace she wanted, but neither of us had enough money."

"Cool."

"Will you come with me, Jer. For moral support and all?"

"'course, Ry. No prob."

The necklace was a flat gold-plated donut with Hebrew writing hung on a red cord, the Kabbalah pendant Susannah never took off. The words meant 'eternal love,' the sales clerk informed us. It cost Ryan seventy-five dollars.

After a week's absence, Susannah finally came home, but she didn't return to school until she'd been back for three days. Ryan wanted me to go to her house and give her the pendant, but I drew the line at that.

I guess I didn't realize at the time how much of a pathetic tool I was. How I was willing to do almost anything, if it could get me near Susannah.

She showed up in art class the following Wednesday. Mr. Wallace had been skittish and moody during her absence, and his relief at her reappearance was obvious. He treated her gently, like a bird with a broken wing in his care, but Susannah showed no sign that anything was wrong except a purple bruise on her right cheek that was well on its way to healing.

There were so many things I wanted to ask her, but my personal vault of secrets prevented me from opening up. If I did, I couldn't be sure I'd be able to stop.

"Um," I whispered, "Your knight in shining armor wanted me to give you something."

She didn't look up from her drawing. "And why doesn't said *knight* give it to me himself?"

"He figured you were less likely to sock me in the jaw."

Susannah looked up, her expressions shifting from sorrow to amusement—as changeable as mountain weather and just as beautiful.

"I would never sock you in the jaw, Jeremy Glass," she whispered, "because you'd shatter." She broke into a tinkling laugh and stopped abruptly when Mr. Wallace gave us the evil iguana-eye. "So what is this miraculous token of forgiveness you bear?" she asked, her face theatrically serious. The pain of wanting to kiss her, wanting to tell her that she was too good for Ryan, even though he'd shelled out seventy-five bucks to win her forgiveness, burned in my throat.

When she opened the box, her eyes lit up like sun through spring leaves.

"Oh," she said. "Oh, this is so…oh." She put it on, and I knew that this time, with my help, Ryan had won her back.

—m—

After school that day, I saw them together, kissing. My gut was stone. I couldn't tell if it was guilt for helping Ryan lie, or just plain old jealousy.

I concluded it was both.

When they'd finally pulled apart, Susannah came over to where I was hanging with some of my track and field buddies. Ryan drifted off to join a cluster of his theater friends.

"Thanks," she said. "He explained everything."

"And that was enough for you?"

"Yeah. I love him."

We'd started walking, though I had no idea where we were headed, and I nodded like a bobblehead, because the words were all clumped up in my chest. "Happy to be of service," I finally choked out. *Happy to stab myself directly through the heart.*

She stopped and looked up at me, arms folded. "Of service? Jeremy, you are one of my best friends, did you know that?"

"Um, I guess?"

"Sometimes you can be as dense as a block of wood. You're always there for me. Steady. Reliable. I never have to wonder if I can count on you."

"Yep. That's me, Old Steady and Reliable Jeremy. Much less breakable, and sturdier than my name would imply."

I must have let a small quaver into my voice, because instead of laughing at my lame quip, Susannah silently studied me. "Is there something wrong, Jeremy?"

"With me? What would be wrong?" Liar. Liar. Liar. But I wore my mask like a pro.

"Never mind," she said. We kept walking.

"Why'd you run away, Suze?" I finally blurted. "Was it because of Ryan?"

She stopped, and didn't look up at me, but spoke in a soft whisper. "Let's go to the park near the library. I'll explain everything."

We sat on a bench nestled in a cluster of trees. Susannah fingered the Kabbalah pendant absently. "I guess you know that things between my mom and me aren't so great. Sometimes I just can't stand it. So I run."

"Your mom…a lot of people don't like her in this town."

"I know. She's an angry person. She's always blaming me for stuff, but she never talks about what's really up her ass."

"Does she…does she ever hurt you?"

Susannah lowered her head. "Not physically."

"Oh," I said.

"I think she's going crazy, Jeremy. The day before I left, I heard her crying and talking to herself. It was like she was having a conversation. She kept calling, 'Dougie, Dougie, Dougie,' over and over, like she was trying to get the attention of someone who wouldn't answer her."

"Dougie? Who's that?"

"Don't have a clue. Maybe one in the string of assholes and drunks she's dated. There's always some loser flung out on our couch."

"Shit," I said, shaking my head. I wanted to fix her pain. If we could be together, maybe both of us could heal.

"It's okay, Jeremy. Soon I'll be out of the house, away at school. I'm going to get a scholarship to Rhode Island School of Design, and my half-brother will cover the rest."

I nodded. She had a plan. Did I have a plan? Dad wanted me to go to Cornell. Maybe getting out of Riverton was the only escape for both of us.

"You're amazing, Suze. They'll grab you up."

Now

The next time I open my eyes, the room is flooded with pale morning light. It's seven AM and the physical therapist is due any minute.

He's a freckled redheaded guy named Chaz Cooper. He looks like Mark Zuckerberg's evil twin, doesn't smile much, and barks short, clipped demands.

I quickly get why. He's not here to be friends. He is here to boss around the stump.

In an hour of relentless abuse, my vestigial appendage is handled like a butcher dresses a cut of rump roast, finally packaged roughly in a tight bandage. Shaping, Chaz tells me gruffly, so my prosthetic leg will fit properly. "You want to walk again, don't you?"—he asks, not unkindly, this time.

After Evil Chaz leaves, I slump into the wheelchair to stare at the birds, the stump still screaming in outrage. It only wants to be left alone like a proper stump, a sad monument to its former glory days, not called upon to masquerade as a living tree.

An old minivan chugs into the driveway. Crap. I'd forgotten Marisa was coming. I'm in my bathrobe with only my boxers and no shirt. I'm sweaty, and the stump feels like a bag of glass shards. There's no time to clean myself up.

Marisa enters shyly, her arms loaded with books. I catch a slight wrinkling of her nose at the staleness of the room, but she's all business, determined not to let my unshaven, half-dressed half-self get the better of her.

I'm not going to make it easy on her, I decide. I don't want any part of AP Calculus and I don't want her.

She sets her stack of books down on Dad's oversized oak desk, the one I've piled with empty cereal bowls, juice containers, history books, magazines, and medicine bottles.

"Will you be comfortable working in here?"

"I guess." I don't tell her that nothing is comfortable any more. Especially having her look at me in the state I'm in.

Marisa busies herself clearing away the debris and carefully shifting aside the papers and books littering the surface, a strand of dark hair falling softly over her fragile features as she focuses on her task. Finished, Marisa sits in the desk chair and smiles at me. "Why don't you come on over and we can get started."

I blow air out from my mouth and roll toward her, feeling as hideous and freakish as the Phantom of the Opera.

"Wait. One minute." Marisa digs in the oversized purse she's hung on the desk chair and pulls out a rectangular object wrapped in a silk scarf. She carefully unfolds the fabric to reveal an old leather-bound book that looks like a lot like a Bible. The gold embossed words are Hebrew. Underneath the Hebrew symbols is imprinted the word *Kabbalah*. On closer inspection, the words *My (very own) Book of the Dead*, are printed in gold ink in tiny, hand-written letters.

Gripping the arms of the wheelchair, I snap, "Where did you get that?"

Marisa meets my gaze and slides the book toward me. "She wanted you to have it."

I sit forward, suddenly eager to write off my spiritual encounters as a product of Vicodin overload. "You've heard from her?"

Marisa smiles sadly. "Not exactly."

"Then how do you know she wanted me to have this?" I ask, my tone acid I know I'm being a bastard and it feels good. I reach tentatively for the book.

Marisa looks away. "Susannah and I—well I wouldn't say we were friends, exactly, but I saw the stuff that went on in that house. What she lived with."

"Like what?"

"Susannah left this for you," Marisa says in a whisper, "Not me."

My head spins. I could use a gulp of vodka right about now. "Where do you think she is? What do you think happened to her?"

"I have no idea, Jeremy. She could be anywhere."

"Dead?"

Marisa shrugs. "I hope not. She's run away before."

"Then why would she leave this for me?"

"Why don't you just look inside and see for yourself?"

The pages are wrinkly and yellow, like the thing has been rescued from a dumpster. In some places, the ink has run so badly that it's impossible to read. From the looks of it, Susannah has disemboweled an old book and inserted her own blank and printed pages from other books, in a crazed patchwork. She's highlighted sentences and scratched out others. Old color illustrations have been either defaced or enhanced by her detailed additions. There are pages of drawings, pages of scrawled writing in her tiny, neat hand. After flipping past a few, I realize Susannah has scavenged information on death and the afterlife and cobbled it together in her very own "best of" Death Remix.

Slowly turning the pages, I come to a sheet of thick black paper, inscribed in silver ink, which is free of the binding, slipped in like a note. Ornate flowers, skulls, and tree roots decorate the margins like an illuminated manuscript.

I suck in a breath and read, aware of Marisa's eyes on me. But I don't care. This is addressed to me.

Jeremy,

1) I know why you run.

2) I know that you drink.

3) I know you've lied to me.

4) I *know you've been in love with me since ninth grade.*
   (*I can't tell you how sorry I am that I threw that away.*)
5) I *know you'll help me.*
Susannah

I slam the book closed and let it balance on my lopsided lap, listening to the breath scuff in and out of my lungs. I want to tell Marisa to leave, but for some reason, I find her presence strangely comforting. We are connected now.

"Where did you find this?" I blurt, finally.

Marisa blushes and looks down. "There was a note rolled up inside—in the box of tampons I keep in my purse. Like she knew I wouldn't find it until—uh, you know. The note said to look in the storage compartment in the back of the minivan. I found the book there yesterday." Marisa's voice falters. "With the pair of turquoise and silver earrings of hers she knows I love."

"Shit," I mutter, at a loss for anything coherent to say.

For a few moments we both stare at the desk, frozen.

Marisa hesitates, watching me. My teeth are chattering against an incoming tidal wave of pain.

"I don't think I can do calculus right now," I say. "The physical therapy took a lot out of me."

"Are you sure you're going to be okay alone?"

"Fine," I mutter. "I'm fine."

Marisa studies me, chewing her lip. "Your father is worried about you, Jeremy. He wanted me to—he thinks you may need to see someone. To talk."

"Talk about what?" I'm shivering hard now. It's difficult to separate the pain from my need for the next fix of meds. I wonder how many more bombshells Marisa intends to drop today, or if she's emptied her payload.

"Jeremy," she says quietly. "You've been through a lot."

The words trigger something wild in me. I grab for my crutches and, despite the screaming agony of the blood as it rushes into the stump, force myself out of the chair and violently upright. Marisa takes a step back as I lurch toward her on my crutches.

"How much is he paying you to do his talking for him?" I shout.

For a second Marisa looks scared, until she rearranges her expression into something neutral. She backs slowly toward the door as I thump unsteadily after her.

"He's paying me to help you keep up with your schoolwork, Jeremy," she says evenly, like she's used to reasoning with deranged madmen. "You know that. It's no secret I need the money."

"That's not what I mean," I say, pressing forward. The veins in my temples throb. I'm being horrible, taking my rage out on this girl so strapped for cash she'd put up with me. But at the moment, I don't care. I'm shouting at the top of my lungs, my voice rasping and hoarse. "What's he afraid of, huh? That I'll end up like my mother? Why does he have to pay you to say it? Why can't he just say it himself?"

Marisa rushes into the kitchen. I thump after her, even though the floor is slanting beneath me, pain peeling away my vision in strips of hot black. Thrusting myself forward on the crutches, I'm not sure where my next step will land. I stop and grab onto the center island to keep from pitching over.

"Let me help you back to your room." Her voice echoes from somewhere nearby.

"No," I say, closing my eyes against the rising darkness. "I can take care of myself. Please leave. I'm sure my dad will pay you either way." I want to take back those last vicious words.

"I'll come back if and when you're feeling more up to working."

"Sure."

I hear her hesitate, maybe checking to make sure I don't keel over. I'm fighting to remain upright, but gravity is winning.

"Sorry," I say, meaning it. Hating myself for being such an asshat.

"It's okay, Jeremy."

Right. I know it's not. There's no excuse for taking my crazies out on Marisa. And she probably won't come back. No matter what my dad offers to pay her.

None of this, I realize, is going to be easy. Or okay.

—◊—

It's a long time before I can crawl back to the study where the Vicodin awaits. Crutches, with my balance all shot to hell, are out of the question.

Eventually the pain and shaking subside. I flop onto the daybed, pondering how much of the drugs I need just to function.

CHAPTER

eleven

Now

Susannah's Death Book sits on the desk. I wonder if it's selfish and stupid for me not to tell the police, or at least Dad. But with the police report discrepancy I'm not sure I can trust anyone. Even Dad, who is stuck under Patrick Morgan's neatly groomed thumb.

It's just a personal thing, anyway. A cross between a diary and a work of art. And Suze entrusted it to me. Me. Even after admitting that she knows about all my filthy secrets.

She has her reasons, I tell myself.

Probably because I owe her.

My memories flash to that night. I know what I saw and no one can tell me otherwise: Ryan pushing Susannah down in the rain. But, beyond that, I can't be certain of anything. The memories end abruptly, washed out in the glare of oncoming headlights.

What if Ryan killed her by accident? Maybe her head hit a rock and she lost consciousness. Wouldn't he call in Big Daddy Morgan to rescue his precious ass, like always? The Morgans couldn't let a small thing like involuntary manslaughter blemish their golden boy's future. What would the Ivy League think?

My thinking is clouded. My head isn't screwed on right anymore.

Somehow, it seems important, but I'm not really sure why.

—☙—

Susannah's Death Book is crammed with scribbled notes and doodles, interspersed with pages from actual books. It has one page torn from The Kabbalah that ruminates on how all life is continuous; a passage that insists that the soul never ends is highlighted in bright yellow marker. Scores of other passages from different books allude to the same concept. I wonder how many used-book stores Susannah has raided to cobble this thing together.

Finally, I get the hint. The summoning kit she left for me was no joke.

It is just the beginning.

And then I see it, written in red, a full page of hastily scribbled notes, much sloppier and more rushed than her usual methodical printing.

> *Jeremy,*
>
> *If you have this book then you know I need your help.*
> *If I could get to you, I'd just ring the doorbell.*
> *But, I guess, if you're reading this I can't.*
> *Maybe you tried once and your first try didn't work.*
> *So you have to try again. To help me find you.*
> *Please.*
> *Susannah*

What follows are a list of YouTube links, with directions.

Follow these IN ORDER. Keep trying until something works.

You've always been very good at following directions, Jeremy Glass. I hope you still are.

I swallow and I read on…

First, close your eyes and think of me. Think how you want to see me again.

I know you do.

I do as she says and close my eyes, taking slow steady breaths. I do want to see her. I wonder if she'd be repulsed by me now.

No. I can't believe she would.

Images and scents flood me. The smell of her hair. The few precious times her lips brushed my cheek. The bright green of her eyes in the sun, so vivid against the dusky bronze of her skin. Her slightly crooked front teeth. Her wild snorting laugh when something I said struck her as funny. The thud of my feet hitting pavement, ragged breaths tearing through my lungs as she rode beside me on her bike, keeping pace as I reached for that final mile.

How can she not be here now?

Tears crowd at the backs of my eyes, but never fall. I imagine my leg slowly sinking to the bottom of the Gorge and joining with the other lost things.

I transfer to the wheelchair and propel myself to where my laptop has been gathering dust. I type in the first URL from Susannah's note and hold my breath as it loads. The link takes me to another YouTube video, this one set as private. At first the screen is black, but instead of one of her animations, this time there's just a grainy image of Susannah, her hair disheveled. She's sitting cross-legged in front of a nondescript white sheet she hung behind her, the red Kabbalah string on her wrist, the pendant hanging over her collarbone. Vaguely, I think of Trudy Durban and her crosses.

I stare and try to muster the guts to hit the play button.

—◦◦◦—

Susannah smiles and tosses the flowing bronze waves from her face. Even though her eyes are hollow with dark circles, they flash brightly. It breaks my heart to see her this way, and I know it's my fault. Somehow, I missed everything. Missed the truth behind her smiles.

"Hi, Jeremy," she says with a nervous laugh. "I feel a little silly doing this, but I guess this means you found the link."

Her voice steadies, the expression sharper as she continues. "And if that's the case, well, that means things aren't very good for me."

My spine stiffens, but I force myself to keep watching.

"So, well. But I hope you're doing okay, carrying on. Running, studying and stuff, the usual Jeremy things," she says. I almost have to stop as my breath catches, but I let it continue.

"Where to start…let's see. Everyone probably thinks I ran away again, right? Do you think so, Jeremy? Well, I didn't. The main thing I need you to do right now is figure out exactly what *did* happen. Let's call that your job. But you're not going to be able to do it alone. You're going to need help. And the only person who can help you, who knows where all the secrets are, is *me*." Pause. She furrows her brow and taps her chest. "Are you still with me, Jeremy?"

Susannah stares at the camera, as if waiting for my response. I nod, unconsciously, as if she can see me, feeling like a complete fool.

"I thought so. So, the first thing you need to do is find me, Jeremy. Not my body, but *me*. The *me* that is everlasting, that transcends death—like the Kabbalah teaches. Yeah, I know you consider that spiritual stuff junk, but think of how you wanted me, Jeremy. I know you did." She laughs, and turns her head to the side in a coquettish pout. Involuntarily, a thrill runs up my one leg to my groin. I shudder, ashamed and freaked out. Getting it up for a dead girl while she talks about her eternal soul. Sicko.

"C'mon, Jeremy. You are the *worst* actor of all time. Every time we were together I caught you undressing me with your eyes." She giggles and lowers her cami, just a little, revealing the tops of her breasts. Oh God. Oh *shit*. Dead girl porn.

"But Jeremy," her voice softens. "I know you. Beneath all that was more. Much, much more."

A relieved smile breaks on my lips. So she knew that, too, at least.

"And I was the supreme idiot, chasing after an even bigger idiot. Ryan Morgan."

Susannah sighs and pauses to sip from a glass of water. "I chose to ignore all the signs. *Chose*. Even though I knew it was killing you. Killing me, too. I was too scared. Scared that if I loved you back I'd ruin it and lose your friendship, your devotion. I couldn't risk that, Jeremy. You were my lifeline. Do you understand?"

Sorrow turns to shock. *What is she saying?*

"I love you, Jeremy. Maybe even more than you loved me."

I pause the video. I want to throw the laptop through the window and stomp it to bits with my crutch.

I've never hated anyone more than I hate Susannah right now for what she's done to both of us.

I hate myself, too, for not seeing it. Not taking a chance and calling her on it.

Fuck us both.

But I press play and continue. I can't stop myself now.

"I know. You're probably pissed. I never really showed it, so how would you know? I'm a master of disguise. A crippled girl with a diseased heart. But that's all over now. All that's left is the essence. The part you loved. Think of it as Susannah Nectar."

I can't listen any more. I pause, wanting to douse her words in a vat of vodka.

The pantry. There's got to be more in the pantry. My phone rings, but I ignore it. It isn't her. I know that can't be possible.

A moment later the house phone rings. I hear my father's voice on the answering machine.

"Jeremy? I heard what happened with Marisa. It's okay. Just call me and let me know how you are. I'm stuck here at the office, or I'd come home to see you right now."

No way. Let him sweat. Let *him* talk to me.

I wheel into the pantry and root through the boxes there. Dad's done a pretty thorough sweep. All I find is the mostly empty bottle left from the last bender I went on. I screw off the cap and chug down the remains. It's not enough to blot out reality entirely, but it's enough to slow the shaking in my hands.

I return to Susannah.

"Did I upset you, Jeremy? I'm sorry. I know you're a sensitive guy and sometimes I lay it on a bit too thick. What I mean by my nectar is my soul. The best part of me. The part I always wished I could give you, but that was too clogged with gunk. Anyway, before we get to that, there's still some life crap we have to talk about."

Susannah cocks her head and stares intently at the camera. "If you can handle it."

My heart starts to pound. There's a jump in the video, and Susannah reappears with her hair pulled back, a T-shirt now replacing the cami.

"Well," she says. "I'll bet you're just dying to know what I mean, aren't you? You always were a nosy guy, Jeremy, with your head buried in all those history books. I mean, the way I see it is—what's history, anyway, but a shitload of other people's gossip? I guess it's just special gossip that goes with the important stuff. Well, here's a piece of history, or as you would call it—a primary source—for you."

She lifts an eyebrow, a half smile forming on her lips. I shiver, and pause it. It's the same expression she'd wear when we'd get into one of our mind-bending philosophical loops that usually ended in extreme silliness, her punching me in the stomach and making faces.

Sorrow tugs at me. Lost, lost. Gone for good.

I press play to continue Susannah's YouTube manifesto. "If you want to know what happened to me," she says, her face suddenly fierce, "go ask Ryan who Derek Spake is."

Derek Spake? I roll the odd name over on my tongue. It sounds familiar, but I can't place it. He's certainly not from Riverton High.

There's a sharp pounding at the back door. I stash the bottle of Absolut behind some pillows and figure I can fill it with water and hide it later. I roll into the kitchen, still a little buzzed. I can handle Dad now. He'll see everything's okay and just go back to the office, relieved there's no threat of confrontation or any real need to talk.

But it's not Dad. It's Ryan, and Taylor Pinski from the track team. Taylor's a good guy, but I'm not sure I want to face him. I roll to the door and gaze up at them.

"Yeah, what's up?"

Ryan is beaming. He's holding up some gleaming metal contraption. "Anyone for a leg?"

I glance at Taylor. He looks incredibly uncomfortable, his fixed smile and shifting eyes a dead giveaway. But Ryan, the actor, is perfectly at ease. "Wanna try it on? Let us in, Jer."

"Is that mine?" I ask, incredulous that I am soon going to become a cyborg—half man, half machine.

Ryan laughs. "Nah. This is a prototype. They'll have to make a custom one just for you. But try it on for size. Take it for a run."

"I don't think so, not right now, Ryan. I'm kind of busy." I don't mention that I'd rather walk on my hands than strap that contraption to my aching appendage.

Ryan smirks and glances at Taylor. "Too busy to meet your new leg?" Taylor returns a hearty guy laugh and they both gaze down at me.

"Okay," I say. "Sure. Come in." I'm buzzed enough so that Taylor's obvious stares aren't going to bother me much. And then there's that thing I need to ask Ryan. I'm itching to confront him about the contradictory police report and the newly named Derek Spake. Right in front of Taylor Pinksi.

I unlock the door and roll back so they can come in. I'm in jeans, one leg cut off so it's just long enough to drape gently over the stump. I catch Taylor's eyes snap to my groin, then snap away. Ryan claps me on the back.

"So. Do you want to strap it on and take a spin?"

I force a laugh. *Jerk.* "As if, Ry. I'm still healing. Thing hurts like a bitch." I watch Ryan's face, enjoying the flicker of discomfort. But his brow creases with genuine concern, and now I'm not so sure he doesn't really feel it.

"Dude," he says softly, kneeling down to my level. His eyes meet mine and I see something puzzling there, something I don't recognize. "I'm sorry, man," he says. "I'm sorry how fucking hard this must be for you."

I don't know what to say to that really, other than, "Thanks, Ry. I appreciate what you're doing. With the leg, and all."

Ryan nods and gets stiffly to his feet. "Yeah. I know you do."

Ryan and Taylor leave and I'm alone with Susannah. I hit play again, but from the progress bar, I can see I'm at the end of this installment.

"So," Susannah says. "Any luck? I'm guessing you got nowhere. In fact, you can look under every tree, every archive but I'm betting you won't learn the truth about Derek Spake. The only one who can set you straight, or should I say is willing to, is *me*. So before you click the next link...find me. Find me, Jeremy."

The screen goes black.

Then

Susannah's summer art classes started the next week, the week Ryan and his family were on vacation in Maine. I'd gotten a job as a camp CIT. I was done every day at three, bone-tired from chasing around bratty six-year-olds, but I ran anyway. No excuses. Rain. Heat. Hurricane. Hangover. Day in, day out.

Susannah got home from the city by four and agreed to be my pacer every day. She'd kept her promise.

That Monday, I rested on the couch, the air-conditioner rattling at full blast, waiting for her to call. I felt a twinge of guilt for planning to see her when Ryan was away, but temptation won out over loyalty. It's not like I was going to do anything. Susannah was way too into him and I wouldn't dare violate that trust.

It was my favorite week of the summer. Maybe my favorite week of my whole miserable life.

Every day, after my run, I'd take a shower and bike to town to meet her for pizza, then the two of us would head to Awesome Cow for fruit smoothies. Later, we'd go back to my house and root through my collection of artifacts for oddball things she could cut up for use in her animations. On my crowded shelves we'd found a reproduction of an old Sears Catalog, circa 1910, as well as an Old Farmer's Almanac. There was even a box of vintage greeting cards I agreed to let her cut up. I'd paid twenty bucks for them at a yard sale just a few weeks earlier, but I couldn't say no to Susannah.

I barely drank at all that week. Barely had a hint of a nightmare.

But, of course, Ryan came home and the afternoon visits with Susannah stopped.

The YouTube links to her first animations started coming through via emailed links. Just for me, Susannah said. Because only I would understand.

Just before her class finished up, without a word Susannah was off again. Ryan's parents had left him on his own for the first time. Patrick Morgan had gone on a business trip and Celia had to make an emergency visit to an ailing relative. The Morgans had asked Dad to keep an eye on things, but Dad, of course, asked me if I would because he was super busy with a case. To make a long story short, Ryan didn't waste any time hosting a huge pool party at his house on a week night. Every kid in town was there.

And everyone was drunk and swimming naked in the pool. Except me. I remained conspicuously stone-cold sober. I hadn't been able to swim in water deeper than my shins since the day my mother plunged her car into the Gorge. Just sitting next to water was challenging enough.

"Dude!" Ryan stumbled into me, slurring his words. "Hold down the fort for me, will ya?"

He disappeared into the house flanked by two freshman girls for over an hour while the music got louder and all hell broke loose in his backyard. Lucky for Ryan, the Morgans' property was so sprawling, I doubt any of their distant neighbors heard the racket.

—⁓—

It was four in the morning when the shrill ringtone of my phone woke me up. I'd been asleep for maybe an hour on the leather sectional in the Morgans' TV room.

"Jeremy?" rasped a hoarse, scratchy voice.

Groggy and disoriented, I raked my hand through my greasy curls. "Who else would it be? Who is this?"

"It's me."

I was suddenly wide-awake. "Shit, Susannah. Where the hell are you?"

I thought I heard her sniffle, but it was followed by a short laugh. "I'm at the Louis Armstrong International airport in Louisiana, waiting for the 4:30 AM nonstop to New York City."

I glanced at my phone for the time. "What on earth are you doing in New Orleans? Isn't it, like, three there?"

"Please don't go there, Jeremy. I have an hour and ten minutes until boarding time. And I thought—I thought you could entertain me." Again, the nervous laugh.

"You sure you're okay?"

"Yes, Jeremy. I'm okay. And if I wasn't, were you going to come down and fetch me?"

"If I had to. Yes."

There was a muffled sniffle on the other end of the line, then silence.

"Suze?"

"I'm here."

"You sure you're okay?"

"I'm still breathing, if that's what you mean. But, I should really go now."

"Don't hang up! You said you called so I could entertain you. What do you want to talk about? What topic? Pick any period of history and I'll cough something up. But whatever you do, just don't ask me to sing."

Another sniffle, then a laugh. "Okay. Ancient religions for five hundred."

"Hmmm. Right up my alley. Okay, what fruit, in Chinese mythology, represents immortality?"

"Good grief. I have no idea. Lychees?" she said, now consumed in a fit of genuine giggles.

"Errrnnnghhhhkk," I honked, simulating a wrong answer buzzer. "That would be '*What are peaches?* Peaches were the immortal fruit the Monkey King stole from the Heavenly Garden. But then Buddha caught him, gave him a slap on the wrist and told him he was a bad, bad monkey boy."

Peals of her exquisite laughter spilled out from the phone. "Yum! I could go for an immortal peach right now."

I smiled, triumphant I could make her laugh. "I'm not sure the grocery store variety can bestow eternal life."

Her voice dropped to a whisper. "Who wants to live forever, anyway?"

I fell silent, tongue-tied, momentarily swept up in my own turbulent thoughts.

"Jeremy? Thanks. You really did cheer me up."

I wanted to ask her why she was two thousand miles away at an airport, at three in the morning, in need of cheering up. But I couldn't bring myself to do it, given the secrets I was hoarding on Ryan's behalf, and clearly she didn't want me to press her.

So I said, "Happy to be of service."

"There's that service thing again. It's not like you get community service points for being my friend. But, Jeremy, I really—you're the best. If you were here with me, right now, I'd kiss you."

Poor love-starved fool that I was, I closed my eyes and savored that statement, practically tasting her lips on mine. "Will it keep?"

"Huh?"

"Will the kiss keep? It won't spoil or get stale, will it?"

"Um, Jeremy? I have to go."

And just like that, she hung up, her theoretical kiss still lingering on my lips.

CHAPTER

twelve

Now

No one tells a history freak he can't dig up the past. Susannah might have believed I couldn't find dirt about Derek Spake on my own, but I'm not buying it. Besides, what else do I have to do?

It turns out Susannah was wrong. I knew the name Derek Spake had rung a bell. There're local newspaper clippings about "Unstoppable Spake's Unbeatable Mile." He's a star runner from Hurley, the next town over, and now that I think of it, I remember him, with his smart-ass smile and the daring challenge in his eyes. I hadn't placed the name because Ryan and I always called him "Unspeakable." Unspeakable had thought he was all that until his team went down last season under our unstoppable winning streak.

The burning question—what the hell does Susannah have to do with Derek Spake?

I vow to ask Ryan about Spake. Just to get his reaction.

The house phone rings again. It's Dad. I toss him a bone and answer.

"Jeremy! I thought maybe you'd want to go out for a change. Get some dinner. I know you had a rough morning, but the doctor says it's fine to go out, if you're up to it. In fact, she says you need to get out of the house, to get moving and get your blood circulating."

I think about Taylor's gawking stare and multiply it by fifty. "Thanks, Dad, but I'm kind of whipped tonight. Can you bring in some pizza?"

A hesitation. Hurt, maybe? A lost opportunity to talk, dad to son? "Sure. I'll be home a bit late, then. You go ahead and order for delivery. Charge it to our account."

"Fine, Dad."

The night is mine.

—⁓—

While combing the Internet for more shit on Unspeakable Spake, I get a brainstorm. No way would cheapo Dad throw away a pirate's ransom of vodka. No damn way. He's got it someplace he thinks I can't get to. Either up in his room, or tucked away somewhere in the basement.

I consider the rickety wood descent to the damp basement and what it would take to navigate that. Not a chance.

But, by lifting my butt backward up the staircase, step by step, I'm at the top in no time. If I find what I'm looking for, then it'll be worth the trouble. My efforts are rewarded. Dad didn't even bother to hide the carton of Absolut, nestled on his closet floor between a pair of scuffed-up loafers and another pair of equally scuffed-up boots. Cheap. Too cheap to buy a pair of decent shoes, and certainly too pragmatic to toss out ten bottles of Absolut.

Getting back down the stairs is harder than I thought, but I make it with a full bottle, white candle and matches in tow.

Everything I need for a date. With Susannah.

—⁓—

I decide I'm going to conserve this bottle to make it last. Exercise some of my old self-control. If I clear out the stash upstairs, Dad will get wise.

Pain nips at the stump, signaling the coming deluge. I pop three Vicodin, fill the old Civil War canteen with my ration, then stow the still-full bottle between the daybed and the wall.

Even before my first heated sip, I'm strangely elated. I've claimed a part of Susannah that will always be mine. A part she never shared with Ryan. And even crazier, I'm almost convinced that the power of my need to be with her will bring her to back to me.

After downing a fifth, I ease myself into Dad's recliner and stare into the lit candle burning on the desk. I've scrapped the tacky old ritual for one of my own. I've written the words on an index card so I don't screw it up.

Flying high on vodka and Vicodin, about to call a girl back from the dead, I know one thing for sure—I've lost more than a leg. I've lost my mind. I really am batshit, cow-jumped-over-the-moon crazy.

But I'm so far over the edge I don't even care. I close my eyes and recite from memory. "Susannah. It's Jeremy. You said if I really believed that love is the glue that binds the universe together, I can bring you back."

Gathering courage, I stare deeply into the candle. I close my eyes and imagine her face beside mine, the warmth of her breath on my lips. I can taste them. Vanilla with a tang of lemon.

My voice catches. "Things have changed since you've gone. I'm changed, too, Suze. I'm, let's say—different than you remember me."

I stop, too self-conscious to be talking to myself. But I have to believe, or it won't work.

Headlights shine in the driveway. I fumble to snuff the candle and flick on the desk light, hoping Dad won't notice the weird lighting effects or the candle smell. I lie back, my head lolling in a convincing imitation of sleep.

"Good evening!" he booms from the doorway.

I open my eyes and stretch as if he's just woken me. He's holding a pizza box and smells like winter, his gray hair dusted with snow.

"Whoops. I dozed off and forgot to call for delivery."

"No problem," Dad says cheerily. "I called Bono's and asked if you'd ordered yet. When they told me you hadn't, I decided to come home and eat with you. But I have to go back. It's going to be a late one for me."

I raise an eyebrow. "Big case?"

Dad nods. "I have two depositions tomorrow. And I'm researching precedents in other counties. I've got to do it all myself, with Cassie out on maternity."

I yawn. "It's okay. I'm pretty sleepy. Chaz practically murdered me this morning. The guy's a bully."

Dad chuckles and sets the pizza box down. "No one ever promised physical therapy was going to be a rose garden. But it will be worth it when you get fitted with that high-tech leg. You'll be jumping around, just like before."

I sigh. I don't know what made me think he'd bring up what else happened this morning. "And running my old five-minute mile, too?"

Dad's smile tightens a notch. "I simply meant to imply that you'll be able to walk reasonably well, Jeremy. Which is definitely a plus. How much more you'll be able to do beyond that is entirely up to you."

"Right, Dad," I say. Pushing myself upright, I hop over to the desk. Dad scowls as I misgauge my last leap and almost crash-land on the pizza box.

We eat at his desk while Dad drones on about Pritchard and Sons vs. Hudson Acres, the new shopping plaza that is suing its builder for damages over a collapsed roof last winter. It's been all over the local papers. I try to feign interest, but my gaze drifts to the half-spent candle I've camouflaged amid my shelf full of running trophies. I fidget, bouncing my single leg with nervous energy. It can't be too soon until he goes back to the office.

I catch Dad staring intently as I chew the last bit of crust. "Hungry, are you? Getting the old appetite back?"

"Maybe," I say, still chewing.

"What happened this morning with Marisa? She said you seemed ill."

I swallow and stare back. "Is that all she said?"

He lets out a breath and blinks quickly. "No."

"I didn't think so."

He wipes his mouth deliberately with a napkin and carefully gathers the paper plates and containers into the box. I watch his hands. They're long-fingered and oddly delicate for a grown man.

"Jeremy. I'm not very good at this stuff, but, uh—but Pat Morgan called and told me that Ryan thinks you're extremely depressed. Maybe even suicidal. He has a good doctor who specializes in teen depression."

I roll my eyes. "Jeez."

He stares at me, expression grave. "Is it that bad? Has it *always* been this bad?"

I heave a deep sigh. "I'm fine, Dad. Totally fine. I'll deal. I've gotten through stuff before."

"I'm just trying to figure out what's best for you. It's hard for me to open up about these things."

I look away. And realize I can't really blame him. It isn't any easier for me to talk about how I feel.

"I'm good, Dad. Really good."

His gaze is still on me. "If you ever feel, you know, that *way*, promise you won't—you know—do anything *drastic.*"

I thump my fist on the table. *There is such a thing as too little too late.* I want to say it, but I don't. "You don't have to worry. I'm not *Mom.*" I stand and realize that my crutches are nowhere around. I'm stranded, left clinging to the table like a sailor to the mast.

"For God's sake, Jeremy. *Please* spare me your drama." Dad rolls the wheelchair over and I plop heavily into it. Parking me in front of the TV screen, he sighs heavily and says, "I brought home some good DVDs. History Channel stuff. Or better yet, just get some rest. Chaz will be back in the morning, but I won't schedule Marisa again for the same day."

After he leaves, I revisit Susannah's Death Book. I root around in the book and discover something I hadn't noticed before. The last third of the book is a dummy, the pages glued together into a solid mass. There's a compartment cut into the paper and sealed with a cardboard lid with a loop of ribbon for a handle. Carefully, I pry it open. Inside is a curl of dark bronze hair and a clunky class ring inside a small plastic packet. It's the ring Ryan gave to Susannah last spring.

I clutch the objects, close the book and the laptop, then relight the match. This time, I'm determined to focus harder.

To believe I can call the spirit of a dead girl into my father's study.

There won't be any script this time. Because there won't be any words.

Then

In the fall of our sophomore year, Susannah moved out of her mother's house and in with the Morgans. They gave her a room of her own on the opposite side of the house from Ryan. On sleepless nights, I pictured him slipping naked under her sheets while his parents looked away with a wink and a nod. The knowledge of what he'd done behind her back burned in my gut like a poison seed. But it had grown thick roots, and to dig it up now meant destroying the healthy flesh around it.

I couldn't hurt Susannah when she was so happy.

Or maybe I couldn't stand the idea of implicating myself in his crimes.

Shortly after the move, I glimpsed Trudy Durban's face behind the wheel of her car on one of my daily runs. I had no idea how she was taking the recent turn of events and wasn't sure I cared. According to Susannah, her mother was getting loopier and loopier by the day.

I asked my Dad if he knew why Susannah had moved in with the Morgans; as usual, his answer was a shrug.

I had my own theories. What better way to get back at her mother than chumming around with the Morgans?

Not long after Susannah moved out, Trudy had studded her lawn with an army of folk art crosses and, a day or two before Halloween, left town for an extended period.

Susannah was happier than I'd ever seen her. Despite the upheaval, her dark golden skin seemed lit from within. Her hair bounced as she walked. And I found it harder and harder to breathe when I was near her. Harder to act like everything was okay with Ryan and me.

But, with the help of my good friend vodka and my steely resolve, I kept my mask in place. I'd played my part well. Or maybe I just liked suffering.

I never told anyone about my obsessive infatuation, but friends were getting suspicious about my inactivity on the dating scene. There was always an eager girl waiting, but I couldn't do it. I'd just be using her, and that wasn't fair.

Susannah and I didn't have art class together anymore, because, mercifully, I was finished with it. Wallace took pity on me and gave me a C. Susannah had moved on to a more advanced unit. But we had Honors English together, a subject I was much better in. We were, at least, on equal footing there.

After the move into the Morgans' house, Celia Morgan had taken Susannah shopping at the pricey designer stores on Fifth Avenue. After her spree, she started showing up in school in a hybrid blend of designer stuff mixed with her thrift store finds. She'd take old men's jackets that she'd covered with poems and drawings, and pair them with Manolo Blahnik boots. "Dumpster chic," Susannah called it. I called it the "killing me with a thousand tiny wounds" look.

On Halloween day, the track team had trounced one of our chief rivals in an off-season regional competition. I'd beaten my own record in the 1500 meters by ten seconds and we'd come home with a thousand-dollar prize that would go for new uniforms for the spring season. I was crowned a school hero.

That night, there was a haunted mansion and a series of celebratory parties. The track stars of Riverton and their friends were in a frisky mood. I didn't bother with a costume. I just stayed in my sweaty track uniform and so did the rest of the victorious team. Of course, nobody saw me stop at home for a sip or two, in celebration of my triumph.

I had to take precautions to numb the agony I knew I'd face when I beheld Susannah in her Halloween costume.

It was worse than I'd imagined. At Bart Raven's party, Ryan, still in his uniform like the rest of us, had his mouth fused to Susannah's. I looked away. Swallowing down the nausea welling in my throat, I mingled crazily, trading quips, getting ribbed for not drinking the spiked punch that sloshed around in everyone's plastic cups.

There was no way to avoid her. Sword in her hand, wearing a silver bikini top, a flimsy gauze skirt which rode well below her jeweled navel, platform heels, and tiny feathered wings, Susannah informed me with a drunken giggle that she was dressed as an avenging angel.

Then, without warning, she threw herself at me, her vanilla scent mixed with sweat and alcohol. My heart slapped like a dying fish as I fought not to give in to my screaming libido. Fought to save her dignity. She was drunk and I wouldn't take advantage of that.

People watched as Susannah stroked my face and cooed in my ear.

"I was keeping this just for you. I let it age a little, like a fine wine."

"What?" I asked, in a state of mild shock.

She planted a kiss on my jaw. "That, you boob. You asked me to keep it for you. Mmmmm. Your skin is so soft. Don't you shave yet, little boy?"

"Y-yeah," I lied. At fifteen, my chin was still as creamy smooth as a baby butt.

"Well, that's some razor you have," she laughed. "I could use one like that for my legs."

I told myself I should wriggle out from under her. Get away while I could. There was something hard in her eyes. Something I didn't recognize.

I didn't get the chance.

"What the fuck are you doing, Jeremy?"

Ryan pulled her off me and swung her so hard she tripped, twisting an ankle in her platform shoes.

But she laughed, got to her feet, and limped off.

Ryan yanked me to my feet. His face was red. "Lay off her, Jeremy. You think I don't know? You think I can't tell you'd fuck her the first chance you got?"

"What gives you the right to care what I think or do? The fact that you've been a perfect boyfriend?"

He pushed me hard back onto the couch. Murderous rage swirled in my veins. I leapt to my feet and swung. Ryan ducked, rebounded, and clipped me on the jaw. Hard. And down I went.

A few of our buddies pulled us apart and forced us to cool our hot heads. They gave me ice for my swelling chin and spent a lot of energy working to calm me down.

After the party finally thinned, Ryan approached me, tears in his eyes, and plopped onto the couch next to me.

"You had every right to sock me. I'm a first class a-hole."

I rubbed my throbbing jaw. "No argument there."

"I don't know why you put up with me," he said.

"History. Habit."

He grabbed my hand and squeezed. "I love you like a brother. But I love Susannah, too. Dude, we can't let a girl come between us."

His blue eyes glowed with sincerity. When Ryan got serious, it was hard not to be touched by his earnestness. I believed him, then. I really did.

"I know you care about her, and it's okay," he said. "You're the best friend a guy could ever have. You'd never do anything with her."

I looked down, not so sure if that was still true. "You've got to stop fucking around behind her back, Ryan. It's not right."

"I know."

"Why do you do it?"

"I don't know. Maybe there's something wrong with me."

"Maybe there's something wrong with all of us."

Someone came over to Ryan and whispered in his ear. "Fuck," he said. "She left. Walked out in those heels on Halloween night. We have to get her."

"We?"

"I'm too pissed to walk a straight line, bro. I'm going to need your help."

Neither of us had our driver's licenses yet, so we got an older teammate with a license and a car to help us search for Susannah. It didn't take long to find her, limping barefoot in the dark alongside the road, heels in her hands.

The car slowed to a halt. Ryan got out and ran up behind her. Susannah wailed and pushed him roughly. Ryan fell backward onto his rump, laughing like a fool. He yelled for me to help; idiot that I was, I got out of the car and went to his aid.

Together, we wrestled Susannah like a baby calf and got her in the car. Ryan wrapped her in his arms, and I held my breath as she melted into him. I looked away as they kissed sloppily, then I slumped into the front passenger seat of the car, wishing I was as drunk as they were.

Our friend drove Susannah and Ryan back to the Morgans' place. On the way we passed the Durbans' old frame house. The windows were dark, but the carpet of crosses was woven with miles of toilet paper.

Curled into Ryan's embrace, Susannah pointed at it, and together they laughed so hard, they could barely catch their breath.

And I laughed with them.

Now

I can't focus on what I'm supposed to be doing. Spidery fingers of pain shimmy from my hip to my spine. I fidget in the recliner and struggle to find a comfortable position, but nothing works.

I glance at the clock. Only three hours since I took the last three Vikes. Alarm bells are sounding in my head. The more I take, the more I seem to need.

But an army of pain is advancing up my back, as if one puny stump isn't enough territory and it's out to conquer my entire body. I take two more pills and wait for the warm waters to soothe the pain away.

Finally comfortable, I settle into the recliner, press the packet of hair and the ring to my chest, kick back, and watch the candles dance.

Time drifts. Silence murmurs. The edges of the room darken until there is only the flame glowing bright at its center. I smile. Susannah's dancing there, waving her arms and legs around in a fugue state, like she did at the Senior Harvest Ball this past November. Her eyes sparkle as she gestures wildly for me to join her.

"Suze," I mumble, my words slurring. The room ripples like windblown silk. "I don't dance anymore."

My lids droop closed and I laugh at the absurd thought of me dancing. I could do great pirouettes, I want to add, but it's too much effort to say so.

You need to go deeper to find me, Jeremy.

"Deeper," I mutter through rubbery lips. A floating feeling tickles my extremities. I'm drifting out on warm ocean water, a raft at sea.

The room is a membrane. If I can break through the thin boundary that separates me from Susannah, I know I can get to her.

My breathing slows, each breath harder and harder to pull in. Sweat breaks out on my brow. I'm nailed to the chair, unable to move.

Susannah's motioning to me, directing me toward her like a traffic cop. But the flame snuffs out. I'm plunged into darkness.

I try to move my lips. To open my eyes. I'm frozen. I'm cold. So cold.

The floor creaks. Voices. Someone shakes my shoulders. Hard.

Dad, I say, but no sound comes out. My eyes flutter up into their sockets and stay there. *Dad, help,* I try to call out again. But it's only a puff of breath.

I'm sinking into the chair. Sinking. The water is cold. And dark.

Shit.

I wanted to bring her back, I think as I fall—*I didn't want to join her.*

—※—

Water sweeps by in iridescent shades of blue and green. I float over piles of debris—gutted cars, furniture, and broken china—until I'm drawn into an open expanse of white flowers dotting the craggy rock floor. Searching, I paddle on, the feel of two working legs pushing against the water indescribably wonderful.

I glance behind me and spot the silky thread that trails in my wake, tethering me to the surface like a scuba diver.

Jeremy. Here!

Susannah smiles up at me, the hair fanned out around her face like the sun's rays. I reach for her hand. She clasps mine firmly. I pull her toward me, and holding hands, we swim upward, until we break the surface.

—※—

Back in Dad's study, it takes a second before I realize that something is not right—for one thing, I am standing on two legs. And I'm not wet.

Red and blue lights bleed through the shuttered blinds. Uniformed people swarm the recliner. I strain for a glimpse of what they're so busy fussing over.

It's me they're gathered around, my face powder blue, lips deep indigo.

"Jeremy," Susannah says. "This is my fault."

I study her, perplexed. She's here. In my room.

I pull her close. Inhale the scent of vanilla that clings to her hair and enfold her in my arms. "You wanted to come."

"Not like this."

The EMT workers fasten paddles to my chest and slam them against me with violent thrusts. I see my body jerk like bacon on a griddle. Zap. *Zap.*

Faint sensations zing through my chest. Susannah smiles warmly and releases my hand. We're pulled apart as I'm sucked down the drain by a whirling torrent.

—∞—

It's so dark. And quiet. I can't open my eyes. But I know she's gone.

Someone lifts my eyelid and shines a spear of light into my cranium. Pain lances through every vein. I can't scream. Warbling voices grind in my ears, marbles rattling in tin cans. Hands touch me. Press at me. Cold. They're so cold.

I can't swim any more—so I sink—this time like a stone.

—∞—

I know by the smells where I am. I pry my eyes open a sliver. Dad sits beside me, hands covering his face.

Every inch of me radiates agony. My leg twitches. The stump bangs uselessly against the bedding. I gasp, my lips moving soundlessly.

Dad peels the hands from his face to reveal reddened eyes and a day's growth of beard.

He leans closer. "Why, Jeremy?"

I let out a breath. Struggle to pull another one back in. It cuts like fingernails gouging into my lungs.

"I…it was an accident."

—∞—

Fuck. They've got me on suicide watch. They're going to keep me in the hospital for four days to wean me off the poison and evaluate me after. I'm visited by Patrick Morgan's recommended psychiatrist, Dr. Kopeck, who has long, dark red hair swept into a loose updo and wears glossy vampire-red lipstick. With her black framed glasses, she looks like a stripper in a doctor costume.

She sits crisply by my bedside, studying me and scribbling notes on a pad.

"What were you thinking when you took those pills, Jeremy? That you wanted to die?"

"N-no!" I shout through my chattering teeth. "I was th-thinking my f-fucking stump hurts!" Life's become a duel between the writhing pain of the withdrawal, the burning fire in my stump, and getting this bitch out of my room.

"I see," she says, and scribbles some more.

The second day, savage tremors rip through my body as the Vicodin reluctantly retreats.

"We're almost through, Jeremy," Dr. Kopeck says.

I'm strapped to the bed to keep me from falling off. I scream for hours on end that I didn't want to die, but I think I'm dying now. It doesn't help much.

On the third day, Chaz visits. Therapy has to be kept up, he instructs mildly, or the leg won't fit into a prosthetic. Isn't the pain worth the chance to walk again, he asks?

"Sure," I grunt, and consider jamming the remains of my leg squarely between his rust-colored eyebrows.

Dad stays by my side the entire time, watching. Saying nothing.

That night, I'm sweaty, limp, and feeling like a discarded banana peel. The pain is constant, and I realize I'm going to have to make peace with it because it is here to stay.

Dr. Kopeck breezes in and addresses Dad. "Good evening. We've determined that your son's overdose was likely an accident, Mr. Glass, and that his rehabilitative needs take precedence at this time. Tomorrow, he'll be released. However." She peers ominously over the rim of her glasses and speaks directly to me. She barely stops to take a breath. "Given the family predisposition to mental illness, you'll be closely monitored, Jeremy, to safeguard against further substance abuse *as well as* to watch for suicidal indications. Have a good night."

She pivots on her spiky pumps, ushering Dad out of the room.

I roll over onto my stomach to let the coolness of the sheets press against my bare chest.

I'm beginning to wish I'd stayed with Susannah.

It's then I hear the curtains rustle. There's a slight breeze. Something cool touches my back, slides up and down my spine. I roll onto my back. There's no one there.

But I know she's come.

Now (December 23th)

It's two days before Christmas. Six weeks and one day since Susannah disappeared. Five days since the Vicodin released its stranglehold on me and I returned home from my third visit to the hospital in as many weeks. Twenty-one days since my right leg and I parted ways.

Chaz brought me new crutches, a sleek pair that cuffs onto my forearms with rubber handgrips to support my weight. They've made bounding around the house much easier.

The town is caught up in its annual holiday frenzy, and one missing girl isn't going to stop that runaway train. I think of Trudy Durban, alone with her collection of crosses and God knows what else in her under-heated old house, pacing the floors in sensible pumps. No one else is worrying if Susannah's lying dead in a ditch, or if she's a runaway, or if she's living as a sex slave in Thailand.

Without the Vicodin coursing through my system, and given my *predisposition*, as Dr. Kopeck so delicately put it, to mental illness—as in, my mother was completely off her rocker—I've started to question my supposed brushes with the afterlife. And maybe just about everything else since the accident.

Just the same, I've torn my room apart in search of Susannah's artifacts and turned up nothing. The history on my computer has been wiped clean. There's nothing to confirm that the Death Book, or the artwork, or even the YouTube links ever existed.

Was someone in here—or had none of it ever happened?

I saw the movie *Shutter Island*. For the main character, the hallucinations were his reality. I wonder if my mother had delusions. And if I can trust my own memories at all.

I'm too embarrassed to ask Marisa about the Death Book. I've nearly gotten myself convinced that my cracked mind conjured the entire pathetic episode to avoid the harsh reality that, just like my leg, Susannah is gone for good. But the echo of a name rings in my ear. *Derek Spake.*

I'm not sure what he has to do with anything, but his name is all I have.

And despite the possibility that I may be starting to lose it, the fact remains—I still need to find out what happened to Susannah—before I *totally* do.

Dad has knocked off work early. His office building held their annual Christmas party and I can smell the liquor on his breath, even from where I sit. The smile comes more readily to his lips. Dad hardly ever drinks since Mom's death, but he stumbles a bit as he steps over the threshold and joins me in the study. *He can't hold his liquor as well as me,* I chuckle to myself.

"The Morgans are having their annual Christmas blowout tomorrow night, and guess who's the honoree?"

"Beyoncé?" I offer.

Dad guffaws and leans against the doorframe. "Very funny. It's *you.*"

My heart plummets. A tsunami of nausea crashes into my stomach. I should have seen this coming, since the Morgans seize every opportunity for media coverage. Each Christmas, the local TV news and papers dutifully show up and run a piece in the Sunday paper. It's their version of community outreach. "Why *me*? I didn't do anything Morgan-worthy."

Dad tears off his jacket and flings it on the desk chair. "C'mon, Jeremy. I think you have an inkling of what they're up to. Ryan's raised nearly half the money it costs for your prosthetic, and Patrick wants to crow about it to show what an outstanding citizen Ryan is."

I roll over on the bed to face the wall. "Just what I need. I think I'm busy tomorrow. I've got to scrub my stump."

Dad pads unsteadily over, sits beside me, and rubs my back. "You can't hole yourself up in this house forever. Soon, you'll have to go back to school."

I close my eyes and shake my head. "I'm not going. I can't."

"This isn't negotiable, Jeremy."

—⁓—

I flip to Disk 2 of Ken Burns' The Civil War, but it's not distracting enough to take my mind off the looming train wreck. Scenarios of tomorrow night play out in my head, each one more humiliating than the last. I sip from the canteen, allowing myself only a few swallows. There's still plenty more in the bottle, but I know I'll have to taper off the vodka. The supply is finite. But the idea of life stretching before me without my last remaining crutch is too terrifying to think about.

I close my eyes and try to envision Susannah sitting across from me. Would she laugh at my horror, facing a houseful of the people I've known my whole life? Tell me I'm ridiculous? Or would she suggest we ditch the party and catch an indie film instead?

Her absence hits me like a kick in the groin. The room's silence roars in my ears. My heart starts to pound. My leg itches for a run, the urge echoed in its shadow twin. I'd give up an arm to be able to bound out the door into the falling snow like I did last winter, when the waters came rushing in like they do now.

Last year, I ran a mile in a blizzard to Susannah's house. She didn't ask questions or laugh at me. She just welcomed me in and gave me hot cocoa.

I gulp down the last drop in the canteen, swirl the sweet heat in my mouth, and let it coat my throat. My famous self-control is all shot to hell.

It's time to face facts. I'm Jeremy Glass. I'm a one-legged alcoholic, Susannah, the girl of my dreams, is never coming back, and it's entirely possible that, like my mother before me, I'm slowly losing my mind.

I slip into a restless sleep, fully dressed.

—◊—

I run naked on a track, a wide groove plowed through a deep field of snow. There's packed ice beneath my bare feet. People line the circuit, cheering, and throw flowers in my path as I run. I'm winded, the ragged breath puffing out in smoky wisps. My feet ache from the cold, but I keep running, each step a blistering agony.

In the distance I see the finish line, but the closer I get, the further it recedes. A figure in a white parka emerges from the haze and walks toward me, headed the wrong way on the track.

Pain knifes up through my feet to my thighs. I glance down. Hairline cracks form on my ankles like old paint, then deepen. Flesh falls away from the bones in meaty chunks, but I keep running, a trail of vivid red in my wake.

The figure stops a few feet in front of me. It's my mother, her face as pale as the snow, her eyes flat and dark like chips of coal.

She points at my legs and laughs. "You can't walk away, can you Jeremy?" She turns to the cheering crowd, and with a flourish bends in a deep stage bow to a surge of applause.

Fully clothed in cold weather running gear, Ryan strides past toward the finish line. I slow as the remaining flesh strips away to reveal bare bone. I run until my stick legs snap simultaneously, like dry twigs, and disintegrate into ash. I drop to the ground onto my back, a half-man beached in the snow.

From the corner of my eye, I see someone running toward me, hair streaming like a banner. Susannah hauls me onto her back and runs the rest of the race like a powerful mare. We edge across the finish line a split second before Ryan. The crowd cheers and pelts us with flowers.

Susannah lowers me carefully to the ground and kneels beside me. "You won't walk away, Jeremy. And not just because you can't."

She leans over me, her lips parted. I open my mouth hungrily to receive her kiss, but she pulls away and whispers, "Ask Ryan about Derek Spake. Tomorrow. Don't forget. And look in your gym bag, Jeremy."

I wake up trembling, the want of her kiss still tingling on my lips. Unable to return to sleep, I study the strip of moonlight that slants across the study floor.

My gym bag is still in the trunk of my car, the last place it was on the night of the accident. I peer out the window. A thick layer of snow covers the long sloping driveway. My car is parked at the bottom under the carport, the same place it's been since that night.

I throw on a jacket and a pair of thick sweats. Letting the empty leg trail, I slip into a sneaker, grab the crutches, and head out the door, knowing the minute my foot hits the ice-coated driveway that I am a complete moron. After a few yards, I'm already sprawled on my butt with no hope of getting vertical. I slide the rest of the way, my crutches serving as ski poles, glad for the isolation of our house so that no one can witness my ridiculous butt-sledding.

Finally, after another Paralympic decathlon event, I reach the car, retrieve the gym bag with my numb hands, and rummage through the dirty socks, spare sneakers and gym towels without even pausing to feel sorry for myself. I'm a man on a mission.

There's a stiff envelope at the bottom of the bag, and I wonder how I'd missed it. I used to run every day, without fail, no matter the weather, and I could swear that envelope had not been there the morning of the accident.

But here it is. Frozen through, I open the seal and slide out a photo printed on plain printer paper. It's a poor shot, grainy, with most of the faces in the crowd out of focus. The photo, I realize, was taken in early October, after we'd trounced Hurley High in a death-defying sweep.

I'm in the foreground, motion blurred, as I wave our team banner over my head. Behind me is a mass of bodies clustered in one celebratory mob. Someone has circled two heads way at the back of the crowd with orange marker. I peer closer, straining to see by the light of the open trunk.

It's Ryan and another guy I recognize instantly as Unspeakable Spake. They're staring at each other, Spake's hand extended toward Ryan, as if to give him something. They're motionless in the midst of the frenetic activity that surrounds them. What does this mean, I wonder, and why was it so important to Susannah that I see this? Did Susannah *know* Spake? It's hard to tell what Ryan and Spake's intense glances communicate. Hatred? Understanding? Had they fought that day? I try to think back, but I don't remember them acknowledging each other, let alone getting into a brawl.

I pocket the photo, return my gym bag to the trunk, close the lid, and begin my reverse sleigh ride up the hill.

I'm cold as hell, my miserable butt is numb, but my jaunty spirits warm me.

I'm not crazy after all.

Not yet, anyway.

—⋙—

Inside, I strip off the wet clothes. The bandage around the stump is drenched, so I peel that off, too, and slip, completely naked, under the covers to try and warm up. In no time I'm hot, so I throw the covers off and lay flat on my back, my eyes closed.

The air has weight. The near kiss from the dream is still driving me crazy. The tingle of her lips on mine. Her breath, warm and sweet. A shiver rushes to my groin and I pull the covers over me to hide my shame. An invisible girl is getting a rise out of me.

But I take my fantasy a step further, anyway. Making imaginary love to Susannah is nothing new. I've been doing it for years. But this time is different. I can *feel* her cool breasts crushed against my chest. Her hands slide up the sides of my ribcage and a hot shudder rolls through me as her lips open to mine.

Jeremy, she whispers.

My eyes snap open, blinking into the pre-dawn light that dusts the room in shades of gray.

Shit. I know what I felt. I glance down. The rest of me is equally convinced, as evidenced by the small hill still protruding from the blanket.

Crap. Either I really am the champion of sick fucks or...

—⁂—

Dad wakes me a few hours later. He's laid out a full-court breakfast buffet of eggs, bacon, French toast, and fresh-squeezed juice on the dining room table—to fortify me for later, he chuckles with his patented half-smile. Apparently only a drunken buzz can enable the muscles on both sides of his mouth to work at once.

The heartwarming moment does little to loosen the clenching of my gut. I can't decide which has me more shaken—my erotic phantom encounter or the prospect of being paraded in front of the whole town like a decorated war hero.

I don't deserve any honors. I'm just a messed up asshat, scarred for life by my own stupidity. Susannah did nothing to deserve her fate, yet there is no dog and pony show planned for her.

Delusional or sane, halved or whole—it doesn't matter. Susannah is lost. Probably dead. And no one in Riverton except for me, and her strange mother, seems to give a shit that she's gone.

And so, imperfect vehicle for justice that I am, it falls on me to shoulder the load.

Susannah has chosen me for this.

Now

Dad stands behind me as I appraise my appearance in the full-length mirror. The gray tweed sports jacket he's loaned me hangs just low enough to hide the stump. Paired with my black jeans and one black boot, I'm cleanly shaven, unruly curls slicked back. I look like a guy who just happened to forget his other leg at home.

"Not half bad," Dad winks.

"Good one," I say to his reflection. I can see how, in jeans, I will look almost normal once I get fitted with a leg. "You're a fast learner, Dad."

Dad pats me on the shoulder. "The car's coming in an hour."

"Car?"

"Pat Morgan is sending one. We'll come in through the garage. Because of all the steps to their front entrance, he wanted to make sure you have the help you need to navigate them."

"I don't need any help." I scowl and attempt to balance on one leg so that I have a free hand to adjust the jacket. Dad rights me before I tip backward.

"Of course you don't. You're Superman." He folds up my wheelchair and carries it to the door. "We'll bring this, just in case."

117

Back in my room. I refill the Civil War canteen and slip it into my inside jacket pocket, grateful there is still a half-bottle left in my emergency stash.

—∞—

At exactly six o'clock, a black BMW with tinted windows rolls up to our back door. A behemoth with bulging arms that strain at the sleeves of his three-piece suit emerges from the driver's seat. Thwarting the man's attempt to toss me over his brawny shoulder and haul me around like a piece of furniture, I insist on bunny-hopping down the three steps that lead to our snow-covered driveway. My boot sinks into six inches of white powder, but I soldier on.

"For crying out loud. Let the man help you," Dad says.

"You could have at least shoveled."

Dad shrugs. "Sorry. That was always your job."

Then

Christmas two years ago, our sophomore year, Susannah was still living with the Morgans—even after Trudy Durban tried to file an injunction to force her to move back home. Anyone could have told Trudy she'd get exactly nowhere in the county courts, that all the judges had long since sworn their allegiance to the Morgans. The injunction was, of course, denied.

According to Dad, the Morgans' attorney threatened to have her parental rights permanently revoked for neglect and abuse, and she backed off.

But not in silence.

The following week, the surveillance camera at the ShopRite parking lot caught Trudy Durban slashing Celia Morgan's tires. She was arrested and slapped with a hefty fine for vandalism. It was in all the local papers. Susannah thought her mother's public humiliation was hysterically funny and relished every minute of it. Secretly, I felt bad for Trudy Durban.

But I'd never tell that to Susannah.

That Christmas, the usual bash was cancelled due to renovation work on the Morgan house, so instead they'd hosted an intimate dinner party for fifty. Dad was invited along with a date, which threw him into a desperate frenzy because he hadn't gone on a single date since my mother died. But he managed to round up a frowzy woman from the office and showed up, freshly shaven and dressed in one of his least worn-out suits.

I was also invited along with a date. And though my heart was barely in it, I'd finally succumbed to the dubious charms of Alicia Finley, a sprinter from the girls' track team. She was as tall as me and about as curvy as a yardstick, but she was funny. And most of all, she liked to run. Fast. She also liked to do a few other things that made her fairly appealing off the track. I can't say I was particularly attached to her, but at least she was good company. We were quickly named the Fastest Couple in Riverton.

For his part, Ryan seemed relieved when I started dating Alicia. Susannah, on the other hand, stopped talking to me. I couldn't figure it out. I'd thought she'd wanted me to date.

At the party, Alicia on my arm, all I could think about was how I was going to get Susannah alone and beg her to talk to me again.

And then, a miracle happened. Alicia got a phone call. Her brother had broken his arm and had to be taken to the emergency room. She needed to get home and stay with her baby sister.

And I got the chance I was hoping for.

I'd been observing Susannah all night. Watching how she smiled a lot, but was unusually quiet, other than the times I saw her whispering and laughing with Patrick Morgan.

Ryan had gone off to play Wii in the game room with some of the guys. And Susannah was nowhere in sight.

I finally found her in the indoor pool atrium. The Morgans had two pools—one for winter, one for summer. I'd made a point of avoiding them both as best I could.

I watched from behind a potted tree, trembling as she peeled off her gown, my heart hammering in a twisted drum solo, caught between panic and arousal.

I felt slimy, a total creeper, but I couldn't look away, half-relieved and half-disappointed when I saw she wore a scanty bikini, as if she'd planned to go for a midnight swim all along.

She slipped gracefully into the water, and I held my breath waiting for her to break the surface. Waiting. Waiting.

Something was wrong.

Without thinking, I was out of my shoes, stripped down to my Jockeys, and cannonballing into the water. I swam the length of the pool, my swimming skills not developed beyond those of a nine-year-old, to where I found her at the bottom of the deep end, hair streaming like sea grass. I grabbed her around the waist and pulled her up to the surface.

"You idiot!" she screamed, hitting me, mascara running from her eyes like black tears. "What the hell are you doing?"

"Getting you to talk to me," I sputtered, panting. She broke free of my grasp and left me treading water.

That's when I realized I was in trouble. Frozen, my heart thumped violently inside my temples. I couldn't breathe or get my legs to kick. Red spots clustered at the edge of my vision.

Weakly, I raked the water with my clawed hands, fruitlessly trying to paddle to the edge of the pool that was a mile away. An ocean away.

"Jeremy!" I heard her scream. "What's the matter with you?"

Hands were pulling at me. Pulling me down to the bottom.

I couldn't answer.

—⁂—

I came to, a dead weight floating at the edge of the pool. Susannah clutched at me frantically, unable to get a firm grip on my slippery skin.

I just wanted to sink like a stone and come to rest gently at the bottom.

"Help!" I heard her scream. "Somebody, help!"

I must have blacked out again, because the next thing I knew I was flat on my back on the tiles, a crowd of concerned faces peering down at me.

I woke in a bed, a towel draped around my shoulders, with a steaming cup of tea and a plate of cookies beside me. Mrs. Morgan sat on the edge, her brow furrowed with concern. Patrick Morgan stood in the doorway to the room, glaring at me.

"Drink some tea," she said, and I dutifully obeyed, slurping down the whole thing.

I was in one of the Morgans' many guest rooms, I realized, nestled under a mountain of soft bedding.

What the hell had I done?

"I'm sorry I ruined your party," I murmured, so groggy I could barely keep my eyes open.

"You didn't ruin anything, Jeremy. Everyone had already left."

"But you did give your father quite a scare," Patrick cut in. "Poor man is so shook up, we sent him home. You'll stay here tonight."

Tired. I was so tired. My eyes were slipping closed. *Had they drugged my tea?*

"Sleep, honey," Celia Morgan whispered, pulling the comforter up to my chin. "It's okay. Just sleep."

I let my eyes close, and snuggled, cozy and warm under the covers, my breathing slow and steady. Celia Morgan adjusted my covers and I thought I could just stay like that forever, soaking in her maternal touch. Feeling safe, protected and cared for, I listened to them talk about me in hushed voices when they thought I was deep asleep.

"I think he's still affected, Patrick."

"Nonsense. It's been eight years. The kid's fine. He just never learned how to swim."

"Teresa was my best friend. I have to take care of him. For her."

"Teresa Glass was nuts, Celia. A total basket case. He's been better off without her."

I tried to cling to awareness, but I was so tired.

I never did catch Celia's response.

—∞—

During the night, I slept dreamlessly, sounder than I had in years.

I woke to darkness, the brief sensation of warm lips against my cheek.

"Susannah?" I whispered, and fell promptly back to sleep.

I woke up to Ryan sitting at the end of my bed munching on a gingerbread cookie.

"Merry Christmas, Jeremy. Your father's here to pick you up."

"Shit!" I said, kicking aside the covers. "What time is it?"

"It's one in the afternoon. You slept so soundly, no one had the heart to wake you. It's not Christmas morning—it's already Christmas day." He plopped a small, elaborately wrapped package on the bed in front of me. "A little something from the Morgans. And Susannah."

I tore off the wrapping and opened the small gift box. Inside was a chain with a tiny sterling-silver lifesaving ring at the end. There was also a gift card for a hundred dollars to Sports Authority.

"The charm is from Susannah."

I turned the charm over. On it were inscribed the words TO MY LIFESAVER.

Ryan's tone was wooden and flat. The skin under his vibrant eyes was sunken and dark.

"Dude, didn't you sleep?" I asked. "Where is she?"

"I slept an hour. Susannah packed up her stuff and moved back home."

"What? Why?"

"Damned if I know. Damned if I understand why she does anything. Fuck her." Ryan stood and started pacing the room.

"It doesn't have anything to do with…"

Ryan whirled on me, his face crimson. "*You*? Not everything is about you, Jeremy. Susannah has *issues*. Big-time issues. Maybe if you fucking woke up, you'd realize that."

I rubbed my temples, a headache pounding. I noticed a fresh scratch on his cheekbone, the skin around it red and puffy. "How did that happen?"

Ryan stared at me, not even bothering to obscure the sorrow tugging at his features with a glowing smile. "I walked into the Christmas tree."

"Give me a break. Dude, did you guys have a fight?"

Ryan looked away, his voice cracking. "No. After we fished your sorry ass out of the pool, she went to her room and started packing. What did you say to her?"

"Nothing. I didn't get the chance. I was too busy drowning."

Now

Cars are parked down the length of Emerson Road. Hedges strung with tiny white lights line the long driveway leading to the Morgans' palatial home.

We pull into the garage and, once again I assert my right to struggle up the two flights of stairs to the main floor without assistance. Dad shakes his head. "Sorry, Jeremy. On our own premises, it's one thing. But it's too much liability for the Morgans to risk."

The Hulk nods grimly and I realize that this mammoth is going to be stuck to me all night like a wad of chewing gum. Heaven forbid I should fall—there might be litigation.

Those Morgans think of everything.

Before I can protest, The Hulk scoops me up over his shoulder and grabs my crutches with the other hand. Dad carries the wheelchair while I'm carted up the stairs like a sack of cattle feed.

Once on level ground, I refuse the wheelchair, opting for the crutches, and survey the room. The opulent space is jammed wall-to-wall with people. Constellations of tiny lights twinkle on the ceiling. A massive Christmas tree towers at the far side of the room.

Every year, the Morgans' tree is themed to reflect the honoree. This year, I fully expect it to be decked out with miniature crutches, wheelchairs, and artificial legs.

Subtlety is not a Morgan strong suit.

The first person to ambush me is Ryan's mother, Celia. Dressed in a red sequined jacket and matching skirt, her blonde bob as solid as a rock formation, Celia Morgan wrings her manicured hands. It's the first time she's seen me minus my leg, so I know what's coming.

I've always liked Mrs. Morgan. Which is why she may be the last person I want to see right now. I smile sheepishly. "Hi, Mrs. Morgan."

Her gaze drops to my bottom half and it looks like she's about to burst into tears. "Oh, Jeremy. Poor sweet, sweet Jeremy." She wraps her thin arms around me carefully like I might break and pats my back. "You brave, brave boy. How *are* you?"

"I'm fine, Mrs. Morgan. Really. And I'm very happy to be here," I lie. "Oh, and thanks for the cookies."

Mrs. Morgan laughs and wipes her eye with the back of her hand, leaving a trail of smeared mascara. "I'm so sorry, honey. It's just—I've known you all your life. I changed your diapers!"

She tries to smile through her tears, and I want to bolt out the front door, down the steps, and into the street. But, of course, that's not happening, so instead I slam a smile onto my face and say, "It's okay, Mrs. Morgan. I'm getting used to it."

From the corner of my eye, I spot my dad talking with a couple. They listen intently. Every now and then, I catch them glancing at me and nodding sympathetically. I think about the canteen in my pocket and look for a place where I can sneak a drink.

Mrs. Morgan draws in a breath, pats her hair, and smiles warmly. "It's Christmas, Jeremy, and you're here to have fun with all your friends. People are *really* happy to see you, sweetheart. Go ahead and mingle."

I want to point out that Susannah is not here, and that no one seems to miss her, least of all the Morgans given how much time she'd spent in their house. But I don't.

Smiling people mill around me. They remark how brave I am, but no one wants to linger. My palms are sweaty on the handgrips of my crutches. I shift forward to adjust my weight. I'm an idiot for refusing the wheelchair. My leg and arms are already tired.

I contemplate crawling under a table to flee the piercing scrutiny of their gazes and decide the bathroom is a good haven. Pivoting, I change directions too quickly, then slip and tumble headlong into Marisa, scattering the tray of hors d'oeuvres she carries across the floor.

The Hulk is on the scene within seconds to plop me into the wheelchair and check that I haven't broken anything litigation-worthy. Red-faced, Marisa kneels to clean up the mess.

"Crap," I say. "I'm sorry. I just keep messing things up for you." I start to lean over in the wheelchair to help, but Hulk sits me up straight.

"It's okay, Jeremy," she says. Smiling, she looks up, a really adorable dimple biting into one cheek. She's wearing a white tailored shirt tucked into black pants. Her dark waves are pulled back in a severe ponytail. "You're looking really great. What have you been up to?"

"Nothing much. Just trying to find the coordinates so I can teleport home."

I want to ask her if she knows anything about the disappearance and reappearance of Susannah's stuff from my room. If someone put her up to taking it. But I've been so rude to this girl that I don't want her to hate or fear me any more than she probably already does. Or to think I'm totally bonkers.

Marisa smirks. "What—aren't you having fun? Make sure you eat before you go. The food's great. But I should get back to work before Mrs. Morgan sees me being idle."

"Hope I didn't get you in trouble."

"Forget it."

Marisa stands, the tray of ruined appetizers balanced on her palm. "Let me get you something to eat after I get rid of this junk. Head over to the table and wait for me there."

The absence of Susannah hangs between us like fog, but I'm not sure what I want from Marisa. Help? Comfort?

Unsaid words gather in my throat. What I really need right now is a drink to wash them down. The canteen in my pocket is reassuring pressed against my chest. She turns to leave.

"One more thing," I say.

Marisa stops and turns around to face me again, her eyebrows raised. "Yes?"

"Why am I the only person who cares that Susannah isn't here?"

Marisa's eyes flash with dark heat. "I miss her, too, Jeremy. But there's not much left to do at this point, except move on."

"What if I can't?"

She leans over and touches my arm. "You have no choice."

She turns to walk away again. I debate admitting my otherworldly encounters, but instead latch onto her wrist. "Do you know a guy named Derek Spake?"

A delicate crease forms between her brows. "No. Why? I really need to take care of this mess."

Marisa is about to flit away when Mrs. Morgan intercepts us. She's holding a plate piled high with food. She speaks into Marisa's ear, which sends her scurrying off even faster toward the kitchen.

"Let's get this to the table for you, honey," Mrs. Morgan says, brightly.

Instead of following after Mrs. Morgan, I pause and watch Marisa's ponytail bounce from side to side as she hustles to the kitchen and wonder why it is I always manage to chase this girl away. I vow to resume AP Calc lessons in earnest as soon as possible.

Mrs. Morgan deposits me at a table and leaves. My insides tense because parting the crowds like Moses with the Red Sea is Patrick Morgan, heading straight toward me.

"Jeremy," he says, patting me hard on the back. Apparently the gesture is one of those manly things they teach you at Patriarch School. "You're looking well. I trust you're enjoying the fête?"

I smile, thinking that fête is probably another word they teach at that school. "Yes. This is great." His look tells me he expects more. "Quite—" I search my mental thesaurus for the right word. *Grandiose? Overblown?* "—impressive," I say.

Maybe my emphasis is wrong, or maybe it's the half-smirk I haven't bothered to wipe off my face, because my clumsy erudition seems to offend him. Pat Morgan's brilliant smile freezes. His eyes glaze with heat. He leans in close enough for me to smell his Ralph Lauren aftershave. Voice gruff, he whispers in my ear. Instead of the charm school valedictorian, he now sounds like one of the husbands from Mob Wives. The hand that rests lightly on my shoulder squeezes hard. "Don't get all wise-guy on me, Jeremy Glass. I'm onto your shit. You think I don't know about you?"

He pulls away, the bright smile gleaming, and waves to some passing guests. Then he turns back to me. The smile still lingers, but the blue eyes have gone ice-cold. "Do you really think this miserable party was my idea?" he hisses. "You think I care if you get a fake leg or if you have to hop around like a kangaroo for the rest of your life? You're just a goddamned stupid kid who ran into the street drunk off your ass and got hit by a car. This party was Ryan and Celia's doing. And, lucky for you, they don't really know that you're such a mess. That you're your mother's son, after all. Lucky for you they don't know about all the dirt I've swept under the rug as a favor to your father and my wife."

He stands and chuckles as if we'd just exchanged pleasantries, pats me on the back, then strides away, the crowd swallowing him whole.

I'm heating up like an ant placed under a magnifying glass in the sun. I need to get out of this hellhole. I need a drink. Now. *What was that all about?*

Drinks are flowing. I spy my dad again, laughing just a little too hard at something Celia has said. She reaches to push a sweaty lock of hair from his forehead with a manicured hand. I'm wondering if it's possible that I've managed to unhinge them both.

I'm about to make my getaway to the bathroom and spend some quality time with my Civil War canteen when Ryan slides into the seat next to me. "Dude! Want a sip of this? It's good stuff."

My eyes go wide. It's one of those things Ryan always did at parties to test my mettle. I'd always made a show of refusing. Jeremy the Teetotaler.

He slides me a glass filled with clear liquid and I'm so grateful I almost hug him. I drain it in one long gulp. Ryan looks at me, baffled as my hidden talent comes to light. "I've never seen you drink like that, Jer. I've never actually seen you drink at all. You sure you're okay?"

I set the empty glass down and stare at him, letting the words that sit on my tongue mingle with the warm afterglow of my elixir. "I am now."

Ryan looks uneasy. Maybe it's because the way my vodka-fueled gaze slices cleanly into his. "What, Jeremy? Why are you looking at me like that?"

"What's up with you and Derek Spake, Ryan?" I blurt.

I note the split second his face drains of color. And how, just as quickly, he layers an easy smile over it.

Ryan laughs. "You mean that guy from the Hurley Wildcats? Unspeakable Spake? What about him?"

I drum my fingers. The room starts to wobble. "What were you guys up to?"

Ryan stands abruptly. "What's gotten into you, bro? The presentation is going to start any minute."

As if on cue, the lights dim. A spotlight flares and illuminates the platform in front of the Christmas tree. Patrick Morgan steps up to the podium.

I turn back to Ryan, but he's gone. Either I really did touch a nerve or I pissed him off for being such an ungrateful bastard. I'm betting it's both. It's dark now, so no one sees me as I fill my empty glass from the canteen. Twice. I figure I've just inhaled what amounts to three-quarters of a bottle. And I'm feeling it big time.

Ryan appears on the podium beside his father. He's brandishing a high-tech object above his head. This one looks more like a propeller blade than a leg. The room falls into a sudden hush. Patrick Morgan clears his throat and his deep voice rolls over the room like mountain thunder.

"I want to thank you all for coming tonight. In the spirit of Christmas, each holiday season the Morgan family honors a deserving member of our community. For my son and for me, this year is more special than most."

Patrick Morgan clears his throat again and sips from a glass of water. Apparently, I've got all the Morgans choked up tonight. He continues. "You all know our star track and field marathoner, Jeremy Glass, without whose efforts the Riverton Devils Track and Field team would never have taken home the Division Championship title this past season. Jeremy's been running faster and longer than anyone else for nearly as long as he could walk. And for most of that time, he's been my son Ryan's best friend."

Again he stops, apparently overcome by my sad tale. I bite back the hysterical laughter that rides shotgun on an incoming wave of giddiness. His delivery is smooth. Smooth as the three glasses of vodka sloshing around in my gut.

"I'm sure you've heard," Mr. Morgan continues, his voice reverberating over the speakers, "that last month, after a terrible accident, Jeremy lost his right leg."

The crowd sighs and clucks. My eyes sting. No mention of the fact that Susannah vanished that same night.

"A life-altering tragedy for a track star. boy who is sure to have won a coveted track and field scholarship from Cornell University . With his promising future now changed forever, his mobility impaired, Jeremy seemed to be in dire straits."

The crowd is silent. A tug of self-pity tightens my throat. Damn, he's good. Even though I know what scum he is, I find myself believing him. Ryan has been well taught by the ultimate Zen master of bullshit.

"But that doesn't have to be the case. Because of new advances, prosthetic legs are better than ever; artificial legs are engineered to allow a natural gait, running at a full sprint. But these devices are prohibitively expensive, and Jeremy's father's insurance only covers a basic cosmetic prosthesis." Here he pauses for effect, the room hanging on his every syllable.

"My son Ryan could not let his gifted friend be sidelined. So, he decided to do something about it. In five weeks, he's raised over ten thousand dollars—about half of what is needed to fit Jeremy with a special high-performance running blade. Because," Patrick Morgan booms, his voice cresting to maximum volume, "of the efforts of my son, Ryan Morgan, Jeremy Glass will run again!"

The room erupts in applause. Ryan bobs the prosthetic leg up and down above his head. It's a community service tour de force, just in time to turbo-charge those college applications.

It's a complete crock of shit.

"Jeremy, will you please join us on the podium?" implores Patrick Morgan's amplified voice.

I sit there for a moment, dazed. I realize I'm seriously smashed. I have no idea where my crutches are, and probably couldn't remain vertical even if I did. Slowly, I begin to wheel myself through the sardine-packed crowd, which draws back like a curtain.

I feel a sudden acceleration from behind. The Hulk, carrying my crutches, has taken over and I'm propelled to the podium in record speed.

As I get closer, I can see the huge tree is festooned with miniature trophies and Photoshopped cutouts of me running with my new blade. The Morgans have certainly outdone themselves this year.

I'm handed the crutches and planted on the podium beside Ryan and Mr. Morgan. The crowd roars.

Swaying like a palm tree in a hurricane gale, I squint at the sea of people. There's an elbow in my rib cage and it dawns on me I'm expected to fawn over my benefactors. I lurch forward and hear my own voice bouncing across the room.

"I, uh—I just want to thank Ryan for raising all this money. And the Morgans, for hosting this great party. And thanks to all of you, for coming out tonight. It means a lot to me."

I pause, trying to focus my vision because I'm seeing double. Looking over the sea of hypocrites, I'm suddenly choking on venomous rage. My next words fall like stones over the silent crowd. "But I'd be a lousy friend to someone who is not here if I didn't take a moment to point out one obvious thing. A girl vanished, without a trace, on the night of my accident. No one has seen or heard from Susannah Durban since November 17th."

Murmurs ripple through the crowd. My leg is threatening to buckle liked cooked spaghetti; my arms are numb. I'm not sure what's holding me up.

My temples are pounding, but I shout into the microphone, "I have only one question, people of Riverton—what the *hell* have any of you done about it?"

The room is freakishly silent. A tidal wave of nausea sweeps over me, the crutches giving way like melted wax. I list, then fall forward into the crowd, the side of my face smacking against something hard.

There are shouts and cries. I feel myself being lifted.

The last thing I think I hear is a voice whispering, *Thank you, Jeremy Glass.*

Now

After four hours in the emergency room, I'm released with an eye that's swollen shut and eight stitches on the side of my head. From the pursed lips and sullen stares, I get the impression the hospital staff is getting pretty sick of me.

Back home, I doze off for maybe an hour. When I wake, Dad is sitting at his desk directly across from me. In the gray morning light he's the same color as the newspaper he's reading. Eyes red, chin sprinkled with salt and pepper stubble, he sips mournfully from a glass of orange juice. "Do you want some juice?"

I sit up in the bed and press the half-melted icepack against the messed-up side of my face. I ache all over, but all I'm allowed is two Advils.

"No, thanks."

It's Christmas morning. Our scrawny tree's lights blink forlornly back at me. There are a couple of wrapped presents for me under the tree. I, of course, haven't been able to shop for Dad.

"Yo. Merry Christmas," I say.

"What's merry about it?" He gulps down the rest of the juice. His tone has changed, ice creeping into his voice like the first chill of winter with a hint of the arctic blast to follow. "What the hell is wrong with you? I've never been so embarrassed in my entire life."

I close my eyes, focusing on the pain of my throbbing head. "What's wrong with Jeremy Glass for five hundred?"

"Quit joking with me, Jeremy," he yells. "I am *so* tired of your bullshit."

I sigh, my eyes still closed. "Which category should we start with then—body, mind, or soul?"

Dad doesn't answer. The chair creaks as he stands and I hear him pacing. "Look at me, Jeremy."

I open my eyes. "So, which one? Let's skip over the obvious. We can both see that I have one leg and eight stitches in my head. That takes care of the physical."

He throws a hand to his forehead, then squats so he can look me square in the eye. "Jeremy. You're my son. I love you. And I think your alcohol problem may be more serious than I thought."

"Really, Dad? I had no idea."

He studies me as if an honest answer will somehow scrawl itself across my forehead. "Why, Jeremy? I can't believe that after drinking destroyed your mother you'd go the same route."

I look straight into his eyes and see the anguish in them. But I want him to feel what I feel. I want him to feel *my* pain deep in his bones. "I've been drinking since I was twelve, Dad. I always got away with it until—you know."

His face twists into a grimace. "What? How can that be?"

I sit up on the bed, the motion sending ringing vibrations through my skull. "Do the math. What would make a kid who has everything going for him start drinking at age twelve?"

Dad paces furiously, shaking his head. "How—how did I not see this?"

"Because you didn't want to?"

"Shit." He paces some more, back and forth, back and forth. Then he stops. "Pat Morgan is livid. He's insisting I put you into treatment immediately, preferably in a residential facility. He is not, of course, making the gift of your leg contingent upon that. He's just concerned about you and your wellbeing. The Morgans have told everyone that you had a dizzy spell. That you're not used to standing around on crutches for extended periods."

"Bet he's worried about a lawsuit now, huh?"

Dad's face turns deadly crimson. "There's no chance we'd sue. Not after all they've done for us. Not to mention all that would come to light about *you*."

"So the Morgans have us by the short hairs?"

Dad grits his teeth. "Enough, Jeremy! I told him that, although a residential facility would probably be the best thing for you, you still need extensive rehabilitation. You'll need to learn to walk with your prosthetic. So, you'll stay home. However, you'll be under strict surveillance. And you'll be seeing Dr. Kopeck four times a week instead of once."

I begin to chant in a monotone, over and over, knowing it's driving him crazy. I just can't resist the temptation to wring more emotion out of him. "Jeremy Glass sat on a wall. Jeremy Glass had a great fall," I taunt, then add, "I hate that bitch. I bet she wears leather and plays with whips in her spare time."

"Jeremy!" he shouts. "Don't you *want* to get better?"

I sigh loudly and sink into my pillow. I want to tell him that I'm afraid there is no thread strong enough to mend the giant tear running right down the middle of me. That all I can manage is to hold back the floodwaters any way I can. That without my right leg to help me fly through the streets of Riverton, the vodka is all I have and now that's gone, too. "Yeah, Dad. Sure."

He gapes at me, his mouth slack like a man in shock. "Try to sound more convincing, okay?"

"Dad. Ever think *why* the Morgans might want me conveniently out of the picture?"

Dad frowns, accentuating the deep new grooves that furrow his forehead. "What the hell are you driving at here?"

I sit up in the bed and lean toward him, even though the motion sends a spike of fresh pain through my jaw and bruised eye. "Maybe they know more about Susannah's disappearance than they're saying, you know? Maybe I touched a nerve last night."

I can see the pulse in Dad's jaw. His eyes shine with something I can't remember seeing before. Fury.

In a blur of motion, he grabs my wrist and wrenches it so hard I see stars. "You shut your sick mouth, Jeremy Glass. How could you say—how can you *think* something like that? You'll accept your fake leg with grace and shut your goddamn stupid mouth!"

He twists my arm around and I bite back a howl. Two months ago, I'd have had him pinned to the floor. "Fuck. You're hurting me!"

Dad drops my arm as if it burns him. His eyes still simmer with rage, but he's holding back on it. His voice is shaky when he says, "All these years, Jeremy. All these years, I've struggled to raise you alone. I've encouraged and supported you. Pushed you to achieve. And—and," his voice breaks. "You'd just toss it all away."

"Dad, it's not like that. I just thought—I mean I have this feeling I can't ignore. About Susannah. It's like she's trying to— like she wants me to help her."

Dad's lips quiver. He's looking at me in a new way, a way I've never seen him look at me before. He looks lost. "What do you mean? She called you?"

"Of course not. Face it, Dad. She's never been gone this long before. If you ask me, she's dead. And I'm pretty sure she's been trying to reach out—trying to reach *me*."

"You're hearing voices?" He's up and pacing, crashing around the messy study. "Oh, no. Not *this*."

"Dad?" Now I'm worried. I've never seen him lose it like this before.

He halts in his tracks, looking completely like a madman, and hisses in the softest, scariest whisper two lips have ever uttered.

"This is how it started with your *mother*." He takes in a deep breath, his voice shaky. "You have three options, Jeremy— Dr. Kopeck, a residential facility, or your blood alcohol report magically reappears."

Stifling a sob, he races from the room, pounds up the stairs, and slams the door.

—∞—

I stare at the blinking lights for a very, very long time, not sure what I'm feeling at all. But I've done it. I've tipped my hand. And now my dad thinks I'm a budding schizophrenic. I can hear the expert testimony now—genetic predisposition, traumatic trigger, onset of delusional symptoms leading to a total psychotic break.

Just the nougat the Morgans will need to have everything I say discounted as the ravings of the town lunatic. I gave them this gift.

What if they're right?

Then what's the deal with Derek Spake? repeats the question in my head.

—∞—

The house is dead silent and dry as a bone. Every last hidey-hole for the vodka has been cleaned out. No one calls. Dad doesn't venture from his room all day. I ease myself into the wheelchair and forage in the kitchen for food. Since I have a slight concussion, the doctors have forbidden me to use the crutches for a week, lest I take another fall. I ache too much anyway, so for once I do what I'm told.

Afternoon slips quickly into grim evening, the lights now blinking like hyperactive fireflies. I roll over to the flimsy tree and slowly unwrap the gifts. One is a massager. I'd complained to Dad that the pressure on my leg when I stand too much makes it ache at the end of the day. The other is a book of photos, quotes, and inspirational stories about disabled athletes. The third is a volume about the Roman Empire. I set them down and roll back to the bed. And wonder.

Am I really going crazy? Or am I just looking for a way to hurt the only person alive who really and truly loves me? Tears slip past my eyelashes, rolling hot down my cheeks.

Jeremy Glass sat on a wall. Jeremy Glass had a great fall.

The Christmas lights buzz, surge brightly, then dim and finally fizzle, plunging the room into complete darkness. A breeze that holds the scent of summer rain whispers through my hair. Slowly, a feather-soft finger traces the damp tracks of my tears, lightly brushing across my lips. My breath catches as a fragile weight settles gently on top of me.

It's her.

The soft cascade of curls falls across my face. I squeeze my eyes closed, afraid that if I open them the moment will dissipate like smoke. Arching my back, I feel her push harder against me, the curve of her skin fitting snugly against my own. Butterfly kisses alight on my eyelids, and when the heat of her mouth opens to mine, I ignite into a white-hot inferno of want.

There's no quenching my thirst until I'm emptied in an all-consuming fire. Does it matter if it's real or a symptom of a deteriorating mind?

Finally, the weight lifts, leaving my heated body to cool, my rapid breaths to gradually slow.

There's a quick pressure against my cheek. The soft words buzz in my ear.

Find Derek Spake.

I'm curled on my side on the sheets, spent and drowsy. On the floor next to the bed is Susannah's Book of Death, splayed open to a spread illustrated with a delicate line drawing of a girl cloaked only in her own hair. Resting across the book is a sprig of evergreen, wet, like it was just brought in from outdoors.

Now (December 26th)

It's the day after Christmas and even though I'm a bruised wreck, Dad has scheduled a torture session with Chaz. The stump must be shaped or it will never fit comfortably into my new leg.

Dad avoids me, except to say that he's arranged for my first visit with Dr. Kopeck afterward.

He can't bring himself to meet my eyes and I wonder if he sees my mother every time he looks at me. I wonder if he already sees me come to rest at the bottom of the Gorge. And he wishes I'd joined her there eight years ago and saved him from all this grief.

"Marisa is coming to take you," he says curtly, before he vanishes back upstairs.

Marisa, I repeat. The sound of her name chimes on my tongue. I remember the photo of Ryan and Spake I tucked away in my coat pocket and hope it hasn't gone the way of most everything else I have of Susannah's. I can't help but wonder if Dad has gathered it all up to show Dr. Kopeck what a nut I am, or even worse, handed it over to Patrick Morgan. But I don't want to throw any fuel on the fire, so I keep my mouth shut.

As promised, Marisa pulls up in the van and bustles about, all quicksilver efficiency. I try to meet her gaze, but she keeps hers averted, busy with the project of getting me situated. Chaz helps me to the minivan and loads the wheelchair in the back. No crutches allowed for six more days. It's the chair for me.

God, I'm tired of being hauled around like cargo. I feel like a piece of bruised fruit. The stump sends shooting pains to my non-existent right foot, as if it wants to make sure I don't forget how it misses the rest of itself.

Marisa's hair is pulled back again in a neat ponytail. I study her profile as she drives, her eyes trained on the road. I note the upturn of her small nose, the dark lush lashes. She won't look at me. I can't blame her. I look like Frankenstein's monster with my stitched-up face.

"You know you're taking me to a shrink, right?" I ask, conversationally.

Voice terse, her hands tighten on the steering wheel. "Under the circumstances, I think that's about right."

"So you think I'm cracked, too?"

"I wouldn't say cracked," she snaps, but her voice gradually softens. "Troubled. Who wouldn't be with what you've been going through?"

I shrug and gaze out the window at the passing landscape, the snowbound hills punctured by skeletal trees. I imagine Susannah's bones buried somewhere in the frozen muck. If Marisa knew what had transpired in my bedroom last night she'd sign the papers for my committal. I consider asking her about Susannah's things and if she knows where everything but the Death Book has gone. Instead, I blurt. "Are you sure you don't know anything about Derek Spake and Susannah?"

Marisa jams on the brakes at a stop sign, jerking me against the shoulder strap. She turns to me, her eyes sparking. "I have no idea who the guy is. Why do you keep harping on that? You *need* to cool it, Jeremy! You've turned the whole town upside-down with what you did Christmas Eve."

"You were the one who brought me the damned Death Book in the first place. Don't you want to know what really happened to Susannah?"

Marisa's soft petal lips slip open. I catch a sliver of dainty white teeth. "I'm sorry I did. I never imagined—you just have to accept the fact that we may never know what happened to her. It's sad and it's tragic, but—but—"

"But what are you so damn scared of, Marisa?"

She pulls the car to the shoulder of the road and brings it to a halt, then turns to me, her small features chiseled to a sharp point. Slowly, she says, as if the only thing between me and a volcanic eruption is her clenched jaws, "I'm not scared for myself, Jeremy. I'm scared for *you*."

"Why?"

She exhales and looks to the roof of the car, clearly exasperated with me. "You just don't get it, do you? You're totally out of control, like a stampeding one-legged bull, knocking over everything in its path, stepping on toes."

Her words scald me. "I'm not trying to hurt anyone. I just want to know what happened to her."

She stares bleakly at the icy road beyond the windshield. "As you might have guessed, Mrs. Durban fired me and now… I'm working for the Morgans and they—by acting out like you've been, they feel you've betrayed them."

"Oh. So that's it." I feel my cheeks go red. "You just need the work. Of course you can be counted on to stay quiet if you happen to know shit you shouldn't."

Marisa pounds the steering wheel in frustration. "I don't know anything! I'm just trying to help you, you fucking goddamned idiot!"

I slump lower in the seat. "I'm sorry. I shouldn't have said that. I don't know what's gotten into me. I've been the ultimate asswipe lately."

Her lips are trembling. I've upset her again. Suddenly, I can't help myself. I reach to shift the damp hairs that have broken loose from her ponytail out of her eyes, but she swipes my hand away. "Cut that out."

"Sorry. I'm crazy, remember?"

She glares at me, and I can't help but appreciate how tiny but fierce she is. "Keep on playing your little games and see where it gets you, Jeremy. I overheard Mr. Morgan tell Ryan that your behavior at the party was the last straw. That he wanted to pull the plug on the fundraiser for your leg, but Ryan talked him out of it."

"Oh," I say, drumming the dashboard. "did Ryan really stand up for me? How touching. More likely Mr. Morgan realized what a public relations fiasco it would be to pull the rug out from under a one-legged kid."

"Jeremy," she says softly and evenly. "Everyone knows how much you're hurting. It's just that you really don't want to piss off Patrick Morgan any more than you already have. He—he has a terrible temper."

I study her closely. "He didn't threaten to hurt you, did he?"

She looks at me oddly. "Of course not. I only meant that you should be focusing on putting your own life back together."

I stare down at my folded-up pant leg. The sad truth is that she may be right—that I'd rather deal with a missing girl than the missing parts of my body. And my life.

Marisa's pity stings worse than her anger. I want to open the car door and slither home down the icy road, like the worm that I am. I'm so tired of being freight that has to be hauled from point A to point B. And I would do it, except there is still the matter of Derek Spake.

I pull out the photograph of Ryan and Spake I've been carrying around with me and look at it again. "This was in my gym bag. You didn't put it there, by any chance?"

"What? I didn't stick anything in your gym bag. Why would I do that?"

I hand her the photo. "Know the guys in the orange circles?"

She takes the photo from my hand and studies it. Her brow furrows and she taps on her teeth with a fingernail. "Well, that's

Ryan, obviously. And the other guy—hmm…" She peers more closely at the photo and her mouth falls open. "Wait a minute. I think I have seen this guy somewhere. Let me think."

"At a track meet?"

She shakes her head. "I don't go to those."

I wait while she scans her memories, then looks at the photo again. "It's him. The guy from that day." Then she looks at her watch. "Shit. We're going to be late for your appointment. Not good."

Marisa pulls back onto the road. More landscape slips by before she speaks again. "I don't know if I should tell you this. If I'm just throwing gasoline on a raging fire."

"What do you mean?"

She smiles sadly. "This could all be nothing. A dead end. And if by fueling your," she pauses and air-quotes the words, "*investigation* I'm just making things worse."

"You're afraid you're aiding and abetting a madman?"

"I don't think you're a madman, Jeremy. Just someone who's," she turns to me and smiles slightly, "a bit lost."

"I don't need you to feel sorry for me," I say gruffly. "Just spit it out."

She shakes her head and sighs. "Fine. Do with it what you want. Just promise you'll keep your head, okay?"

"Okay. I promise."

"Well," she starts. "I was working one Saturday afternoon at the Durbans'." She continues, her soft accent and the van's rickety motion soothing my jangled nerves somehow, and I realize that I like hearing her speak. That I like watching her as well—the way her lips shape her words, the way her hair bobs when she wants to emphasize a particular point.

"Papa dropped me off, so there was no car in the driveway. Mrs. Durban had me going through boxes of papers in the basement she wanted to dispose of. What a mess. That woman hasn't thrown away anything for the past ten years. And she has crude handmade crosses everywhere. I'm Catholic, but to tell you the truth it makes me nervous."

Marisa stops to wet her lips. Her voice quavers as she continues. "At about four-thirty, a car screeched into the driveway. There's a pretty good view from the basement window so I stood on a chair and peered out. I didn't recognize the car, but it barely stopped long enough for Susannah to stumble out. This guy got out of the car and followed her, but she shoved him. Somehow she managed to get into the house and slam the door. He kept banging on it and calling her name."

"How long ago was this?"

"This past October, I think. Anyway, the guy storms back to his car and peels off. Susannah's sobbing hysterically. It doesn't stop. Finally, I can't stand it anymore, so I go upstairs and find her at the kitchen table. I asked her what happened. She looks up and tells me 'nothing.' Nothing happened. Then she added that if anything did happen, 'what did it matter, since the Morgans control everything?'"

"That's weird. Do you—do you think maybe he—"

"Raped her? I wondered. It could have been anything. But, I'll tell you one thing—I've never seen her so upset. And this was that guy."

I stare at my knuckles and wonder if I'm missing something. "Did you ask her what Derek Spake had to do with the Morgans?"

Marisa nods and answers softly. "All she said was, 'One day, I'll tell you everything, Marisa. But not today.'"

"Do you think Ryan knew about this? Maybe it had something to do with that drug bust that sort of went away." I swallow and peer at the photo with her. This leads me to think about my own blood alcohol report, which has also magically vanished. It seems that anything remotely inconvenient for the House of Morgan simply disappears.

I'm starting to wonder if Susannah fits in that category as well.

Marisa shakes her head, her hands clenched on the steering wheel. We pull into the parking lot of the professional building and she slides the van into a spot, then turns to me. "I don't know, Jeremy," she says softly. "But I'll tell you one thing. In this town, it's safer to let the dead rest. Or you could end up joining them."

She gets out of the car and tugs the wheelchair out from the back, rolls it over to the passenger side, then guides me down from the van's high seat. I feel the strength of her tiny body as she helps me ease into the chair.

Shame washes over me. I want her to touch me. But I should be the one sweeping her into my arms. Sorrowfully, I wonder if I'll ever be able to do that to a girl.

Self-pity is crowded out by a cresting wave of anger. I'm disabled, but I'm still alive. A perk Susannah lacks.

No, I am not going to walk off quietly into the sunset on the leg the Morgans bought and paid for. Not while this entire town wants its secrets to stay buried along with its dead.

I'm one-legged Jeremy Glass and I'm an alcoholic. And I'm going to dig until I unearth every last shred of the truth.

Silently, she pushes me up the ramp to the entrance.

"Marisa, will you take me to find Derek Spake after this session?"

She holds the glass door to the building open for me to roll in. Once inside, the only sound is the swish of my wheels on carpet and the soft tread of her sneakers as she walks beside me. I stop and pivot toward her. "Marisa. Will you?"

She closes her eyes and raises her hand to her mouth. "I'm going to regret this. But I'll take you. For Susannah."

—◊—

Dr. Kopeck flashes a brittle smile when she sees me. It's the kind of smile the victor smiles at the vanquished, a smile that Roman generals probably wore when they surveyed their new conquests. She's out of her white coat, dressed in a black turtleneck and an alarmingly short red skirt, her dark red hair pulled back in a severe bun. She's a symphony of mixed messages, and I can't help but think that she's got a sharp blade ready to slice through my rib cage so she can rip out my still-beating heart.

She settles into a chair and gestures for me to sit on the couch. I refuse and remain in the wheelchair, even though its unforgiving vinyl digs into my back and chafes my stump. Not a minute into our session and she plunges mercilessly into the events surrounding my mother's death, my recurrent nightmares and the dark waters that choke me in my sleep. I'm wondering how she knows all this and if I'd told her myself in the hospital as I flailed around in my detox delirium.

I'm like a guppy thrown in the tank with a piranha. There's no way I'm getting out of this with the flesh still on my bones. She is going to eat me alive.

Looking up from her yellow legal pad, Dr. Kopeck regards me coolly. "So, it seems, Jeremy, what we have here is an early childhood trauma from which you've never fully recovered. I'd like you to tell me about that day, moment by moment. Everything you can recall."

Dr. Kopeck manages to strip away my onionskin, layer by layer, to reveal the shriveled little kernel of misery at its center. I recount the day my mother died, from the watermelon ice fight I had with Michael Fishkin to the game of tag where we all jumped on top of Dave the counselor. I describe the sharp pain in my stomach when I saw my mother's eyes and the raw terror as we flew over the embankment into the water.

Had my mother screamed? she asks.

I grip my temples. "I don't know. Can we stop now?"

At this point I'm having a panic attack that has me hyperventilating so violently I'm sure I'm going to asphyxiate right here in her office.

She hands me a glass of water. "Very good," she says, a slight smile curling the corners of her mouth. "Can you tell me about the recurrent dreams you have?"

I gulp down the water, still gasping for breath. "Please. I can't."

"You wouldn't want me to report to your father that you've been uncooperative, would you, Jeremy?"

Still struggling to breathe, I realize that I hate this woman and wonder where the interrogator's lamp is. Between breaths, I wonder if she really wants to help me.

Or break me.

"Jeremy," she says. "You know I have your best interest at heart. Paranoia is a common symptom of people suffering delusional disorders. We'll talk more tomorrow."

She smiles, and holds the door open for me as I wheel myself out.

In her own way, Dr. Kopeck is more of a terrorist than Chaz. And this is only the first session.

Back in the van, I'm shaken and stirred, jittery as the time when I'd made the mistake of riding the Jaws of Death at Six Flags and seen my life flash before me.

God, I'd kill for a drink. And my stump is throbbing like a second heart.

"You okay?"

I can't take my eyes off the dashboard. For some reason, the patterns and lines in the faux leather fascinate me. "It depends how you define okay."

"So, it was that bad."

I shiver and nod. I'm going to have to beg Dad not to send me back. Play the suicide card. I can't imagine how this torment is going to cure me of my drinking problem. But I know what he'll say. Our hands are tied by Patrick Morgan.

"Sometimes when a bone is set wrong," Marisa says, her gentle accent like lapping waves, "it needs to be re-broken so that it can mend straight. And that's gotta hurt."

"So, now you're a doctor?" I mutter. I know I'm being unfair, but I'm a raw, bleeding piece of meat. The only way to feel better is to inflict pain myself.

But Marisa doesn't back down. "I'm interested in medicine."

"How nice for you. Why?"

Marisa's cheeks color. She looks away. "Sick relatives with no insurance. Maybe if I became a doctor, I could help."

"Oh."

"You're hurting, Jeremy. But sometimes you have to let a wound bleed out."

I wrench my gaze from the dashboard. "Why are you being so nice to me?"

Marisa tilts her head and shrugs. A smile creeps across her face, setting fire to her coal-dark eyes. "You're my meal ticket?"

I chuckle mirthlessly. "Touché. Nicely done."

"I like you, Jeremy," she blurts. "Even though you're working overtime to make sure I don't."

I return to the intricacies of the dashboard. The indents in the plastic remind me of the gullies that form in mud after a hard rain. My throat catches. Mud conjures the image of Susannah's bloated body lying in a gully, coated in it. Forgotten. Abandoned. I squeeze my eyes closed tight so I don't sob out loud.

"I should take you home," Marisa says, touching my shoulder.

"No. We need to see Derek Spake. You promised." I know I sound petulant, but I don't care.

"Do you think that's a good idea? Look at you."

My eyes still closed, I pull my arms in tight to stop my shaking. "It doesn't matter if it's a good idea or not. It's what has to be done."

Now (December 26th)

It's a five-minute drive to Hurley from Riverton and I'm lost in a current of thought as I watch the dirty snow piles whizz past. I imagine the steady thud of my feet on pavement, the calming rhythm that kept at bay the waters that threatened to drown me.

Now there are so many cracks for the waters to seep in and suddenly I see myself, balanced on one leg like a stork, peering down into the depths of the Gorge. Wondering if I should jump. Join Susannah and my mother after all.

Maybe it's the only way to cut this noose from around my throat. Stop this physical and mental agony.

Not yet. If I don't finish what I've started, no one will ever know what happened to Susannah. The guilty will walk away, scot-free.

Before I go, I decide, I'm taking them with me.

"What's on your mind, Silent Sam?" Marisa says cheerily, back to playing nursemaid.

"Things you wouldn't want to know about." I clam up and she goes silent, too. I see her mind working, trying to figure out how to navigate the winding roads of my wild mood swings. She's getting paid to do this after all, to tolerate me, and Marisa Santiago, I have learned, has one killer work ethic.

We coast to a stop in front of a nicely landscaped house on a neat little block. The houses in Hurley are more closely packed than the winding country lanes of Riverton.

It wasn't hard to find his address online and her GPS helped us locate it easily.

The house looks quiet. It's winter recess and I wonder if the Spakes have gone out of town.

We sit in the car for ten minutes, watching.

"So what are you going to do if we do see him, Jeremy? Have you thought of that?"

"No," I admit. Maybe I just want to look him in the eye and see what's there. I'm not sure. "I guess I'm just going to ask him how well he knows Ryan and Susannah."

We're about to leave when a sweaty, exhausted Derek Spake slows to a stop in front of his house. He bends over, catching his breath, hands on his knees. I'm wrenched by a tug of deep longing for that feeling, the burn of my muscles, the satisfaction of knowing I just ran twelve miles without stopping.

No. Life isn't fair. I want to break Unspeakable Spake's neck with my bare hands.

"Open the window."

"Be careful, Jeremy." Marisa rolls down my window.

"Hey, Spake!" I call. "Derek Spake!"

Spake straightens, squints at the car, and then ambles cautiously over. "Who's that?"

"Come a little closer and find out."

"I'm getting a bad feeling," Marisa says.

"It's fine," I say, my eyes pinned on Derek Spake.

"Whoa. Look who it is. Dude, I heard you had an accident. We even gave to the fund. Sorry, man."

"Yeah," I say. "But I didn't come for your pity. I want to talk to you about something."

Spake squints at me. "Huh?"

"I'll be real quick."

From the corner of my eye, I see Marisa squirm in her seat. "Jeremy," she warns, "Don't say anything stupid, if that's possible."

Spake saunters to the car and eyes me cockily. "Okay, spit it out, Glass."

"You and Ryan Morgan—are you guys kinda, you know—*tight?*"

His face colors, the sculpted features screwing up into a snarl. "What the fuck do you mean by *tight?*"

"It's slang for friend, asshole. Are you guys friends is all I'm asking."

Spake is breathing heavily, his face getting redder by the minute. "What are you driving at, Glass? Because I don't fucking care if you have one leg or if it's been shoved up your ass—you start with me, I'm gonna finish it."

My arm hanging out the window, I drum the car chassis. "I'm not trying to pick a fight, Spake. I'm just trying to ask a few questions. Do you know Susannah Durban?"

At this, his face deepens to a hideous maroon. Veins are popping out in his neck. He lunges for my arm and yanks it backward in a painful twist. "Why don't you just get the hell out of here?"

"I would," I say, "But you've got my arm. Can you just answer the question? Is it that big of a deal?"

"I'll let go when you come out of this car and tell me to my face why you're taunting me! I didn't do anything! I didn't hurt anyone!"

He bends my arm painfully backward and I yowl. "Fuck! Okay, Spake, you win. Let me go!"

At this point Marisa jumps out of the car, opens the back of the van, and storms around to the passenger side. She's holding a baseball bat. "Let go of him," she threatens.

Spake looks at her and laughs. "This is your bodyguard?"

Marisa glares and I don't doubt she'd swing the bat and happily knock out his perfectly white front teeth.

"Okay!" I shout. "Back off, everyone. I'm coming out."

"Jeremy. Don't," Marisa pleads.

I slide open the van door, unlatch the shoulder strap and pivot around so that my leg rests on the step plate. I ease myself down to the asphalt so that I'm leaning against the car body for support. It takes a second for Spake to find his voice. "Whoa. They never said it was the whole fucking thing. Shit."

"My leg's not the only thing that's missing, Derek," I say. "The night this happened, Susannah Durban vanished. She hasn't been seen since."

Spake walks away backward, palms raised. "Dude. I'm sorry for you. I don't know anything about Susannah."

"Did you ever, you know, *hurt* her?"

"*What?* No way. Never."

"What is your relationship with Ryan Morgan?"

He starts trotting away. "Fuck off, Glass. If you ever come back here, I'll break your fucking pogo stick."

Marisa helps me back in the car, gets in herself, starts the engine, and closes the windows. I shake out my sore arm.

"That was productive," she says.

"Actually, it was. Unlike Ryan, Spake's no actor. I think he's hiding something."

"Or he's pissed off about being stalked."

"I think it's more than that."

"What if Susannah had something on him and Ryan, and that's what the crazy shit with him and Susannah was?"

"Maybe. But I don't know. There's something weird going on with him and Ryan, and I need to find out what it is."

CHAPTER
nineteen

Now (December 26th)

When we get to my house, the sky is indigo blue, almost nightfall. Dad's car is in the driveway. The light's on in his bedroom, so I know he's home, but the house is silent when Marisa helps me inside. He's left half of a meatball hero wrapped in aluminum foil and a Caesar salad in a plastic container on the kitchen counter. Bono's again.

It's been a long, weird day. I'm exhausted, sore, and perplexed. The answer to the riddle of Derek Spake's role in Susannah's disappearance is within my grasp if I can just connect the dots. I think about a book I'd read once on forensic historians, people who solve longstanding historic mysteries. Like them, I need to take a more systematic approach.

One thing I know I don't want to think about is the bleeding wound Dr. Kopeck has opened in my soul.

Rooting around in my neglected book-bag, I fish out a pad of grid paper. I tape four sheets together and spread them on the desk. Along the tops of the pages I pencil dates. I start with early October, when Susannah fought with Spake, and write each date across the whole length of the paper until I get to the present day.

I plot out each noteworthy event of the past three months, including our upset win in late October, the day the snapshot of Spake and Ryan was taken. I note Susannah's departure to Rhode Island, her return and ultimate disappearance, fights Susannah and Ryan might have had. The YouTube animations. The day I found the cigar box with the picture of Ryan as a vampire. The package from Susannah with the conjuring kit. The drawing her mother gave me in the hospital. The surgery that took my leg. Messages on a drinking glass. My overdose. Hearing voices. Marisa. My confrontation with Spake. I record all of it.

I stare at the network of dots drawn onto the graph paper and let my eyes blur, hoping the answer will leap out at me from the grid.

The longer I keep my mind occupied, I realize, the longer I'll be able to hold back the avalanche of pain the sadistic Dr. Kopeck unleashed earlier today.

Thinking about the session is like touching an infected bedsore, so instead I fixate on the large red X I've made to indicate the day of my accident, the day Susannah disappeared.

The X grows until it swallows my vision, a single glowing red eye. My fingers are made of rubber. I can't feel the pen anymore and it drops from my grasp.

The room fades to black and I'm blind to my surroundings except for the burning red eye.

Panicking, I flail at the darkness and wonder if my head injury has spawned a fatal blood clot. These could be the last few moments of my conscious life.

My searching hands brush skin. Velvety soft, heat-kissed skin. I trace the swells and folds of her body and a thrill of electric pleasure shoots through me. It only takes an instant before I'm an arrow of white-hot desire.

Jeremy. The disembodied voice is both next to me and apart from me all at once. But the touch. The touch is real and immediate.

I moan as gentle hands torture me into a state of exquisite agony. "Susannah?"

There's no reply. Only her touch.

Oh, her touch.

"I can't see anything," I gasp in staccato bursts. If she stops, I'll burn down to ash. I might as well be blind right now, and I don't fucking care. "Are you here? Why won't you let me see you?"

Fingers plumb the contours of my face, the hollows of my eyes, my lips. My heart crashes against my rib cage. I think of her eyes the last time I saw them, in the theater lobby the night she disappeared. Sorrow rushes to shore, a breaking wave.

I'm making love to an echo. A memory.

"Is it really you?" No answer, only soft fingers traversing my skin.

I squint into the black heat of my room. I may be dead, too, for all I know, making love in hell. Or I really may be crazy. Totally, Dr. Kopeck-sign-the-papers-lock-the-door-and-throw-away-the-key crazy.

I'm simmering all over again, my bare skin sheened with sweat. "Can you speak?"

Nothing. Just a lightening of her touch, as if she's pulling away.

"Please don't leave yet," I moan and rake my hands through hair I'm not sure is real or in my imagination, desire eroding my veins, melting me to a pulsing core of want.

I am crazy, I think. Or this is the final hallucination of a dying boy.

Either way, I don't care. If this is insanity, I'll take it. If I'm dying, this is worth it.

In the pulsing dark, I see a form, dust particles floating in sunlight. A girl made of stars. I crush her against me, and laugh.

It's the ultimate cosmic joke. I've found the love of my life.

Only she's dead.

Your mother says..., says a disembodied voice, barely louder than a summer breeze through grass.

Cold dread shivers down my spine. I'm suffocating, trapped in this way station between life and death. "What?"

I claw at the dark, my throat closing, lungs filling with cold water. There's no air. No breath.

A nightmare. I'm having a nightmare.

...to look in the attic, Jeremy.

The attic? Why the attic?

Go look in the attic.

—⁓—

Lamp light filters between my lashes. Shattering pain pounds my skull. It's four AM.

I'm seated in the wheelchair, slumped over on the desk exactly where I was before, my hand slack around the red marker.

A blotch has formed in the place where its point has bled into the paper. On closer inspection, I see it's a word scrawled into the shape of a tiny red heart.

Truth.

Then

The winter of our sophomore year was an endless blur of snow and ice. For some reason, Ryan had abruptly decided to start talking to me again. I figured he was as bored as I was, and since I was tired of clawing at the walls of my cage, I accepted the unfreezing of his cold shoulder without judgment.

But Susannah was still freezing both of us out. I was secretly glad that I had company on Susannah's shit list, but I didn't tell Ryan. The spring musical hadn't been cast yet, and without Susannah and track to occupy him, Ryan also had a lot of free time on his hands.

We spent our weekends together playing poker with the guys, playing violent bloody video games, and cracking immature jokes like old times. I watched my friends get drunk and high, but only indulged when I was alone, as always.

And, as always, I studiously maintained my 96 average. It was that spring the teachers started murmuring *scholarship,* Dad started thinking *scholarship to Cornell,* and my coach started thinking *track scholarship to any school you want.*

Without Susannah to wedge herself between us, Ryan and I had quickly reverted to the great friends we once were.

Susannah, meanwhile, had started dating a slick and handsome guy in his twenties, Reingold Sheehan, the manager of Riverton Arms, the fanciest of the three restaurants in town. He was also supposedly an exhibiting artist with gallery shows in Manhattan, which possibly explained why she'd bother with him. We didn't know because she wasn't talking to us.

I nearly chewed through my lip when I saw her step out of his black Volkswagen Jetta each morning and climb back in after school. The thought of his groping twenty-something-year-old paws on her tender skin had me praying every night that someone would arrest the creeper for statutory rape. It bugged Ryan just as much as me, but as the winter wore on, and Susannah kept seeing Sheehan, dissing them just got old, so we stopped.

Mr. Wallace had arranged for Susannah to have one of her sculptures entered in a juried show, and her work, *Mother Figure*, the grisly plaster figurine with a gaping mouth of broken razor teeth, won third place, netting her $1,000 and a lot of buzz around the school and community. The piece was installed in a permanent showcase and the whole thing was written up in the local newspaper.

Ryan said nothing, apparently unfazed by all the attention she was getting. But I was stewing in my own stomach acid.

Each night, after dutifully studying and completing my homework, I proceeded to drink myself to sleep. One night, when Dad had driven to a case two hours north, the light snowfall that had been predicted turned into an intense blizzard. Dad had to book a motel room and I was alone for the night, stuck in the drafty old house with my vodka and my night terrors.

I hadn't ever spent the whole night alone, and even the vodka couldn't dull the pulsing ache of raw loneliness that came bursting in like a flood-swollen river.

The recurring horror of my mother's death, the nightmare plunge into the Gorge was nothing compared to life without her. To live with the knowledge that she had wanted to die. And she'd hoped to take me with her.

Was it so I'd never be this alone?

I drank that night until I passed out. And woke the next day at noon. Luckily for me, school had been cancelled due to the nearly two feet of snow that had fallen.

The hollow ache was still there, growing teeth, gnawing at me from within.

Who could I talk to?

I couldn't tell Ryan that I was as raw as an exposed nerve. That every year, I was breaking into smaller and smaller pieces, and that one day all that would be left of me was a smudge of dust.

In theory, I could only tell Susannah. Not that I actually had.

But it didn't matter anyway, because she wasn't speaking to me.

I needed to get outside. I needed to run or I was going to suffocate under the weight of my own misery.

I threw on sweats, sneakers, and a wool cap, and braved the silent, white-blanketed streets of Riverton.

What I did was more like slogging than running. In minutes, my feet were frozen and packed with snow. My hands had gone numb.

But I couldn't go back to that empty house.

So I trudged on, mile after mile, growing weaker, losing chunks of time. It wasn't until I stood before the lawn full of crosses poking up from the field like a miniature mountain range that I realized I was in Susannah's front yard. There was no car in the driveway. But there was a light in the window.

Sleepily, I trudged through the knee-high snow to the front porch, collapsed onto one of the snow-covered wicker porch chairs and fell asleep.

It couldn't have been that long before Susannah discovered me, or I would have been dead from hypothermia.

"Jeremy! What the hell? Are you fucking insane?"

She yanked me to my feet, led me into the living room, and shoved me onto the couch, all the while keeping a running dialog about what a complete moron I was. She pulled off my soaked sneakers and socks, threw a blanket at me, and matter-of-factly told me to strip. She heated up water for hot chocolate while I lay under the covers in a daze, shivering uncontrollably and wondering how I had gotten there in the first place.

I had the chance to look around, and it dawned on me that I'd never been inside the Durbans' house before. It was neater than I expected, and much more welcoming than our shabby man cave. The small living room was filled with antique furniture draped with lace doilies, frilly lampshades, old oil paintings of flowers, china cabinets bursting with knickknacks, and, most of all, crosses. It was as though Mrs. Durban had carefully preserved her parents' house and squeezed her own additions into all the empty spaces. Crosses made from matchsticks, from old tin cans, from torn-up cereal boxes, Mexican tin crosses, and tiny ivory crosses covered every bit of space between the paintings and bric-a-brac. There was a shelf crammed with framed black and white photos, mostly of unrecognizable people in fusty old clothes. I picked up a photo of Susannah as a little girl in her mother's arms, and was surprised by how strikingly beautiful Trudy had been. How her gray eyes blazed from her sculpted face. I put the photo down again, wondering what the woman could have been through to age her so terribly. Beside the photo, there was a framed yearbook page of a high school football team, a dried flower pressed behind the glass. Next to one of the smiling faces, the words *love you forever* were scrawled inside a hastily drawn heart. I pinpointed the guy's name, the team captain, *D. Lewis.* This was Riverton High, yet the name didn't ring any bells. The guy, whoever he was, must have had the good sense to move on and move away.

Susannah reappeared and tossed me a pair of sweatpants. "Sorry, I have no idea who these belonged to. But they're dry, at least." She set the mismatched mugs of hot chocolate on the upholstered bench that served as a coffee table, then sat across from me on a wingback chair, her legs tucked under her.

"Thanks," I said, cupping the mug's warmth between my freezing hands. "Your place is nice. Really cozy."

Susannah glared at me, eyebrows drawn into a frown. "You could have died out there. Why didn't you at least knock?"

"I didn't think you wanted to see me."

"So you decided to come and die on my front porch?"

I stifled a shiver and snickered. "I was out running and—I don't know. I saw the light on. I'm not really sure what I was thinking. If I was thinking at all."

"Jeremy, you're really strange."

"Strange, yet reliable."

"Reliably strange."

I smiled and sipped the hot chocolate. It was the most delicious thing I'd ever tasted. "Why on earth does your mother collect all these crosses?"

Susannah just shrugged. "My mother is a mystery. She never goes to church or anything. I mean, technically, she's Jewish. Which means technically I am, too. It's by the mother's bloodline. So you're not technically Jewish because your mother was…"

"Episcopalian," I stammered and contemplated bounding back into the snow, but it had gotten dark and my clothes were soaked.

She must have noticed my squeamish expression, because she quickly changed the subject. "So when does team practice start up again?"

I gaped at her. "For fuck's sake, Susannah. Do you really expect me to believe you give a shit about track practice when you haven't spoken to me for months?" I slam my mug on the coffee table, emboldened, caught up in the heat of my hurt. "Was it something I said?"

She looked down into her mug. "You didn't do anything. You didn't do anything *at all.*" She swallowed and looked up at me, "Jeremy—I—you're the best friend I've ever had and I should never have shut you out of my life. I just needed some space. That's all."

"Oh."

"I'm sorry."

"It's okay. Really."

There I was, reading from the same dumbass script. Nothing ever really got said. Nothing ever really got resolved. I could have leaned over and kissed her. But I didn't dare risk breaking the fragile bridge we were building between us.

"I met my father two weekends ago," she blurted.

"You're kidding."

She shook her head. "I mean, I saw him. He's a musician from New Orleans named Slimfinger Jones, if you can believe it. He was giving a concert."

"Did you get to talk to him?"

Susannah squeezed her eyes closed and shook her head. "No. I didn't stay for the end. About midway through, someone helped him onto the stage. He could barely walk. He couldn't see. He'd had a stroke not that long ago, someone said. Somehow, though, the guy could still play the harmonica and sing." Tears made a glistening track down her cheek.

I reached for her hand. "I'm sorry. I'm guessing he never knew you were there?"

"What was the point? It would just have confused him. He isn't that old, really. Just—I guess he had a hard life. Why would he need more complications?"

"I don't know. He might have been happy to meet you."

"Whatever," she said "I caught my mother at a lucid moment, one of those rare times she wasn't cussing me out. I asked her if she'd loved old Slimfinger then. It seemed important for me to know that two people loved each other, at least for a little, and chose to bring me into this world."

"'The old bastard's real name is Nelson Buttersmith,' my mother barked, 'and the only person I've ever truly loved is Douglas Bernard Lewis. Who is quite dead, by the way.'"

Susannah stared at the floor, her knuckles pressed against her lips. I walked over to her, took her hand, and guided her onto my lap. I held her, rocking her slowly until her sobs went silent and she fell asleep in my arms.

Now (December 26th)

The attic might as well be the South Pole. Distant, remote, and out of my reach.

And like the Norwegian adventurer Roald Amundsen, I'll either make it there and get away clean, or like his rival Robert Falcon Scott, whose frozen remains were found months later, I'll fail. But I'm going to have to try.

The wood ladder folds down from the ceiling trapdoor in the hall outside the bathroom. I know I'm going to do it. The question is how I'm going to do it without making a racket.

Dread thrums in my eardrums. More for what I might find out if I'm successful than if I succeed in cracking my spine.

I get myself up the stairs and miraculously haul myself up the creaky pull-down attic ladder, rung by rung, without waking Dad. The attic is cramped, musty, and piled high with crap he never bothered to throw away.

The story of our family told in junk.

Boxes of toys, baby clothes, rusted bicycles, sleds, coats. My mother's furs. Boxes of documents, books, albums, old TVs. Some of it, I suspect, dates back to my great-grandparents. I slither on the floor, not wanting to awaken my dad with the thump of my graceless hops. But I have no idea what I'm looking for.

"Susannah," I say, "If you're listening, help me out here."

Nothing. Only the settling of the house and the ticking of an old watch? too stupid to quit keeping time. I try to think like a forensic scientist. If my mother wanted to leave me a message for when I was older, when I would understand, where would she leave it?

Probably in a place that meant the most to her.

The image of her old jewelry box, the one with the twirling ballerina that had been her great-grandmother's, flashes in my mind. But I have no idea where to start my search.

Something catches my eye and my heart does a little flip. A plastic zippered bag stuffed with neatly folded floral bedsheets sits on a carton. The memory of playing with Matchbox cars on the bed while my mother brushed her hair bubbles up. My dad probably threw them up here after she died. These were the sheets my parents used to lie on together, after all.

I balance on my knee and remove the bag of sheets. Inside the carton, carefully wrapped in tissue paper, is my mother's collection of antique perfume bottles and the little decorative boxes she'd bought from her childhood travels with my long-dead, globe-hopping grandparents. But there's someone else's touch here. Dad would have just tossed them in the box.

There are layers and layers of yellowed newspaper, all from about thirty years ago. Most of them have rectangles cut out of them, as if they'd been clipped for coupons. Mom was a big coupon clipper, always combing the newspapers and cutting them up, but I can't imagine why she'd save these.

I dig down, past the paper. Beneath the accumulation of objects is the jewelry box. My heart speeds up unexpectedly. It's like finding a living piece of my mother that got left behind. Inside the box are her demure gold chains and simple stud earrings. There's a charm bracelet with baby shoes that have my name engraved on them—that makes my breath catch—and a half-heart pendant on a tarnished chain. I picture the necklace dangling over Mom's pale collarbone. I remember her wearing this all the time when I was little.

I look closely, and realize the half-heart charm is actually a locket. I pick at the hasp and pull the two halves of the locket open. My heart sinks. Fixed into the left side of the locket is a scratchy photo of a little girl, so old and beat-up it really could be any little girl and not necessarily my mother. I try to swallow the lump sticking in my throat and ease myself back into the cool mind-set of a forensic historian. What I really want is a long, hard swallow of liquor to obliterate the pain, but my dad's scourge of terror has apparently reached up here. There's not even a bottle cap.

It's hard to see in the scant light. The charm is engraved. I hold it up to the single dim light bulb.

Trudy and
Best frien.

I sit and study the inner half-heart of the locket. Obviously, the rest of the words continue onto the other half.

But *Trudy*?

Trudy Durban, Susannah's mother, is the only Trudy I know.

Trudy Durban? I can't imagine Trudy Durban and my mother as best friends. Acquaintances, maybe. I can see my mother looking down her nose at someone like Trudy. But people change. Maybe Trudy had been bearable, once.

Pocketing the pendant, I begin my long slog to safety. By the time I get to my bed, I'm filthy, sweaty, and jittery with exhaustion. I strip to my underwear, slip under the sheets and fall asleep, the necklace clutched in my fist.

The next morning I wake to a note from Dad. He's been sucked away by the irresistible draw of the office.

Marisa has offered to take me for my first leg fitting. I know she isn't enduring my mood swings and abuse as a hobby, but I'm glad to have her with me. Something about her presence quiets the turbulence in my head.

I wonder how long Dad thinks he can parent by avoidance. When he'll be able to look me in the eye again. I finger the necklace and wonder what he knows.

CHAPTER

twenty-one

Then

I'd let Susannah sleep, her head resting against my chest. Her shimmery curls rose and fell with her soft guttural breaths.

I could have sat like that all night, content as a cat after a full bowl of milk. But the air smelled funny. Like cooking. No, it smelled like something was burning. Carefully, I slipped off the couch and let her head rest on a throw pillow.

I padded into the kitchen and let out a terrified shout. Flames spewed from a pot on the stovetop and shot up to the wooden cabinets above.

"Susannah! Fire! Wake up!" I raced into the living room. "Where's the fire extinguisher? Go onto the porch and call 911!"

"What the hell?"

"The fire extinguisher! Where is it? Get out of here! Now!"

"What?"

"Get the fuck outside!" I roared.

She did as I told her. I found the fire extinguisher in the pantry where she said it was. Flames were chewing their way up the wall and racing over the cabinets. I shot a blast of foam at them and hoped it was enough.

In seconds, it was all over. The kitchen had a swath of blackened cinder down its middle, but the fire was out.

I found Susannah shivering on the porch. After about ten minutes, the fire truck pulled up onto the driveway, followed by a Jeep with a plowhead. The firemen leapt out into the snow in emergency mode, but quickly realized they'd come for nothing. Two figures emerged from the Jeep. Ryan and Patrick Morgan. Ryan trotted up to the porch with Patrick right behind him.

"What happened?"

Patrick Morgan had a police scanner, and when he'd heard the call out to Susannah's house, Ryan and Patrick had followed the fire truck.

Patrick Morgan drove us all back to their house and we stayed the night. Ryan never did ask me what I was doing at Susannah's in the first place, but by morning he and Susannah were back together yet again.

Now

The Lyle Hoffmann Center for Orthotics and Prosthetics is in its own building situated right outside the main drag of the Riverton Business District. From its parking lot, there's a panoramic view of the Hudson River sprawling in the distance like a giant silver snake.

Marisa wheels me up the ramp but agrees to let me enter on my own. I roll into the waiting room, which has the same hushed, faux-homey feel of a doctor's office, to find Ryan sitting there among a scattering of amputees.

He moves to the chair closest to where I park myself. I feel a snarl rise up inside of me, but squelch it. I'm going to owe Ryan for life, and even though it's not going to stop me from my quest for the truth, there's no need to be rude about it.

I sneak a quick glance at him. Dark circles ring his eyes. There's a bit more golden stubble than usual. His skin is so pale he's nearly translucent, like some kind of mutated mole rat.

"How are you, Jeremy?"

"Fine," I grumble. "What about you?" I want to spit fire and ask him what the hell he's doing here, but it's obvious he's been sent to oversee the investment.

"I'm good." He shifts in his seat, clears his throat, and sucks in a breath. I sense a soliloquy coming on. "Look," he says, "I know you're basically angry at the world these days, but I've been doing some reading. It's normal. I've read you kind of go through the same steps you go through with grief. You know, denial, anger, bargaining... I figure maybe you just got sort of stuck in the angry part."

I stare at him in disbelief. "Fuck. You're serious."

Ryan rests his arms on his thighs and lets his head drop. "I'm just—things have been hard on everyone. I can't help but feel responsible for what happened to you. If I'd never messed around behind Susannah's back, maybe we wouldn't be sitting here."

The muscles in my jaw tighten. "So basically, you just feel sorry for yourself and you want me, fucking Saint One-legged Jeremy to bless and absolve you of your guilt."

Ryan closes his eyes. His lids tremble and I begin to wonder if this is his best performance ever, or if he is actually troubled.

"Shit."

"Maybe you'd feel better if you unloaded your terrible burden and tell me what really happened that night. And what Derek Spake has to do with it."

"You don't let up, do you? I should have known all that displaced energy of yours had to go somewhere if you couldn't run."

"What are you saying, Ryan?"

Ryan presses the heels of his palms to his eyes. "That you should focus on your rehabilitation. Think how much better you'll feel when you can walk, and even run."

"Nice try, dude. Translation: quit poking your nose where it doesn't belong and focus on yourself like a normal person."

Ryan groans. "You're in a rut, Jeremy. You can't change the past. You can't bring Susannah or your leg back. You have to move forward."

"Why the fuck do you think I'm getting fitted with a fucking fake leg? To sit in this chair?" My voice starts to rise, but I'm just hitting my stride. "I can multitask, Ryan. I can figure out what happened to Susannah and walk and chew gum, all at the same fucking time!"

"You're making a scene, Jeremy," Ryan says between clenched teeth.

The people in the room glare at me. The receptionist comes out from behind the desk and says firmly, "Please calm down, or you'll be asked to reschedule, Mr. Glass."

Gripping the arms of my wheelchair, I hiss, "Just tell me why you and Spake get so jumpy when I mention one of you to the other."

Ryan sucks in air. "I wish, Jeremy, that you would please stop asking me about Derek."

"So it's Derek, now? What is it with you two? Did you conspire to throw the championship meet? Or are you both overlords in a steroid smuggling ring?"

"We're friends, okay? We—I just figure it's best if no one knows—you know, with our teams being archrivals and all."

"So you're friends. How quaint. Are you afraid I'd be jealous of being supplanted as best friend-in-chief?"

Ryan flashes me a wounded look.

"Was that it? Was Susannah upset that you were hanging out with Spake more than with her?"

"That was some of it. Look. It's complicated, okay? Susannah and Derek—let's say they had some words. But I swear I didn't hurt Susannah. And neither did Derek." Ryan slouches, his skin clammy. "I guess it makes sense that you'd blame me for what happened to you. I mean, if it wasn't for what I did, you wouldn't have come out on that miserable night in the first place."

I lean forward in the chair. "Whoa. You think I'm pissed because I *blame* you for my accident?"

"That's what the team thinks."

I shake my head. I want to tell Ryan *I* had emptied my silver water bottle, and then tried to save the world because I couldn't live with my own shame. "Well, the team is wrong. I don't blame anyone except myself."

"Oh," Ryan lapses into silence. I glance at him. He seems deflated. And for once, I don't think it's an act. I'm pretty certain whatever he's trying to hide is eating away at his insides.

—∽—

Ryan excuses himself and wishes me luck with the fitting. I'm ushered into the showroom to meet Lyle Hoffmann, the prosthetist. I'm surprised to find a shaggy-haired walrus-mustachioed guy who looks either like a fugitive from a seventies country-rock band or the stunt-double for Cousin It. His getup is so incongruous with the white lab coat he wears that I have to stifle the urge to laugh out loud. Dozens of electric guitars hang on the wall above the rows of realistic-looking legs, arms, hands, eyes, and ears. Fancy metal gadgets with only a passing resemblance to human limbs are stacked in towering piles.

Mr. Hoffmann comes around from behind his desk and leans over to shake my hand. "Pleased to meet you, Mr. Jeremy Glass. I hear you're a track star."

I nod and shrug. "Was."

"Welcome to the art of the possible, Jeremy." Mr. Hoffmann's eyes twinkle mischievously as he gestures to his body part menagerie. "With these hands, I can restore your life."

I nod some more. I don't want to insult the guy, but I find him a tad overdramatic. I wonder what would make a megalomaniac like him want to build artificial limbs.

"Not impressed? Have you ever seen that commercial for the Hair Club for Men? The one where the guy says 'I'm not only the owner, I'm a client?'"

"So that's not your real hair?" I say, smirking.

For a minute Hoffmann doesn't catch my ribbing, then chuckles broadly. "Ah, a joker. I was referring to this." Dr. Hoffman lifts his pant leg to reveal a blue and silver metallic pole. "Lost it in a motorcycle accident when I was just out of college. Way above the knee. Like yourself." He prances back and forth and I watch his gait closely. Not bad, but now that I know I can see the slight catch in his step.

"Yeah, but can you do the mambo?" I ask.

"No," he says, eyes twinkling, "But then again, I was always a lousy dancer. But I can ride my motorcycle and do killer lunges at my gigs."

I gaze at the collection of guitars on the wall. "You're not going to fit me with one of those for a leg, are you?"

Hoffman's laugh is more like a merry wheeze. "Oh, my. No one warned me about what a comic you are. Jeremy Glass, you and I are going to get along very, very well."

"Wait until you get to know me better."

Hoffmann's handlebar mustache turns down. "It's always hard at the beginning, Jeremy. It's a loss. It takes a while to accept the fact your leg is never coming back." He paces over to the wall of black propeller-like devices. "Wait until we fit you with one of these blades. You'll bounce like you're on springs."

But will I feel the pavement beneath my sneaker? Nope.

He's right. My leg is gone forever, just like my mother. And Susannah. My mind drifts toward the times when she has felt so close and real. So warm. And I wonder about myself. If maybe my brain just can't accept losing one more thing.

The room goes silent, its fluorescent lights eclipsed by darkness shot through with sparks of light. A hand runs through my hair, the touch maddeningly tender. Shivering, I blink rapidly and the darkness dissolves like ink in water.

Hoffman is staring at me. "It was like I lost you there for a moment, Glass. Where'd you go?"

His voice is tinny in my ear. The bright room is stained with sepia at its edges. "Sorry. Just daydreaming."

Hoffmann nods and his big mustache bobs with him. "Can't do that when you're out strolling with your new C-Leg. Learning to walk again is tough work, Jeremy. It requires complete concentration."

Hoffman launches into a detailed explanation of the hydraulic knee joint and spring-loaded foot in the revolutionary titanium C-Leg model. He's already in negotiation with my dad's insurance provider over upping the funding to cover one. A boy of my level of activity, he says, can have nothing less. With the money collected by Ryan, I can also buy the high-performance running blade and get back to serious running.

"Did anyone tell you about Team Hoffmann, Jeremy?"

"No. What's that?" I offer a weak smile to feign interest, but in my mind I'm envisioning some kind of parade of freaks.

"It's our Paralympic team. We've got a kick-ass trainer. Last Paras we took home three golds."

I imagine what I know of the Paralympics. Down's syndrome kids laughing with raised arms as they shuffle across the finish line.

"Sounds inspiring."

"Oh, it's more than that. It's a lifeline." Hoffmann smiles, his twinkling eyes backlit by the fervent gleam of a zealot. And, despite my wish to wall myself off in my airtight fortress of gloom, I have to admit I may like this crazy spare-parts-dealing dude.

Hoffman takes a cast of my stump and tells me I'll have my walking leg in a little over a week, but that it might take a few attempts to get the fit right. I should expect it to take many more weeks to learn how to walk again—it's not like I'm going to be running right out of the gate. The fancy blade attachment will be fit after I've adjusted to walking.

And suddenly, like sunlight streaming into a cave, the thought of throwing away the crutches and the wheelchair forever sounds a little bit like heaven to me.

—∞—

After my session with Hoffmann, Marisa suggests getting coffee at Awesome Cow. I beg off, but she persists and drags me inside.

"You can't lock yourself in a cocoon forever. You have to face the world."

"I'm tired of the stares. I'd rather wait until I get the leg."

"Jeremy," she says. "If you don't do it now, you'll just keep finding excuses. You have to learn to power through this stuff.

Focus on what you want, not on what other people think about you."

"Is that how you do it?"

Marisa fixes me with a steady stare. "What do you mean?"

I look down at my coffee mug and shift it back and forth. There's no quick way out of the corner I've painted myself into. "You know. Assumptions based on the, uh, snap judgments people make."

Marisa's soft voice has developed an edge. "You mean about my culture? My accent?"

I clear my throat and look directly at her. I'm certain she can see the evidence of my own rush to judgment in my eyes. "I— well yeah."

Marisa holds me in her gaze and lays her hand over mine. "That's *exactly* how I do it, Jeremy."

—⁂—

I'm relieved that the Cow is virtually empty at this hour. The breakfast crowd is gone and the lunch crowd hasn't arrived. I feel safe, nestled in the dimly lit interior. Marisa folds up the wheelchair and puts it out by the back exit. Sitting deep in the round corner booth where no one can see I'm missing a piece of me, I feel relaxed, almost normal. Maybe it's just sitting next to Marisa that makes me feel better.

I glimpse a familiar Oldsmobile sedan pull into the parking lot. It's Trudy Durban. I pat my pocket. My mother's half-heart locket has joined the photo of Derek Spake there. I'm going to have to speak to Trudy Durban about it sooner or later. Suddenly, the need to confront her sits on my tongue like a pill that won't dissolve.

"Marisa? I'm kind of tired. Want to get going?" I ask innocently.

Ever diligent, Marisa helps me into the chair and wheels me out to the van just as Trudy Durban walks out of the dry cleaners, a pile of plastic-wrapped clothing draped over her arm. Her bush of wiry hair is pulled back in a messy bun, and an enormous pair of sunglasses perch on her hawk nose, giving her the look of an oversized bug.

Dragging myself forward with my single leg and pumping at the wheels with my hands, I pull away from Marisa, propelling myself forward. "Mrs. Durban!"

"Oh crap! No, Jeremy!" Marisa hisses from behind me.

Trudy Durban whirls around, not expecting a shout-out from so low to the ground. As always, she's dressed monochromatically in a plum pantsuit, a tangle of necklaces hanging from her neck. But her face is more worn and haggard than ever, like a piece of driftwood that's been left out to dry and bleach in the sun.

Her gaze falls first on Marisa. Her mouth sets into a scowl as she strides toward us. I feel the tug of Marisa trying to yank me backward, and I dig my heel into the sidewalk to act as a brake.

"Jeez, Jeremy. Let go!" Marisa says, tugging harder on the wheelchair. But it's not budging.

"How nice to see you both," Trudy says, coldly. It's impossible to see her eyes behind the dark glasses, but her face is twitchy, the skin saggy and almost a grayish white. "Especially you, Marisa." Her words are pointed, each one a dart tipped with acid. "How are you feeling, Jeremy?

"Um, hello, Mrs. Durban," Marisa says softly. "We should get going, Jeremy."

"Such a hardworking young lady. The problem is, you see, she steals from her employers."

Marisa draws in a breath and tugs harder at my chair.

"If you mean that package, Mrs. Durban," I say, "That was addressed to me."

"So it was," she says in a low voice. "I suppose I can't expect much help from this town. You're all against me."

Marisa huffs and stomps around the wheelchair, hands on hips. "I'm sorry, Mrs. Durban, but Jeremy lost a leg *clear up to the hip* because he went out on a terrible night to help *your daughter*. Have you ever thanked him?"

I find I'm starting to regret this. "No one has to fucking thank me," I say softly. "I'm not a hero."

"I lost a daughter." Mrs. Durban blurts, her lips trembling. She turns her bug eyes on me. "You were *there*. You could have stopped it. You could have saved her from that bastard. She's with the devil now because of you!"

I gape at her, open-mouthed. Trudy Durban may be losing her tenuous grip on sanity, but her words sting like slaps. I might have saved Susannah, if I hadn't tripped. I wouldn't have tripped if I hadn't downed a half pint of vodka. And I might have saved Ryan from himself.

His haunted expression flashes in my mind. Yes. There was guilt written there, in the tracery of blue lines around his eyes, but there was something else. Something I can't define. Regret? Desperation?

"I'm doing my best to figure out what happened to Susannah, Mrs. Durban," I say, my voice cracking. Marisa was right to back away. I'm not strong enough for this verbal assault. Tears well in my eyes, hot and bitter.

It's my fault she's dead. I may not have done the crime, but I did nothing to prevent it.

"Susannah's disappearance is a police matter, Mrs. Durban," Marisa says, defiantly. "Jeremy has enough to deal with."

Mrs. Durban leans over me, her face close enough so that I can smell her breath, cloves and cigarettes. "You should know better than anyone, Jeremy," she says, "that the police in this town are under Patrick Morgan's thumb."

I think of my mother's necklace in my pocket and the connection between her and Trudy Durban it implies. I'm about to ask her about it when black rims the edges of my vision and moves inward. Harsh silence fills my ears, swallowing all sound. Bright pricks of light swim and dance around me. Someone squeezes my hand. So warm.

I hear snapping fingers. It takes a second before I can see them, too, right in front of my face.

"What's wrong with him?" I hear Mrs. Durban demand shrilly.

"Jeremy! For a minute there, you were totally out of it." Marisa sounds panicked.

It happened again. Like in the prosthetist's office. And in my room. I'd gone away.

"Nothing. I was just thinking of something I forgot."

Mrs. Durban is staring at me with an expression of sheer horror. "Demonic influence. I can feel it."

"Do you remember my mother's locket? The half-heart?"

A deep crease forms between her thin brows above the insect sunglasses. Her lips press together and she speaks as if in a trance. "What locket? Your mother never wore much jewelry."

I fish out the locket and let it dangle from its chain. Trudy Durban's face turns brick-red. She speaks in a low, menacing whisper. "Where did you find that? *Nobody* knew about that locket."

"What about this, Mrs. Durban? What does it mean?"

Mrs. Durban's eyes go wide, the color draining from her face. "Never mind that. It's all in the past. Doesn't matter. What matters is that my daughter was murdered. And her mortal soul is in the clutches of a demonic power. Do I have evidence? No." She removes her glasses, the burning gray eyes burrowing into mine. "The cops in Riverton don't investigate crimes that involve Patrick Morgan."

I glare at her and snap, losing patience. I'm not backing down this time. "Please tell me, Mrs. Durban, what on earth Susannah's disappearance has to do with Patrick Morgan. You want to help me find her, don't you?"

But Mrs. Durban doesn't answer. Instead, she fingers her crosses, her gaze distant again, then turns and walks away.

"Don't you, Mrs. Durban?" I call out, and try to follow, but Marisa has a firm grip on the wheelchair. I'm stuck.

I consider Susannah's drawing with the tiny tree on a massive pile of roots, skeletons, and body parts, with the little leaf that says *truth*, and realize it's a portrait of the town. Gnarled roots that twist deep into the rock, binding their occupants to each other and to the past. Roots that, when ripped out, cling to things you wish you never knew.

"*God*," I murmur, finally. "I think Trudy Durban really has finally lost it."

"See? Compared to her, you're a saint," Marisa says, still tugging on the wheelchair. I lift my foot and we hurtle backward.

"Jeremy! Really!" She shoves me lightly on the shoulder. "Cut that the hell out."

"But it's just for the money, right?" I say, swiveling around. "It has nothing to do with my wit and dashing smile."

Marisa's cheeks flush. She tosses her river of black hair behind her shoulders and I shiver a little. "Nothing at all. You're a huge pain in the ass. And if you ever want to take me to a movie, that will cost you a king's ransom."

"Is that an offer?"

Marisa's eyes shimmer. "It was a joke. But I'd do it, Jeremy. I'd go to a movie with you. It would be good for you to get out more."

"So would you be on the payroll or would it be…"

She tilts her head and smiles. "…two friends enjoying a night out."

"Wait," I said. "You just said we're friends."

She nods. "Yeah. Crazy me. I did."

I smile back at her, but dark presses at the edge of my vision, the light sliding away. It's as if I'm being drawn into a cosmic meat grinder. I cling furiously to the arms of the wheelchair. Solid reality. I'm breathing hard, sweat popping out on my forehead. The dark skitters away, leaving me weak. I slump in the chair.

Marisa has her cell phone out.

"What are you doing?" I ask.

"Calling your father. Did you hear me calling your name? Two times in one hour, you snapped totally out of it."

"It was a dizzy spell. The room started spinning."

She slants her head and eyes me skeptically. "You were staring straight ahead like a statue. I waved my hand in front of your eyes and you didn't even blink. Your head injury may be worse than they thought."

"Whatever you say, Dr. Santiago."

But my head is pounding and I can't help but wonder—is this a medical problem, a mental problem, or a metaphysical one?

And if you summon someone from beyond the grave, can you send them back?

Then

The morning after the fire, to celebrate Ryan and Susannah's reconciliation, we were all treated to a feast of a breakfast in the dining room. Celia Morgan had gone all out, heaping our formal place settings with pancakes, sausages, and hash browns. I wolfed it all down. I don't remember a meal ever tasting better.

Susannah ate her sausage in small nibbles, her coppery cheeks lit by a rosy glow. The name of Reingold Sheehan never came up again. I vowed never to set foot in the Riverton Arms.

We were a threesome again. It was the best that I could hope for, and it was time I finally accepted my position—the base of the triangle. I would never rock our shaky boat. I'd set a course on calm waters as the first mate, the deckhand.

"Let's make a pact," Susannah said, eyes glittering. She raised her glass of fresh-squeezed orange juice. "To never hurt each other again."

"Hear, hear." Ryan raised his glass.

I was tempted to throw my juice in his face and ask him if he really could keep that promise. Instead, I raised my glass, too. "To triangles, the strongest form in geometry."

We gulped down our juice with Celia Morgan looking on, smiling. "The Three Musketeers," she said, "Together again. As it should be."

"Forever and for always," Susannah said.

After we'd helped Celia clear the table, Susannah pulled the two of us into a huddle with her. "After the reservoir thaws, I have a surprise for you guys."

"What?" asked Ryan, as excited as a child. "An adventure?"

"I'm not telling." Susannah put her finger to her lips. "It's top secret."

I smiled vaguely, trying to think of something clever to say, but Celia Morgan cut in, her brow furrowed. "Never go skating on the reservoir. You can't tell where the ice is thin."

"Mom," Ryan said, rolling his eyes. "No one said anything about skating or doing anything on the frozen reservoir. Relax. Susannah's talking about—"

"Taking out a rowboat, Mrs. Morgan. Don't you guys have one?"

"Yes," said Celia, her face still tense. "In fact, we do. Patrick uses it for fishing sometimes. But you have to wait until it's *completely* thawed because..."

"Because why, Mom?" Ryan asked, draping an arm around her shoulder. At nearly sixteen, he already towered over her.

"Just, well. Let's say people weren't always so careful. Things happened."

"Like what?" I asked, suddenly curious.

"Nothing. I have to get ready for a luncheon now, kids. I hope you enjoyed your reunion breakfast!" Celia added brightly and walked out of the kitchen.

"Wonder what that was about?" I asked.

"Who cares?" Susannah gazed up into Ryan's blue eyes and I resumed my position as third wheel. "Everyone who grew up here is crazy anyway."

"Maybe it's in the water." Ryan said.

"Once we're done with high school, we should all leave, so we don't go crazy, too," Susannah glanced at me. "We should put it in writing. Make a pact. A Three Pirates Manifesto."

"Sounds like a plan." I wondered if, by then, I'd have mastered the art of making myself go numb. Ryan leaned over and kissed Susannah on the mouth as the full weight of what I'd signed on for truly hit home.

Many nights of hard drinking lay ahead.

Now (December 28th)

They run a battery of tests on my brain to see if there's some residual bleeding or damage from my fall or the accident, but I come up clean.

On the car ride back from the hospital, Dad is ashen. He's aged years in the three days since he's bothered to be in the same space with me. I consider showing him the locket but I'm afraid he might accuse me of engraving those words myself. He flips on the classical music station, the absurdly sweeping notes of Vivaldi filling the silence between us.

In his mind, he's probably watching my future slip down the drain.

"Dad, I know what you're thinking."

"You don't," he says after a lengthy pause.

"I'm not crazy."

Dad glances at me, eyes rimmed with red. "I love you, Jeremy, and we'll face whatever we need to face together."

"I swear I'm not crazy. Yes, I have a drinking problem. Yes, I have one leg. You have to trust me."

"I don't know what to believe anymore. Your mother's doctors said there was a one in ten chance you would inherit her illness."

"Who were Mom's doctors? Are you totally sure Mom was crazy?"

Dad screeches the car to a stop and shouts, his face a mask of rage. "Why are you doing this, Jeremy? Please!" He breathes rapidly in little shuddering gulps. I'm afraid he may have a heart attack. Finally, his breaths slow and he manages to speak in a more controlled lawyerly tone. "I'm sorry. Jeremy, your mother was a paranoid schizophrenic. You know what that is? Someone who imagines everyone is out to get them. Your mother was consumed with the notion that someone was trying to kill her."

An icy chill climbs up my neck. My hands shake. "What if she was right?"

Dad glares at me with such fierceness I fully expect fire to shoot from his nostrils. "Please be quiet now, Jeremy. I need to think."

"Okay. But first answer my question. Who was her doctor, the one who made the diagnosis?"

Dad shoots me a puzzled glance. "Dr. Kopeck, of course. She has the best credentials in the area."

Out the window, the bare branches grope the air like skeletal hands. "If I find someone else, will you promise not to send me back to her?"

—⁓—

Back in my room, my heart won't slow. The walls have eyes and ears. On top of everything else, my dad I'm thinks I'm a paranoid schizophrenic. I can't decide. Am I? Or have I actually begun to untangle the poisoned roots that twist beneath the underbelly of Riverton?

The savage need for a drink ambushes me and coils itself around my throat like a boa constrictor. There's no chance I'll find even a drop in this house. To calm the pulsing ache in my throat, I throw myself into practicing the gait exercises Chaz prescribed and that Lyle Hoffmann has urged me to do. Chaz promised that I can park the wheelchair for good if I get my balance back. It will also help prepare me for walking with my new leg. It's a goal. If I can run again, I can control the panic.

I go at the exercise with grim determination, hoping to either exhaust or outpace the dark waters that lap at my ankle.

But the reptile mind doesn't understand logic. Whether my mother tried to kill herself and take me with her, or someone else drove her off the road, I'm still going to be forced to relive the day she died. Until I die, too.

And I can't get Trudy Durban's voice out of my head. What was she getting at—that Susannah's disappearance is somehow linked to my mother's death?

To a rational mind, it seems unlikely. And Trudy Durban is not rational.

But I'm probably not either, which gives me the perfect excuse to see what other dirt I can dig up.

—ᴍ—

I thrust the crutches forward and kick out my leg in the smoothest approximation of a walk I can manage. It feels weird. Unnatural. But, over and over, back and forth, I walk, trying to keep a heartbeat ahead of the water that has started to rush in. If I sweat it out, maybe the nightmare will recede.

Finally, exhausted, I collapse in the wheelchair. I never knew walking could be such hard work, but at least I've chased the panic away.

Post-traumatic stress disorder, that bitch Kopeck called it. The reason I drink. The reason I run. All to avoid the terrifying loop of our car plunging into the Gorge over and over again.

But this is the same Dr. Kopeck who diagnosed my mother as a paranoid schizophrenic. I have no doubt my mother drank. Too much. But was she crazy? Was there more to it than that? Maybe she had her reasons, too.

I have to wonder what mangled roots my mother might have unearthed. A brief internet search pulls up some interesting intersections. Both Dr. Kopeck and Patrick Morgan serve on the board of directors of the same pharmaceutical company. Over the years, Morgan Associates has helped her make huge land investments in upstate New York.

Nothing damning. But enough to confirm my suspicions. She's an affiliate of Patrick Morgan's, and though I'm not precisely sure what that implies, it makes me trust her even less.

Just as I'm about to click on another link, the screen goes black along with everything else. Darkness steals away my vision. Sensitive fingers work their way up my back, exquisite shivers rushing to my nerve endings. My mouth falls open. The taste of her lips floods my senses with longing.

I shudder with desire and naked fear.

Susannah visits whenever she wants these days.

In the dark void, tiny sparks soar and cluster. An outline materializes in the form of a shimmery, girl-shaped constellation.

I blink. It's Susannah, or at least an outline of Susannah made of stars.

I gasp as she leans over me, the soft curls I can't see brushing my forehead. Barely visible lips kiss the tip of my nose and I moan, a riptide of urgent want dragging me out beyond the waves.

I can't stop kissing her long enough to ask her why she invades my senses without permission. By now, I don't know. I ravage her, my searching mouth desperate to quench the fire she's lit inside me.

Susannah traces the entire length of my body with deadly slow kisses, burning me with her touch. By the time she presses her lips to the stump, I'm ablaze, close to a core meltdown. The sensation is indescribable, a witch's brew of pain and ecstasy. I arch my back as the violent spasms of release sweep over me.

I slump in the wheelchair, nerveless. The fever in me rises again. I'm ravenous. An animal. Consumed by a flash fire, I kiss the neck and hair I can't see, the scent of vanilla and summer rain scorching my lungs.

I exhale in a tremulous shudder. I have no breath. My words burn to cinders in the flames that lick at my skin.

I'm ready to follow her. Ready to sink into oblivion with her so I can burn with her forever.

Panting wildly, I pull away, an unstable compound, about to go nuclear at the slightest touch. Trembling on one leg, I want to scream—*why did you have to leave me?* And I find I'm filling with rage for the one who took her from me.

The room echoes with whispers. *Join me, Jeremy.*

She torments me with kisses until my heat explodes in volcanic eruptions of legendary proportions.

"Yes," I murmur, tears sliding down my cheeks. "I'll do it. But first, I'll make sure whoever took you from me will pay for it."

Her form brightens, then fades. Within the haze, I tell myself I see a smile. My surroundings solidify. She's gone.

I'm left standing naked, my arms empty, balanced tenuously on one leg like a stork in the middle of my room.

I lunge for the bed in a few clumsy leaps before I fall. Feverish, I'm shaking violently, cold and hot all at the same time. I pull the covers over my head and try to think.

I've somehow managed to find an even more toxic addiction than alcohol.

CHAPTER

twenty-three

Then

Somehow, as winter dragged on, our threesome held steady. I had started to believe that the triangle really *was* the strongest form in geometry.

My sixteenth birthday was March 14 and Ryan's March 30. We'd always made a habit of celebrating the weekend between. This year, Susannah suggested the three of us go bowling. I wasn't a big fan of bowling. I might have been a champion runner, but I was not known for my stellar hand-eye coordination. Ryan was only marginally better. But Susannah was a natural, hitting strike after strike.

After her triumphant fist-pumping victory, Susannah presented us each with oversized black envelopes, both elaborately printed in white with our names and decorated with glitter, sequins, and feathers. Very Susannah.

I carefully opened mine and pulled out what looked to be a giant ticket.

Trip to Pirate Island, it said. *Passage for One. April 23.*

"April 23?" Ryan looked baffled. "What is this?"

"A boarding ticket." I said.

Ryan still looked confused. Susannah laughed and roughed up his hair. "That's *my* birthday, silly," Susannah said. "We're going on a little trip to Pirate Island. And neither of you are ever going to forget it."

—⁂—

Eventually, April 23 rolled along. It was a mild night for the season. Susannah insisted we all meet by the rocks that descended to the reservoir. "Bring flashlights and dress like a pirate," she'd said. I'd brought her birthday gift in my knapsack, a pair of turquoise and silver earrings shaped like feathers. I very much wanted to see them mingling with her curls.

Ryan and I rode together. We'd both wrapped our heads in bandannas and Ryan who had no problem with theatricality, had slipped on a black patch over one eye. He'd already gotten his driver's license, though it was a junior license and he wasn't supposed to be out after nine o'clock in the evening. Down by the water's edge, Susannah waited.

My heart nearly stopped. She wore a filmy black dress that flowed to mid-calf, a silver shawl wrapped around her waist, spiky boots, and a necklace of pearls. From under a silver bandanna, her hair flowed loose. Her vamped-up version of a Pirate Queen. The rowboat floated beside the rocks, lit by about a dozen votive candles.

The effect was mythical and dreamlike. I was so consumed with want, I thought I'd pass out from lack of oxygen to my brain.

"Beautiful," whispered Ryan. "You're so beautiful, Suze. This is beautiful."

Mortified, yet insane with desire, I climbed in the boat, unable to croak out a single word.

We rowed in silence across the moonlit reservoir to the tiny island almost clear on the other side.

"Welcome to Pirate Island, the lair of the Pirate Queen," Susannah said, getting out of the boat. She'd placed dozens of votive candles to create a path to the center of the small island.

My insides churned, my heart pounded. *What was I doing?* I was terrified to be out on the water, certain my terrors would come back. Worse was the knowledge that my situation was unsustainable. I couldn't go on this way. I couldn't go on being old reliable Jeremy Glass, trusty triangle side and third wheel.

It was killing me. Heartbeat by heartbeat.

I don't remember Ryan's reaction. I don't remember much from that night, except for the sculpture at the center of the island Susannah had surrounded with more votive candles. It was an abstract tree she'd made from plaster, embedded with a mosaic made from tiny bits of colored glass and ceramic tile. The tree had three trunks that twisted around each other and ended in branches made of grasping hands.

"A shrine to us," Susannah said dancing around her creation. "A tree with three trunks whose roots are so intertwined that, if one of us should wither, the whole tree will die."

She and Ryan kissed tenderly by the light of the votives. And inside, I withered just a bit more.

Needless to say, I drank a lot when I got home that night.

Now

I spend sleepless hours staring at the ceiling, part of me hoping that she'll return, the other part dreading the same thing. Finally, I slip into a fitful sleep.

—⁂—

I'm flopped on the shady rock ledge that borders the reservoir, near the spot where Susannah disappeared, my legs fused into a massive iridescent fishtail. Susannah stands at the water's edge, her bronze curls glinting in the sunlight. She laughs and motions for me to come down to the shoreline, but I balk, knowing the sharp rocks will gash the tender underside of my tail. She insists; not being able to refuse her, I slither down, my heavy tail sliding over the jagged rocks. Sharp points scrape against the scales and pierce the soft flesh. Blood stains the rock. The pain is terrible, but I don't want to disappoint her.

I finally reach the water's edge and Susannah dives, slicing gracefully into the water without a splash. I heave my cumbersome body off the rocks and submerge myself in the cold water, the powerful fin propelling me after her. I follow Susannah to the darkest depths where the sunlight doesn't reach.

At the reservoir bottom, a woman sits at a vanity. My mother. Methodically, she brushes her hair, the ballerina on her jewelry box spinning in a continuous pirouette.

Susannah frowns and gestures for me to keep swimming. But I halt beside my mother, who turns to me and nods. She picks up the jewelry box that sits on her vanity. Susannah has doubled back and is angrily pulling on my arm.

But I remain where I am, riveted by what my mother is doing, as if she is about to reveal the secrets of the universe.

She lifts the jewelry box, holding it like a book. And then, in the strange way of dreams—it is a book.

—⚬⚬⚬—

It's still dark when I wake. My sheets are tangled around me like vines, the dream tattooed on my eyelids. Buzzing with restless energy, I take to the crutches to begin my tedious gait practice until my leg and elbows are stiff with the effort.

My body is limp with exhaustion, but my brain won't shut off. I review the dream and try to puzzle out its meaning. There's something I'm just not getting, so I haul myself up again and pace some more until my arms are about to fall off.

The persistent tick of Dad's old desk clock reminds me of what I need to do. Part of the dream's meaning clicks into place. If I don't solve Susannah's murder, her eternal spirit is going to drag me down to join her.

Apparently, the dream version of my mother doesn't like that. Yet, she was the one who drove me into the Gorge strapped into the back of our car.

Or did she? *Has my mother been trying to get a message to me all these years?*

I'm just not sure what the symbolism means. A jewelry box turning into a book seems like the nonsensical language of dreams. But great scientific breakthroughs have often been sparked by dreams, like the scientist, Kekule, who solved the molecular structure of the chemical benzene after dreaming about the *ouroboros* symbol—a snake biting its own tail.

I'm not sure I'm ready to face the attic and the secrets buried there just yet. But there's a person who is ripe for the picking.

I call Ryan at ten AM and he answers immediately, breathless. On edge.

"Everything okay, Jer?"

I tell him I want to meet him in our old elementary school playground. On the swings. There's a silent pause.

"You're not serious, are you? There's a foot of snow out there. How will you—"

"You worry about you. I'll worry about me. I want to clear my chest about some things. Stuff about me you don't know."

I hear him swallow and hope that my somewhat lame strategy will work. If I confess my darkest secrets, maybe Ryan's paper-thin veneer will tear, revealing the truth behind it.

"I can pick you up and drive us there," Ryan offers. I grit my teeth. Why does he have to be so fucking considerate? I want my own wheels. Dad thinks he's hidden my car keys, but I know exactly where they are.

"No. I can get there myself."

That is, of course, if I can make it to the car. It's still parked at the bottom of our steep driveway under the carport. I peer out the window. More snow has fallen. There's about a foot on the ground now, but at least Dad has had someone shovel and plow the driveway, so I have a fighting chance.

Getting to the car is a little more of a challenge than I'd imagined, but my gait practice has paid off. I only fall twice.

Fortunately, there's enough gas in the car to get to the Riverton Elementary School. The playground is the one where I first met Susannah. It seems a fitting place to untangle the mystery of her death.

But is Ryan a murderer? It's clear he's been falling apart lately, his actor's bravado slipping off him like an oversized coat.

I'll be doing him a favor. Relieving him of his burden. It could have been an accident. Or he could have witnessed something. I have no idea. But I need to find out. And soon.

—⁓—

It's totally weird to be in my car. The last time I'd been in here, I had two legs. Susannah was alive.

But you only need one foot to drive a car, so I'm golden.

When I get to the school, I find that, while the parking lot has been plowed, the long path to the playground hasn't.

The wind cuts across the field, whipping ice particles into a face-scouring blast. It takes a fair amount of grunting and sweating to ford my way through the foot-deep snow, but at least Ryan hasn't gotten there yet to witness my Discovery Channel adventure—one-legged boy braves the wilds of a suburban schoolyard in blizzard conditions.

My hands are nearly frozen onto the grips of my crutches. I stab at the snow, then vault, stab, then vault. It's brutally exhausting, but I finally reach the swing set, spear the crutches into a snow bank, and collapse onto a swing. But I can't resist the urge for motion, so after a bit of single-leg pumping action, I'm airborne.

Ryan plods through the snow and sits on the swing beside me. I slow and return to earth.

"How the hell did you make it here, Jeremy? I could barely get through."

"Ski poles," I say, nodding toward the crutches planted like a flag in the snow.

He shakes his head, a small smile creasing the smooth lines of his face. "So what were you going to tell me?"

I let myself sway on the swing. The motion feels good. I vow to come back here when I'm feeling sorry for myself, to hop on a swing.

"I'm tired of hiding behind a mask," I say, choosing my words specifically to unnerve him and peel away his facade. I see a slight shift in his posture, but Ryan being Ryan, he's still in character:

The Interested Listener. But his hands betray him. He clenches the fingers of one hand tightly with the other.

"What mask? You're always the same."

"That's because my mask is so excellent."

Ryan rocks back and forth a bit. He shivers and snorts out a puff of mist. "Jeez. Get to the point, Jeremy. It's cold out here."

"The point is, I'm an alcoholic."

Ryan squints at me, like he's suddenly gone hard of hearing. "That's a crock, Jeremy. Just because you drank one shot of vodka, then made an ass of yourself?"

I arch an eyebrow. "You couldn't have known about the flask I had in my jacket pocket. Or the silver water bottle I always kept in my car. When no one was looking, I drank. A lot."

Ryan's brows furrow. He really is shocked, and I smile inwardly at how well I've kept the ruse going for so many years. And surprised his father hadn't told him.

"You never drank a sip at keg parties. You've helped us win two division championships, and maintained a 3.8 GPA. Why are you laying this bullshit on me?"

I swing a little harder. "I was wasted the night I stepped out into the road to get to you and Susannah. It's not your fault. I lost my leg because I'm a drunk." My voice cracks on the last words. I am speaking the pure, honest truth.

Ryan gapes at me as if giant tusks have sprouted from my face. "You're serious."

I nod. "I've been a closet drunk since I was twelve. The running was never enough to—" My words fail to penetrate the lump in my throat. My eyes burn.

"Wow," Ryan says. "Why now, Jeremy? Why are you unloading this now?"

I rock myself back and forth a bit. And realize I'm telling him this not only because I want to play tit-for-tat, but because I want it to end. Talking about it is like my gait practice. A first step.

Ryan is still looking at me and nodding. "That's a lot of baggage to carry around."

"You're telling me. It's even heavier on one leg."

Ryan shakes his head and looks down. "I feel terrible about what happened. I feel terrible that we don't seem to be friends anymore. I miss—I miss our talks, bro. You know, the way we'd analyze the stupidest shit until four AM? So you drank. You're still you, Jeremy. You're still the same cool, weird kid I've always known."

"Yeah. I guess am." I stare at him. He's relieved. He seems to think this is the reason I brought him here. I feel almost guilty probing him like this. I wish I could let it go. Go back to the way we used to be. The three of us. But all those years of doing his bidding, cleaning up the mess he made, fester under my skin like an infected splinter. "What about you, Ryan? You're just a basic red-blooded American guy. What you see is what you get, right? No dark secrets? No skeletons in the closet?"

Ryan's face crumples. It happens as if in slow motion and I almost regret the grief that flashes briefly across his features. "Is this about Susannah? Is that why you dragged us out here? Fuck, man. I told you already."

"Just tell me the truth, Ryan. I just need to know for myself," I say softly.

Ryan buries his face in his hands. He looks up and makes no attempt to hide the raw emotion that twists his features. "I have my own problems, Jeremy, hard as that may be for you to believe. I don't know what happened to Susannah. If I'd killed her, I swear, I couldn't live with myself."

"You couldn't?" I ask, "I hated myself for drinking, yet I'm still around. There's all kinds of ways we make excuses for ourselves."

Ryan shudders. He's fighting tears, I realize.

"I-I have to go," he mutters. "I can't, Jeremy."

"You can't what?"

"I *can't* live with myself anymore."

He stands and bolts out of the playground like he's been shot from a cannon.

"Hey! Don't do anything stupid, Morgan!" I call. I certainly can't run after him. "You can still talk to me!"

I watch his car peel out of the parking lot. I swing some more, then finally pick and lunge my way back to my car.

Now

Once home, I fall onto the bed, my limbs twitching with exhaustion. It felt good to have some physical exertion. Really good. I decide to take a nap and to do some more gait practice afterward. When I get that bionic leg, I'm going to break records for the time it takes me to be walking again.

My phone rings and I jump like a startled cat. Barely anyone calls me anymore.

It's Marisa.

"Hi!" I try not to sound too eager. But I want to talk to someone. I want to talk to *her.*

"Do you have any plans for New Year's Eve?" she asks hesitantly.

I opt for deadpan to hide the thrill that heats the back of my neck. "I was thinking of going ballroom dancing."

She giggles. "I-uh. Well, my family is having this party. I kind of don't want to be there, so I thought we could go to a movie, I mean, if you want, then you can come over for a bit and say hello."

My stomach does a back-flip off the high dive. "You want to me to meet your family?"

"They know all about you. They won't be weird or anything."

"N-no." I imagine myself in a spotlight, everyone staring. "But I promise, once I get my leg, I'll make it up to you. I'll—I'll even go ballroom dancing if you want."

Marisa snickers. "I would never ask that of anyone. But what about the movie?"

"Yeah , I—" My voice dies in my throat, the phone in my hand lost to a sudden wash of blackness. I hear nothing. Feel nothing. See nothing.

Not now. Please not now.

Shimmering with light, a figure stirs the absolute darkness. My body leaps to attention as if flipped on by a switch.

I feel her weight as she climbs onto the bed and straddles me, her hipbones sharp against my groin, the feel of silken hair hanging in my face. Soft lips rake my chest with kisses, then slide lower until my body is a wire pulled taut enough to snap.

There's no escaping this.

The room vibrates with whispers. *I love you, Jeremy. Love you.*

Who else can love you?

"No," I whisper, live wires threading under my skin. Pleasure crackles along my nerve endings, but beneath it is the slightest hint of violence, like the calm before a lightning strike.

No one.

I would cry out, but my breath has been sucked away. I can't help but wonder if she knows how I covered for Ryan. How I hurt her. And if this is her revenge.

Her faint shimmer fades to black and I'm shot from the sky and falling fast, the words lingering in my ears. *No one else will love you like I do.*

—⁂—

I know I'm not dead, because my heart slams madly against my ribs.

It's an eternity until the terrorized scream explodes from my lungs. I don't know how long I lie immobilized, unable to see before my vision clears and I can sit up again. I'm wired, as if ten thousand volts are ripping through my flesh. I gulp in air in shallow gasps.

—⚹—

I find my phone. There are ten missed calls from Marisa. It's only been fifteen minutes.

My hand freezes on the call button.

A chill crawls up my spine.

She's watching my every move.

CHAPTER

twenty-five

Now

I need a drink more than I need my next breath. But I know there's nothing to be had.

Another ten minutes go by before I can find my voice. Shakily, I dial Marisa. Maybe Marisa is just trying to be nice. Maybe Dad is even paying her to drag me out of the house. Despair turns my weak little bubble of happiness to lead.

"What happened? We got cut off and then I tried to call like seventeen times and you never answered."

"My battery died. I couldn't find my charger," I say tersely, trying to modulate my voice to its normal tenor.

"Oh. Weird timing. Now about the movie—there're a couple of good things playing in Manor Woods, and I thought maybe you'd be more comfortable there, anyway."

"Yeah, about that. I, uh, I don't think it's such a great idea."

"What? You just said you'd—Jeremy, what is it? Are you okay?"

"I'm fine." I know my voice rings flat and unconvincing, but it's the best I can do with my heart smashing its way out of my chest. "I just overdid the gait exercises, so I'm a little tired and sore. And I'm just not up for a night out yet."

"You sound different. You didn't have another one of those spells, did you?"

"No. I—"

"You sure you don't want me to come over?" There's an edge to her voice and I realize that, for some reason, maybe Marisa actually wants to be with me. But no. I'm delusional. Why would she want to be around an amputee with an attitude problem?

"N-no. I—I'm going to rest awhile. I'll, uh, call you later."

But I'm not going to rest. I may never close my eyes again.

I need to think. To feel the cold clear air pushing in and out of my lungs, even if I'll never feel the road under two feet again.

—m—

I make it down the driveway to the road with only a little slipping and sliding. The bitter cold air slices into my lungs. But it feels good. I press forward, my gait smooth despite the icy patches. I hurry on, awkwardly lunging and stepping, lunging and stepping. I glance over my shoulders, unable to shake the feeling that the woods have eyes. But, seduced by the sheer pleasure of moving forward, even at my old man pace, I fall into a kind of a rhythm until I've almost lost track of how far I've gone.

I lurch along so lost in thought I don't notice where I am until I recognize the guardrail and how the road bends at an almost ninety-degree angle. It's the place where I was hit. The place Susannah disappeared. Through the network of tree trunks, I see the hungry waters of the reservoir.

A great heaviness tugs at me, as if the water has a magnetic pull. The air is elastic, a wall of resistance, and I'm so tired of pushing against it.

I can slip into the water and float free of this life.

It's always been a fight to take the next step. The next breath.

With one leg, it's even harder now.

Snow flutters down in powdery flakes. I gaze longingly at the rocks that slope to the reservoir's edge, and begin to climb down.

Somehow, I reach the shoreline without falling. I stare deep into the murky water. I can see the smooth boulders that line the bottom. Beyond the dam, the rushing waters of the Gorge collect.

Like the tangle of roots that twist beneath the soil of Riverton, the water connects us, too. I'm gripped by a sudden aching desire to see my mother again. To curl up in her arms like the little boy who used to ask her to chase the monsters away.

A thought drops into my head. The jewelry box in my dream. I'm missing something. Are the clues to my mother's death concealed inside it? Did she really never mean to leave me?

Tears pool on my lashes and slip down my cheeks. The water, dark and welcoming, calls me to be with my mother again.

Darkness catches me and descends like a shroud, blotting out the desolate terrain. I sink onto the rocks, consumed by it.

All you have to do, says the wind through the trees, *is slip into the water. We can be together.*

I'm sprawled on the rocks beside the reservoir. Alone, the scent of vanilla lingering in the bitter air.

It would be easy enough to fill my pockets with stones like Virginia Woolf and sink to the bottom. The thought of the black water filling my lungs, choking off my air until my lungs explode, sends me into a panic. I can't do it.

I'm even too freaking afraid to kill myself.

Instead, I gaze across the gray water. Tiny Pirate Island sits, a monument, a blip on the horizon, a hiccup of happiness in our pathetic history. I think of my Pirate Queen, the tree with three trunks, the Buffalo nickel—and what will never be.

I begin to haul myself back up the rock pile leading to the road, but slip, my palms grazing the sharp rocks. I cry out as a crutch slips from my grasp and clatters down the hill into the reservoir.

Heaving myself over more rocks, I climb until I make it to the road, relieved it was just my crutch and not me that met its end.

By now it's getting dark. Snow falls steadily, blanketing the world in a lacy white haze. Cold penetrates my layers of clothes and finds its way into my bones.

With one crutch I can only move in awkward hops. The way back home is uphill. My crutch isn't getting much traction. I debate calling Marisa to rescue me, but decide against it. I don't want to explain what I'm doing out here. And I just can't face her.

I jerk at the sound of a car rolling to a stop behind me. A door slams. Patrick Morgan strides toward me, chuckling softly. "Most people have the sense not to come out on a night like this."

"It was daylight when I left," I say through clacking teeth. "I just wanted to get some air."

Patrick Morgan laughs thunderously. "You can take the boy off of the road, but you can't take the road out of the boy, huh? It won't be long, Jeremy, before you'll be running for real."

I nod, shivering too hard to respond.

Patrick Morgan helps me into the passenger seat, then turns the thermostat up to toast. As the warmth heats my bones, I steal a glance at the craggy lines of the elder Morgan's strong features. Thick silver hair stops short of the stunning blue eyes, like a patch of crystal-clear sky breaking through storm clouds. I'm sure that in his day Patrick Morgan was just as extraordinary as his son, though these days Ryan is a pale shadow of his former glory, as tightly wound as an over-tuned guitar string. But the elder Morgan is almost Zenlike in his steady calm.

Patrick Morgan drives in silence, the black BMW hugging the snow-sheathed roads. It seems to be taking us a good bit longer than it should to reach my street.

His deep voice shakes me out of my daze. "I wonder what your father would say if he knew the risks you've been taking. The poor man has been through so much."

"Risks?"

"I would consider hiking in a snowstorm on one leg to be a potential risk."

"You have a point, there."

"And trudging through an unplowed playground to sit on a swing. Not the smartest move."

"Ryan told you we met?"

I glance out the window. Patrick Morgan is driving very slowly, and I realize we've passed the turn off for my street.

"Ryan was extremely upset when he came home this afternoon. What did you say to him?"

"I—" Suddenly the car is too hot. I tug at the zipper of my jacket. "I told him about—some of the things I've been going through."

"Of course. It must be very hard for you," he says mildly, "but is that all?" I can't shrug off the feeling that I am on the witness stand and Patrick Morgan is cross-examining me.

"He said he was upset that we haven't been that close. I told him it's not his fault about the accident. It isn't."

The car rolls to a stop on a deserted, dark portion of Route 112. "That was very charitable of you, Jeremy. But I'm certain you brought up a few of the other things that have been on your mind. Like what you blurted out at our annual Christmas party, for instance. It wasn't very polite."

"I-I—," I stammer, completely at a loss in the face of Patrick Morgan's penetrating gaze.

"Ryan tells me you spoke about Susannah Durban's disappearance." He pauses while I squirm. "Jeremy, we all know how fond of that girl you were, and maybe your devotion made you a bit blind to her many flaws. Susannah was very troubled, as Ryan can attest."

I hang my head, wondering how much of this so-called behavior I'd missed while I was busy laying flowers at the altar of my lovesick obsession. Was I truly that blind?

"It's understandable that so much loss would be hard on a boy," Patrick Morgan continues.

I nod, my voice trapped in my throat.

"But you've deeply upset my son with your line of questioning, Jeremy. Your very odd and provocative accusations." His eyes blaze. I shrink lower in the seat, my heart thudding.

"That's how it started with your mother." His words ring in my ear like the crack of a judge's gavel. "First the paranoia. The visions. The complex intrigues. The conviction that people were out to get her. Then came the drinking. Then…"

I'm hunched in the seat, jumpy with the pointless urge to run. Doubts flutter inside my stomach like moths in a jar. *Am I really just crazy like her, after all? I did almost jump in the reservoir.*

"In Riverton, we all pitch in to help each other. Mrs. Morgan tried everything she could to help your mother. It was heartbreaking to watch her best friend unravel. But in the end, no one could save her from herself." Patrick Morgan's deep voice drips with the mournful tones of an undertaker.

"But you, Jeremy. You can still be helped. I've spoken to your father about appropriate facilities once you're fitted with a leg. Very progressive places that will help you cope, deal with your addictions, and help you learn to manage your illness."

I have no response. He's tied a noose around me with his words. And he very well may be right. I might be full-out insane. A danger to society. A danger to myself.

After all, I'm the guy who's been fucking a ghost. And then, the memory of the locket bubbles into my addled brain. *Trudy knows.*

"What about Trudy Durban? Did she try to help?"

For a moment, Patrick Morgan's face contorts into a twisted mask of rage and I'm afraid he's going to reach over and snap my neck. But his flexible features smooth and his voice oozes out, calm and reasonable.

"Trudy Durban is a reckless woman who cloaks herself in religious trappings. She never could face the fact that her daughter was out of control. That others had to step in and try to save the poor girl. She couldn't have helped your mother even if she'd wanted to."

He stares at me, his face lit eerily by the glow of the dashboard lights. "Remember to mind your manners, Jeremy. I'm going to speak to your father to ensure that you visit Dr. Kopeck regularly and get the meds you need to control your illness before it consumes you."

He drives me home, physically carries me into the house, settles me onto my bed and says with an odd smirk, "and Jeremy, I think we should keep our little talk to ourselves. You can keep a secret, too, can't you?"

Now

The light on the answering machine is blinking. Five messages from my dad.

He'd been trying frantically to reach me for hours. He got called out of town on urgent business for the remainder of the week. He'll be back sometime during the day on New Year's Eve. He will have Marisa stop by to bring food, check in on me, and bring me to my appointments.

So I've got the house to myself. I can tear the house apart and hope to find the liquor I know my dad couldn't bear to throw out and drink myself to death instead of the more watery alternative. Or I can figure out what really happened to Susannah. And my mother.

The answers, I'm convinced, are in the attic. If I can connect the dots, understand the clues, it will come to me. This can't be that different than the way historians piece together facts. If they can do it with artifacts and lost civilizations, I can find the root of my own mysteries.

With one crutch gone, I sit on the bed and contemplate the damn wheelchair, vowing to figure out an alternate mobility device. After a flash of inspiration, I fashion an ad hoc crutch from a mop handle. The attic climb is easier with the strength I've built in my arms, and the good news is that I can clomp around to my heart's content without worrying about Dad hearing me.

The jewelry box is exactly where I'd left it the last time, buried at the bottom of a carton of yellowed newspapers and my mother's trinkets. I pull it out and sit it on the floor in front of me, frightened of what I will find.

And what I might not.

I turn the box upside down and hold it up to the light. There's nothing unusual. I tap it and there's an odd, hollow sound. Carefully, resting the box against my leg, I dig my fingernail into the bottom side and pry open the false bottom.

Jammed in the hollow space is a yellowed envelope stuffed with neatly folded newspaper clippings dating back thirty years.

The missing rectangles. But these aren't coupons.

They are all articles of varying length about the accidental drowning of a boy named Douglas Bernard Lewis. He was an extremely handsome kid, a football quarterback. He died when the ice on the reservoir cracked and he'd fallen in. There'd been no one there to save him.

I'm struck by the horror of it. To die alone in the cold depths of the reservoir with no one to hear your screams. To drown in black water.

My mother seemed obsessed with the death of this boy. The name is vaguely familiar. Shivering, I wonder if she was thinking of him when she drove her car into the Gorge.

In addition to the newspaper clippings, there are snapshots of a house at 115 Garden Crescent. My mother's neat handwriting has labeled it, *The Lewis' house*. Then, there is the photo of a modest house with a For Sale sign in front. Next, the house boarded up, vacant. Each photo, dated on the back in my mother's neat handwriting, tracks the neglected state of the house as nature reclaimed it, until ten years later, when the house was torn down and a new house was built in its place. Still, there are photos of the new house that date right up to the week my mother died. There are also photos of Douglas Bernard Lewis' grave, a single flower laid on the stone, year after year, dated in the same manner.

There are images of the boy, frozen in youthful exuberance. My heart squeezes with sympathy for his family. If my mother felt this badly, how terribly did his death impact the people he left behind?

I sprawl on the dusty attic floor, trying to tease out the thread that connects my mother's death to Susannah's death, to the drowning death of Douglas Bernard Lewis. The answer hovers somewhere just out of sight.

Supported by my makeshift crutches, the papers tucked under my arm, I clomp to the staircase, then set them down. I'm tentatively easing myself down the ladder, rung by rung, when dark spots crawl across my vision like caterpillars on a windshield.

I don't feel myself let go of the ladder, but I'm falling backward, the papers releasing from my hand. They flutter around me in slow motion, like stop-action moths. I sink into darkness and remember exactly where I'd heard the name of Douglas Bernhard Lewis.

—m—

Susannah sits hunched on a rock by the reservoir dressed in the clothes she wore the night she disappeared. Behind us, Trudy Durban is building a raft made of crosses.

Smiling, her eyes vacant and bruised with dark circles, Susannah pushes up her sleeve to reveal her inner arm, purple veins visible through the fragile skin. I watch, horrified as she punctures the skin with a fingernail. Dark red blood pools around the wound. Digging into the skin with a finger, she rips out a strand of veins like pale blue tree roots. "You never know what you'll pull out if you keep digging," she says, laughing. "Come with me, Jeremy. You know you want to."

She dives smoothly into the water, and despite my hesitation I follow, diving deep into the turbid waters. But I lose her in clouds of brown mud, somehow ending up inside my mother's car as it plunges into the Gorge, yet again.

CHAPTER

twenty-seven

Now

I wake, choking and gagging. I'm lying on the hallway floor on my side, covered in yellowed newspaper, my arm twisted beneath me at an awkward angle. It hurts like hell, but somehow I manage to prop myself up to a sitting position. Two limbs down, two to go.

My ears are ringing. Salty liquid collects in my mouth. I put my fingers to my lips and they come away bloody.

There's the faint squeak of the back door swinging open. Light, hurried footsteps patter on the kitchen tiles.

"Jeremy?"

"In here," I call out hoarsely.

Marisa peers down at me, cell phone in her hand. I sigh, my eyes flickering closed.

"What happened?"

My thoughts are mixed up. Deranged. I see things. In the darkness behind Marisa, lights shimmer. Susannah's here. Watching. Always watching.

"The guy who died… I know who he is."

"What guy? Jeremy, you're not making sense. Lie still. The ambulance will be here in a minute. I'm going to call an ambulance."

"Susannah." Over Marisa's shoulder I see her outline, a shape made of stars glittering against the void. She stands at the center of a tempest of whirling papers, hair whipping around her like tentacles.

In the ambulance, under the glaring lights, I waver between bright and dark. Light streaming through leaves. Susannah's green eyes blaze from within the water that rises around me, an oily black whirlpool. Bony fingers rest on my shoulder. Digging into my skin, pulling me down. Down. I cling to Marisa's warm hand.

"I'm t-trying to help you, Suze," I choke out. I squeeze Marisa's hand but I can't see anything through the crash of the waves. I'm so cold. "You wanted me to find out, Susannah, didn't you? That the guy...the guy who died was your mother's boyfriend. The one in the yearbook photo with the heart drawn next to his face."

"Jeremy," Marisa says from somewhere nearby, "lie still." The rhythmic rocking of the road beneath us lulls me quiet. My head pounds, but the rest of me is numb. I close my eyes and try to float on the surface of the water. Try not to sink.

"They're going to lock me away," I hear myself mutter. "Because I'm nuts, Suze. Stark raving mad. Like my mother."

"No," Marisa whispers, leaning next to my ear. "You're not crazy. You've just hit your head one too many times."

―���―

The nurses in the emergency room let Marisa stay, since my dad isn't able to get a flight home due to storm delays. I'm laid out on a bed behind a curtain. My skull feels like it's been skewered through the temples, then roasted on a spit.

"Jeremy," she says softly, trying to gauge if I'm all there or not. I blink to clear my vision but everything is surrounded by a fuzzy aura.

"What were all those newspapers on the floor in your house?" she asks.

"Just stuff from the attic," I mumble.

"You said something weird. About some guy who died. What were you talking about?"

Did I? My head throbs. Behind Marisa, a hazy Susannah figure floats, cloaked in midnight. Her disappointed eyes burn through my haze and tell me that I haven't solved her murder because I'm such an accident-prone yutz.

"You shouldn't listen to me, Marisa. I'm crazy. *Estoy loco.*"

Marisa squeezes my arm. "I was coming over to tell you that Derek Spake called me. He was trying to reach you. He said he needed to talk to you, but you wouldn't answer your phone."

I try to sit up, but the white lights shoot needles behind my eyes. I quickly fall back against the pillow, eyes squeezed closed. "What did he want?"

"He wanted to explain about him and Ryan. To come clean. That it's not at all what you think."

"Just more lies to cover the truth," I mutter.

The doctor steps behind the curtain and gestures for Marisa to leave. He prods my shoulder and forearm. I wince.

The hazy Susannah form watches me hungrily from the falling shadows.

I'm trying, I say, mouthing the words. I don't want the doctor to see me talking to a ghost. Or a hallucination.

"I'll be sending you for x-rays to see how serious your concussion is, but at a glance it doesn't look so bad," the doctor says. "And your arm is just a sprain—" His words are broken off by a commotion. Shouts and scuffling feet fill the emergency room. An urgent voice blares over the loudspeakers.

"I'm sorry, but you'll have to excuse me," the doctor says calmly, "a code blue just came in." He dashes through the curtain, but it slips back in place before I can see what the hell is going on. I call out to Marisa, but no one could possibly hear me over the ruckus. I'm alone, in pain—disoriented and stranded.

Finally, Marisa rushes in, her large eyes dazed with shock.

"What the fuck is going on out there?" I ask, my speech slurred. I try unsuccessfully to sit up again.

She falters before her words rush out and lash me like a whip. "Ryan tried to hang himself. They said he's in cardiac arrest. But—but he's alive."

I fall back on the table and close my eyes, dizzy. No.

CHAPTER

twenty-eight

Now

Marisa and I wait for almost an hour for the doctor to return. Though I'm more alert, I'm still not much company. I steal glances at the dark fringe of her downcast lashes as she dozes off. She may look as fragile and as precious as a glass doll, but underneath she's forged from steel and concrete.

If I believed for a minute that she would be interested in a one-legged loser like me, it would only serve to prove how crazy I am. It's a business arrangement for a financially strapped girl. And that's all.

Just the same, I'm not sorry she's here.

—◊—

When the doctor comes back, my head is somewhat clearer, though the scent of vanilla still lingers in my nostrils and I catch vague glimpses of Susannah from the corner of my eye. I don't tell anyone.

I press the doctor for information about Ryan. He's in the ICU, but the doctor is tight-lipped about offering any further details.

It's long past midnight when the x-ray results come in. I've got a bad sprain and a mild concussion. My arm is secured in a sling that's strapped to my chest. The doctor gives me a warning about taking more care. That's it's easy to get hurt when you've got only one leg.

Since I'm under eighteen, the staff won't release me to Marisa's care, so I'm wheeled into a room for the night. Marisa offers to stay, but the hospital staff insists on sending her home in a cab.

Once she leaves, I lie on the bed, unable or unwilling to sleep, though my eyes sting with exhaustion. Thoughts of Ryan circle my brain like vultures, ready to pounce the moment my eyes drift close.

I have to see him.

The wheelchair is folded up and parked behind the door. I make one of my usual mad hops, and pray that I don't lose my footing and fall flat on my sore arm.

—⁓—

The ICU floor is deserted and silent save for the beep and hum of the machines. I make lopsided progress, my single foot dragging me forward, my good arm pumping the wheels. Peering into mostly empty rooms, I finally find the bed with Ryan in it and roll cautiously to his side.

His neck in a brace, Ryan is unconscious. He's entangled in a network of tubes and wires, like the briars that surround Sleeping Beauty's castle. But there's nothing beautiful about him. His skin is so pale it's almost transparent, the veins in his thin eyelids etched like a topical map of a tributary system. I stand and whisper into his ear, slightly sickened.

"Ryan."

There's not even an eye flutter.

I rest my head on his chest and listen to his heart thrum steadily. "I'm so sorry, Ryan. Please, wake up."

The clonk of boots on linoleum jars me out of the moment. I fall back into the wheelchair, cornered as Patrick Morgan thunders toward me, rage burning in his blue eyes like gas jets.

"What the hell are you doing in here, you fucking bastard? Did you come to gloat over your handiwork?"

Black spots cluster like ink stains, and against the dark backdrop Susannah's image ripples like backlit silk.

I hear Patrick Morgan hurtling toward me and fight for my vision to return.

I'm certain he is going to kill me.

I kick out blindly and land a lucky bull's-eye right to the balls. Patrick Morgan yowls and stumbles back. I scramble to wheel past him, my surroundings still gray and hazy. There is a scuffle, then silence. Before the dark peels away, I feel myself pushed from behind, propelled forward.

A familiar voice asks, "You okay, dude?"

When I can finally see and breathe again, I'm looking up at Derek Spake, his eyes puffy and bloodshot, his hair a wild spiky mess.

"I think that asshole was trying to kill me." I say.

"Welcome to the club," says Spake. "I had to get you out of there. He was like a charging bull."

I lift an eyebrow. Why on earth is *Derek Spake* in this hospital? I don't get it. Spake registers my confusion and offers, "I was the one who found Ryan hanging in the garage. Another minute and…"

"How did you know to look?"

"He called me to say goodbye."

I slant my head. "He called *you?*"

Spake rolls me down the hall to an empty lounge room and sits on a couch opposite me. He chuckles, tears sparkling in his eyes. "He's been trying to tell you for months. But he was scared, Glass. Scared of Patrick Morgan."

My insides twist.

"Ryan and I," Spake continues softly, "we're…together."

"Ryan and *you?*"

Spake nods, a wistful smile curling his lips. "Ryan put up an amazing front, didn't he?"

I close my eyes and shake my head. Fucking Ryan. All those years, I never had an inkling. I was too busy wishing I *was* him.

"He was a better actor than I thought." My eyes snap open. "But what about Susannah? Did she find out?"

Derek Spake doesn't get the chance to answer.

There's a violent energy in the lounge, as if lightning is building inside the fluorescent bulbs overhead. The lights crackle and dim. Sweat breaks out on my forehead. I see only Susannah's eyes as the room explodes into bits, the pieces raining down around us in slow motion like we're two people trapped in the world's weirdest snow globe.

Now

The lights flicker, then brighten. The room is intact as if nothing had happened. "What the hell was that?" Spake asks.

I swallow hard. Spake apparently saw something, but not what I saw. I'm hallucinating. I'm sure of it. I wonder how long I have until I slip into a world where fantasy and reality merge into a single nightmare.

Is this why my mother took the plunge?

"I don't know," I whisper.

—m—

Derek Spake wheels me slowly back to my room. Standing on the threshold, he says, "Somebody should lock Patrick Morgan up and throw away the key."

My good hand draws into a fist. All those years prancing around naked in locker rooms. What was Ryan thinking? How did he hide it? "Why didn't he tell me? I'm his fucking best friend, for chrissakes."

Spake's face reddens. "Would you still be?"

I'm a little queasy, and I'm not sure I know the answer. "I hope so," I whisper.

"His father found us together in his room," Spake says in a monotone. "So reconstruct that scenario. I don't know if Ryan's ever told you what life was like living under that man's roof. It's a wonder he's lived this long. Ryan is an expert at hiding bruises."

I lower my head. Another thing I'd missed. It never occurred to me that Ryan might be suffering in his own private hell. I'd been so worried about Patrick Morgan messing with me, I never suspected he would lay a hand on his own son.

"Do you think he'll come out of this?"

"God, I hope so," Spake says, shuddering.

—◦◦◦—

I wake to find my dad staring down at me with a bemused half-smile. "I really can't look away for a second with you, or you wind up here."

"One-legged people tend to fall over a lot."

His smile collapses. "Marisa says you'd been rummaging around in the attic. What the hell were you doing up there?"

"Digging up the past. That's what historians do. In truth."

Dad flops into the plastic chair opposite me. I sit up to face him, my leg dangling over the side of the bed. My muscles are twitchy and restless from lack of use. I want to run. Or at least hop.

"You don't have to sneak around, Jeremy. You can just ask me about things."

I laugh. Really hard. "Right, Dad. That's you—the guy with the lantern, ye old truth seeker of Riverton. Either that or you are the blindest man alive. Or," I pause and let my smile fade, "you're the biggest fucking liar this side of the Hudson."

Dad's brows slam down over his eyes like he's strapping on a battle helmet. He catches himself before he grabs my wrist. "Take that back, Jeremy," he says, his jaw quivering.

"Or what? You'll beat me like Patrick Morgan beats Ryan?" I pause and watch the storm clouds gather in his eyes. "What are you so fucking afraid of, Dad? Did you know what was driving Mom crazy? You *had* to know."

Dad folds in on himself, crumpling into the chair. "You found out."

"There's an attic full of shit, Dad. Do you know why Mom would have been obsessed with an accidental death that happened over thirty years ago? Or don't you?"

Dad's eyebrows spring up. "What the *hell* are you talking about? What death?"

"The articles Mom saved. There must have been hundreds. I found them."

Dad's mouth drops open and hangs slack. "She saved articles? About what?"

In truth, Dad never has been much of a liar. An Olympic-gold medal avoider of unpleasant topics—but skilled liar? No. His face twists in confusion that solidifies into shock.

"So you didn't know." I scratch my head. "What the hell did *you* think I found out?"

Dad is gray. Literally. His eyes shift from side to side. He exhales in a long, weary sigh, as if he's finally let go of a breath he's been holding in for years. I feel the tug of another root pulling free. "Celia. Celia and me."

Now it's my turn to take the bullet that slams into my gut. "What are you saying, Dad? That you've *been fucking* Celia Morgan?"

"Yes. For years."

"What? Did Mom know *that*?"

Dad slumps forward in the chair, his face resting against his palms. "You figure it out. You're the historian."

But I don't say anything. My lips are too numb. His face still buried in his hands, Dad mumbles. "Celia and I were together in high school. We broke up soon after. Only we didn't."

Dad raises his head and looks at me, his face haggard, exhausted. "We were poor, Jeremy. Both of us. Dirt poor. I lived in one of the apartments over the stores in town with your grandmother. I could never have afforded law school without your mother's help. She was so beautiful and kind. And rich as hell. But she was fragile and breakable. I think her parents were relieved someone would take her off their hands."

"Didn't you love Mom?" My insides are writhing, full of slithering snakes.

"I suppose. Though I knew there was trouble ahead. But she was totally dedicated to me. Dependent. She willfully overlooked everything. I guess you could say she loved me more."

I lower my head, my eyes tracing the pattern of the linoleum tiling. I want the waters to rush in between the cracks and wash me away. "You fucking bastard."

Dad hesitates, and continues. "Celia waitressed at the Riverton Diner. After her parents died a few years later, she had no inheritance and could barely afford the taxes on their house. Patrick wanted her because she was the one girl who *didn't* want him. When she finally went for him, it was like planting his victory flag straight through my heart. Only an arrogant ass like Morgan couldn't see the truth behind our masquerade."

I shake my head slowly, the room spinning in a slow-motion whirlpool. From its edges, I think I see Susannah looking on, smiling, arms folded over her chest.

Poison roots, toxic roots. I wonder how far down into the earth they reach and ask myself how I feel, now that Dad is finally revealing his full hand. I decide that maybe I preferred his polite silences.

But once roots are unearthed, you can't put them back into the ground.

Dad continues, but I'm looking past him, darkness teasing the edge of my vision. Susannah's image is coming into focus. And she's not so pretty. Her hair is bushy, as disheveled and wild as an abandoned bird's nest. Her hands reach for me with skeletal, dead tree fingers. I'm following in my mother's footsteps. I'm losing my mind, just like her.

"Jeremy," he says, his voice growing tinny and distant. "I hurt your mother. Terribly."

I swallow hard and blink back the cresting wave of darkness, force Susannah to the edges of the room. I feel sorry for Dad— first a crazy wife and now me. "So that's why you let Patrick

Morgan walk all over you all these years? Because you were fucking his wife. Does he know?"

"Of course not. I wouldn't be alive if he had any solid evidence," Dad says miserably. " But lately, I've been beginning to wonder if he does know. And only a sick fuck like him would enjoy the leverage it gave him. Patrick Morgan inherited his law firm from his father, and from his grandfather before that. They built this town. They have connections that reach all the way to Albany, and some say right to the White House. No one can touch him, Jeremy. He could do any crooked deal he wanted and assume I'd stay silent."

My frenzied mind crawls over the facts at hand. "Have you ever heard of a guy named Douglas Bernard Lewis?"

Dad's face colors. "That was the accident you were talking about—Doug's death. He was my best friend. An amazing guy. A big guy. Star quarterback, and smart as hell. We were all friends. Me, Patrick, Doug. Your mom, Celia, and Trudy. We did everything together. Until Doug fell through the ice on the reservoir and drowned."

Dad continues, lost in the memory. "Back then Trudy and Doug were the *it* couple. She was a stunning girl. But I don't think Trudy ever had her head screwed on right after Doug died. She started distancing herself from the rest of us. Getting into trouble. After high school she moved away, some say to have a child. But she came back years later, twisted and strangely religious."

"Your mother was petrified of Trudy," Dad says. "I wouldn't be surprised if Trudy Durban killed Susannah herself, buried her in the backyard under a rosebush, and then prayed for her immortal soul."

Dad and I stare at each other blankly. My head is spinning, but my mouth can't shape words. The darkness rises like floodwater. Susannah is walking toward me, shaking her head.

"And what about Mom?"

Dad squints at me and slants his head. "Your mother was always sensitive and prone to depression. I couldn't really say when things started to take a turn for the worse. I guess I never realized how much his death upset her. I always thought it was because of me."

I want to tell Dad I'm sorry. Sorry for being too much like Mom. Sorry for what lies ahead for us both.

—∽—

"We should get going," he says finally, and stands, straightening his rumpled clothes. He walks to the wheelchair, rolls it over beside me, helps me in, then leans down, and looks me in the eye.

"I don't blame you if you hate me, Jeremy. But no matter what I've said, the horrendous choices I've made, I will always love you. I can't stand the idea of anything happening to you. Do you understand?"

He hugs me, careful not to jar my sprained arm. I reach around him with one arm and hug him back. "I'm sorry, Jeremy. I'm sorry for all the shit I've put on you and put you through. It's no wonder you drank."

I don't answer. I just stare at the untied lace of my single sneaker. I don't want to slip into insanity. I want to fight this. If I can solve Susannah's murder, I can be free of her terrifying visits. I can be free of the madness that wants to claim me.

"I just want you to get better, Jeremy. I want you to kick the drinking, get help for all the demons that are tearing you apart. And most of all, I want you to walk."

"I know that, Dad."

"Chaz is coming in the morning. Your leg will be ready soon. He says once it's in, you need to be fit immediately, even with this setback, or you'll lose muscle tone you may never get back."

This shocks me out of my numb state.

"Huh?"

"Lyle Hoffman put in a rush order on your electronic C-Leg. He's gotten the insurance company to cover most of the cost and he's donating the rest. He'll also cover the remaining cost of the custom running blade, which he wants to fit as soon as you get used to your new leg. You must have made quite an impression on the guy."

Suddenly, I'm hyper-aware of the wheelchair seat chafing against my butt and I want, more than anything, to be vertical. Despite the toxic roots, the bombshells, and the hallucinatory ghosts trying to drag me with them to the grave, a small thrill of excitement works its way through my insides.

"A leg," I repeat.

Then I remember that Ryan is lying unconscious, hovering near death. "How's Ryan?"

"Alive. As far as anything else, the doctors are still trying to figure that out."

As Dad wheels me out to the hospital lobby, I imagine the rhythm of something I never once gave a thought about—putting one leg in front of each other. Human locomotion, unassisted by crutches or wheelchairs. Or mop handles. I close my eyes and vow when I get that leg I'll make everything up to everyone. I'll quit drinking for good.

I'm so deep in my own thoughts, I miss the initial blur of Patrick Morgan pushing through the revolving hospital doors. He storms straight up to us.

Dad pauses, his hands frozen on the grips of the wheelchair. Patrick glares at my dad with the weirdest expression I've ever seen. It's anger, but underneath is something harder to pin down. Triumph. I think of Dad's metaphor about the flag of victory stabbed straight through his heart.

It occurs to me that Patrick Morgan isn't sorry about what happened to his son.

He's happy. Because whatever secrets Ryan was going to divulge, now he can't.

"You," Patrick Morgan says, glaring at my dad, his voice cold and low. "Do you think I don't know? Here's a pun for you, Glass. Get ready for your world to shatter. I'm going to ruin you for what you've done to my family."

Dad is frozen. Speechless, his mouth trembling. Patrick Morgan pushes past us and strides to the bank of elevators.

There's a shout from the revolving doors that lead into the lobby.

Trudy Durban stands at the entrance. "You bastard!" she screams crazily. "You fucking bastard! You deserve your filthy spawn to die! I know you killed her! You killed my daughter! I know what you did to her!"

Patrick turns calmly around to face Trudy. She's waving a gun, her eyes wild, the jangle of crosses thick at her neck.

"You don't mean that, Trudy," says Patrick in his soothing baritone, walking toward her. "You know I would never hurt Susannah. She was like family to us."

"Why wouldn't you?" she shrieks. "We kept your secret. You have no soul. No conscience!"

Patrick's voice is choked. "You're just upset. This isn't the proper time for this. My son is in the ICU, barely hanging on. Susannah was a troubled girl. You've known that for a long time."

Dad pulls my wheelchair toward the wall. Trudy Durban's face contorts into a mask of grief. Darkness claws at me, trying to drag me under.

Trudy's face becomes serene. "The devil wants your soul returned," she says, calmly, taking aim.

A whooshing sound zips past my ear. Blood spurts from the back of Patrick's neck in a red arc. He folds to the ground like a marionette whose strings have been cut.

Trudy Durban stands in the lobby entrance, her expression blank, the barrel of her pistol now pointed right at Dad and me.

"What about you, Paul?" she screams. "Did you know? Did your wife tell you what she saw?"

Dad shouts and lunges for me, knocking me out of the chair. I hear a blast and I'm on the floor, Dad on top of me.

CHAPTER

thirty

Now

I manage to push my dad's weight off me. Darkness speckles my vision, turning my sight to negative Swiss cheese. Between the bright spots, I see Susannah gliding toward me in a flowing black dress that billows around her like smoke.

"Dad?" I say, though I can't see him. I can't see anything but her.

"Jeremy? Are you all right?"

The dark devours me. Susannah stands before me, her rippling image like reflections on water. *I thought you loved me.*

I hear Dad's voice, tinny and distant. "Jeremy, are you hurt?"

I slither backward, pushing out with my sneaker. Susannah drifts closer, an invisible breeze rustling her hair. Her eyes burn bright green through the dark mist, glowing like a firefly. *You know I love you, Jeremy, don't you?*

"Dad?" I call out, weakly. I know I'm not hurt. But I'm in a waking dream I can't pull out of. "Please, help me."

"It's okay, Jeremy," I hear him say. "You're just in shock. We're okay. We're both okay."

"Where are you, Dad?" I'm trembling as Susannah's shadow expands around me. *You're just like the rest of them, Jeremy Glass, aren't you? Using me for your own selfish desires.*

I feel Dad's hand gripping mine, pressing it hard. Shaking it. No matter how hard I try, I can't get to him. I can't snap out of this nightmare.

Susannah's shadow reaches down into the ground and pulls up a root. But instead of tree roots, they are bloody veins. The floor cracks and breaks apart beneath me as the roots pull free. The ground gives way, and I'm falling, falling.

Choking for air, I land with a silent splash in the dark waters of the Gorge.

—∞—

The breath returns to my lungs. A blurred face peers into mine. Chaz.

"You blacked out, buddy. Your dad had to talk with the police, so he asked me to wait with you."

Someone's moved me to a waiting room where I'm sprawled on a couch.

"But you're okay," Chaz adds. "Your dad's going to be awhile. He asked me to take you home and stay with you."

"I don't need a babysitter," I huff.

Chaz smirks. "Apparently, your dad thinks you do."

Marisa bounds into the waiting room, breathless. She sits beside me smelling of snow and whatever she'd been cooking. "Oh, God! Jeremy! It's all over the news!"

"Is Patrick dead?"

Marisa shakes her head grimly. "As good as. He was shot in the throat. The bullet lodged right at the base of the skull. He's on a ventilator."

I let out a breath. I'm still shaking, but less so. "Does anyone know why Trudy did it?"

"She thinks Mr. Morgan killed her daughter," Chaz offers. "But, I don't know. Why the hell would a guy like Patrick Morgan kill a seventeen-year-old girl?"

I stiffen. Somehow, all the roots spring from Patrick Morgan. I can't help but wonder. If he's unable to speak, how will we ever know? A fresh wave of shaking rips through me. *If I can't solve the mystery behind Susannah's death, how will I ever be rid of her ghost?*

"I'm betting there's more to it than that," Marisa adds. "Mrs. Durban may be crazy, but she's a schemer. Nothing she does would surprise me."

—‿‿—

As we file out to Chaz's car, what I don't expect are the TV trucks and the reporters that surround us like flies trying to land on shit.

I duck my head as Chaz barrels through, using the wheelchair like a battering ram. Marisa strides ahead, palms to their cameras lenses. Once we're in his van, Chaz puts the pedal to the metal and we peel off, leaving the crowd of reporters jockeying for a shot of our retreat.

The shooting of Patrick Morgan is apparently big news.

Once we get to my house, Chaz busies himself in the kitchen, rummaging around. Marisa and I are alone in Dad's study.

"I'll stay awhile, if it's cool with you," she says shyly. Her cheeks are flushed, her eyes dark as the river at night. "I figured you could use the company. Chaz is not the most brilliant conversationalist."

"Isn't tomorrow New Year's Eve? Weren't you supposed to go to a party?"

She lifts an eyebrow. "Weren't you supposed to go to a movie?"

My cheeks heat. I look down. I'm not going to do it this time. I'm not going to lose my heart to someone who will keep it and never give it back.

"Yeah," I mutter. I can't look at her. And I'm sorry I let her come back here. It won't be long before Susannah returns. Then Marisa will know how deeply disturbed I really am.

She glances around, her nose wrinkled. "This place is a mess. And it smells. I think I'll straighten up a bit. Why don't you rest?"

"You really don't have to do that."

"I want to, okay?"

I have no strength to argue. I sigh wearily and ease myself from the chair to the bed. She's right. I'm exhausted. But I'm afraid to sleep. Afraid what unwelcome guests might drop by.

Marisa leaves, then returns a few minutes later with her hands full of yellowed newspaper clippings. "You were going to explain what all these articles were and why they were worth nearly cracking your cranium open."

"They were my mother's," I say, shaking again. I pull the blankets up around me, but still I can't seem to draw in enough warmth. "They're about the death of a guy named Douglas Lewis thirty or so years ago."

"Why would your mother be so obsessed with it?" Marisa whispers, skimming through the old articles. I take them from her as she finishes, wondering what I'm missing.

"He was a friend of hers. Maybe she felt responsible, somehow."

"The drowning was ruled an accident."

Ruled an accident means nothing in Riverton, I realize. If Patrick Morgan wanted the truth altered, police reports could always disappear. Maybe witnesses do, too, or are at least persuaded not to speak up.

The temperature in the room drops measurably, and I shiver. "What if," I say, "Trudy's convinced that Patrick Morgan killed Susannah because he's killed before?"

"Who?" Marisa bites a nail, deep in thought. "Who would he have killed?"

Dark mist pools in the corners of the room. My stomach clenches. In moments I'll be blind to my surroundings. Marisa will know how sick I really am.

I try to focus on the light. On ignoring the figure of Susannah that's emerged from within the shadows, her dress now ragged, hair whipping like storm-lashed branches. I press my hands to my ears to mute the sounds of the howling wind.

"What if Douglas Lewis's death was not an accident?" I shout above the noise only I can hear. "What if Patrick killed him?"

"Why are you yelling, Jeremy?"

The wind screams, a piercing, nerve-abrading shriek.

No, it's Susannah.

226

The light sucks out of the room. I'm deaf to all other sound. Papers lift in a swirling vortex. Susannah is at its center. *You brought me back and now you don't want me.*

I grit my teeth until my eyes bulge. I will her to leave. "Please," I whisper, my hands pressed to my temples. "Let me think."

"I didn't say anything," Marisa answers.

"Headache. Just a headache." I breathe in deeply; under my breath. I hiss, "*Go.*"

The shrieking dies away. The light returns and I let out my breath.

"What if," I say, "my mother knew for a fact that Patrick murdered that boy? That she saw it happen and was forced to stay quiet. Maybe it's why she drank in the first place."

Marisa's dark eyes widen. Blood rushes to my face. I want to pull her in closer to me so her heat can warm my chill. I want to hold her against me and never let go again.

"That's just conjecture. There's no proof. And even if that's true, it still doesn't mean Patrick Morgan killed Susannah."

"What if Susannah found out?"

And then I'm looking at Marisa, forgetting the murders, the deaths, my own almost certain insanity.

It's as if I'm seeing her for the first time. She's shimmery and glowing and so, so achingly beautiful, I wonder how I never noticed. Suddenly, all I want is for all of this mystery and craziness to go away, so I can lean over, touch Marisa's jet hair and kiss her shining lips.

I shudder, guilt scraping at my insides. I should have left well enough alone.

I'd wanted to be with Susannah so badly I'd believed I could bring her back from the dead. I pray it's just my sick mind playing tricks on me. That Susannah is in a better place, not lurking desperately in the shadows.

And, here I am, falling for someone else. As if I stand a chance with Marisa.

Chaz bursts into the room and we both jump—we'd forgotten he was in the house. The phone to his ear, Chaz nods repeatedly. A rare smile lights up his face. "Great. Thanks. That's excellent."

"Well, buddy," he says, pocketing his phone. "Good news. That was Lyle Hoffman. Your leg is in."

"So soon? Are you serious?" I ask, genuinely bowled over with the news.

Chaz winks. "Would I kid about a PT matter? Lyle says you can take it for a test run right away. Well, not exactly a run. More like a halting stroll. But you need to use it so he can make adjustments for fit and programming. Why not start tomorrow?"

Marisa beams, her eyes shining. "Tomorrow is New Year's Eve."

Chaz lifts an eyebrow and shrugs. "What better way to ring in the New Year than on two legs? Lyle's ready if you are."

"Thanks, Chaz," is all I can choke out.

"We have to be there at eight AM, team, so get some sleep. If you don't mind, I'll crash here tonight. Your dad will be home late."

He leaves. Marisa still smiles shyly at me. I'm painfully aware that we're alone in the room. Me, her, and my rampaging libido.

And then I yawn.

"Are you trying to get rid of me?" she asks, smiling.

I'm completely wiped out, my eyes drooping closed, but the last thing I want is for her to leave. "No. Not at all."

She pulls her chair closer. "Good."

My palms are damp. Sweat pops out on my brow. Great. In a minute she's going to see what a loony tune I am and make a run for the hills. I bunch up the blankets so she won't know what's going on under there.

Marisa leans in closer. So close, I can see her teeth glint behind her parted lips.

"I like you, Jeremy," she whispers. "I like you a lot."

My skin prickles with electricity. My good arm lifts like it plans to wrap itself around her without my permission. What the hell am I doing? What am I saying?

"I like you, too. A lot."

"I'd like to be there to see you walk, Jeremy."

"Of course," I say. But I'm just plain gone. I'd say yes if she asked to watch me fly.

Her lips press against mine, and my mouth slides open to hers. It occurs to me that my dad wouldn't be paying her to do *this*.

I kiss her tenderly, carefully, as if my heat might melt her. As if in a moment she'll realize she's kissing the frog who won't be turning into a prince anytime soon. As if the spell will break and the pumpkin coach will arrive at the stroke of midnight to steal her away.

She draws back, hand over her mouth. "Oh, crap. I—I'm sorry. I don't know what I was thinking. I hope you don't think I was too—forward."

I smile and lay my hand on hers. A persistent alarm sounds somewhere off in the distance.

I shouldn't be doing this. And not because she won't like me.

Marisa shifts closer. "I—I wasn't sure. I'm kind of—I'm never really around boys. Boys like you, that is."

I laugh. "Really? You don't hang out with emotionally twisted amputees much? Wow. You don't know what you've been missing."

"Jeremy. You really should stop putting yourself down like that."

"It's just a hobby of mine. I've never really considered going pro."

This time she laughs. "What I was trying to say, and believe me, this is hard, is that I used to watch you run with the team. Those guys—all those guys treated me like I was invisible. A shadow. I know you never noticed me, but I always thought you were different, somehow."

"I am now. All those guys have two legs."

"Jeremy!" Her eyes flash with sudden anger. "You aren't listening. It's not like I planned to meet you! Like I schemed for you to lose your leg and for your father to hire me as a nursemaid. It just kind of happened."

"What kind of happened?" My heart is speeding up again. But the alarm in the distance is growing louder. Dark spots are dancing at the edges of my sight. Soon, when I go zombie, she's going to realize that I am decidedly not boyfriend material.

"You make me laugh." She moves closer. "Even when you hurt. Your eyes are…" she swallows hard. "so…warm. There's so much behind them."

Darkness pulses all around me. The room is getting dimmer. No. Not now.

But now would be exactly when Susannah would come.

Marisa leans in, her mouth parted again, but the room is sucked into a whirling black hole of darkness. She's gone.

Susannah's form stands in the center of the room, dark as smoke.

A muffled voice calls from far away. "Jeremy? What's happening?"

I reach for Marisa, but I can't feel anything.

You're just exactly *like all the rest of them, Jeremy Glass.*

I try to edge away, but I'm numb, frozen in place. I grope for Marisa, but there's no sign of her.

She's just using you. Like all of you used me.

Finally, I find my voice. "That's not true!"

I search for Marisa in the dark and find her hand.

"What's going on? Should I call Chaz? Can't you see me, Jeremy? I'm right here."

I struggle to block out the dark world beyond the grave and see the real one again. *You brought me here, Jeremy.*

The faint silhouette of Marisa is superimposed against the dark. I'm shaking, tremors jerking my body. My heart shudders and spasms.

A shadow draws closer. Papers fly around the room, caught in a wet wind.

She'll never love you. No one will ever love you. But me.

She lunges for me, but I realize too late she's grasping for Marisa's throat.

Light slashes through the black void. The room flares into focus. Marisa is sprawled on the floor, unconscious. My mother's newspaper articles scatter the floor. Susannah is gone.

What the hell did I do?

I stumble to the floor and check her pulse. Normal. Her eyelids flutter, then open. Marisa sits up and rubs her head. "What on earth happened? First, you went limp. It was like you were seeing something that wasn't there. I thought—I don't know what I thought."

She wraps her arms around her chest. She's shaking and I want to hold her tight to stop it. But I don't dare.

"Then, it was as if the lights went out. I couldn't see anything. And then—" Marisa closes her eyes, shuddering, tears dotting her thick lashes. "You're going to think I'm crazy, Jeremy, but I felt—I felt cold hands. Fingers like icicles. They wrapped around my throat and I couldn't breathe. The next thing I knew, you were looking down at me."

Shock pings through my nerve endings.

I'm not crazy after all.

I'm haunted.

Now

Marisa gets to her feet and helps me climb back onto the bed. "So, uh, you don't think I'm *loca* do you? Sometimes I get dizzy when I don't eat enough."

I stare at her, not a trace of a smile on my lips. "You're not *loca*. Not by a long shot. Unless there's a crazy virus around and you caught it from me."

Marisa shivers. "What's really going on here, Jeremy?"

I take her by the hands. "I'm sorry I dragged you into this."

I tell her everything. From the first wave of YouTube links, to the cigar box with the photo of Ryan hinting at what I learned later—that he is in love with another boy—to the package containing the summoning kit, to Susannah's Death Book. I describe how she re-entered my life, at first a subtle presence, gradually strengthening to an entity that could seize control of my psyche at will.

"Demonic possession. We have legends about that. I just never—" Marisa squeezes her eyes closed and hugs herself tighter. Her eyes snap open. "I've just always opted for the rational. But this, Jeremy—I have no doubt it was a hand from beyond the grave around my neck."

We discuss Susannah's interest in Kabbalah. Researching online resources, we finally turn up information on a form of disembodied spirit from Jewish mythology called a dybbuk, a soul that will not rest.

"I think that fits what we have here," Marisa says, matter-of-factly, "And there's got to be a ritual for dealing with a situation like this. A formula for returning her to where she came from."

I study the delicate lines of a face that conceals the fire and spark behind it. A thrill rises up inside me. "You make it sound like a science project."

Marisa folds her arms and purses her lips. "Jeremy Glass, we are two of the smartest kids in Riverton High. If we put our brains together, solving this should be as easy as cracking a differential equation."

"I love it when you talk calculus to me. Except, I'm probably failing calculus right now. I haven't been to school since November twenty-first."

Marisa leans over and rubs her nose against mine. "That's what I'm here for."

"I hope that's not the only thing you're here for."

"That's billable hours. The rest is strictly pro bono."

I close my eyes and breathe in the scent of her, my heart picking up steam again. "You mean that, Marisa?"

I want to tell her that my heart's been safely locked up with all my other collectibles. It's not durable enough to get kicked around without shattering into bits.

She gazes into my eyes. From the close proximity, her two eyes have merged into one massive one. She giggles. "You look like Cyclops. But much cuter. And yes, Jeremy. Pro bono means voluntary. I am choosing to be here. With you. This close." She snuggles next to me on the bed. "No, this close."

My breath comes in rapid gasps. I'm generating enough heat to melt my bones. "I hope you mean it, otherwise you'd better call the fire department to hose me down."

We lean into a kiss, and for thirty seconds, her small frame crushes against mine, I smolder in the fire of pure need.

Until darkness steals the light from the room.

"Don't let go of my hand," I shout.

Seeing nothing, I barely hear her muffled response. Wet wind scours my skin, and my hair blows back as gales ravage the room. In flashes of light, I catch a glimpse of Susannah, her back arched, arms splayed at her sides. Her scream pierces like a thousand fingernails on a chalkboard.

I squeeze Marisa's hand until the light returns.

—⁓—

The room is in shambles—papers scattered everywhere, furniture turned on its side, books splayed all over the floor.

"Well," Marisa says, hands on hips, surveying the mess. "We've got ourselves one hell of a bossy chaperone. No kissing until we solve that problem."

I nod, too stunned for words, still buzzed with adrenaline. I've tampered with things I should have left alone.

We resume our research. Marisa's called up a long list of sites detailing facts about dybbuks. I hop over, pushing my wheelchair like a walker. I'm so ready to ditch this thing I could slam it through the window.

"Jeremy," she says. "This says a dybbuk is the discontented soul of someone who died—or more like an angry echo of the person's soul, with all the better parts taken out. What if Susannah's ghost wants to punish someone living?"

Her question jolts me like the crack of a whip. "Susannah asked me to solve her murder. Why would a ghost lie?"

Marisa swivels around to look at me, no spark of humor in her eyes. "Wouldn't the ghost of a liar *be* a liar?"

Squinting, the reflex to defend Susannah sends blood rushing to my face. Maybe I have Marisa wrong. Maybe I just don't get girls at all. "Susannah's never been a liar."

Marisa shakes her head. "If you're raised by a liar, you become a master of the art form. Mrs. Durban and Susannah lied to each other constantly and asked me to cover for them.

What if Susannah's ghost has been lying to you? What if all these accusations she's made are just—false?"

I grit my teeth, my face hot. For all my fear of Susannah's angry ghost, I never for a minute questioned the sanctity of her memory.

But what if Marisa is right?

"Why the hell bother to come back from the dead to tell *lies?*"

Marisa shrugs and slants her head. "I don't know. Vengeance on her killer? Unfinished business? She may be angry at people other than her murderer. Susannah had secrets. It was like there was something broken inside her that she spent a lot of energy trying to hide."

I chew on a nail, gazing at the computer screen. "Just like the rest of this town."

Marisa turns back to the monitor "This website says that a dybbuk is a soul's cry for help to resolve what's keeping them here. She may not want to be here at all." She turns back to me. "So, it's kind of like you said. The only way to get rid of Susannah's ghost is to help her to leave."

Now (December 31st)

Chaz wakes me at seven AM. Marisa pulls up at seven-twenty. By seven-thirty, we're hustled into Chaz's van, headed for Lyle Hoffmann's Emporium of Legs and Assorted Spare Parts.

My nerve endings crackle with energy. I know I'll never again really feel the rhythm of both feet hitting the pavement, one after the other, but I close my eyes anyway and recreate the sensation from memory.

Marisa slides next to me in the backseat and my body warms with her touch. But by the time we get to Hoffman's Prosthetic Center, I'm sweating, my heart palpitating. What if the leg doesn't fit? What if I can't get the gait right? A million worries race through my head.

Chaz wheels me in and Marisa holds my hand. Lyle Hoffmann bounds into the empty reception area and ushers us into a room with soothing lights and soft music. There's a set of parallel bars and a wall of mirrors, almost like a dance studio.

The way Lyle Hoffman sprints around like one of Santa's strangest elves, it's easy to forget he's got a fake leg, too.

"I'll be back in one minute," he pronounces. "Please, make yourselves at home." Lyle Hoffman dashes from the room, his handlebar mustache trailing like facial coattails.

"The suspense is killing me." I drum my fingers on the wheelchair arm. "This is like meeting my mail-order bride for the first time."

Both Chaz and Marisa laugh. I just keep tapping my sweaty fingers to the rhythm of my racing heart.

In a few minutes, Hoffmann returns with a gleaming metal contraption that reminds me of C-3PO from Star Wars after he was taken apart.

He sets it down on the floor in front of me. "Meet your very own state of the art C-Leg, Jeremy. This beauty was developed by Otto Bock, and features an electronic microprocessor knee joint with three settings."

Hoffmann goes on and on as if he's talking about the latest computer operating system, or at least the love of his life.

I nod, trying to look interested, but I just want to strap it on and get walking.

"I think I'll call her Veronica," I say, finally.

Marisa lifts an eyebrow, one corner of her mouth quirking up. "Veronica?"

"People name their cars, right? Veronica's going to be a part of me, so we might as well get off on the right foot. Literally."

Lyle Hoffman slaps his normal thigh and guffaws heartily. "See, I told you this kid was a comic! Okay, Jeremy Glass, are you ready to test drive your brand new C-Leg?"

"Is there a better word for ready? How about *hell, yeah*?"

Chaz helps me to the bench, and I realize that, with my sprained shoulder, this is going to be doubly hard. I can't even strap on the leg myself.

Hoffman covers my stump with what looks like a little white hat, then carefully eases it into the cup at the top of the prosthetic leg. It feels weird, like I'm being stuffed into a toilet plunger. Chaz has me by the waist. Hoffmann takes me by the arm and eases me upright to my feet.

Feet. The plural of foot.

I sway, dizzy like when I'd climbed to the top of the Statue of Liberty but was too chicken to look down.

Marisa claps. "Woohoo! Look at you!"

I glance in the mirror. There I am—one bare, hairy leg and one metal robot leg. I don't know why I forgot that I wouldn't actually feel the ground under the fake foot, just the stump pressed into the socket.

I swing my hip out and the thing lurches forward, like Frankenstein's monster.

Chaz guides me to the parallel bars and Hoffmann explains the stepping process. It's like learning to drive. You have to do things in precisely the right order or you'll fall on your face. It's hard keeping my balance with only one hand to grip the bars, and I have to struggle to keep totally focused, but in a few minutes, I'm taking my first halting steps.

Walking. It's like being a one-year-old all over again

Chaz, Hoffmann, and Marisa applaud wildly and I have to laugh. I've gone from winning twenty-mile races to this.

But that's life, I guess.

—m—

I walk out of the Hoffmann Center on two legs, with a single crutch to support me in case I tip. I'm not all that steady and sometimes the leg just seems to lock on me. With practice, Hoffman assures me, I'll be practically jogging. But the real running won't come until later, when I'm fitted with the even freakier-looking running blade.

Marisa and Chaz flank my sides like proud parents. The steps are tough, but I make it to the car, amazed at how tiring the simple act of walking can be.

"I want to visit Ryan. I want him to see me walk."

I think of him, lying immobile, lingering near death. My best friend.

He's been an enigma, a vessel of secrets. But so have we all.

And I realize I can't stay angry with him.

I never could.

Though I was once so sure, I'm beginning to wonder if he killed Susannah. I want to hear him deny it, once and for all. *I hope I get the chance.*

By the time we enter the hospital lobby, I'm barely leaning on the crutch, so I hand it to Chaz and I'm walking on my own. It still feels like I'm the Tin Man, but I'm getting the job done.

I catch a glimpse of Marisa and me in a mirror. My curly head towers a good eight inches over hers. At 5'11', I'd completely forgotten how tall I am. And how short Marisa is. I smile. With my sweats falling to my shoes, I look like a regular guy with a really bad limp.

In the ICU, my jubilation turns to dread. I stop and lean against the wall, water pushing into my lungs. Ryan. *How could he do this to himself?*

I fight the desire for a drink. It's a fight I'm probably going to be battling my whole life.

"You okay, buddy?" Chaz asks.

I nod, swallowing down the cold lump in my throat. "Just tired. This is hard work."

"You're doing great," he says. "The best I've ever seen. But I think, after this, it's enough for your first day out."

I nod again, wipe the sweat from my brow and push on, one foot in front of the other.

Even though my stump feels like it's tied to a steel girder, I insist on visiting Ryan by myself and send Marisa and Chaz to the coffee shop lounge to wait. Chaz relents, on the condition I agree to take the crutch.

As I limp past the coffee shop, a small blonde woman wearing sunglasses and a running suit dashes into the hall and reaches the bank of elevators before me. When I finally get there, the woman is still waiting. The elevator doors open and we go in. It's only after the doors slide closed and she lifts her dark glasses that I realize it's Celia Morgan.

Her face tight, Mrs. Morgan's glance cuts from my feet to my face. Her eyes light with her smile. "It's good to see you back on your feet, Jeremy."

I try to block unpleasant thoughts of her face-sucking my dad, but can only replace them with equally unpleasant thoughts of the present.

"H-how's Ryan?" I blurt. I don't ask about Patrick Morgan because, frankly, I don't give a flying shit.

Celia Morgan's eyes fill with moisture. "Thanks for asking, dear. He's awake now, but we won't really know—" she breaks off and wipes her eyes with a tissue. "We won't really know what the future holds for Ryan for another day or so."

Her words vibrate in the small space like tolling bells. The floor, which only part of me can actually feel, seems to tilt. My brain is oversaturated with news I do not want to hear and can no longer absorb. I shoot a glance at the elevator display and curse silently that the thing is so slow, and can't help but wonder how many people have died in this thing while it creaked to its destination.

Celia Morgan blows her nose. "I'm sure Ryan will be happy to see you walking again."

—m—

Derek Spake stands outside Ryan's room, pinching the bridge of his nose. He looks up as I approach. "Well, if it isn't Glass and his brand new peg-leg."

"Next year's model comes with Bluetooth and a phone. How's Ryan?"

Spake's smile evaporates as he motions me inside. "It's hard to say."

Celia Morgan settles in the seat beside the bed and holds Ryan's hand in hers.

Ryan looks a hell of a lot better than he did yesterday. His cheeks are flushed, his lips moist, and his blue eyes clear. But his neck is still immobilized in a stiff plastic collar and his eyes seem unable to focus, like two butterflies flitting from flower to flower.

"He's doing so much better, Jeremy. Let him know you're here," Celia says, her smile overly bright.

Ryan's eyes jitter as his gaze skims past mine.

"Can he see?"

"They think so. But the muscles in his eyes are messed up," says Spake, angrily. "They don't focus or respond to light. He can't talk either, because his vocal cords have been damaged."

I shudder and lean closer to Ryan. "Dude, it's Jeremy. Can you hear me?"

The corners of Ryan's mouth twitch into a slight smile. He blinks rapidly, his eyes rolling but never fixing on me. My insides clamp up.

Celia Morgan blows her nose. "I told you he'd be glad to see you."

I take Ryan's hand. It's warm and limp. Tears spring into my eyes. This can't be my fault. It can't be.

"I-I've got to go." I swivel and lurch from the room as fast as my metal leg will carry me. The fluorescent light sears my retinas. If there is such a thing as hell, I decide, it probably looks and smells like this hallway.

Spake catches up with me in a few long-legged strides. Which is easy enough, since I'm moving only marginally faster than the hour hand on a clock.

Spake motions me to a row of benches that line the wall. It occurs to me that, compared to the brain damage that Ryan probably has, losing a limb is a paper cut. I stare down at my mismatched feet. My stump throbs.

"Christ," I say. "What if he stays like that?"

"He's a fighter. He can get back to normal eventually, with lots of therapy." Then, Spake clears his throat. "You still aren't thinking that Ryan had anything to do with Susannah's disappearance, are you, Glass?"

I meet his gaze. Spake's pale eyes burn into mine, and it occurs to me that Derek Spake might actually love Ryan more fervently than Susannah ever could. "My gut tells me no. But I still have no idea what happened to her."

Spake lets his head droop, then straightens. "Ryan didn't hurt her. I can prove it."

"How do you know? Were you there, too?"

Spake sucks in a sharp breath. "She knew about us, Glass. She was going to blow the whistle and ruin us both."

I narrow my gaze. "So *you* killed her?"

"Fuck no. Neither of us laid a hand on her. She just disappeared into thin air that night."

"Sure," I say. "It sounds like you both had pretty good motives for shutting her up. But how did she find out about you two? Even I had no clue."

Spake stares at his palms as if the appropriate answer is written there. "Two years ago, Susannah and I met at a summer art class in the city. I thought art was my thing before I found track and field. I was going through a lot of shit then. So was she. We got kind of close. Started telling each other stuff we'd never tell anyone else who lived in the same town. So I told her I was gay. That I knew since I was nine. That I hadn't come out to my parents yet."

Her summer art class. I think of the tangle of roots that apparently stretch beyond Riverton, all the way to Hurley.

"She told me stuff, too. Stuff I'm pretty sure she wishes she never did. Because when she tried to threaten Ryan and me, I threw it back at her."

"She threatened you?"

"Fuck, yeah. And I told her I'd post all her pathetic secrets all over Facebook if she started trouble with me."

"So that's why she was crying the day you took her home."

"How the fuck did you know about that?" Spake asks, frowning.

"Never mind. What did she tell you?"

"It was pretty harrowing stuff, actually."

My spine goes rigid. "Like what?"

"She was such a lost soul. Stuff with her mother, with other guys. Older guys, too. What a mess. I felt sorry for her. But after the class ended, we didn't stay in touch. The next time I saw her was as Ryan's arm candy at a meet last April. Susannah introduced us, and from that moment on I couldn't help myself. I was in love. The most amazing day in my life was the day Ryan came out to me. I'm the first person he ever told."

A twinge of jealousy flashes through me. Ryan told this guy, but hid the truth from me. Forced me to lie about his hookups. But would I have accepted him if I'd known? I'm not sure.

"So she confronted Ryan the night she disappeared? Did she suspect you guys right away?"

"A few weeks before that. She expected him to dump me, but he wouldn't. I'm not really sure how she found out. But I was furious, knowing about some of the shit she had done. She didn't deserve him."

My insides twist with nausea. It's as though Spake is talking about a different girl. Not the girl that I knew.

Spake's voice trembles. He squeezes his eyes shut and tears leak through his lashes. "She refused to break up with Ryan. She would not let go. I don't know what that girl was thinking. Ryan loves *me*."

The linoleum pattern on the floor reminds me of roots. Roots that connect and weave into a twisted tangle.

"I'm sure he does," I mutter absently. "When you were in Ryan's room all day yesterday, did Mrs. Morgan ever visit her husband? Isn't he, like, paralyzed from the eyeballs down?"

Spake nods. "Yeah, it's pretty gruesome. I heard the doctors talking. Dude can't even blink. If you ask me, he's probably better off dead, and I wish he was. He's a first-class bastard."

"Did you hear anyone mention what room he's in?"

Spake cocks his head. "Why?"

"I just want to see the guy. He may be a bastard, but he practically raised me. I didn't have the heart to ask Mrs. Morgan. She's got enough troubles."

Spake assesses me and either falls for my flagrant bullshit or just doesn't care enough to keep sparring with me. "There's a special ward on the next floor for patients who can't breathe on their own."

"Thanks, Spake. You've been a big help."

He heads back to Ryan's room, and I text Marisa to come and get me because I'm running on empty. The stump screams in rebellion with every dragging step I take, outraged at the abuse.

Marisa helps me to the elevator. It's slow going, but she steadies me.

Patrick Morgan's room in the ITU, or Intensive Treatment Unit, is guarded by an elderly private security guard who snores gently on a chair outside the room. Marisa and I slip inside.

Patrick Morgan lies in state behind a see-through tent, a plastic tube inserted straight into his throat. His eyes are frozen in a perpetual stare, as if he is dead. The sky-blue eyes shift ever so slightly and a chill shrieks up my spine. Unlike his son, the eyes are shrewd and aware, but the face is immobile. The machine that registers Patrick Morgan's heartbeats bleeps faster.

"Oh, my god," says Marisa. "He's wide awake in there. How awful."

"It is, isn't it," I say, drawing closer. Patrick Morgan doesn't blink, his face as still as sculpted marble. But the monitor's bleep rate speeds up.

"So," I say leaning over him, staring deep into those wide-open eyes. "A tree with the deepest roots starts with a single seed, Mr. Morgan. All the trouble in this town leads back to you, doesn't it?" Blip, blip, blip.

"Jeremy," Marisa warns. "I think you're upsetting him. If his heartbeat gets too erratic someone's going to come rushing in here. We should go."

I turn to her. Sleek black hair frames her face, obsidian eyes shining with fear and worry. "Why shouldn't he know how it feels to be completely powerless, like the people he's victimized all these years?"

It's time to test my theory. Before she can protest, I pull Marisa into a kiss. I want to punish Patrick Morgan for hurting Ryan. For being a tyrannical bastard. And any other crimes he had his filthy hands in.

My groin presses against Marisa's pelvis. The thrill of standing and kissing her all at the same time washes over me, even though I know the curtain is about to come down on my stolen moment of bliss.

As if on cue, the lights snuff out. Damp wind circles the room, buffeting Patrick Morgan's plastic tent. Blip, blip, blip, blip goes the heart machine.

Feeling for Marisa, I hug her close against me. I see nothing but Patrick Morgan, his plastic tent illuminated as if by an eerie spotlight. The heart monitor is going wild. In moments, a medical team will be stampeding in to keep the bastard alive.

I feel her presence in the swampy air. Hear her cries swallowed in the howl of the sudden wet wind that tears at our hair.

"Did he hurt you, Susannah? Was Patrick Morgan the one who killed you?" I shout.

A black mist in the vague shape of a girl hovers close to Patrick Morgan, wind shrieking and lashing our faces. Marisa trembles violently and I press her tiny frame tighter against me.

The nebulous form passes through the plastic tent. The heart monitor races, the lines on the screen jagged with zigzags.

"No!" I hear Marisa cry.

The heart monitor stutters.

"Stop this, Jeremy!" Marisa screams.

"Let's get out of here," I say. Dragging Marisa with my good arm, I head blindly toward the door, shreds of light ripping through the dark veil of gloom. By the time we reach the glare of the hall, I can see again.

"What if she kills him?" Marisa asks, her voice trembling.

"Then she'll have done them both a favor."

"Do you really think Patrick Morgan killed Susannah?"

I stop and wince at the grinding ache in my hip, tempted to rip off Veronica and hop the rest of the way to the car. "I guess we'll find out soon enough."

Back in Chaz's van, Marisa helps me unstrap Veronica. I can almost hear my stump sigh with relief as I peel off the sweaty sock it wears like a newborn's cap. Marisa doesn't flinch at the sight of the raw, raised scar, or the pink hairy slab of flesh and bone jutting a few inches past my hip joint. Veronica sits beside us on the seat like a third passenger.

My head resting on Marisa's slight shoulder, I let my eyes drift close, lulled by the movement of the car tires as they roll over winding roads. I slip into the peaceful sleep of a tired baby after an outing at the playground.

—⁓—

And I dream.

Sunlight dapples the reservoir in lazy ripples. The lapping water sparkles in diamond-bright glints. Her back to me, Susannah stands on the rocky shore tossing daisies into the water. The current takes the flowers toward the center of the reservoir in a single line, like a string of beads.

In the distance, Pirate Island rises from the water like a shark's fin.

Marisa, Chaz, Dad, and I spend New Year's Eve eating pizza. Afterward, Chaz puts me through my paces, making me climb the stairs again and again, backward and forward. Then, he makes me do it with my eyes closed.

I collapse into bed, exhausted, and dream, yet again, of Susannah tossing flowers into the water, the floating bouquet stretching across the reservoir in a long yellow line.

And each morning, I wake, no closer to understanding the message of the dreams, no closer to solving Susannah's murder. I can't find any concrete evidence of Patrick Morgan's involvement, but I don't want to believe it could have been Ryan. It doesn't seem like Spake could have done it. Which leaves me with zero suspects. And a persistent headache.

I've felt Susannah's grip on me slip into a holding pattern, like a storm that lingers, refusing to blow out to sea. She makes her presence known each night, soft breathy advances alternating with violent tirades. Through it all, I remain still, eyes closed against the turmoil, impervious to her touch.

It's not the same for me, anymore. Her power over me has diminished, yet she's still with me, this restless spirit I've summoned from the grave.

Each night I drift into sleep to the sounds of her muted sobs.

And with Susannah's presence watching our every move, Marisa and I don't dare do more than hug.

Which is killing me faster than going cold turkey from vodka ever could.

Still, it's been nearly two weeks since I've wanted a drink.

—⁓—

The days have slipped into a kind of routine. Dad has temporarily moved in with Celia to help her through her ordeal. Even though the town is talking up a storm, a weight seems to have lifted from his shoulders. I've even caught him smiling with both sides of his mouth. Ordinarily, I'd be jealous that Dad can be with the woman he loves without the fear that a vengeful spirit will kill him. But he's lived under the tyranny of Patrick Morgan for so long, I figure we're even.

I'm left in Chaz's merciless care—PT torture sessions in the mornings, afternoons doing calculus with Marisa.

My insides still burn for a drink. I won't be able to hold out forever, but for now there's too much else to do.

Yesterday, Ryan was transferred to the rehab wing of the hospital. This bright and bitter afternoon, every surface glazed with ice, Dad decides to gives Marisa the afternoon off and takes me to the hospital himself. He makes a strange detour that takes us down a hilly, deserted road glistening with ice-coated branches. A low stone wall banks the road, punctuated by a pair of wrought-iron gates and a sign that reads, *Upper Westchester Memorial Cemetery.*

"Why are you stopping?"

"Your mother is buried here."

I gnash my teeth. I think I hear the faint rhythm of water lapping against my eardrums. "Shit. Why now, Dad?"

"I don't know. I guess—you know, Celia and all. I always thought—"

"You always thought what?"

Dad doesn't answer. Instead, he gets out of the car, comes around to my side, opens the door, and holds his arm out for me. "Please, Jeremy. Just for a minute."

"There's all this ice—I don't know if I can—" It's true, I've gotten pretty good with the walking thing. I've ditched the crutch and graduated to a cane. Though I get tired much less easily, I'm still mastering the art of walking on uneven terrain. So I'm not lying when I look at the frozen path with real trepidation. But that's not what's holding me back.

I let Dad help me out of the car. Sheets of rutted ice glisten in the sunlight. Dad grips my arm firmly and helps me along, my footfalls uncertain. "I've got you, kiddo."

On either side of us, monuments poke from the shimmering snow cover. My heart races, my frozen breath like razors in my lungs. My gait is hesitant and tentative, each step like wading into a void. "Dad, I—"

"We're almost there, Jeremy. Promise."

And then I see it, set a few feet back from the path. A headstone engraved with the name *Douglas Bernard Lewis. Beloved son. Born 1961—Died 1978*

The brisk air echoes with whispers, with secrets long buried. I jerk away from Dad and do my best approximation of a run.

"Hey," Dad calls, "Be careful!"

Then I'm slammed by a wall of darkness, as though a black hood has been thrown over my head. I feel myself going down, my stomach and palms slamming against the ice. Within a halo of dim light, the silhouette of Susannah takes shape, perched on Doug Lewis' grave.

You're not even trying anymore, Jeremy.

"I'm trying!" I shout.

You did this. You brought me back.

Dad hoists me to my feet, my vision shredded by darkness. I fight to regain my bearings and force her away.

"Relax," Dad says. "I have you."

"Yeah, well," I say, still half-blind and clinging to him for support. "I told you it was too icy."

"Sorry. I shouldn't have brought you. It's just that I'd been thinking about what you said. About Dougie's death. And about what if it wasn't an accident. I just—I guess I just wanted to find some answers."

I stare really hard at Dad for a beat, trying to blink away the darkness. The questions thrum around me, vibrating through the tangle of roots that twist under the cold hard ground of Riverton, connecting the past to the present, all of us to each other. I can't help but wonder if I, one-legged, alcoholic-in-recovery Jeremy Glass, really do have the courage to dig them all up to find the answers.

"Don't we all," I say, my vision clearing. "And," I add, "don't ever make me go back to that Dr. Kopeck again, okay?"

"But, Jeremy. You still need to—"

I cut him off. "I haven't had a drink in three weeks. I know what I need to do. If I fuck up again, you can find someone else. But not that bitch."

"It's not that simple. It took years for you to become an alcoholic. It's not going to just magically go away in a few weeks."

"I get that, Dad. I really do."

Dad nods grimly, and silently helps me back to the car without visiting Mom's grave.

—◊◊◊—

At the hospital, Dad walks me to the rehab unit where Ryan's been moved. It's a long and confusing route and he doesn't want to risk me falling again.

Spake is there as usual, helping Ryan eat. Visits from the track team have dwindled as Ryan's inner circle has whittled down to just me, Dad, Spake, Celia and sometimes Marisa.

Ryan is propped up in a cushioned chair with a tall back. Spake looks on as Ryan tries to spoon oatmeal into his mouth with his working left hand. His blue eyes drift and roll, unfocused, until he notices me and smiles the smile that has lost none of its wattage. Seeing him this way tears me in two, but I'm careful not to show it.

He's still unable to speak, and the doctors don't know if it's due to the damage done to his vocal cords, brain injury, or both. With his right side weakened, walking is an epic struggle. It's going to be a long road for Ryan, months of rehab and psychological evaluation. And there's still the matter of his attempted suicide.

There's no way I can ask him, yet again, if he killed Susannah.

And I'm not sure I want to.

Ryan rests the spoon on his tray and makes the same gesture he has every day since he's been fully conscious. Two fingers walking.

He smiles and his scattered gaze tracks my movements as I get to my feet and make my usual circuit, my limp still pronounced.

He never seems to tire of watching me walk with my new leg.

I pull up a chair alongside him. We may have switched places, but Ryan is a much more agreeable patient than I am.

"Hey, bro."

Ryan nods and grips my hand. He squeezes hard. Harder than I'd ever suspected he could. His wavering gaze struggles to lock in on mine. Finally he gives up and squeezes his eyes closed tightly.

"He looks forward to when you come, Jeremy," Spake says. "It means a lot to him."

But Ryan seems agitated today. His eyes snap open, and he blinks rapidly. Pressing his lips together, he huffs out repeatedly through his nose. I can feel his frustration, the words locked inside him, as he repeatedly taps the tabletop with his palm.

"What's the matter with him?" I ask.

"I'm not sure. The nurse said that sometimes at night he has these fits where he shivers and breathes heavily. They have to give him a sedative to get him to sleep."

I frown and turn to Ryan. "Are you in pain?"

Ryan shakes his head no, vehemently. But his lower lip quivers as he fights to keep his unsteady gaze on me. Tears slip from the corner of his eyes. His mouth opens and closes, but only a raspy wheeze comes from his throat, which prompts a coughing fit so violent, this time the nurses have to be called to give him oxygen.

Pacing the room, Spake looks as tightly wound as a coiled spring. The nurses transfer Ryan to his bed and he falls asleep quickly, snoring lightly.

I stare at his peaceful form, his chest rising and falling. Ryan is still as beautiful as ever, his injuries and scars masked by sleep.

Spake leans over and plants a kiss on his cheek. "I'm sure he's been trying to tell me something. I've gotten him pad and paper, but he can only make meaningless scratchings. I think the frustration of not being able to communicate is driving him crazy."

I peer down at Ryan, wishing I could crack open his skull and peer inside. What secrets are locked in there? "What do you think is keeping him up? You don't think—"

Spake's jaw sets as if he's read my thoughts. "Don't go there, Glass. He didn't do it. Ryan couldn't hurt anyone. It's not in his nature." He paces the room, a cyclone of bristling energy. "It's probably nightmares about his monster father. Seeing him like this, while the person who's responsible is still alive, is tearing me up inside, Glass. Have you ever seen the bruises on Ryan's back?"

I think hard and realize I never have. Ryan would often swim wearing a T-shirt. But since I wasn't much for water sports myself, I'd barely taken note. I'd seen him in the shower, but never noticed anything odd.

"Asshole was careful not to beat him during track season. But the rest of the year—all bets were off. You should see what his back looks like now. It's no wonder he preferred to die rather than face that man's wrath."

Spake meets my gaze, his jaw trembling. "Patrick Morgan threatened to kill me, Glass. He said if he ever caught me within a country mile of his son, he'd cut off my—my—and toss me in the reservoir with everyone else who'd crossed him." Spake spits out his words. "It's that bastard's fault that Ryan tried to kill himself. And I'm fucking glad he has all the time in the world to think about what he did."

"That's assuming," I say softly, "he has a conscience to bother him."

CHAPTER

thirty-four

Now (January 9th)

In the morning, Chaz orders me to walk up and down the staircase twenty times. I'm so tired, I'm ready to whip off Veronica and beat him to a bloody pulp with her. But Chaz is unflinching in his grim determination. For my next tasks, he has me walk around the house holding books in my good arm, balance plates like a waiter, and mop the floor one-handed.

My stump howls with pain, but Chaz isn't interested in my whining. And my effort has been paying off. As my gait improves, and since I've been sober for over three weeks, Dad has been experimenting with letting me drive the car for short stints, apparently unaware of my few sojourns.

Marisa and I meet at Awesome Cow for lattes and sandwiches. I never thought being able to get out of a car on my own and walk into a café on two legs would feel so good. We're still cautious in our behavior—all giggles, flirtations and snuggles, but nothing more. And I'm starting to wonder if desire denied is going to be the default setting for the rest of my life.

After lunch, I drive Marisa home and I'm off to visit Ryan on my own. She smiles at me, sunlight tripping across the black gloss of her hair, as she walks to her door. And I think how unfair it is, how we are both prisoners of the inconsolable spirit I've brought back from the dead.

And how we won't be free unless I can send her back.

—⁓—

Spake sits with Ryan, as usual, talking to him. Ryan nods and grimaces, his head turned away. Celia leaves to go for coffee.

Once his jittering gaze lands on me, Ryan's left hand drums the tabletop incessantly. He starts to breathe heavily, making deep huffing noises as if he's trying to speak but has none of the necessary equipment.

I pull up another chair and throw an arm around him.

"Do you want to see me walk today?"

Ryan pounds the table with force and shuffles his feet.

"The nurses say he was up all night, bug-eyed. It's like he's scared to death. They say they want to have him transferred to the psych ward as soon as he's stronger," Spake says. "I have to do something."

I glance at Ryan, who sighs and slumps lower in his chair, defeated.

"What do you actually think you can do?" I'm not sure I like or trust Spake's tone.

"Maybe if Ryan knows that Patrick Morgan is really gone, he can start to heal. I'm not sure he gets that his father can't hurt him anymore."

Ryan's mouth moves, fish-like, making the same wheezing and huffing noises. His lips twist and contract into strange positions, as he struggles unsuccessfully to form words.

"What is it, Ry? What are you trying to tell us?"

Ryan nods and exhales, left hand patting his chest, then points to his mouth and shrugs as if to say he's not sure why he can't talk. He taps his chest again, points to his shifting eyes, then circles his finger next to his head, the universal sign for crazy.

"No one thinks you're crazy, Ryan," Spake says. "You've had a huge trauma. It's just going to take awhile to get your body to work right again."

Ryan blows more air out of his mouth and shakes his head. This time he does the *crazy* gesture and points to his eyes.

"Wait," I say. "Do you mean you've *seen* something crazy, Ryan?"

Ryan smiles, his head bobbing yes, enthusiastically.

I pull my chair closer. Spake crosses his arms defensively. "Go easy on him. He didn't do anything wrong."

"What did you see?" I ask, ignoring Spake.

Again, Ryan paws at the air, but his rapid gestures are not getting us anywhere. He contorts his mouth into a trembling O. His eyes flutter closed, his face red and strained into a grimace. His tongue finds the back of his teeth. He lets a puff of air escape to make the sibilant sound of an "s." It's little more than a gruff whisper, a rasp of air.

Breathing hard through his mouth, Ryan's clearly spent from the effort, but he tries again. "Suh—" This time he purses his lips in a tight little "o" and blows out a new rush of air.

Ryan shakes his head, wildly, clutching my arm. "Sooosssss— soooosssssssssss…"

"Susannah?" I prompt, wondering if this, when I've finally accepted his innocence, is his confession.

Ryan nods furiously, and smiles. Tears stream down his cheeks. I pull him close to my chest as hissing sobs vibrate through his body.

"You're upsetting him, Glass, just by mentioning her name."

Ryan pulls away, fighting to form words. "H-h-h-eerrrrrrrre."

My scalp pulls taut, my hands shaking. It can't be. Ryan's not confessing to anything. "Here? Susannah is here?"

Ryan squeezes his eyes tight and nods.

I pull him closer, and rub his arm. "It's okay, Ry. It's okay."

—m—

I ask to spend the night in Ryan's room. I wait until he's asleep, then carefully unstrap Veronica and slip her under the cot. In no time, despite the hospital noises, I fall into a fitful sleep myself.

I wake to near-total darkness, punctuated by the vigorous rattle of the hospital bed. I make out Ryan as he swipes with his good hand, the breath hissing and huffing wordlessly through his lips. There's no sign of any presence in the room, and I wonder if he's having a PTSD episode, similar to the ones that I suffer from.

"Ryan. I'm here, buddy. Settle down."

Then I smell it, a vague tang of vanilla and earthen dampness, a scent of the wet wind that blows in with a summer storm. Ryan thumps his head against his pillow. The windows blow open, admitting a gust of biting wind that lashes the room in a violent frenzy.

I leap off the cot and lunge to close the window, then hop to Ryan's side. There's no time to fuss around with Veronica. I climb onto the bed and enfold him in my arms, his chest heaving and shaking with tremors.

A chill claws up my spine. The moment I touch Ryan, I see the silhouette of Susannah against the dark.

"Is he your killer or isn't he?" I shout. "Just say it!"

He hurt me. All of you hurt me.

A freezing squall whips the curtain that surrounds Ryan's bed. He exhales in a breathy hiss, edging as far away from her as he can get in the bed.

You were supposed to help me, Jeremy.

My voice booms out from my chest. "Wouldn't a murder victim *know* who killed them? Why all the hints and clues?"

Ryan flails and swats, eyes wild like a startled horse.

"Well?" I press. "Did he or didn't he? Or was it Patrick Morgan? Why all the intrigue? Is this some kind of game to you?"

Ryan heaves and shakes, achieving nothing louder or more defined than a series of tremulous exhales.

"Leave him!" I bellow, "Go back to where you belong. You're dead!" I'm shouting, pointing at her shadowy form with a trembling finger.

Ryan turns toward me, blinking helplessly, his mouth opening and closing like a fish.

The shadow recedes. *You've always lied for him! You never loved me!*

"Once, I did. I really did." I close my eyes and hold Ryan's quaking body against me. "Who killed you, Susannah? Just tell me."

All of you killed me.

The silhouetted form flickers and sputters out, taking the dark with it like smoke drawn through a vent.

Ryan sobs in silent gasps, his head pressed against my chest.

I stroke his damp hair and cradle him, her words ringing in my ears.

Dreams don't lie, Jeremy.

Now

I fall asleep on Ryan's bed, jammed against the bedrail.

Spake shuffles into the room first thing in the morning, looking more like a ghost than Susannah did.

"He's dead," he says flatly. "Patrick Morgan is dead."

"What the hell? I thought you went home."

"I started to. Then I thought about it. As long as Patrick Morgan could breathe in oxygen, I wouldn't be able to rest."

"Shit." My heart starts to pound. "You didn't."

Spake walks to the bedside. Ryan lifts his head and huffs softly.

"I didn't have to. When I got to his room, there was this strange wind. His heart monitor was going nuts. I slipped outside and seconds later the doctors came stampeding in. But it was too late."

Spake leans over and kisses the top of Ryan's head. "You don't have anything to be afraid of anymore," he says.

I stare at my knuckles and wish, more than anything, that it were true.

—⁓—

I walk to the handicapped spot, a perk I'll have the pleasure of enjoying for the rest of my life. Overnight, the cold snap has thawed. The air is unseasonably warm. Water drips in tiny diamonds from the glittering branches, and the skin of ice encrusting everything has started to liquefy. The slick ground under my feet is spongier. I make it to my car without fear of falling on my butt.

I turn on the car radio and try to blast away my exhaustion. Dad wasn't thrilled that I missed my appointment with Chaz, but my whole body is sore from my twisted sleep, hunkered in the bed with Ryan.

Our triangle has completely caved in on itself, I think.

I'm the only side left standing, and even that's just barely.

And not for long, if I can't figure out how to put Susannah back where I should have left her in the first place.

To try and calm down, I switch on the radio full-blast and let an ancient hip-hop song shake my bones. For reasons I can't explain, I turn down the same route Dad took the other day and pull to a stop. Turning off the radio, I open the windows and cut the engine, the only sound the tinkling of a thousand drips as the melting ice plinks from the skeletal branches. The sun beats down in a slanting mimic of spring. The air carries a teasing hint of life, which has no place in the middle of January.

Before I know it, I'm out of the car, leaning on my cane just in case the uneven ground rears up to meet me. Then I'm hobbling through the gates and up the slushy path, past the eternal resting place of Douglas Lewis to the ground where my mother's bones lie.

Breathless from the effort, I make it. Without falling once. Without the sky going dark around me, I stare at her tombstone.

Teresa Winston Glass

Born January 10th, 1961

Beloved wife of Paul. Beloved mother of Jeremy Michael.

I gulp in air. I'd forgotten today is my mother's birthday. Had she drawn me here? By opening the door to the beyond, did I make it easier for Mom to get a message through?

I'm overwhelmed with a sorrow deeper than any grave.

Slowly, I ease myself to the slushy patch of ground in front of her headstone and curl up in front of it. And for the first time I can remember, I allow the tears I've bottled up for nine years to flow.

Somehow, despite the cold wetness seeping through my pants, I fall asleep, cradled in her arms.

And dream.

In the distance, I see Susannah stroll across the frozen terrain of the graveyard, her black dress in sharp contrast to the sun-washed whiteness of everything else. Her bronze hair gleams in the bright light, and blows ragged though there's no breeze to speak of.

It's the dream Susannah, not the dark revenant that's been haunting me. But her features are obscured, blurred by a bright haze. I squint and realize I'm not sure who it is, after all.

Silently, the figure approaches and I realize Veronica is gone. I'm one-legged and stranded, hopping crazily from tomb to tomb to get away. *I'm dreaming. This is still the dream.*

I make it to the edge of the cemetery, but there's no place left to go except straight into the water of the Gorge.

The figure draws closer. I see it is not Susannah at all.

It's my mother.

Silently, she stops at her own grave and smiles at me. Then she leans down and pulls at the ground, but instead of clumps of earth, she's pulling up the wood planking of a floor.

I wake suddenly, the sun sinking between the crosshatch of branches, gripped by a chill deep in my bones. And I know I hear it, borne by the wind that whistles between the graves.

Dreams never lie, Jeremy.

CHAPTER

thirty - six

Now (January 10th)

It's almost dark when I get home, soaked and freezing. I try to slink up to my room, but with a metal leg sprouting from my thigh, the art of sneaking is going to require a lot more practice.

Dad calls out to me from the dining room. "Jeremy!"

I find him seated at the table behind an avalanche of papers, reading glasses perched on his nose. He stands abruptly, scattering more papers, and peers at me over the rims. "Where the hell were you?"

"I went for a drive.

"You could have called."

"Cell battery died."

Dad throws up his hands and sits down with a sigh. "Some things never change."

"What is all this?" I ask, gesturing at the blizzard of papers.

"Paperwork for Trudy Durban's murder trial."

"You've got to be kidding. *You're* going to represent her? "

"Of course not. I'm just helping out. You know, for old time's sake."

"Old time's sake." I drum my fingers on a part of the table that's not covered in papers. Ever the historian, on the lookout for details and the things others miss, I scan the mess. "Just how close were Mom and Trudy?"

"They were inseparable in high school," Dad says, returning to his work. "But after graduation, they stopped speaking to each other."

"You think Trudy Durban is fit to stand trial?" I ask, working hard to sound casual, my eyes combing the pile.

Dad scribbles something on a yellow pad and mumbles. "She's being evaluated, but I doubt it. She seems to have snapped completely. She keeps repeating, over and over, that Patrick Morgan is the devil. And Ryan is the son of the devil. And the town must be expunged. And a whole bunch of other nonsense about the Lord's justice and an *eye for an eye*.

"Her ravings aside, there's nothing to suggest that Patrick Morgan killed anyone. However, there's plenty of circumstantial evidence that Ryan did kill Susannah, and Patrick was helping him cover it up."

I stand so quickly, Veronica locks on me and I fall back into the chair. "Ryan didn't kill anyone. Maybe *Trudy* did it herself! The woman is clearly insane."

"I don't know," says Dad. "There's no sign of Susannah anywhere. It's been two months, and the police are about to declare her presumed dead. And with Patrick gone, people are talking. It appears the initial police report *was* tampered with. Everyone with a grudge against the Morgans, and believe me there's no shortage of them, has come out of the woodwork. I'm going to be busy for years helping Celia fend off the lawsuits."

I scratch my head. "I know Ryan didn't do it. I just have a gut feeling that…"

Dad cuts me a look. "Not that again, Jeremy. Weren't you the one who suspected him in the first place? Are you feeling okay? You're not having hall—"

"Dad! I am not fucking nuts. I'm saying that, based on the evidence at hand, I just don't think he did it."

"Jeremy, there's enough damning evidence to support the possibility. You may even be called in as a material witness."

"This is ridiculous. How can Ryan stand trial? They can't send someone as—as messed up as him to jail."

Nestled in the white mountain of papers my roving gaze lands on a small manila envelope labeled *keys*. I note it for future reference.

"Disability is not a 'get out of jail free' card," Dad says, "The fact that Ryan tried to kill himself is very damning." Dad takes off his glasses. "If it's determined that he is mentally competent, he can stand trial."

—∞—

Tired and frozen, a nasty cold coming on, I clump up the stairs to my room. I strip off my wet clothes, remove Veronica, throw myself onto the bed, and stare at the ceiling, wondering if I can summon Susannah at will.

Come, I think. *We need to talk.*

Time passes, an hour maybe. My eyelids are so heavy. But before they slip closed, darkness descends. The room goes cold. Gusts of wind hurl papers around and tear at my curtains. I feel her weight lower on top of me, and automatically, despite myself, my body responds.

But no. This is business. I roll over on my side and curl in on myself like a millipede.

"C'mon. Did Ryan kill you or not?" I ask wearily. "If you say he did, I'll believe you. I'll make sure he pays for it. I swear."

Wind slams my door shut.

I sit up and speak into the blackness that engulfs my room. "Or do you want an innocent person to go to jail?"

The door reopens and slams shut again. The lights in my room flicker back to life.

I fall asleep. I do not dream.

—∞—

The morning of January eleventh dawns bright, another unseasonably warm day. It's also the day Patrick Morgan will be cremated at his wife's request, his ashes sprinkled into the Gorge. It's a small ceremony, just Dad, Celia, and a few relatives. It's decided that Ryan, still recuperating from his injuries, is not well enough to attend. And I flat out refuse to go.

Because I've come down with a cold, I get out of PT for another day. But I'm restless and lonely in the big stuffy house, just me and Veronica. She gets me where I need to go, but she's not very supportive beyond her job description.

Chaz's PT boot camp really has paid off. I can walk for miles at a pretty fast clip without getting too tired. Slowly, Veronica has become an extension of me. The stump feels lost without her warmth to cradle it.

The same way I feel about Marisa.

Jittery, my head spinning with loose ends and anxiety, I call Marisa to come out for a walk since it's such a nice day. Before I leave to meet her, I shuffle into the dining room where Dad has left his paper mountain range. The envelope labeled *keys* beckons from its place under the pile.

I slip it open and know I've hit pay dirt. The keys are stuck with a Post-it—*Trudy Durban, 38 Melrose Park Drive.*

Do I dare?

For a flash, I feel sorry for Dad and the trouble I may cause him. Despite everything I've put him through, he still doesn't get just how devious, and cunning, and downright sneaky I can be when I've set my mind on things. I stick the keys in my pocket, not precisely sure if I'll ever get the nerve to use them or why I'd need to. But something tells me I should.

I drive to Awesome Cow to meet Marisa. We walk the first mile through town and up Greenbrook Road in comfortable silence, our breath hanging in vaporous puffs on the crisp air. I've gotten used to the alternating pressure—foot, thigh, foot, thigh.

It's become second nature to me. But between the steady beats, I wonder if I'm making the same mistake all over again. If I'm letting personal bias color the truth. I viewed Susannah through the lens of my obsession, never really seeing her for the way she was. Maybe now I'm doing the same with Ryan because

I feel sorry for him. And because I'm guilt-ridden. What if I'm wrong about him, too?

And if I'm not, then who killed Susannah?

Patrick? Trudy? Spake? The possibilities swirl in my head.

Marisa and I have walked fast and I'm a bit winded. I stop to catch my breath. Between the bare trees, the reservoir glitters in silver patches.

Marisa looks up at me, and smiles. "I can barely keep up with you. You and Veronica are Team Awesome."

"We make a strange love triangle—me, you, and my bionic leg."

"I have to admit, I'm a bit jealous. She's the one who always gets to be close to you."

I crack a one-sided smile. "Yeah, but she'll never really warm up to me."

Marisa giggles. I cup her face in my hands and sigh. I don't mention the true third side of our triangle. Leaning in closer, my breath quickens.

"I want you so much," she says, her lips parting. "I can't stand this anymore."

"Me neither." I close my eyes and let my mouth find hers. *What's the harm of one quick kiss?*

But I pull back, shaking a little. I can't risk Marisa getting hurt.

"This sucks," Marisa says.

We trudge along some more. I look up, surprised to see we've gone much further than the two miles we'd planned to walk. My thigh throbs. I've overdone it.

"Tired?" Marisa asks. "I can go back and get the car."

"No. I'm fine. In fact, why don't you head back? I have a quick errand to do."

Her voice drops, and her lip curls. "Jeremy, my bullshit detector is bleeping code red. You may think you can put one over on everyone else, but I'm onto you. What are you really up to?"

I finger the keys in my pocket and think about the dream in the cemetery. My mother pulling up boards from the floor of her grave. If Susannah can return from the dead to haunt me, why can't my mother return to warn me?

I stare into the middle distance, lost in thought. *Dreams don't lie*, Mom said in the dream.

"Earth to Jeremy?"

I turn to her and smile. "I, uh..." and realize quickly that I can't lie to Marisa because she sees clear through me. Transparent Jeremy Glass. "I have the keys to Trudy Durban's house."

"What? Why? You're not thinking of—Jeremy, don't tell me you want to go in there."

I glance up at the street sign. We're at the intersection of Melrose and Monroe. It must have been in the back of my mind all along. "Look, Marisa. You don't have to come. In fact, I insist that you don't. It might be dangerous."

"You really are insane. You could slip and fall, and who would be there to help you?"

"You worry too much. Look. They're getting ready to file charges against Ryan. Not only will that mean an innocent, totally fucked-up guy who can barely see, walk, or even speak for himself could be blamed for a crime he didn't commit, but it still won't get Susannah off our backs because I don't think he did it, and, quite frankly, I don't know if she wants us to know who really did."

"Are you saying Susannah wanted to *frame* Ryan? Why?"

"Maybe. I don't know. But I had this dream. About floorboards and stuff. I think there's something in the Durbans' house that will unravel the whole thing."

"Isn't that breaking and entering?"

"Not if I have the key."

Marisa bites her lower lip, looking so adorable I want to scream.

"Why on earth did I have to get mixed up with the biggest lunatic on the planet?" she moans, mock dramatically, hand to her chest.

"I take that as a yes?"

"Yes. To make sure you don't get hurt, Mr. My Ass is Glass."

The Durban house has a forlorn and deserted look. Snow has drifted onto the porch in thick piles and the dirty white of the front lawn is pitted with tossed newspapers left where they'd landed. I realize it's a good thing Marisa has decided to come with me, because Veronica and I are going to have a rough go crossing the filthy, melting mess.

The sun has disappeared behind a thick cloud cover. The sky has the close dark look of imminent rain, unusual for early January. A drop falls, and then another.

We get to the porch just before the deluge. I'm gasping for breath and embarrassed to be so winded from a simple dash across a yard.

"It'll get easier, eventually," Marisa says, reading my mind.

Again, I'm overcome with the urge to kiss her and the anger rushes to my cheeks. It's not acceptable, I think.

Not acceptable at all, that I can't.

I place my cold hands on either side of her face and look into her eyes. Electricity passes between us, drawing me closer and I can't pull away. I want this too much.

So I kiss her anyway, soft and sweet and urgent, right there on the porch, knee-deep in snow. Practical, no-nonsense, quicksilver Marisa. Her lips are cool, her mouth warm. Joy rolls through my nerve endings. Cold as I am, I could stand like this forever, kissing her.

But my memory roams to the time I almost died of hypothermia on Susannah's porch. It's only then that I remember where I am.

There's a sudden gust of wind and the screen door flies open, slamming hard into my back.

"Ouch. Shit!"

"Weird," Marisa says, looking warily around.

"It was just the wind. That's all."

But Marisa's eyes are wide and I'm not sure she believes me.

—◊◊—

Inside, the air is stale, but as always the Durbans' house is meticulously neat. If anything, though, there are more crosses cluttering every spare inch. Trudy Durban has even hung them on the slats of the staircase banister.

Rain patters the roof and streams into the gutters in small waterfalls. Wind pounds at the windows. I don't dare turn on the lights, in case a neighbor or passing car might notice intruders. The whole town knows that no one is home at the Durbans'.

Lightning flashes strobe the dark room into intervals of intense brightness. Marisa looks around and shivers. "It's really spooky being back here. Now, remind me. Why exactly *are* we here?"

"Because I had a dream."

Marisa laughs nervously. "So, now you're Martin Luther King."

I poke her with my elbow. "Funny, funny. I had a dream about something hidden under some floorboards. And I think whatever it is is hidden somewhere here, in this house. But I have no idea what *it* is, or where Trudy would hide something."

Marisa's face creases in a frown. "Well, she never did let me clean under her bed."

There's a bright flash and an earsplitting crack of thunder. We flinch, and then, without saying a word, we're racing up the steps to the master bedroom as fast as I can manage, Marisa right behind me.

When we get to the top, a squall of wet wind blasts the hall window open. We hit the floor and creep on our stomachs, commando style, to Trudy's bedroom. Above us, the blackness gathers and billows in an iridescent cloud.

Once inside the master bedroom, the door slams behind us. With violent pops, all the glass in the room shatters. Shards bombard us in a glittering blizzard, the deadliest snowfall ever. Thunder rattles the floor. Rain slams the roof and pelts the window.

A lamp smashes into the wall behind us, followed by a picture in a glass frame. Small objects, paper, coins, and dust whip into a vortex that whirls around us as we drag ourselves toward the king-sized bed like soldiers to a foxhole. Marisa screams as a sliver of glass grazes her cheek, narrowly missing her eye.

I help her squirm under the bed beside me. "I shouldn't have brought you here."

Marisa presses her scarf to her bleeding cheek. "It's just a scratch. Let's make this worth the trouble."

As we huddle under the bed, the room shrieking and groaning around us, a hurricane of flying objects batters the walls as we grope around for loose floorboards which may or may not be here.

And I wonder if I really am crazy *and* haunted. If I've led Marisa on an irresponsible and dangerous wild-goose chase.

My knuckles knock against hollow floor. Digging my fingers between the planks, I pry a single board free, revealing the shallow space beneath.

I poke around, my hand scuffing against something soft, and extract what looks like a large wedding album.

As soon as I open the album, the howling wind stops. The glass shards clatter to the floor.

There are pages and pages of loose-leaf paper slipped under the plastic sheeting of the photo album. Some pages are crowded with ballpoint pen, written in a backward-slanting loopy script. Some are covered, collage-style, with photographs, torn bits of menus, book covers, magazines, and matchbooks. Then come the pages and pages of defaced photos. Patrick Morgan with his eyes torn out. Scribbled on. Gouged. Even burned. Each subsequent page more violent and disturbed, as if the book is a timeline of Trudy's devolving mental state. Her rabid hatred for Patrick rises from the images like toxic fumes.

A pendant on a chain slips from inside the book. It's the other half of Mom's heart locket, embossed with the words.

Teresa

ds forever.

Marisa and I sit by the window in the waning light and leaf through the strange book that documents the anatomy of Trudy

Durban's rage. But it's not Trudy's insane scribblings that hold my interest. Instead, it's the pristinely penned essay on loose-leaf paper that draws me in.

Teresa Winston and Trudy Durban
My Version, December 24th, 1978

Paul had the flu and Celia was out of town visiting relatives. I didn't want to go out on the ice with Patrick, Trudy, and Doug that night. But Trudy insisted.

"Wear a hat," she said.

"I hate hats. I get hat hair."

"Give me a break, Teresa."

It was just going to be Trudy, Doug, Patrick, and me. And I already knew the scenario. Trudy and Doug would be all over each other, X-rated style, and Patrick, without Paul there, would have his hands all over me. I never did have the nerve to tell Paul that, whenever he turned his back, Patrick swooped in.

It was weird, but I kind of liked it. Patrick was gorgeous. And if I thought for a minute he actually wanted me, I'd have ditched Paul in a second. But everyone knew he was crazy about Celia.

I always ended up doing whatever Trudy wanted. She was wild, willful, beautiful, and fun. And I was afraid she'd drop me for a more interesting and lively friend. Then I'd have no one.

So I went.

Since that day, I've spent every waking moment wishing I hadn't.

It was a bitter and clear night, the full moon beaming down on the ice-bound reservoir. Patrick had stolen some of his dad's good brandy and we chugged it straight from the bottle. By the time we staggered out on the ice, we were a pack of stumbling fools, laughing madly and howling at the moon.

I let Patrick kiss me. His lips tasted like brandy and oddly, mint, like he'd brushed his teeth extra hard that night. In the cold moonlight, his breath misting, Patrick Morgan looked like a Norse god.

I really liked the feel of the brandy sliding hot down my throat, but not as much as Patrick's warm mouth on mine.

Out on the frozen reservoir, we skated and slid in our boots, hooting, yelling, and singing Christmas carols at the tops of our lungs. We made up our own zany words to the songs. I felt free. Happy. I wanted to stay out until the gray light of dawn crept over the ice.

We got so drunk that, at one point, Trudy and Doug lay down as if they were in bed together. Patrick thought it was hysterically funny and twirled me around until I plopped onto my bottom.

Then, laughing crazily, he pulled Doug's knit Yankee hat right off his head.

Some hint that they'd had a falling out. That they were bitter rivals, now.

"Give it back, Morgan. "

But Doug was not laughing. He stood up, glaring at Patrick.

"Give it back, Morgan. You know that hat is special to me."

Instead, Patrick tossed the hat to me; giggling, I caught it and threw it back to Patrick.

"Give him the hat!" Trudy said, her speech slurred.

"Shit, asshole. It was my fucking dad's. Give it back before I knock out your teeth."

Patrick circled Doug, pretend jabbing at him like a boxer. "C'mon, big shot. Let's see what you got."

Doug swiped at him, reaching for and missing the hat. "Look, Morgan. I thought we talked this through. I was just kidding. I swear I wasn't going to tell anyone."

"Take it. Go ahead," Patrick said, no longer laughing, his eyes the cold blue of a mountain lake.

"Tell anyone what?" I shivered. Somehow, all the fun had gone out of the night, along with my buzz. Doug's gaze flashed to mine. There was desperation in his eyes. Fear.

Then, linebacker that he was, Doug sprang at Patrick in a tackle. But lithe and sleek Patrick leaped out of the way. Doug crash-landed in a belly flop. The ice, thick as concrete where we stood, supported his bulk. Laughing, Patrick flung the hat far into the center of the reservoir.

"Fuck! What'd you do that for?"

"Leave it, Dougie!" Trudy shrieked. "Let it go!"

Patrick stood up and shrugged. "No reason. I know we're cool, asshole. We've been friends forever. Now get your hat. Let's go home. I have a headache."

"The ice could be thinner over there," I said softly.

"Oh, for crying out loud." Trudy stumbled to her feet. "I'll get the damn hat."

"No," Patrick snarled. "Let Lewis get his own goddamned hat. I was going to give it to you, asshole. You didn't have to tackle me for it."

Doug chewed his bottom lip and stared at Patrick, as if he was considering breaking his jaw, and then Doug stalked across the ice. I'd always thought Patrick and Doug were the best of friends, but what passed between them in that moment looked a lot like pure hate.

It had been a viciously cold winter, so none of us thought the ice was actually thin. Just the week before, our dads had all gone ice fishing together.

Still, as I watched Doug walk further and further out onto the reservoir, to the place where his hat had landed, I felt uneasy. The brandy no longer had the power to warm me. I was cold to the bone.

"C'mon," Patrick said. "I'll take you home."

"What about Doug?"

"Fuck him."

I couldn't help myself. The brandy had loosened my tongue. "What did Doug promise not to talk about?"

Patrick had me by the arm, almost pulling me along. "Shut the fuck up, Teresa!" he screamed, and smacked me across the cheek. The look in his eyes was colder than the ice below our feet.

That's when I knew that, under the beautiful surface, Patrick Morgan had no heart.

That's also when I heard the crack, as loud as rifle fire. Half of Doug's body was submerged in the freezing water. He called out for us to help him, pawing vainly at the slippery sides of the hole he'd fallen in.

Trudy started to run to him, but she didn't get far.

Patrick grabbed her by the feet and sent her sprawling onto her stomach, and then dragged her by her ankles toward the shore.

"Let me go!" She wailed and kicked, but Patrick wouldn't let her go free.

I stood paralyzed as Doug screamed and pleaded for us to help him.

If only I'd run when I had the chance. I could have saved him. I've relived that moment, again and again. Me, watching as Doug struggled to climb out of the hole. But the ice kept cracking under his weight, the hole getting wider and wider.

Trudy stood up again and skidded wildly across the ice toward Doug.

Patrick grabbed her by the arm, spun her around, and punched her in the face. Hard. She fell unconscious.

He turned to face me, a weird half-smile on his face. "You're not going to try to help, are you Teresa? We both know the ice is too thin there. You'll fall in with him."

The smile didn't match with the warning. It looked, I know this sounds weird—but Patrick Morgan's smile looked triumphant.

Doug had stopped struggling, bobbing in the water at the center of the hole like a buoy. Moments later, he slipped quietly under the surface and didn't come back up.

"If either of you ever say a word about tonight," Patrick whispered, the triumphant smile still curling his lips "you'll join him."

—⁓—

I never did find out what secret Dougie Lewis was keeping for Patrick Morgan.

It died with him under the ice of the reservoir.

But the memory of that night has festered inside of me, ever since.

They didn't find his body until after all the ice had melted two months later. He washed ashore down near the dam, three miles away.

Now

The neatly written account is signed by Teresa Winston and Trudy Durban, dated March, 1979. Below the signatures are two fingerprints, apparently stamped in their blood. Articles about the accident clutter another double-page spread. At the bottom, scrawled hastily in red marker in the same sloppy printing are the words:

PATRICK MORGAN IS A MURDERER. PATRICK MORGAN IS A RAPIST.

"What the hell do we do with this?" Marisa asks, breaking the silence.

I stare at the open book in my hands, at the only words written by my mother that I have ever read. "Nothing. It doesn't change anything."

"Jeremy. Do you think, maybe, Susannah saw this and acted on it? Tried to threaten Patrick Morgan? Covering up one murder would certainly be a motive for another."

I'm still blank, numb, staring at my mother's girlish handwriting. My voice, when I finally find it, comes out strained and hollow. "I'm not sure. And if she did, there's no evidence she did anything about it. And Patrick wouldn't care. He was beyond that. There's nothing I can really do with this information. Let's just get the fuck out of here."

I return Trudy's book to its hiding place under the floorboards.

—∞—

Outside, rain slashes down in blinding sheets, the melted snow rushing down the road in torrents. Spears of lightning slice through the bare trees. Thunder shakes the ground. There's no way we're going to make it home on foot in this mess. Water will short out my high-tech leg.

Reluctantly, I phone Dad and ask him to come get us. I tell him we'd had to find shelter under Susannah's porch when the clouds broke open. I say nothing about the keys I stole or what I'd found under the floorboards. Someday, I will. But not now.

In the car, Dad eyes me skeptically, but seems too exhausted to interrogate me further. Once we get home, I slip the keys back in the envelope under the pile of papers where I found them.

—∞—

I lie on my bed, puzzled, my mind skimming through the information at hand. Nothing adds up. Nothing in Trudy's book really gets me any closer to solving the mystery behind Susannah's disappearance and death. There's no mention of the secret Patrick Morgan and Dougie Lewis shared that got one of them killed. It's all just a guessing game. Maybe she really doesn't want me to know, after all. *But why?* Why come back from the dead only to confuse the only person who gives a shit?

Patrick Morgan was a murderer, no doubt, and possibly even worse, something that doesn't surprise me in the least. And it's just as likely my mother drove herself into the Gorge because of guilt over what she'd witnessed and kept secret all those years. As far as my mother's death, it doesn't look like I'll ever know the whole truth.

But there's nothing to link any of this to Susannah. No evidence that she found her mother's book and tried to use it. She'd certainly found out about Ryan and Spake, and threatened to expose them. Which still makes Ryan the prime suspect, since he was there at the scene. But that still doesn't sit right with me. How would he have had time to dispose of her body?

The reservoir will eventually give up its dead. When winter ends, we'll know.

The answer drifts between the shadows, eluding me. Susannah's ghost has quieted and retreated. I wonder if this is a sign that I'm close to a breakthrough.

How many historians have been confronted with bits of information that baffled them? Did they solve age-old historic mysteries in their sleep, or in bursts of intuition?

All I can hope for is another dream to guide me to the truth.

—⁓—

I do dream. About the night Susannah took Ryan and me on the candlelit boat ride to Pirate Island to seal our pact.

I wake up crying.

For my lost illusions. My lost leg.

And for my mother, whose own guilt may have destroyed her.

But mostly for the Susannah I lost. The one that never really was.

Because, finally, I know.

I know where she is.

—⁓—

It's the middle of the night, but I drive to the place on Reservoir Road where Susannah disappeared. The temperature has dropped again and it's snowing lightly, a thin powder of white dusting the asphalt. Striding smoothly across the road, Veronica and my natural leg working together in a passable stroll, I pause at the guardrail that marks the craggy decline to the water's edge. A sliver of moon peeks through the cloud cover to light a path. I climb over the rail and proceed to pick my way gingerly down the jagged rocks.

I'm much steadier, now, I assure myself.

Veronica protests and whirs as she tries to adjust for the uneven terrain. Still, I make good progress and reach the edge.

I stare into the fathomless deep, thin sheets of ice coating parts of its dark surface, and think of those who met their end in the cold waters of Riverton. Mom. Douglas Lewis.

My dream of a line of daisies drifting on summer water superimposes itself over the water's surface.

The line points to our tiny island on the far side of the reservoir. Pirate Island.

Dreams don't lie.

There's a pile of old rowboats turned upside down a few yards away. I climb over the rocks to the jumble of boats. One boat has a set of oars. With the recent thaw, most of the ice has melted. If I'm lucky, I'll have a clear path to the island.

I unstrap Veronica. Just in case I don't make it back, I stand her in a place where someone will notice. Where someone will find her and maybe hook her up with a nice stump that will love her as much as mine does. There's no reason to waste a perfectly good leg.

I push the boat into the water.

I pause to stare at the moon. It looks back at me, a white eye, and I wonder if I should be baying at it like all madmen do, because what I am about to do can only be classified as insane.

In the frigid air, I think I hear Susannah urging to me to join her and Mom in the depths. Already, I can taste the rank water gushing into my lungs.

Drowning is still my deepest dread.

But there's no other way. I have to do this.

Now

I suppress my terror and suck in quick breaths. The motion of rowing hurts my sprained arm, but I press on, navigating the ice sheets like a cheap re-enactment of the Titanic. But the moon dips behind a thick tuft of clouds and I'm plunged into near darkness. Lights wink on the distant shore and I question the wisdom of this slow cruise to hell.

I hit a snag fifty feet from the banks of Pirate Island. A crust of ice still surrounds the island and the boat can't get through. I have no choice but to climb out onto the melting sheets and pray the water won't swallow me like it did Doug Lewis.

I lie on my stomach and propel myself across the frozen surface, since hopping on one leg won't do. I'd laugh at myself gliding across the ice like a seal, if the fear of falling through the perilously thin crust and into the black water below wasn't chewing through my intestinal wall.

I'm a few feet from the shore when there's a creaking groan and a sickening crack. The ice gives way, and I crash into the water, sputtering. It's so cold it burns. But instead of slipping into panic mode, I fight wildly for my life. I flail and paddle until the ice that blocks my path breaks into pieces and my single foot finds a ledge. Miraculously, I flop onto to the rocks, my heart firing like an adrenaline-fueled machine gun.

The wind tears at me. In my soaked clothes, with the temperature well below freezing, it won't be long until I'm flash-frozen. My phone is waterlogged, so there'll be no eleventh hour rescue if I can't get myself out of here.

I shimmy on my butt across the craggy snow-covered terrain. Blanketed in dirt and leaves, as if someone had tried to conceal it, is a rowboat beached on the shore. I shiver, and not just from the cold.

Because I know, somewhere on this island, *our* island, she's here.

The ground evens out and I slither on my side, not sure what I'm looking for other than a place to get warm.

But something does catch my eye. In the center of the tiny island, surrounded by a stand of trees, is a snow-covered canopy. On closer inspection, I realize it is a half-collapsed old army tent and wonder if it's a neglected campground from long ago.

And then I see it. Her shrine to us, the papier-mâché statue made of three twining tree trunks. Faded and nearly unrecognizable, it's bedecked with garlands of shriveled flowers.

Cold penetrates my wet clothes, the chill squeezing deep into bone. By now, I'm quaking so violently, it's hard to think. I'm not really sure why I'm here and why, suddenly, all I want to do is curl up and sleep.

I've had enough bouts with hypothermia to know the signs. If I go to sleep, I may never wake again.

I haul myself into the tent and root around for anything to warm me up, but it's too dark, impossible to see much of anything. And it smells indescribably bad. There's a jumble of clothes in the center of the tent. I feel around. It's a sleeping bag, but it's stiff and frozen as if it had been wet. I stumble on something colder and harder.

A hand.

My insides twist wildly. I'm going to retch.

I throw back the tent flap and a strip of moonlight falls across the body inside the sleeping bag.

I scream.

Susannah's open eyes are sunken and filmy like dried-out eggs. Leathery gray skin has begun to draw back over her skull, her teeth bared in a ghoulish smile. Both hands are palm up, the ragged slashes where the tender flesh of her wrists has been slit black with dried blood. In one hand is a cell phone, in the other a small notebook sealed inside a plastic bag.

Shaking, I zip open the sleeping bag.

Susannah died in a black dress painted with skeletal white lines. But they're not meant to represent bones. They're roots.

For a moment, I'm lost in the strange beauty of the scene. In the dim moonlight, her hair splayed around her, Susannah in her death shroud looks almost like she's asleep.

Susannah: *Then*

Ryan had his secrets, too. I wonder what he would have done if he knew mine.

The moment I saw the way Derek Spake and Ryan looked at each other at the meet last spring, I knew that something had changed between them. I guess I just didn't want to admit it to myself. I'd known about Derek's orientation from our weekend art class together. I shared stuff with him, too. Mostly hinted about my things with older men.

How being with older men made me feel protected. Safe.

I just never happened to mention one of those men was Ryan's father.

Yeah. I know. How low can you go? But Patrick was indescribably kind to me. I know he was old. But he was so hot. He was fascinated by me. Enchanted, he used to say. At the same time, he took care of me like the father I never had. Bought me things.

Try and understand what it feels like to grow up a stunted tree in a barren wasteland, always straining your face to the sun for a warm ray. Sucking on stones for water. I took sustenance wherever I could get it.

Patrick hated his wife, he'd tell me. He'd married the wrong woman. Someone who loved someone else. He was lonely. We clung to each other as a matter of survival.

And Ryan. Odd as it sounds. I loved him, too. Switching between the father and the son was like drinking two similar yet different wines, one rich and aged, the other light, sweet and new. Their love warmed the killing frost in my soul. I would have shriveled up and died without it.

And of course, there was sweet, awkward Jeremy Glass. His eyes were as dark and wise as the earth, but he hid them behind a joker's mask.

I knew he loved me from the moment we met. But I also knew his love was a weight that would drag us both down. Jeremy was always there when I needed him. But he deserved better than me. I could never provide the kind of love he needed to keep him afloat. I just didn't have it to give.

Yet, selfishly, I took what I could from him. I made his sweet obsession with me a side dish to Patrick and Ryan. I used him as a back-up flotation device to keep myself from drowning.

I supposed I thought I could go flitting between lovers, like a honeybee gathering pollen, forever. If I stopped, I'd have to look at myself. It was easier to look outside of myself for answers.

I guess I had it coming. Ryan was like a drug I couldn't kick. His ocean-blue eyes. Perfect lips. Hair like woven sunlight. Body like a god—except those scars he never showed to anyone but me. Scars he said he'd gotten in a boating accident.

I never considered that he didn't need me the same way I needed him.

That he needed something else.

—⁂—

Last spring, when I'd suspected something was brewing between Ryan and him, I had it out with Derek. I threatened him to get him to stay away from Ryan. Insisted Ryan was mine. But he'd thrown the threats back at me. Told me he'd tell Ryan I was fucking older guys. I'm not sure if he knew about Patrick. Maybe it was just a lucky guess. Spake may be a jerk, but he's devious and smart. I couldn't take the chance of Ryan finding out about me and Patrick.

So we were at an impasse, Derek and I.

This past October I caught them. I'd been out walking, looking for branches and twigs for my new art project. They were parked on one of the little-used dirt service roads that run through the nature preserve, the windows fogged up from their breath. I came right up to the car and peered in.

They didn't see me. But I saw enough. There was no doubt what they were doing in there.

Instead of confronting Ryan, I invited him to dinner at my house. I needed to know if he was serious about Derek, or if it was just a fling. I was well aware of all his past lapses. Who was I to complain, with my track record?

But Ryan always came back to me. I was the default. I was home base.

Mother was out of town for the weekend, as usual, and I didn't expect her back until Sunday evening. That Saturday night I made roast chicken and potatoes with peas. I lit candles. Poured wine. Dressed in my Pirate Queen outfit. Lit a roaring fire in the hearth.

Ryan smiled at me, candlelight dancing in his eyes. He took hold of my hand.

"I'm always going to love you, Suze. You know that. But I finally realized who I am. And what I need. I'm different. I just never understood."

I sipped at my wine. I glanced appreciatively at my reflection in the dining room mirrors. The effect was hypnotic, sensual. Yes. I've always been able to work my special brand of magic.

"You don't mean that, Ryan. This is just a phase."

"It's not a phase, Suze. I'm gay. I've always sort of known it. But, you know, with my dad, I just couldn't go there."

I sipped at the wine again and tossed my hair over my shoulder. I was tipsy, on my fourth glass. I'm not sure what I said. I know it was crazy, but I still felt certain he was mistaken. That he wanted me. I leaned over to kiss him, but he pulled away, spilling his wine all over his plate of food.

"I'm sorry, Suze. I didn't know for sure until I met Derek. I didn't mean to hurt you."

He was apologizing. Not begging, not pleading. *Apologizing.*

It was true. Ryan didn't want me.

But I couldn't let go. I threw my glass at the wall behind him and stood. I told him that I'd been fucking his father. How his father was the *real* man, and a better one than he'd ever be.

And that if he broke up with me, I'd tell his father all about him and Spake.

Ryan turned every shade of red imaginable, then whiter than a sheet.

"You're crazy."

"I know."

"Let me go."

"I can't."

Ryan stared at me silently, his lips moving, then stormed out.

I sat at the dining room table, gulped down the rest of the wine bottle, and cried.

—⁂—

Jeremy Now

The white painted roots form a delicate filigree at the edges of Susannah's death shroud, coiling and twisting toward her abdomen, culminating in a large skull and crossbones.

The poison seed and its toxic roots.

No one murdered Susannah.

She did it to herself.

Nearby, on the tent floor, is the artist's blade that made the cuts. Leave it to Susannah to end her life methodically and artistically, with the tools of the trade.

I swallow back nausea, but it's no good.

I'm going to be sick.

I haul myself out of the tent and spew my insides out onto the snow.

Chest heaving, I lie on my back and stare up at the moon, tremors exploding through me in violent spasms.

I'm tired. So tired. I'll sleep for a moment and then find the strength to go back in there and wrap myself in that filthy blood-encrusted sleeping bag.

No. If I sleep, I'm going to die out here. "I don't fucking want to join you, Susannah!"

Why did you do this to yourself? Do you want to take me with you?

Darkness steals over the moon and I slip down the rabbit hole of oblivion.

—⁂—

She settles beside me in the snow, silver light glinting in her eyes. She's never looked more beautiful, and the animal urge inside my dying brain refuses to go quietly. She strokes my hair.

So much power, I think. Enough to give a dying boy a hard-on.

But I have no strength left to act on it. Even within the hallucination, I can feel the life force ebbing out of me.

"It only hurts a little after you cross over," she says gently.

"Fuck you," I spit. I hate her. Hate her for turning my love for her into a weapon. If it would do any good, I'd sock her in the teeth, but she's a ghost, and I can't move anyway.

"We'll have so much time together, Jeremy. Isn't that what you always wanted?"

"I didn't know what I wanted, Susannah. I was just a horny idiot."

But I know that isn't entirely true.

It was just that I loved a different Susannah. The one who didn't exist.

"No. You were different."

I take in a shivering breath. My cells are shutting down one by one. This is it. I'm going to die for nothing other than my own stupidity.

Maybe fate always wanted this. I'd cheated death twice before.

Third time's a charm.

"No. I wasn't. I was just dumber. Why did you do this?"

Rage shudders through me.

It's amazing the clarity one has in the moments before dying, I think idiotically as my breaths wind down.

"You used me," I shout.

A single tear rolls down her cheek. I gulp in one long shivering breath, then fade into darkness as the sky drops down on me.

CHAPTER

thirty - nine

Now (January 13th)

I wake to the sensation of being burned alive. I'm encased in plastic, the ground under me shuddering and grinding. A face peers down at me.

"Good thing you left your leg out there like that, kid, or you'd be a goner."

I fall back into oblivion, convinced I'm in hell.

—⁋—

I finally realize what's going on from the newspaper someone has left on the table beside my bed.

MISSING GIRL'S DEATH RULED A SUICIDE.

I don't have enough strength to read the rest.

—⁋—

But it's the notebook that has my name on it that tells the truth. Finally.

Inside is just one line.

A link to YouTube.

—⁋—

It takes a few more days for me to gather the courage to look.

Spake and I visit Ryan every day. He's making slow and steady progress. He's up walking, his wavering eyes have begun to focus better, and he's begun to speak in a slow, halting, and somewhat garbled manner. And he smiles. A lot.

His night terrors are gone.

So are mine.

But I can feel her waiting. Waiting for my final act.

I know how. But Susannah still needs me to know *why*.

Susannah: *Then*

I sat at the dining room table, head resting on my arms. When I looked up, Mother stood there, cradling a big white book.

"So," she said, conversationally. "I just saw Ryan."

"Oh, God. You were listening?"

"I tried to warn you, Susannah. I tried to help you understand that the Morgans are the devil's spawn. But what did you do?"

She took a seat beside me, her voice suddenly dropping to a whisper. "Bitch. Slut. I heard everything. *Everything*."

She set the book on the table. What I'd thought was a Bible was the furthest thing from it.

Mother opened the book, leafing through page after page of gruesomely defaced photos. She pulled out a firsthand account of the death of her high school sweetheart, written by Jeremy's long-dead mother, Teresa. The note claimed that Mother's long-ago boyfriend, Douglas Lewis, was left by Patrick Morgan to die in the icy waters of the reservoir.

I didn't want to believe it.

Then she pulled an envelope out from the back of the album. On it, she'd printed in her same messy hand. **HUSH MONEY**.

She pulled out a thick sheaf of photocopied checks, some for as much as $5,000.

"If it isn't true, why do you think he paid me all this money to shut me up? Who do you think owns the deed to this house?"

I stared at Mother, speechless, as she tossed the envelope with the checks into the fire.

"I'm sick of taking his blood money. Teresa took it, too. But then she stopped. We didn't talk much, but she called to tell me she was going to go public."

The blood rushed to my head and I felt dizzy. "What? What are you saying?"

"I'm telling you that the man you have been sleeping with is the monster who murdered the love of my life, and who ran Teresa Glass off the road to her death. And do you want to know why he killed Dougie? Do you?"

I tried to stomp out of the dining room, but Mother grabbed my wrist and squeezed with the strength of a man.

"He killed Dougie because one night, in some town upstate, Dougie watched Patrick rape, then kill, a younger girl. A girl of thirteen. Patrick always liked them young."

I was sobbing, trying to free myself from her iron grip.

"Where do you think you're going?" Mother's voice grew progressively louder, until she was shouting. "To see your demon lover? He's enslaved you, and now your soul is going straight to hell!"

"You're crazy!"

"Am I? What do you think of your precious Patrick Morgan now?"

I pulled free and ran up the stairs to the bathroom, threw up my dinner, slumped to the floor, and cried some more.

Patrick Morgan, my savior, my surrogate father, the man I'd come to idolize, was a murderer. A monster. How could someone who could be that cruel truly love me?

He used me. Used me to punish my mother. Tormenting her and extorting her wasn't enough. He had to destroy me, too.

And Ryan. His love for me was a sham. A masquerade.

What did that leave me with?

Only Jeremy. Who I cared too much about to taint with my poison.

I heard the clomp of Mother's heels on the staircase as she headed to her bedroom and slammed her door.

In the medicine cabinet, I kept razor blades to refill my shaver. I sat on the tile, the sharp edge hovering a millimeter away from my wrist.

I would have sliced deep into the flesh, severing the vein. I would have bled myself out all over the bathroom floor.

But that would have been too easy.

A plan started to form.

Now:

At last, on the night before I'm to return to school, I click on the link.

Susannah speaks directly into the camera. Directly at me.

—∽—

"Okay, so you loved me."

She tightens her ponytail, clears her throat, and looks straight into the camera. Straight at me.

Straight into me.

"That was only because you didn't really know me."

Susannah looks away.

"I decided to end it all. Not in a fit of desperation, but in a way that would shame the people who'd wounded me to my core. Maybe, if I was really smart, I'd take them down with me."

She looks at me again and I shiver at the feral coldness there, and wonder how I never saw this side of Susannah before.

"I had plenty of time to plan."

A smile curls her lips and it's even more chilling than her cunning stare.

"And you, Jeremy, would be my unwitting accomplice.

"If you're as smart as I think you are, you'll have unearthed the truth by now."

She swallows, her voice is cracking. "And maybe, someday, you'll be able to forgive me."

—∽—

Susannah's image fades to black.

To the tune of a single lilting cello, words write themselves in white script across the black screen.

For Jeremy, with Love and Squalor

The writing fades, and a wavering, white line cuts across the black. Below the line, a single red seed pulses and sprouts hairline-thin roots that fill the black space in an intricate tangle of scratchy squiggles. Curling tendrils pierce the ground and draw a white tree, its branches fanning out like skeletal fingers.

The image dissolves and the cello music fades to silence.

I stare, unable to rip my eyes from the dark screen, paralyzed with emotions I can barely identify.

"Roots," Susannah's voice whispers. "You always loved history, Jeremy. But what if that history, and those roots, are the very things that want to strangle you? Drag you down back into the dirt with them? Jeremy, all the roots in this town, all the poison roots have a single poison seed."

—∽—

I suck in a breath and begin to shake. I want so badly to shut my computer and turn it off. But I can't. I hug my arms close to my chest and force myself to listen.

The blackness gives way to Susannah, seated in front of the wrinkled white sheet, alive. So alive.

"I'm sorry for manipulating you, Jeremy. For using your love to get back at the ones who hurt me."

"And most of all, I'm sorry for the nonsense about raising me from the dead. I hope you didn't fall for that. When I kill myself, I mean to stay dead. I only threw that in so you'd really believe I was gone."

She looks straight into the camera and says flatly. "I want you to find Mother's book. I was going to use it and expose all those roots to the light…but, Jeremy, it wasn't enough reason to live. I just wanted to end it. And to take them all with me."

"I knew you wouldn't rest if you'd thought someone had killed me. That you wouldn't rest until you'd uncovered every last secret. I'm sorry."

She looks down, hair falling like a curtain over her face. When she looks into the camera again, her eyes are shiny with tears. "I wish I could have loved you back, Jeremy. But my heart died a long time before I did."

—⁓—

I turn off the computer and cover myself in blankets, waiting for the dark to claim me, for her to come so I can apologize for not getting it. For missing the gnawing emptiness behind the radiant smile.

But she never does.

EPILOGUE

Now (April 7th)

Once the ground thawed enough, we chartered a boat and buried Susannah on her island, the island Celia Morgan bought from the state and had officially renamed "Pirate Island."

With Spake's help, Ryan shuffled up to the grave's edge and tossed the silver Kabbalah pendant on top of the traditional Jewish oak coffin I insisted she be buried in.

"Ashes to a-a-ashes, d-dust t-to dust," he said in his faltering stutter. And I began to shovel in the dirt that would fill her grave.

In his own way, I guess Ryan really had loved her, too.

Beside Susannah's three-spired sculpture, we'd installed a simple headstone that read:

Here lies the Pirate Queen. At peace at last.

But, sadly, I know that isn't true.

Not yet, anyway.

—⁂—

Trudy Durban was declared unfit to stand trial. In jail, her weak hold on reality tore loose and she slipped completely into madness, her ravings about murders and devils ignored. Strangely, the day after her commitment to the psych ward, Trudy Durban's house mysteriously burned to the ground, the evidence of Patrick

Morgan's crimes gone up in smoke along with the last traces of Trudy Durban's sanity.

In the end, Patrick Morgan got to take his good name to the grave, his esteemed memory marked by a statue of his likeness erected by a grateful town.

What waits for him on the other side, who can say?

I'll never know if Patrick Morgan really did drive my mother off the road or if she was driven to madness by her own personal demons.

I'm happy to let her rest in peace.

With the poisonous tree cut down, the roots are better left buried. Let some future historian dig them up.

For me, at least, the drowning dreams have stopped.

At my dad's, Celia's, and Marisa's insistence, I've been attending Teen-Anon meetings three times a week.

And though there are times I would have cut off my other leg for a just a sip, I haven't had a single drop of alcohol in four months.

—⁂—

Often, I walk down to the reservoir and gaze at Pirate Island. On clear nights, when the moon is blazing over the water, I think I see her waiting by the shoreline, her dress rustling in the breeze, and my stomach twists in knots.

I don't think she expected me to bring her back. She thought it was a joke. What I summoned from beyond the grave was just the angry, hurt part.

I prefer to remember the girl from my art class with the magical smile.

But before I can do that, I have to set the sad, desolate echo of Susannah free.

—⁂—

It's a mild day for early April. There's a small crowd gathered at the Riverton High track. I spot Lyle Hoffman, but he's not looking at me. He's staring at Ralph, my new running blade, a deranged smile twitching under his mustache.

I give Ralph a test bounce. The stump balks a little. It's used to snuggling up to Veronica. But change is good.

Ralph is pretty weird, though. He's a lot like Veronica at the top, but after the knee joint he curves into a wicked black piece of metal, like a bent helicopter blade.

I spot Ryan walking slowly, without a cane or walker, clutching Spake's arm, an orange ski cap perched on his head. He's still a bit too unsteady to walk on his own, but he's getting there. The mirrored glasses are Spake's touch to hide his "googly eyes," as Ryan calls them. He still gets headaches from eyestrain, and his speech is a little slurred and halting, but that doesn't dim his smile.

Marisa jumps up and down next to Celia and my Dad. She's landed a full scholarship to Columbia and plans to study medicine. We worry about how it will be for us when we go our separate ways in the fall, her to Columbia and me to Duke.

It was Marisa who convinced me to write the essay that won me the full track scholarship to Duke University, the first ever granted to a disabled applicant at that school. It documented in gruesome detail the ordeal of losing my leg—minus the drugs, alcohol, and sexually abusive ghosts, of course—and argued the point that, even with one leg, I can run faster than most candidates with two.

I'm here, today, to prove my point.

—·ᴍ·—

There's also a horde of TV crews and news reporters. I've gotten kind of used to them following me around. After all, I'm the one-legged miracle boy who solved the mystery of Susannah Durban's disappearance.

—·ᴍ·—

I take off running. The wind whispers through my hair like a hundred kisses. My stride is uneven at first, the hard thud of one sneaker against pavement alternating with the springy bounce I can only feel in my thigh and pelvis. But I run, laughing, my speed increasing, the steady thump of my heart against my ribcage like the beat of a ceremonial drum.

I'm back.

And life is good.

—⚏—

Later that day, the setting sun stains the sky a brilliant vermillion. Marisa and I climb the rocks to the water's edge. Veronica still doesn't like the uneven terrain, but with Marisa to steady me we make it to the shore. I set down the knapsack I've loaded up with artifacts, things I might once have added to my collection.

I've finished clearing out most of the junk gathering dust on my shelves. I've located each of Susannah's things, squirreled away in odd corners of my room.

I'm not so sure if history is my thing anymore. I've dug up enough dirt and unearthed enough roots for a lifetime.

But Susannah's presence hovers at the edge of my awareness, still tethered to this world.

Until I let her go.

Marisa's eyes gleam in the waning light, her dark hair loose and blowing wild. Like it always does, my heart leaps into a full gallop at the sight. My mouth slips open and I edge closer. She sighs, her eyes closing and we kiss, softly at first, the heat that lingers under my skin simmering quickly to a full boil. I press her against me, my breaths quickening.

When I hold Marisa close, I have a hard time letting go. But she pries herself free, laughing, and reminds me that we have work to do.

"Later," I murmur, my nose in her hair. "My reward for a job well done."

Marisa's not a theory of a girl or an ideal of a girl. She's not the desperate fabrication of a troubled, miserable boy. She's the real deal.

I'm not sure how I'll manage at Duke without her to keep me warm at night, but that's life, I guess.

Like I did on my last disastrous trip to the island, I leave Veronica standing tall, a beacon. Just in case.

Marisa helps me out of the boat, but I've brought my crutches so I won't have to crawl this time.

I take in a deep gulp of cool air, shivering. Though there's no sign of her, I can feel Susannah's essence inside the marrow of my bones.

Marisa sets out the candles in a five-pointed star and marks the space with masking tape. Since we're not really sure how you return the dead to the great beyond, we've improvised our own ritual.

In the months since my ordeal, my anger has faded.

Susannah nearly took me down with her. But that's what cornered animals do.

We were all strangled by the same venomous roots that grew and twisted from the same toxic seed.

Patrick Morgan.

I count myself as the lucky one. I just had to lose a leg to get free.

But it's hard for me to stay angry at anyone, really. After all, I'm reasonable Jeremy Glass.

We build a circle of rocks inside the five-pointed star. I ease myself to the ground and carefully arrange Susannah's personal effects in the middle: the Death Book, which Ryan stumbled upon in his late father's study, the drawings, the cigar box, the photos, the jewelry she'd left for Marisa. I've deleted all my YouTube links to her videos and animations, though they will exist in cyberspace forever.

After piling the artifacts with dry leaves, I set it all ablaze. I hold Marisa against me and together we watch the smoke coil in a white spiral against the indigo sky, taking the last of Susannah with it.

T H E   E N D

ACKNOWLEDGEMENTS

I'd been writing a fairly long time before I wrote *Breaking Glass*. My transition from artist to writer was neither easy nor smooth, and I needed a lot of support along the way. My path to publication was also bumpy with many off-road adventures—so I have a lot of people to thank for believing in me.

First, I must thank my wonderful mother, Sherry Amowitz, who always reminded me not to leave my creativity behind in childhood, to always carry it with me for all of my life. For filling our house with books and encouraging me to read them.

To my daughter Rebecca, who while growing up endured so many nights of my writings as her bedtime stories. And to my son Benjamin, who still managed to read at least parts of every book I wrote, including *Breaking Glass.*, and make intelligent suggestions.

To my husband, Richard Zank, who patiently endured his artist wife's transition from a somewhat nutty artist to a full-out crazy writer, and gradually accepted the change.

When I first began writing, I filled countless spiral notebooks with my ramblings. It's hard to believe I found anyone who would read that, but I did—my dear true-blue friend and sister-of-choice, Joanne Flaster, who read the entire monstrosity, along with my cousin Mark Stein. To this day, they both insist they enjoyed the beast, which will never again see the light of day.

To another dear friend and sister of choice, Jill Danenberg, who tolerated my strange behavior and was so unfailingly supportive that I tried to talk her into becoming my agent. To her son, David Lichtenberg, who also played his part in cheering me on.

And to yet another dear friend and sister-of-choice, Debbie Cohen, who not only stood by me, but is the unofficial creator of Jeremy Glass. Debbie, a psychotherapist, is the first person I run to when I need counsel on either a personal or writing matter. When I described Jeremy and his drinking problems to Deb, here is what she said, "Well, no wonder he drinks! You should have his mother die in a way that really traumatized him, that way he drinks to self-medicate his post-traumatic stress disorder."

There you go. Jeremy in a nutshell.

That morning I started writing *Breaking Glass.* and never looked back. Thank you, Debbie—for jump-starting this book and being a wonderful friend!

I can't really go on without also mentioning Debbie's son, Josh Karp, a voracious reader, who also read parts of every book I wrote and encouraged me every step of the way. And to his dad, Andy Karp, Debbie's husband, and one of my favorite people in the world, for just listening to my long-winded gab sessions for the last bazillion years.

While we're on the subject of the Karp family, I must also mention that the town they live in, Croton-on-Hudson, NY, with its twisty wooded roads, rivers, gorges, and cool Commie past, is the model for the fictitious Riverton, NY.

A special shout-out to my former student and current tutor, Christian Santiago, who read all of *Breaking Glass.* and peppered me with endless Facebook messages (usually in all caps) to broadcast his concerns and freak-outs. Thank you for being my very first fan, Mr. Santiago.

And to all my graphic design students at Bronx Community College—you are the spark that fuels my creativity and keeps me young. Just knowing all of you, I feel I can live forever. I know so many of you spend a lot of energy thanking me—but seriously, the pleasure is all mine.

And now, with the deepest gratitude, I want to thank my writing family. To the Cudas, my writing group of over eight years who basically taught me HOW to write and talked me down from the ledge more times than I can count—Heidi Ayarbe, Pippa Bayliss, Linda Budzinski, Dhonielle Clayton, Trish Eklund, Lindsay Eland, Cathy Giordano, Cyndy Henzel, Christine Johnson, and Kate Milford. You guys are the keepers of my soul. And—Dhonielle and Christine—you know how much I rely on you both, my two little on call Muses.

To Colleen Rowan Kosinski, my dear "twin" and tireless beta reader—I am rooting for you. To Michelle McLean, my crazy partner in all matter of schemes—you are my human Red Bull—if only I could keep up with you.

And lastly, but in no way least—to the wonderful family that is Spencer Hill Press. I had no idea that signing with you would be an exciting new chapter in my life that would not only provide a home for my future works, but also launch my career as a cover designer. There aren't enough pages for me to express my love of this wonderful motley crew. Kate Kaynak, the miracle worker—you have created a company in your own big-hearted, genius image. To my die-hard editor, Vikki Ciaffone—I just love you. To Rich Storrs, thank you for your laser eyes. To Laura Ownbey, for ripping this ms to shreds so I could put it back together even better than before. And to Jennifer Allis Provost, for being my total kickass go-to girl.

To all my fellow writers at SHP—you all are so supportive and wonderful. It is an honor to be a part of this amazing family.

Jenna Oliver doesn't have time to get involved with one boy, let alone two.
All Jenna wants is to escape her evaporating small town and her alcoholic mother. She's determined she'll go to college and find a life that is wholly hers—one that isn't tainted by her family's past. But when the McAlister twins move to town and Jenna gets involved with both of them, she learns the life she planned may not be the one she gets.

Ian McAlister doesn't want to start over; he wants to remember.
Ian can't recall a single thing from the last three months—and he seems to be losing more memories every day. His family knows the truth, but no one will tell him what really happened before he lost his memory. When he meets Jenna, Ian believes that he can be normal again because she makes not remembering something he can handle.

The secret Ian can't remember is the one Luke McAlister can't forget.
Luke has always lived in the shadow of his twin brother until Jenna stumbles into his life. She sees past who he's supposed to be, and her kiss brings back the spark that life stole. Even though Luke feels like his brother deserves her more, Luke can't resist Jenna—which is the trigger that makes Ian's memory return.

**Jenna, Ian, and Luke are about to learn there are only
so many secrets you can keep before the truth comes to reclaim you.**

SPENCER HILL CONTEMPORARY • spencerhillcontemporary.com

PODs
A Novel
The end of the world is only the beginning.
Michelle Pickett

THE LOST IMPERIALS ~ BOOK ONE

SHERRY D. FICKLIN & TYLER H. JOLLEY

EXTRACTED

An infamous brother and sister have been stolen from history and drafted to opposite sides of a war no one can win—a battle for time itself.

Founded and run by the disembodied head of a mad genius, the Tesla Institute is responsible for locating, retrieving, and training teens with the ability to Rift through time and space. Seventeen-year-old Ember has no memory of her life before being brought to the Institute, but she's made a home there. Just as she's about to officially join the ranks of the Rifters, memories of her bloody past begin to slide through the cracks. Now she's forced to question everyone she loves and everything she's been taught.

Ex still bears the scars from the fire that killed his entire family. The newest member of a group of rogue Rifters known as The Hollows, he thinks he's finally found his place in the world. It's gritty and treacherous and the only place he feels completely free. But his partner and best friend Stein is dead, and he's to blame. The only chance of saving her is a dangerous mission inside the heart of the Tesla Institute itself. But what he finds there is more than a piece of tech. It's the key to changing his whole life. Now that he understands what's possible, he's willing to break all the rules to put his family back together.

Also available as an ebook • SPENCER HILL PRESS • spencerhillpress.com

photo by Ben Zank

A b o u t   T h e   A U T H O R

Lisa Amowitz is an artist and graphic designer by trade, but writing has always been a deep and abiding passion. As a mom of an actual teen, she's not just writing YA; she's living it.

Lisa is a member of Enchanted Inkpot, a YA fantasy blog (enchantedinkpot.blogspot.com), and she also can be found online at lisa-amowitzya.blogspot.com

DATE DUE

CPSIA information can be obtained at www.ICGtesting.com
Printed in the USA
LVOW04s2225230814

400624LV00003B/3/P

9 781937 053383

JAN 05 2015